The CALL of HOME

The CALL of HOME

A Novel of Family, Friends, and Love

Anne Arkins

Printed in the United States of America
ISBN: 978-1-946425-69-0

Book Design by CSinclaire Write-Design
Cover Design by James Hislope

• WRITE WAY •
PUBLISHING COMPANY
RALEIGH, NORTH CAROLINA
www.writewaypublishingcompany.com

To Jim,
my best friend and husband of 55 years.
I love you more than yesterday
and less than tomorrow.

And to my four adult children,
Erin, Matt, Corrie, and Josh.
You each are special gifts from God
who continually bless me beyond measure.

Acknowledgments

I ONCE READ THAT THE WRITING of one's first novel is akin to childbirth. I can't remember the exact year I began *The Call of Home* but I do recall my oldest grandchild, Orion, at age 4 asking me, "Baba, have you finished your book yet?" He's an adult now!

The genesis of this novel began sometime during my high school years when I first started dreaming of writing a book. That dream was shattered in my first semester of college as a journalism major while taking freshman English. My teacher was a graduate assistant working on her Masters. Returning a paper I had written, she had made numerous grammatical corrections. At the end of the class, I asked her what I could do to improve my writing skills. She asked me why, and I explained my dream of someday writing a novel. Her response remains etched like a tombstone in my memory. "You need to consider changing your major, because it is obvious you have no writing skills," she said. Devastated, my shattered dream resulted in me changing my major from journalism to library science.

I carried this secret wound of disappointment for years until sharing it with my husband, Jim. His response was 180 degrees opposite to the graduate student's. He said, "Sweetheart, you need to forgive her for her cruel and inappropriate words and relight that dream. Psalm 37:4 says that 'we are to delight ourselves in the Lord, and He will give us the desires of our heart.' I know that you indeed delight yourself in Him, so to me that means your desire to write was given to you by Him."

Without any doubt, I believe this desire, this dream began with Jesus, and I thank Him for fulfilling His promise to me.

~ ~ ~

This novel would not be possible without the tireless encouragement of Jim; of each of my children, Erin, Matt, Corrie Rusch and her husband, Mike; Josh and his wife, Jennifer, the support of each of my grandchildren, Orion, Tyler, Ryan, Isabella, Cate, Connor, Wells, John Michael, Will, Conley, Melly and Sosi. I thank each of my parents, Charles and Catherine Wuest, for your years of love and encouragement.

My "sassy sisters," my soul-mates in Jesus, Sallie, Suzy, Sandie, and Stephanie remain a blessing in my life. My dear friend Kathy Rusch, this novel is an answer to your years of faithful prayer.

Gabrelle Idlet, you were my first writing coach. Your patience and your wisdom on wordsmithery remain an inspiration and guide to me even after all these years.

My editor and publisher, Lee Heinrich of Write Way Publishing, you have become my dearest friend. You have encouraged me, challenged me, inspired me, eased my anxieties, calmed my fears, and are now high on my "hero list." THANK YOU!!!

My freshman English 101 teacher, I not only forgive you but thank you for a hard lesson in my life journey.

Last of all and again to You, Lord Jesus, for fulfilling a desire of my heart.

Addendum: I recognize that there are so many of you who have impacted my life but are not mentioned in this acknowledgment. As a family member, as a friend, your name may not be listed, but you are engraved on my heart. Thank you!

The Call of Home

TWO PEOPLE FROM TWO VERY DIFFERENT lives find themselves called to a small Ozark town. For Claire Westfield and her son, Mason, it's coming home to a place her great-great-grandfather founded. For Dr. Seth Bradley, it's a begrudged but necessary stopover on his way to a prestigious big city medical practice. But the town and its residents, particularly Reuben Walker—a man who walks close to God—have their own plans in this warm, touching family saga with best friends, old friends, new friends, heart and soul journeys, and perhaps a spark of romance.

The CALL of
HOME

~1~

CLAIRE WESTFIELD STOOD AT THE BEDROOM window in her upscale home looking over the suburbs of San Francisco. She no longer found it strange to be standing there, gazing out at the neighborhood she and Randall had lived in for the last seven years. It was not something she had been prone to do before. She had been far too busy for that. But here she was again, and somehow over all these months, she had found a certain comfort in being here at the window.

Claire Mason and Dr. Randall Westfield said their vows eight years ago, promising to love, honor, and cherish till death do us part. *Till death do us part . . . would the ringing of this phrase in her head ever end*, she wondered. It wasn't supposed to be this way. *We were young, healthy, and madly in love.*

And what about Mason? His daddy had been taken from him so soon. Who would teach him to be a man? Who would play catch with him or go camping or teach him to fish?

She ached for her young son and his great loss. And she ached for herself. How could life ever have real meaning again? It was thoughts like these that brought her back to this place at the window day after day.

Claire knew something had to change. She couldn't go on this way—for Mason's sake. He deserved more than a mother physically present but emotionally numb.

"Oh, Randall, what do I do?" she cried aloud. "Tell me how I move forward without you. You were so strong, so sure of yourself. I admired you so. I know you always said I was the gutsiest woman you ever knew and that I was not afraid of the devil himself! Randall, it was a show. I'm not gutsy, and I am afraid of the devil and of life without you. Who's going to show me the way now that you're gone?"

Claire heard Mason come in the front door calling, "Bye! See you tomorrow. Mommy, I'm home," and willed herself out of the desperation she felt. She called back, "Hi, sweetie, up here."

She made a quick check in the mirror and saw someone she barely recognized. This wasn't Claire Westfield, wife of the prestigious orthopedic surgeon, Dr. Randall Westfield. She had been known and admired by much of San Francisco society. Now she cowered like a wounded animal in its den, fearful of what lay outside. She applied a quick touch of lipstick and gave her hair a few brush strokes.

Mason, home from kindergarten, ran into his mother's arms. Kneeling, Claire held him close, feeling the warmth of his soft skin next to hers and inhaling the smell of baby shampoo in his hair. Her heart overflowed with love and thankfulness for their child, the legacy of their love.

With tears streaming down her face, Claire knew she had to begin living again. She had a son to raise, a love to cherish, and memories to carry her through. But her heart, flayed raw by her emotions, refused to heal. Feeling a small hand pressing against each side of her face, Claire opened her eyes and stared into the concerned face of her son.

"Mommy, don't cry, please don't cry. I'll take care of you, Mommy, just like Daddy always did." Mason lifted his hands and placed a kiss on each cheek. "Mommy, why did Daddy have to die?"

His searching stare and trembling voice wrenched Claire's heart, sapping any reserve strength she possessed. In this long year and a half since Randall's death, not once had Mason asked this question. And to be honest, she was thankful he hadn't, because she didn't know what she would've said.

Looking into the face of her stoic little soldier who had tried so hard to be brave in accepting this mysterious thing called death, she saw large crocodile tears forming and finally spilling down his cheeks. A new surge of pain sliced her heart, razor-sharp.

"Oh, Mason, sweetie, I . . . I don't know. Mommy doesn't know why Daddy had to die. It was an accident. It shouldn't have happened, not to him. Your daddy died trying to help someone who was hurt. You know how you make your Rescue Heroes do things that help others because they're the good guys? That's why they're called heroes. They put the needs of other people first. Well, that's what Daddy was doing."

She sat down on the floor and pulled him to sit in her lap. "There was a bad car wreck that night when daddy was coming home from the hospital. He wanted to come straight home to see you and me because he missed us so much. But that night Daddy knew the people in those cars were hurt and needed his help. So, instead of driving by and not helping them, your daddy became a Rescue Hero. When the ambulance came to take the hurt people away, Daddy started walking to his car so he could come home. But a man was driving his car very fast. He'd been drinking too much of something called liquor, and it made him not pay attention to what he was doing. Instead of driving his car where he should have, he drove it on the side of the road where Daddy was walking. The car hit Daddy so hard that Daddy died."

"Mommy, I wish that man didn't drink that bad stuff. I miss my daddy, and that man made him go away. Will we ever see Daddy again? Will we, Mommy?"

She looked helplessly into her child's questioning eyes. "I hope so, Mason. Oh, I do hope so, sweetheart."

"Mommy, I'm hungry. Can we have our snack, and then can I go over to Billy's house? He wants to play pirates."

Mason's smile and cheerfulness caught Claire off guard. A lump filled her throat. How like a child to move from the deepest questions of life to the pressing concern of the moment. Was it a lesson for her to move on as well? Certainly, her perspective was far more encompassing than her five-year-old son's, but she would have to think on this. Maybe later today or maybe tomorrow at her window.

"Mommy! Mommy! I said I'm hungry. Starving! I need food." Mason scrutinized his mother impatiently, anxious to go downstairs. Claire couldn't help but laugh.

"Okay, little man," she said, lifting him off her lap and standing up. "Let's go fill that tummy." Giggling, they tromped down the stairs, pretending to be soldiers. Next to playing pirates, playing soldiers was Mason Westfield's favorite thing to do.

After inhaling a glass of milk and several oatmeal cookies, Mason ran to his room to gather up his pirate sword, hat, and black eye patch.

"Bye, Mommy, I'm going to Billy's house. We're going to dig for buried treasure today. He has a big, new shovel, so he says we're sure to find treasure now. Love you, Mommy." Looking back over his shoulder, Mason smiled and threw her a kiss. Claire followed him out the door, pretending she'd caught the kiss and with great exaggeration, threw it back to him. She stood at the front porch, watching to make sure he made it safely a few houses down the street to Billy's.

Returning to the kitchen, she cleaned up the glasses, plates, and remaining cookies, but her thoughts were still on her son. Mason definitely was the source of any joy in her life now. She reached for the latest addition of *Country Living* magazine. Staring at the cover, she wondered again why she always seemed drawn to this magazine. It certainly wasn't typical of her decorating taste.

Curling up in her favorite comfy chair, she allowed her mind to wander as she turned the pages. Then, without warning, she was staring at an image that brought a rush of memories. A picture of an older home set in the middle of a grove of huge trees. It was spring, and the house obviously belonged to a prolific gardener. An old iron fence surrounded the place, standing guard over all who lived there.

Claire found herself embracing the memories that flooded her thoughts. No, this wasn't her grandparents' home, but there were so many similarities. The simple style of the house, its weathered wood, paint-needy shutters, and large, old shade trees spoke to her. There were peonies planted along the fence and hydrangeas off to one side of the house. She recognized lilac bushes and spirea cascading onto the lawn. She did notice one difference. The fence. Her ancestral home had a stone wall around a sizable section of the yard.

Her thoughts went back to a time when she was sitting on her grandfather's lap, listening to him tell the story about the wall. Potch told her of the colored folks who worked for her great-great-granddaddy and built the wall.

"Your great-great-grandparents were much opposed to slavery, child, so they were among the first who hired colored folks after the Civil War. They never owned slaves. Remember that, Claire. It's an honorable heritage you come from."

The image was so clear in her mind she almost felt Potch's strong arms enfolding her, the smell of his bay rum aftershave filling her senses, and the coarseness of his beard against her cheek. It was only then that she realized she was actually curled up in his very chair—a gift from her father when her grandfather died.

Claire traced the outline of the picture with her finger, deep in thought. "Is this coincidence?" she asked aloud. "Is it fate or karma? Or is it something or someone much greater?" She found herself caught up in so many happy memories of her childhood visits to see her Potch and Honey. She ached with regret for the wasted years of youth when she was too caught up in herself to have time for them.

She replayed days of swimming and fishing at the creek and sneaking behind the waterfall named Mason Falls after her ancestors. Memories of riding her bike into town for ice cream at the local drug store and climbing the wonderful old trees scattered across the yard at her grandparents' home flooded her thoughts, which then turned to her son. What a wonderful experience it would be for him to see what life in a small town was like. Maybe they could make a visit, she thought. But in the next instant, she was struck with the idea of moving to Mason Falls.

"Absolutely not!" The words were out of her mouth before she knew it, but somewhere in the recesses of her heart a question arose. *Why not?*

"Because your life is here," she said aloud. "What do I know about living there? It was a long time ago. Everything we have and anything that means something to us is here." She found herself speaking aloud, as though that would put a stop to the feeling escalating inside her.

It seemed an eternity as she sat there wrestling with the questions pounding in her head. What began as a resolute mindset against the idea of a move to Mason Falls slowly gave way to a wistful yearning for the security and serenity she remembered. She felt profoundly drawn to return.

~2~

Tying up loose ends to complete his family practice residency proved more complicated than Seth Bradley had thought. The schedule of a resident was grueling at best but the last month had tested his energy to the limit. Now the last patient had been seen, every medical record updated, and final farewells and handshakes extended to staff and friends. He knew he should be celebrating. Most of his cohorts were doing so with great exuberance, and he longed to share their joy and anticipation at what lay ahead. But for him it was payback time.

After applying to several medical schools, he had accepted the offer in Little Rock, Arkansas. He'd needed a change and had no family to consider, plus the school provided a way he could afford to go there through a Rural Practice Loan program. He knew he'd never regret the education and experience he'd received in Little Rock. The program was just what he'd wanted, lots of hands-on experience. His residency here in Kansas City had challenged and thrilled him, and he loved this city. He hoped that someday he'd return to practice here.

His stomach churned every time he thought about having to turn down a highly sought after position with the top clinic in the city. But now that he'd completed his residency, he had a commitment to honor. It was a struggle for him, a born and bred city boy, to imagine himself living and working in a small town in the Ozark Mountains of Arkansas. Seth shut the door to his apartment and walked down the stairs for the last time. He pitched the last of his bags in the back of his beat-up Honda that he affectionately called Old Red.

~ ~ ~

The road stretched before him for what seemed like forever with no other car in sight. It was an unnerving thought when he considered the condition of Old Red. Seeing a place to pull over up ahead, he decided to take a break and stretch his legs. He steered the car to the side of the road and stopped next to an old tree. Out of habit he reached for his Kansas City Royals ball cap and put it on. Going to the Royals games anytime he had the chance was one of the few ways Seth had given himself permission to relax. For some reason, going to the games helped him feel like he belonged, that he wasn't completely alone.

Seth leaned against his car to do some stretches for his shoulders and legs, feeling the tension of the last few days ease from his body. His normal routine of stretching and running had been replaced over the last week with the mountain of paperwork facing him before his departure. Those loose ends were never as easy as they looked to be in the beginning.

After doing a few stretches, he studied the old tree. Its swaying branches seemed to beckon him to come and rest awhile. He accepted the offer and brushed aside a few small rocks from a hollow between two large roots. He sat down, his back up against the rough bark of the tree's trunk. Closing his eyes for a moment, he let himself listen to the sounds around him. Unfamiliar sounds to a city boy.

As his body and mind relaxed, he allowed himself to take in the world around him. He watched as a good-size turtle slowly ambled its way across the gravel, heading toward the road. He laughed out loud as he watched two squirrels play hide and seek with each other. The mooing of cows grazing in a nearby pasture content with the world around them gave him a sense of peace.

Slapping his neck at the attack of some insect, Seth jumped up and took the turtle across the road to safety. He surprised himself by this act but experienced a rush of pleasure in it. He watched the ancient-looking creature continue its slow progress, like an old slow-motion movie. He wondered if that turtle knew what was ahead of it. Did it have a plan, or was it simply going wherever the moment led it?

Walking back to his car, his thoughts turned to the small town that would be his home for the next three years. He climbed into Old Red and began the last part of his own journey.

What did this part of his journey hold for him? Driving along the deserted highway, a thought struck him like a bolt of lightning. He realized he was leaving all signs of life as he'd known it behind him. The gently rolling hills spread before him mile after mile and reminded him more of the serene result of the Old Masters' paintings than reality. He had to admit the landscape was not only picturesque but also quite beautiful. It had the look of being manicured with the precision of a surgeon and the heart of a gardener.

Seth pushed the button to let the windows down and inhaled the pungent smell of newly cut hay. The ground was covered in neat, tufted, half-moon rows of hay ready to be formed into the bales. Fields that were probably being reserved for planting crops were precisely plowed in parallel rows. Everywhere he looked showed signs of order, quiet, and a kind of oneness between man and the land. He was surprised by the impact it had on him.

The car crested a hill after a long, slow incline, and there before him was Mason Falls, his destination. Estimating the town to be about two miles away, Seth slowed the car and looked with new interest at what spread out before him. It was almost dusk, and the air was golden.

As he approached the town limits, he couldn't help but think of the towns in some of the old movies he used to watch with Gran. Tree-lined streets had neat, medium-size homes with simple but attractive landscaping. He had to admit this place looked picture perfect. If given half a chance, it could grow on him. He wasn't at all sure he wanted that to happen. This was to be just a job—a place where he could gain some experience and pay off his loan. Nothing more.

Seth had no desire to settle down in the rural South, no matter how charming it looked. His hopes and dreams were much higher than some quaint town. Tightening his grip on the steering wheel, he took a deep breath and guided the car into the next three years of his life.

The first thing on Seth's agenda was to get something to eat. Then he'd find the motel he'd called earlier in the day. It was getting late, at least for a small community, and he began to wonder if he'd find anything open. Would everyone have already shut the doors of their business establishments and retreated to their homes for a quiet end of the day?

Arriving at what looked to be the main street, Seth stared in amazement at the spectacle before him. The street bustled with people of all ages. Paper lanterns were strung across the modest thoroughfare on each side of the square creating a warm glow as dusk announced the coming darkness. Music floated on the gentle breeze, drawing him like the well-known voice of a friend. The smell of food reminded his stomach of its need for nourishment.

Seth began searching for somewhere to park the car. He spotted an empty space in front of a place named Hank's Hardware Store and pulled in. He was watching all the activity in the town square as he got out of the car and managed to plow right into a man coming from the hardware store. The older man's hat fell out of his hand, and Seth reached down to retrieve it. When he stood up, he found himself gazing into the most amazing blue eyes he'd ever seen. Gran would have said they were as blue as an October sky.

The man, probably in his seventies, had collar-length, white hair, a mustache, a full white beard, and a broad, contagious smile. He held his hand out to Seth, giving him a strong handshake, and introduced himself as Reuben Walker, handyman by trade.

"I was just closing up for Hank, so he could take his family to the festivities. Are you passing through or do you plan to stay awhile?" Reuben asked with a smile.

"Stay awhile. I'm moving here. I just got into town."

"My, my that's a fine thing. We need more young folks coming here, believe me. Don't think I got your name, son," Reuben said.

"I'm Seth Bradley, sir. Nice to meet you." Once again, the two men shook hands, and Seth felt the strong yet gentle grasp of Reuben Walker's workman hands.

"Tell me, young Mr. Bradley, are you hungry?"

"Yes sir, I am," Seth laughed. "In fact, I'm starved!"

Reuben placed a hand on Seth's shoulder and began steering him toward the lively gathering across the street. Several white tent tops glistened in stark contrast to the darkening night sky as laughter and music fused into a melody all its own. The square, the typical hub of countless small Southern towns, resonated with the richness of Americana. The tangy sweet smell of barbecue hung heavy in the air, drawing everyone to the feast that awaited.

Reuben explained that it was the Mason Falls annual barbecue cook-off. All the while he smiled and exuberantly greeted everyone they passed, adding a handshake, pat on the shoulder, or personal greeting of affection for each person.

"Hey there, Clovis. How's that new barn coming?"

"Well, I'll be. Joe Young, how you doing? Haven't seen you since the night that new baby was born. How is that darlin' little girl doing? Must be about what . . . five months by now? Give my love to Mary. Edna Harper, how are you? Sure have missed those oatmeal cookies. My mouth waters just thinking about them."

And so it went, man, woman, and child. Reuben knew them all. And to each person they met, Reuben introduced Seth as his new friend who just moved to town. *Yes indeed*, Seth thought, *this was a small town, and he couldn't help but smile.*

~ ~ ~

The two of them stood in line waiting to sample the final contestant's effort to win the judges' accolades and prized blue ribbon. Seth wasn't sure he could put one more bite of food in his mouth, but Reuben had assured him that these ribs would put the others to shame. Seth had never eaten or even seen so many varieties of barbecue, potato salad, baked beans, and coleslaw. Looking over his shoulder, he was astounded to realize he'd followed a trail of food from one side of the square to the other side, sampling everything in sight. Reuben engaged in lively banter with a large, bearded man wearing a chef's hat and apron and dishing up two more plates of ribs. Both men smiled and motioned for Seth to join them.

Seth took the plate handed to him and with a deep sigh bit into the most wonderful barbecue rib he'd ever eaten. He heard Reuben's gusty chuckle as he introduced Seth to the cook, George

Meyers. It was clear they were friends who had enjoyed one another's company over many years.

"George was the reason I came to Mason Falls," Reuben said. "We were army buddies. Started boot camp together before the Vietnam War. To hear George tell it, Mason Falls was downright perfect. Course, no place is really perfect, but I gotta tell you, after all these years, guess I would have to say I agree with him."

George grinned with affection, slapping Reuben on the back. Looking more closely at this hulk of a man, Seth saw a tear glisten at the corner of one eye. No doubt this friendship had seen good times and times not so good.

Seth found himself wondering what stories formed the friendship between these two. Then he heard his new friend saying, "George doesn't always cook up barbecue. His family has had the finest dairy farm in the county for three generations. With the help of his six sons, the biggest and strongest boys you'll ever see, George has taken that dairy business to a new level. He's also a man blessed with a prize of a wife in Jenny."

George's face turned rosy red as he gave a slow nod of his head, clearly touched by Reuben's praise for his family.

"Young Mr. Bradley, I just realized I never did ask you what you plan to do here." Both men gave Seth an inquisitive look.

"Well, fellas, I guess you could say I'm here to pay back a loan." Seth could tell from their expressions the idea of a stranger coming to do such a thing was intriguing. "I'm here to practice medicine. It's payment for a loan I took out to help put me through medical school. I'll be here with Dr. Angus McQuarry for three years."

"Well, I'll be. You're the new doc. Fancy that. Welcome to our town, Dr. Seth Bradley," Reuben said. "I've been hearing that Mac was bringing in some young doc."

"High time we got some help around here for old Doc McQuarry," added George.

Seth knew there would be a learning curve in getting used to small town life—like everyone wanting to know all about you. He'd already decided there was only so much he was planning to tell. After all, he didn't intend to be here that long. He was simply taking the first step toward something bigger and better. It didn't seem like a good idea to get too close or involved with people, no matter how nice they were.

"I've had a long day today, and I sure would like to get a hot shower and a good night's rest before meeting with Dr. McQuarry tomorrow. I have reservations at a place called the Sunset Motel. Could one of you give me directions?"

"Sure thing, Doc. Let's get our cars and you can follow me," said Reuben. "See you around, George. That may be your best barbecue yet. Give my love to Jenny and tell the boys hey for me."

"Will do, buddy. You and Doc here need to come out for dinner real soon. There's nothin' Jenny likes more than feeding a house full of hungry men!" George reached out and shook hands with Seth then gave Reuben a friendly hug before starting to pack up his cooking gear.

Seth couldn't remember ever seeing two men who had such a warm friendship. It sent a twinge of longing through him. He had to admit it would be nice to have a friend like that. It wasn't that he didn't have friends, but he'd never experienced a long history with someone like these two men seemed to share.

"Here we are, Doc," Reuben said. "I'll go 'round back and get my truck. You can follow me over to the motel, and I'll introduce you to the proprietor, Mabel Porter."

Seth sat in Old Red with the driver's window down waiting for Reuben to return. The musicians were packing up their gear and laughter had subsided, but the sounds of the night engulfed him.

Crickets were playing their symphonies; tree frogs, he supposed, serenaded one another, and the sound of what he guessed might be an owl filled the air. These were the sounds he'd read about in books but never heard growing up in the older part of a large city with little grass and few trees. He couldn't decide if this new environment would lull him to sleep or drive him crazy. He didn't have time to draw a conclusion as he saw Reuben pulling in front of Old Red in a dilapidated truck. He waved for Seth to follow him. Seth couldn't help but chuckle at the sight of the vehicle. *And I thought I was driving a piece of junk. Man, Old Red has class compared to that!*

Seth soon discovered it didn't take long to reach any destination in Mason Falls. A turn to the right, then go past the elementary school on the left with its large shade trees and assorted playground equipment. After two more blocks, there was the sign in all its flashing glory, the Sunset Motel. It sure didn't look like much and that was being generous. He hoped it was at least clean. One thing was certain. Paint must be a scarce commodity for the owner. But the main thing he wanted right now was a shower and a good bed. He hoped that the Sunset Motel could provide both.

Noticing only one other car, Seth felt a little uneasy about going in, but there was Reuben, smiling and motioning him to follow once again. It dawned on Seth that most of what he'd done since arriving in town was adhere to Reuben's "follow me" messages. *Interesting*, he thought. He couldn't remember that happening with anyone else. And there was something about the way the man said it that made it okay, even kind of mesmerizing. So once again, Seth followed Reuben Walker, thinking he'd probably meet a lot of interesting people in this small town over the next three years.

Reuben knocked on the screen then called out, "Mabel, Reuben Walker here with a customer." After several minutes, a short, heavy-set woman, probably in her late fifties, stomped into the office from a back room. She didn't seem too enthusiastic about a new customer but grudgingly allowed him to sign in and handed him the key to room #4. Before they turned to leave, Reuben coaxed a trace of a smile from her when he complimented her on the afghan she was crocheting. Seth almost choked trying to squelch the laughter building inside him. But the man seemed completely genuine in his comment. For the life of him, Seth couldn't see it the way Reuben did. Mabel had chosen the most unbelievable colors he'd ever seen. In fact, he was trying to imagine where she could have found yarn in those colors, much less why she would have put them together.

Glancing around the motel office while trying to get his silent laughter under control, a thought struck him. What in the world would his room look like? When they stepped back out into the night air, Seth thanked Reuben for all his help and assured him he'd stop by the hardware store tomorrow to meet Hank, the owner.

Seth walked to the door marked #4, sucked in a deep breath, and slipped the key into the lock.

The sight that assailed him was unlike anything from his wildest imagination. "How could a person bring together so many colors and patterns in one small room and think it a pleasing sight?" Seth whispered. He'd heard his grandmother refer to a crazy quilt. That was what she called a quilt with a hodgepodge of colors and patterns. Mabel Porter had done just that with an entire room. Shaking his head, Seth could only gawk at what must be considered by the motel proprietor as a decorative masterpiece. He was too tired to check out any other rooms, but he wondered if it was humanly possible to fall asleep in such absurd surroundings. He would find out soon enough.

Dropping his suitcase next to a gold velour chair, he went to take a shower, hoping this was all a fabrication of his weary mind. After a shower long enough to turn the hot water to icy cold, Seth grabbed a towel to dry off and got ready for bed. As he walked out of the bathroom, reality hit him. The room was not a fabrication. Right now, he couldn't care less. Seth crawled into bed determined to prove again what had been true in all the years of his medical training. If you are tired enough, you can sleep anywhere, even in a room decorated by Mabel Porter. Within moments the sounds of crickets, frogs, and an owl like the one he'd heard earlier that evening lulled him to sleep. He had answered his own question.

~ ~ ~

Reuben drove slowly, allowing the inky blackness of the night to embrace him. The night air was cool, and he was glad this old truck fell short of modern necessities like air conditioning. Pulling up to a stop sign, he took advantage of the moment to marvel at the night sky. There seemed to be a million stars dusting the sky. Creation's display never ceased to astound him. Thankfulness filled his heart in that moment, but the glare of headlights behind him broke the spell.

Guiding the truck down the familiar road, his thoughts drifted back to his time with Doc Bradley. He'd taken an immediate liking to the younger man and hoped they would become great friends.

His keen intuition told him there was a wall or barrier the young man had erected to keep people at a distance. It reminded him of the common signs posted on most farms in the area. "No Trespassing–Private Property." Yes, Doc Bradley may be the new doctor in town, but he was going to need some tender care himself.

Reuben hurt for the young man. He edged the truck to the side of the road, letting the stillness quiet his soul. Only the stars looked on as a simple man spoke his heart. "*Lord, You know I'm not an educated man like the Doc, and maybe I'm all wrong, but it seems to me Doc Bradley is carrying a heavy load. Let Your light shine through me so maybe I can help him with that load. Thank You, Lord.*"

~3~

"Claire, you can't be serious!" Robyn moaned. "You just need some time to think, maybe a trip somewhere. But move—that's ludicrous! Where would you go? What would you do? I know you don't have any family, so that's why your friends here are important to you, especially now. We're here for you. You know that, don't you?" Robyn stopped, catching her breath while keeping her eyes locked on Claire.

"Of course, I know you and the others are here for me, Robyn. I couldn't have gotten through this time without you." Claire slowly sipped her iced tea while trying to pull her thoughts together. She knew how crazy this all sounded, and that's why she'd delayed mentioning it, even to her dearest friend.

"Robyn, you know me better than anyone except Randall. Now he's gone and so is a big part of me, especially a big part of my heart. You know I'm not impulsive about much of anything, so these thoughts and feelings that keep creeping into my mind are strange to me as well. You also know me well enough to realize I'm not someone interested in spiritual things, but there is something—or someone—drawing me back to Mason Falls." Claire gazed out the kitchen window to see Mason playing in the sandbox, moving his trucks in single file on an imaginary highway.

"When was the last time you saw your counselor, Claire? It seems to me that you should run all this by her." Robyn fidgeted with her napkin, looking first at Claire, then at Mason. "What in thunder does a small hick town like Mason Falls have to offer you? You don't even have any relatives left there. If you want to move, why not go to Montreal? You always said you would love to live there."

17

"No," Claire said, "I don't have anyone in Mason Falls, but I would have my roots, the place my ancestors carved out of nothing. Robyn, I understand it doesn't seem to make sense, and at this point, I'm not sure if it's what I'll do, but I need some solid ground in my life right now, especially for Mason. I don't think I can keep going like I am here. It hurts too much to see all the places and people that were part of Randall and me as a couple. It's like I've fallen into a big sinkhole, and I can't get out. I have to find a way out, Robyn, for Mason's sake, I must!"

Claire reached across the table grasping her friend's trembling hand and held it for a long, quiet moment. "Robyn, walk through this with me just as you have in the past. Please." Neither woman could hold back the tears that began to flow. Claire stood at the same time as her friend, and they embraced, each with her own sense of loss and pain.

"Mommy, where are you?"

"In here, sweetie, in the kitchen with Robyn." Both women dabbed away the tears and greeted the happy, sand-covered little boy who came bounding into the kitchen.

"Hi ya, Aunt Robbie!" Mason squealed, running to jump into the outstretched arms awaiting him.

"Hi yourself, Tiger. How's my favorite guy in the world?" Robyn smothered him with huge kisses, laughing as he groaned and rubbed them off.

"Aunt Robbie, I'm too big for kisses," Mason teased.

"Mason Westfield, you'll never be too big for my kisses, you hear?"

"Oh, okay. I guess it's all right for you and Mommy to still kiss me. Are you going to stay and have dinner with us, Aunt Robbie? Please, please!" Mason pleaded.

"Sure, honey, if it's okay with Mommy." Robyn glanced over at Claire.

"That's a great idea. Is spaghetti all right with you two?" Claire looked from her son to her best friend.

"Spaghetti! Spaghetti! We love spaghetti!" Mason and Robyn shouted, waving their arms in the air and dancing around the room.

Claire put the pasta on to cook while Robyn and Mason began setting the table. Pulling a container of her sauce from the refrigerator, her thoughts turned to the past. She loved the aroma of spaghetti sauce simmering on the stove. The blend of herbs and spices in the rich sauce filled the air, always bringing to life again the memories of her honeymoon with Randall in Rome.

Oh, what a city it is, she thought. She and Randall had savored every moment of their time there. When they returned home, she was determined to come up with the most wonderful sauce ever, created just for him. With all the enthusiasm of a young bride for her Prince Charming, she set about with her plan. It wasn't as easy as she'd expected. Remembering all her failures and the way her husband choked down each new attempt brought a smile to her face. Her determination finally began to waiver. Disheartened, she set before him what was to be her final concoction. Randall slowly raised his fork and less than enthusiastically took a bite. Then, with great relish and eagerness, he devoured what became "the best spaghetti sauce ever." At least it was to Randall. He used to say it was soul food to him and that he loved her.

Oh, if she could hear him say those words right now. Instead, she chided herself. *Claire Westfield, get a grip on yourself and come back to reality. There are hungry mouths waiting to be fed.*

"Mommy, can we make it like a restaurant with a candle and the red and white checked tablecloth? Daddy always liked it when we made our own restaurant. Can we, Mommy, please?"

Claire and Robyn exchanged glances, each remembering many happy, shared moments like this with Randall.

"Sure, we can do that, Mason. Daddy would be so pleased you thought of it," Claire said, choking back tears and the urge to cry out *why* once more.

Robyn immediately distracted Mason by asking, "Is that tablecloth still in the drawer by the dishwasher, Mason?"

"Uh huh, you know that, Aunt Robbie, but I'll get it for you."

"Thanks, Tiger. You're such a good helper. I'm hungry! How about you?"

"Yeah, me too. I could eat a horse!"

At this, both women broke into laughter. The little boy gave them a quizzical look, not at all sure what he'd said was that funny, but he joined their laughter, delighting in the lighthearted moment.

The meal was soon prepared, and they sat down to their own restaurant table, as Mason called it. He had turned the dimmer switch down for the lights and seemed quite proud of the ambiance he'd created. Mason was full of stories from kindergarten and as any five-year-old boy, he adored being the center of attention.

After dinner, Robyn tried to help with the dishes, but Claire assured her it was fine to go see Mason's newest acquisition, a gerbil he had named Sammy. This furry little creature had become his pride and joy. Standing at the sink, Claire could hear laughter coming from her son's room, and it made her smile. It had been a day full of roller coaster emotions, but that wasn't out of the ordinary anymore. She was glad Robyn had come by—for herself and for her son, who adored his Aunt Robbie.

It was only in the last few months that Claire realized what a blessing it was to be able to end the day on an upbeat note rather than in a minor key. Her heart felt lighter at times like these, and she caught herself believing there was a glimmer of hope out there for her and her child. Where it would come from, she didn't know.

After putting the last glass in the dishwasher, Claire added the detergent, punched start, and headed upstairs to indulge herself in playful antics with Mason and Robyn.

A gasp escaped her as she walked into the room and saw Robyn. She sat in the middle of the floor, transformed from a chic prosecuting attorney into Captain Hook, all by one small boy. She was adorned with a genuine Captain Hook hat, make-believe hook, and black eye patch. A dark green sash was tied around her waist, and her slacks were shoved into a pair of Claire's knee-high boots.

"Hi, Mommy! You sit over there in the chair, and Aunt Robbie and me are going to show you what pirates do."

Claire obediently went to the chair and settled in. For the next half hour, she was entertained by a quite swashbuckling performance. At times Claire laughed so hard she felt the tears flowing down her cheeks. They were good tears, healthy tears, and full of happiness. It had been a long time since she'd abandoned her pain and felt truly alive.

Mason and Robyn took a final bow, adding a resounding high-five to finish their performance. Claire stood, clapping vigorously, and joined in the improvised victory dance until all three of them collapsed on the floor, relishing the moment, experiencing the contentment that comes from being with those you love.

"Mason, sweetie, it's way past your bedtime. Let's go get your teeth brushed and your jammies on," Claire said, pulling him into a monstrous hug. She knew he was tired by his willingness to obey rather than give a lengthy list of all the reasons he needed "just a little more time, Mommy, for some really 'portant stuff I need to do."

Claire and Robyn kissed the little boy good night, making sure his covers were just right and a veritable fortress of stuffed animals encircled him.

They slipped quietly down the stairs, each trying to squelch their giggles. If Claire didn't know she'd just left her five-year-old son's room, she would have sworn she was back in the boarding school of her youth.

"Want a cup of tea before you go?" Claire said.

"Sure, sounds great."

Claire filled the tea kettle while Robyn found two mugs and the cream and sugar. After the kettle gave its familiar whistle and their tea was steeped and sweetened, they sipped the hot liquid and replayed the evening with great animation.

"Claire, it's getting late. I'd best be going. Can I ask you to do something for me?"

"Of course. What is it?"

"Would you please talk through this moving idea with your counselor before making any decisions?"

"If it will help you feel better, yes, I'll talk to Meredith at my next session." Claire patted her friend's hand as they got up from the table.

"Be careful on the way home, okay?" she said, giving her friend a big hug.

"I will. See you soon." Robyn smiled and headed for the door.

The house fell silent, welcoming Claire into the moment. Though tired, she wasn't ready for bed. Instinctively, she grabbed her grandmother's afghan and sought out her solace chair, as she called it. Wrapped in the warmth of the afghan she'd seen her grandmother use so many times throughout the years, she felt a sense of peace wash over her, allowing her thoughts to take on a life of their own.

Claire awoke startled. She had no idea how long she'd been sleeping curled up in the chair. Her mind felt fuzzy for a moment the way it does after a long nap. But one thing was certain, she knew exactly what she had been thinking about before she fell asleep. She hadn't moved from her position in the chair, but now she was completely awake.

The plan was as clear as though it had been scripted and handed to her by some unseen agent. Her hands trembled as she ran them through her hair, pulling it back from her face. It would take all the courage and fortitude she could muster to do what seemed—what was the word Robyn used—ludicrous. And what would Robyn think? Claire knew for certain she must at least keep her promise to Robyn and talk to her counselor, but it would simply be a formality. There was no question in her mind—or her heart—that she must go back to Mason Falls. Everyone she knew was going to think she was crazy. That was a given. And she had to admit it did sound crazy, but she knew it was right even if she couldn't explain why, not even to herself.

Claire went to the kitchen and started water for tea once again. *Ginger peach would hit the spot right now* she thought, rummaging through her tea box. She opened her desk drawer and pulled out a pad of paper and a pen. With her tea close at hand, she sat down at the desk and began to draft what would become The Plan.

First, she would call Meredith and reschedule her appointment for as soon as possible, hopefully within the next two days. Second, she would make an appointment to see a Realtor and begin the process of leasing the house. She would ask for a one-year contract that would assure her of a home to come back to if things fell apart and all of this was some mixed up dream. Of course, she would need to tell Mason what she was planning. Third, she would contact a childhood friend of her dad's in Mason Falls and ask him to check on her grandparents' old homeplace to make sure it was in livable condition.

Claire sipped her tea to calm her nervousness. On one hand, she felt new life welling up inside her, and just as quickly, she cringed in fear at the unknown. It had been years since she'd ventured into an unfamiliar situation, especially all on her own. She sat there for a long time, simply weighing the magnitude of what she was contemplating.

Finishing her tea, she cleared the desk. She gazed around the tidy room that had been the center of her world for the last several years. Was she actually brave enough to go through with this plan? Right now, all she had to base her plan on was an overwhelming sense, in the depths of her soul, that this was what she was meant to do. Well, tomorrow she'd put herself to the test. She would do the first thing on her list and call Meredith.

~ ~ ~

The sound of thunder cracked the silence causing Claire to sit upright in bed. Rubbing her eyes, she yawned before glancing toward the window. It hardly looked like a day of new beginnings. Her first instinct was to crawl under the covers and let this day pass her by, but the blare of the alarm made her jump. "I will not be defeated by some thunder and rain," she said, pointing her finger at the window. She jumped out of bed and slid into her slippers and robe. It was time to get Mason up and ready for school, so she'd have to put the thoughts of last night aside for a while.

"Come on, sweetie, it's time to get up," Claire said, sitting on the edge of his bed as she did every morning, stroking his hair and rubbing his back. As energetic as her little guy was during the day, he was almost impossible to get up in the morning. "Mason, honey, it's raining really hard, so we'll have to leave early because of traffic. I need you to help me by getting up right now."

"All right, Mommy, if I really have to. But I'd rather stay right here with you, and we could snuggle." An impish grin spread across his face as he peeked out from under the covers.

"You rascal you." Claire reached out to tickle him. Mason giggled and wrapped Claire in a bear hug, pulling her down beside him.

"You really want to stay here too, don't you, Mommy?"

"Yes, sweetie, I do, but today I have some things I need to take care of, okay?" The little boy held her tighter, pressing his head against her. He felt warm and soft in her arms. She was doing this for him, she thought, setting about with this plan of hers. She wished she could talk to Randall about her plan. She hugged her little guy, picked him up, and headed for the bathroom. A new day was about to begin.

～4～

WHILE MABEL PORTER'S SUNSET MOTEL DIDN'T do a thriving business, her coffee shop was the hub of early morning traffic and talk in the hamlet of Mason Falls. By eight a.m. Mabel had served innumerable cups of coffee, a variety of her homemade fruit or nut breads, several pounds of bacon, and dozens of eggs.

On Wednesdays she also served her famous sausage-egg casserole. Many mornings there was standing room only, but no one seemed to mind. This was the place to be. Customers stood holding coffee mugs filled from a self-serve urn while waiting for a table. Their conversations were lively and jovial.

Most of the clientele were state highway workers, business-men from town, and farmers who'd been up since dawn and already finished their morning chores. There were telephone and propane company employees headed out to job sites and random travelers just passing through who had dazed looks from long days of travel.

People leaving were extended a typical parting—a slap on the back or wave of the hand accompanied with "Bye y'all," "Take it easy, brother," or "Catch y'all later."

In room #4, Seth opened one eye, rubbed the other, then stretched. For a moment he thought he was napping on one of the beds in the doctor's lounge at St. Luke's Hospital. When he opened the other eye, he knew exactly where he was. Mabel Porter's Sunset Motel in Mason Falls.

Hearing voices and car motors, he got out of bed and pulled back the yellow gingham curtains. There was a traffic jam between the motel and the coffee shop where the night before it had been Old Red and the car belonging to the guest in #6. Deciding to take it easy a little longer, Seth crawled back into bed, stuffing a pillow over his face to block out the sunlight now invading his room. He quickly dropped into that delectable, stolen-moment kind of sleep. That lazy Sunday afternoon nap on the couch kind of sleep.

The hearty farewells of the last of the coffee shop crowd woke Seth once again. Glancing at the bedside clock, he became instantly alert, another ability honed by countless nighttime interruptions in medical school and residency. Propelling himself out of bed, he ran to the bathroom, took a quick shower, and shaved hastily. He had less than half an hour before his appointment with Dr. McQuarry. He stared bleary-eyed at himself in the mirror and realized how much he needed a haircut, something he'd intended to do before leaving Kansas City. But, as usual, he was hard pressed to accomplish all expected of him even to the very last moment in town.

Seth couldn't remember the last time he had done anything at a relaxed pace. The fact that he had been able to throw all his stuff in the car and get out of town on time was monumental. Maybe he could get that haircut today. Turning away from the sink, he saw a coffee pot on the desk and decided he had just enough time to make himself a cup while he dressed.

Seth pulled on his navy blazer and straightened his tie. He rubbed his shoes on the back of his pant legs to shine them up a bit then grabbed a cup of coffee and headed out the door. He wasn't sure where Dr. McQuarry's office was located but hey, how hard could it be to find? Wasn't he in small town USA? Before getting into Old Red, he caught a glimpse of Mrs. Porter through the coffee shop windows, scrubbing a table and setting things straight. She would know where to find McQuarry's office. Seth opened the door to the café and waved as she looked up from her work.

"Good morning, Mrs. Porter. How are you today?" he asked, smiling.

"Same as yesterday, I guess."

"Well, ma'am, I find I'm running a little late. Could you tell me how to find Dr. McQuarry's office?"

It was obvious she was not pleased about the interruption to her work. She looked at Seth for several moments as though she couldn't make up her mind whether to answer him or not. She verbally hurled the directions at him, saying them so fast he wasn't sure he'd caught them. He felt like a little league catcher trying to catch a ball thrown by a big league pitcher.

"You're all alike!" she growled. "Always in hurry, always late. Everybody else is supposed to be at your beck and call. Why didn't you get up earlier and not sleep so late?"

Seth found himself holding up a hand in defense and backing toward the door. "Sorry, Mrs. Porter, sorry I bothered you. You're right, ma'am. I should have set my alarm. Really, I'm sorry I bothered you." He couldn't get to the door quickly enough. Jumping into his car, he backed out, wanting to gun the car for all it was worth but knowing he would bring on the full fury of Mabel Porter's wrath if he did.

"What was that all about?" he muttered. "That woman has problems, and apparently, I have already landed on her list." What a way to start his first day in town. He felt like Public Enemy #1. Now where did she say to turn right? Something about a white house with a white fence? Carefully trying to replay the hurled directions, Seth finally pulled up in front of a small, neat, red brick building. The colonial style sign hanging from a post at the sidewalk read: J. Angus McQuarry, M.D.

Seth opened his visor mirror, brushed at his hair with his hands and straightened his tie once again. "Here goes," he said, opening the car door. He patted Old Red for luck and walked up the sidewalk to the front door. Seth hadn't felt this nervous in a long time as he stepped onto the porch and opened the door.

The waiting room was empty except for a mother and her little girl. He walked to the front desk and introduced himself to the young woman on the other side.

"I have a meeting with Dr. McQuarry at ten, I believe," he said.

"Oh yes, Dr. Bradley, we've been expecting you. Dr. McQuarry kept the morning schedule light so he could show you around. I'm Nell Meyers. My father-in-law is George Meyers. You met him last night. I'm married to his son Billy. We were at Mom and Dad's when he got home, so he told us about meeting you." Nell smiled warmly and put out her hand to him.

"Glad to meet you, Mrs. Meyers."

"Oh, Dr. Bradley, just call me Nell."

Seth smiled back, inwardly thanking her for making a significant improvement to his morning. Her warm smile washed away the caustic words thrown at him earlier by Mabel Porter.

"I'll just sit here and wait for Dr. McQuarry," Seth said, looking back at the waiting room.

"Thank you, Dr. Bradley. It won't be long. Dr. Mac is with a patient and then needs to see little Jill over there."

"Peggy, let me introduce you to our new doctor. Peggy Stevens, this is Dr. Seth Bradley. He just got to town."

Peggy smiled and nodded. Jill looked up with a shy smile, and when Seth waved at her, she ducked her head, then peeked up at him with huge, dark eyes, slowly waving her small hand.

Seth sat down and got comfortable. He looked around the room. It was nothing fancy. Warm rather than cold or sterile. There was a nice landscape painting of mountains and a stream. It looked like the work of a local artist, simple but appealing. A card hung below it with the artist's name and the asking price.

There was the Norman Rockwell print he'd always gotten a kick out of where the doctor is getting ready to give the boy a shot. The boy has a troubled look on his face and his pants are hanging down around his feet. Seth chuckled every time he saw this picture.

The one that held his eye the most was a tranquil scene of a valley in the early morning. Mist was rising above the grass and a few sheep grazed next to a stream. Looking at that painting, he found himself becoming quiet inside. It was pleasant—pleasant to just sit here and not feel he was in the middle of some crisis or trauma.

He felt strangely calmed by the atmosphere of this room. He decided the room had a cozy feel to it. The colors drew you in and made you feel at ease. Comfortable, well-used chairs were arranged in friendly groupings with end tables between them, magazines scattered across their tops.

He heard Jill giggle. He saw that Peggy was reading *Green Eggs and Ham* by Dr. Seuss to her daughter. Jill would crumple her face in a disgusted look at the mention of green eggs and giggle with delight. Seth looked around. It made him feel good to know patients entered a warm, relaxed environment when they came to this office.

At that moment Nell Meyers came out from the office and scooped up Jill in her arms, giving her a big hug. The child responded immediately by placing both chubby arms around Nell's neck while planting a kiss on her cheek. Nell looked over at Seth and smiled. "Not much longer now, Dr. Bradley. Why don't you come along, and I'll take you back to Dr. Mac's office?"

Seth rose obediently and followed the two women and the child. They were engaged in a lively discussion that was apparently about frogs, Jill's newest infatuation.

After ushering Peggy and Jill into an exam room, Nell asked Seth if he might like a cup of coffee. He accepted enthusiastically, remembering the weak brew he had made at the motel.

"Do you use cream and sugar, Dr. Bradley?"

"No thanks, just black. Never seemed to be time during my training to spice it up, so I just got used to the straight stuff."

"Well, here we are. You go in and make yourself comfortable. Dr. Mac will be with you in a few minutes." She smiled at him. Her reddish blond hair, blue eyes, and sprinkling of freckles reminded Seth more of a mischievous child than a married woman working in a doctor's office. He had a feeling Nell Meyers met each day with eager anticipation. His first impression of this charming young woman led him to believe she was a rare asset for any employer.

Glancing around Angus McQuarry's personal office gave Seth a fair amount of information about the man he would be working for. The style was definitely antiquated, but he did admire the beautiful, rich mahogany book cases filled with worn medical books and an assortment of framed photographs. Nell Meyers appeared with a tray holding a china cup and saucer. The coffee smelled delicious.

"Thank you, Nell. This will hit the spot. What I made at the motel was awful."

"Dr. Bradley, just relax. You're going to like practicing with Dr. Mac," Nell said as she left Seth to collect himself.

He took a long, appreciative sip of coffee then finished the cup, carefully setting it back on the tray before investigating what he had wanted to check out since he'd entered this unique space.

He found himself drawn across the room. He had the strange feeling that he'd entered a time warp. A rocking chair, which he would later learn had been passed down to Angus McQuarry all the way back from his great-great grandfather, served as the focal point. The warm glow of old wood spoke volumes about who had cared for the chair over the years. The cane seat and back were in excellent condition. *What stories this old chair could tell,* Seth mused, *if only it could speak.* An unusual looking vest hung across the back of the rocker. It had many pockets housing a variety of interesting items, most of which were unfamiliar to him. A fishing rod of some sort leaned against the wall next to the rocker. Beside it was an old woven basket with a well-worn leather strap. Seth knelt to inspect it more closely, running his hand over the leather, soft and supple from years of use. Memories of museums and old black and white movies flooded his thoughts as he stood up, brushing a bit of lint off his slacks.

Looking around, Seth spied a small rectangular table, very old by its look, which held a vintage lamp, a thin black book on opera, and a small brown leather case with the initials JMQ. Maybe it had belonged to Dr. McQuarry's father or grandfather. Curiosity about the contents of the case almost overpowered him, but in the end, caution and his natural reserve reminded him that as sure as he opened it, in would walk Angus McQuarry. Staring at these items, he was touched by their simplicity. Seth felt convinced that what he saw in this fascinating corner revealed much about the man he would soon be working for. Seth heard a rustle outside the door and before he could move, a tall, lanky man with gray hair took two long strides across the room and greeted him.

"Dr. Bradley, welcome. It's so good to see you. Can't tell you how much I've been looking forward to this day."

Seth stepped forward and said, "Dr. McQuarry, I've been anxious to meet you also." *That was an understatement,* Seth thought.

The two men shook hands. Seth instantly sensed the character of this man through the firm, steady handshake. The older man's steel gray eyes were penetrating, yet compassionate, giving Seth the distinct impression McQuarry had seen straight through to his heart. He couldn't help but wonder what McQuarry was thinking at this moment.

"Sit down, Dr. Bradley, and tell me about yourself." He pointed Seth to a comfortable chair next to his desk. Seth did as instructed while McQuarry edged back against his desk, straddling the corner.

Having made a mutual decision to begin an employment arrangement without a formal interview due to Seth's tight schedule and the practice's need for immediate help, Seth assumed Dr. McQuarry might be experiencing some of the same anticipatory anxiety he was feeling. He couldn't help but visualize two chess masters meeting for the first time, each one scrutinizing the other for any sign of intimidation or weakness. Seth sat up a little taller in the chair as McQuarry repeated, "Dr. Bradley, tell me about yourself."

"Sorry, sir, I, uh, guess I was just collecting my thoughts. Let's see, I did my undergraduate work at Pelham College, a small but very thorough liberal arts school."

"Excuse me, Doctor. I have all your records from college, medical school, and your residency program. That's one of the reasons I hired you, very impressive credentials. What I want to know, Seth, is who you are."

Seth hadn't blushed in years but at the moment he was certain his face was crimson. Trying to regain his composure, he took a deep breath. Seth faltered then said, "Dr. McQuarry, I guess I don't know where to begin."

"Well shoot, son, right from the beginning," McQuarry replied, slapping his leg at the same time.

"There's not much to tell, really." Seth hesitated. He wasn't ready to divulge to a perfect stranger, kind as he may seem, the painful history of his early years. What did he feel comfortable telling the man at this time? He decided to keep it simple. No need for a blow-by-blow discourse of the past.

"I grew up in St. Louis. My maternal grandmother raised me.

I never knew my parents. Gran was a schoolteacher. She taught sixth grade students for thirty years. We didn't have a lot of extras, but Gran gave me a love for books and art. I have to credit her for developing a very strong work ethic in me as well. She was a stickler when it came to doing a job right and finishing what you begin.

"Gran spent years saving money to help me go to college, then she died of breast cancer before I graduated. She never knew I decided to go to med school." Seth paused a moment to clear the catch in his throat. He saw the understanding gaze of a man who had probably also experienced loss.

"Well, Gran was the reason I went into medicine, Dr. McQuarry. She was diagnosed with cancer when I was a junior in high school. She had a radical mastectomy, and at the time of surgery, three of the lymph nodes were positive. The physician recommended post-operative adjuvant chemotherapy.

"Of course, I didn't understand much of this at the time, but watching her through those several years made a great impression on me. It was heartbreaking to see her enduring such pain and discomfort. She put up a valiant fight. I felt so helpless. I mean, what can a nineteen-year-old college kid do?

"This experience started me thinking about medicine; not seriously early on, but it grew with time. When Gran died, it just seemed to be the natural response to go to medical school. I had been too young to help her, but maybe I could help someone else."

Seth ran his fingers across his forehead and leaned back in the chair. He felt drained physically and emotionally. He couldn't remember the last time he had turned himself inside out and shared his own pain like this. And it was only half the story.

Both men were silent for several moments, neither feeling the need to comment further.

Dr. McQuarry broke the silence. "Thank you, Doctor. I like to know the man behind the title, if you know what I mean. And let me say, your grandmother must have been a lovely and gracious woman."

Seth nodded his thanks, relaxing his grip on the chair arm and waiting for the older man to continue.

"It is only fair that I tell you something about myself since you've been so transparent with me," he said as he re-positioned himself on the edge of the desk.

"I was born and raised in Mason Falls. My father, John McQuarry, was also a physician. While he was well respected, I grew up watching him and my mother struggle to make ends meet financially. You see back then patients tended to pay their bill more with produce, baked goods, and other services than in cash. For as long as I can remember, I dreamed of becoming a physician— but not a poor one! In my dreams, I was the rising young star in a grand practice in a large city like Dallas, Houston, or Chicago." Dr. McQuarry hesitated, obviously reflecting on the past, a faraway look in his piercing eyes. "Oh what dreams a young man can have. Would you agree?"

Seth nodded, lost for a moment in his own reflections.

"I also had another dream not related to my career. During high school, I fell in love with the most wonderful, beautiful girl any man could imagine. We had grown up here but didn't really discover each other until high school. I was determined to marry Helen Pierce but knew it would be years before it became a reality. Helen must have been pretty set on marrying me as well. She waited six years! By my second year of medical school, we knew our long distance romance couldn't continue. We were married that summer."

Dr. McQuarry shook his head and said, "Well, that's enough about me. You're probably ready to get a look at the clinic, and then Helen is fixing lunch for us. I wanted you two to have some time to get to know each other." Dr. McQuarry stood, stretching his lanky frame and motioned to the door. Seth rose and followed him into the hall.

～5～

LUNCH WITH THE McQUARRYS HAD BEEN delightful. Seth was embarrassed about how much he'd eaten, but it seemed to please Mrs. McQuarry immensely. His time with them had been relaxed and cordial. He was certain Mrs. McQuarry could make anyone feel welcome and at ease. He was a good case in point. Initially, he was ready for some alone time after the thorough tour of the clinic, but he had to admit he felt refreshed by the presence of this lovely woman. Seth certainly could understand why a man would marry someone like Helen McQuarry. He smiled as he remembered her parting words.

"Now, young Dr. Bradley, I expect to be seeing a lot more of you. This house can be far too quiet. Mac and I get to acting our age when we don't have young folks around. You know what I mean, talking about our aches and pains and what we ate that didn't agree with us," she said with a laugh. "So please, Seth, don't be a stranger here."

She reached out and took his hand in both of hers and smiled with such warmth he almost choked up. It had been a long time since anyone had looked at him like that. It reminded him so much of the way Gran used to look at him, her eyes twinkling, her love shining through her remarkable smile.

"Thank you, Mrs. McQuarry. I would love to come back. I had an enjoyable time, and your cooking is wonderful." He and Dr. Mac, as everyone seemed to call him, shook hands; each assuring the other they felt it would be a great working relationship.

"See you tomorrow, Seth," Dr. Mac said. As Seth turned to walk away, Mac called him back. "Seth, I'm such an old fool at times. Forgive me. I didn't ask about your living arrangements. Do you have that worked out?"

"Well, sir, it's somewhat unsettled at the moment. I spoke on the phone with Mr. Lawson, the real estate agent you suggested, about rental property. He said there isn't much available at the moment, but he'll keep working on it for me. I think I'll be fine at the Sunset Motel for a while. Thanks for asking."

"If Helen or I hear about any possibilities for you, we'll let you know. Have a good afternoon, Seth."

"Thank you, sir, you too." Seth ambled to his car still experiencing the contented satisfaction of a wonderful meal and enjoyable company. Sliding behind the wheel, he yawned and thought of returning to the garish motel room for a much-needed power nap, but he remembered his promise to meet Reuben Walker at the hardware store. He turned the car toward the main street of town.

As he approached the square, Seth was surprised to see such a thriving community. Men and women of all shapes, sizes, and ages bustled about, stopping often to exchange bits of news and catch up, he assumed, on the latest happenings. Small children swarmed like bees around many of the younger mothers' legs. Some were playing hide and seek, some crying, wanting to be scooped up in their mother's arms and held, and one was angry and throwing the proverbial temper tantrum. A few banker-types stopped to chat, while several old timers sat on benches, probably solving the problems of the world—and in short order.

Thinking back on the whole process of coming here, Seth realized how little information he had about Mason Falls. He'd been in such a terrible mood about turning down the promising and very lucrative opportunity with the Hawthorn Clinic in Kansas City, he actually had said yes to the first rural practice position he was offered. Angus McQuarry gave him some basic information: rural community, population about 3,000, nestled in the Ozark Mountains, simple lifestyle, lots of great fishing, hospital about 14 miles away, and friendly people.

Seth had signed on the dotted line and braced himself for a long, boring three years, convincing himself the experience would be worthwhile. He continued to hold onto the hope that the Hawthorn Clinic would be ready for yet another bright, energetic

M.D. when he completed his obligation in Mason Falls.

Seth found a parking place close to the hardware store. He removed his tie and blazer, neatly folding them and placing them on the back seat. He found himself anticipating seeing Reuben again. There was something intriguing about the man. Reuben Walker may only be a self-described handyman, but he exuded a genuineness that even Seth's inclination to cynicism couldn't reject.

The rusted handle on the screen door felt warm in Seth's hand as he entered the store. He'd never experienced anything like stepping into Hank's Hardware—hinges, hardware, & other helpful things according to the sign in the window. The floor of wide wood planks creaked with each step he took. A musty smell, accented by the odor of 3-in-1 oil, made him sneeze.

A large mounted deer head stared down at him from one wall with seeming disapproval. The sign underneath attested to Hank being the taxidermist for this scraggly creature. While Seth knew little about the art of taxidermy, he didn't have much trouble discerning this as an amateurish job. A clacking sound caught his attention. Looking up, he saw it came from an old wooden ceiling fan suspended from a quite beautiful pressed tin ceiling. *Quaint*, he thought. His first impression of the entire place was total chaos, and he wondered how anyone ever located what they were looking for.

Stuffing his hands in his pockets, Seth began making his way along rows of wooden bins, all holding differing shapes and sizes of bolts, nuts, screws, and nails. There was even a hand-lettered sign on one stating "Rags for sale – 1 handful 25¢." The more he peered into these awkward looking catchalls, the more he realized what had initially seemed chaotic was simple, well-thought-out organization. Seth felt a friendly clap of a hand on his shoulder. He found himself once more staring into the eyes of Reuben Walker.

"Hey there, Doc," Reuben said, smiling, obviously pleased to see the younger man again.

"Hello, Mr. Walker, how are you?"

"Well, I'm just fine, mighty fine indeed, but I would be a whole lot better if you'd call me Reuben instead of Mr. Walker. We don't hold much to formality around here." Reuben grinned. His smile was contagious and Seth smiled back.

"Sure, Reuben, I'd like that."

"Well now, let me show you around. I've been out on a delivery, so I'll have to see where Hank is hiding out. Since it's so quiet around here, he must be back in the storeroom. It's just over there," he said, pointing to a door. He led the way through the aisles of wooden bins. His heavy leather work boots came down hard on the creaky, old floors. It sounded like a small army marching through the store instead of just the two of them. Reuben opened the door and called out, "Hey, Hank, are you back there? We have company, come on out."

A moment later, Reuben was introducing Seth to Hank Simpson, owner of all these hinges, hardware, and other helpful things. The two of them shook hands, Hank first wiping his hand on a leathery apron. Seth thought he looked like a character out of an American Revolution era novel. He was small and thin, wore rimless glasses, and had his hair pulled back in a short ponytail. He was clutching a broom. He was so soft-spoken that Seth had to strain to hear his greeting. He estimated Hank to be about forty years old. Though of slight build, Hank had an athletic look to him.

"Hank has a charming wife, Karen, and two lovely daughters. Kelly is fourteen, Holly is twelve," Reuben said, patting Hank's shoulder.

Seth noticed that when Reuben spoke to someone, he had a habit of touching them with a pat or friendly slap on the shoulder. He'd never been around a man who so naturally affirmed others by his words and touch. Yes, Reuben piqued Seth's interest. Something he found both pleasant and somewhat irritating.

Seth was a loner, always had been. Except for Gran and one other person, Seth never got too close to anyone. If he admitted the truth, it was probably out of fear of being rejected. And besides, developing strong relationships right now didn't fit his agenda.

Reuben, however, collided with Seth's self-erected barricade, knocking a chink in it and opening a tiny portal of light. Unnerving as it was to him, Seth gravitated to that light. What was the key Reuben seemed to hold to create these connections?

At times like this, Seth had a strong urge for a cup of Starbuck's coffee. He could almost smell the aroma and see the table where he'd spent so many hours reading or reflecting. There in that quiet corner in Starbuck's on the Plaza in Kansas City, Seth Bradley felt right with the world around him. He was known, admired even, and his privacy respected. Here in this new place, he felt unsettled. The safe, secure world he had created was no longer available. In less than 24 hours, he was experiencing emotions that had been conveniently tucked away for a very long time.

"Say, Doc, how about a cup of coffee? I'm due for a break," Reuben asked.

Startled, Seth nodded in agreement. What was it with this man? Could he also read minds? He shook hands with Hank, then he and Reuben made their way to the door. The floors creaked as they walked away, the fan clacked, the deer continued to stare, the screen door slammed behind them, and Seth stood in the sunlight feeling bewildered.

"Doc, are you hungry or just want coffee?"

"Just coffee, thanks. I had lunch with the McQuarrys, and I'm still full."

"I bet you are. That Helen is known around here for her cooking. Well then, let's go by the bakery, get some coffee, and then find a bench by the fountain on the square. Reuben started walking, and Seth stepped into place beside him.

"Who won the cook-off?" Seth asked, trying to make conversation.

"Jack Hagerity," Reuben replied, a trace of disappointment in his voice. "I was sorry for George, of course, but Jack has been struggling with some hard times, so I think winning the cook-off helped him feel better about himself. Sure is a beautiful day, don't you think, Doc?" He gazed around, inhaling the fresh air.

"Uh, yes, I guess it is. I hadn't noticed," Seth answered with a quick look around.

"Don't they enjoy the outside world where you come from?

Round here that's real important to most folks. Where are you from anyway? Never got around to asking you last night."

"First off, I don't know how people feel about the outside world where I come from. I haven't had the time or the interest to ask, to be honest." Seth immediately felt terrible about being so curt with his answer, but Reuben's gregarious personality overwhelmed him.

Seth's thoughts drifted back to comments fellow med students and residents had made when they assumed he couldn't hear them—comments he heard more than once. "Man, what's up with Bradley? Is he always this uptight?" "Watch out for Bradley, he's snapping today. Looks docile enough, but when he comes out of his shell, he'll snap your head off."

Those words still stung, but he knew they were accurate. He'd been so focused on accomplishing the task in front of him, there was little interest given to cultivating relationships. Seth gazed at nothing in particular while trying to think of a way to apologize.

"Forgive me if I spoke out of turn. Sometimes my words get ahead of my thinking. I sure didn't mean to upset you." Reuben stopped mid-stride with a contrite look.

"Sure, Reuben. It's no big deal. Guess I'm a little touchy—so much on my mind. I'm sorry too."

"Let's get that coffee then, okay?" Reuben's smile lit up his face in a way that was hard to resist. The two men walked down the street each in his own thoughts.

"Here we are, Earl's Doughnut Shop," Reuben said, pointing to a sign ahead of them. "Earl makes a mean cup of coffee as well as mighty good doughnuts, but we'll save the doughnuts for another day."

After several introductions to other customers and Earl himself, Seth and Reuben ordered their coffee to go. Bidding everyone farewell, they walked across the street to find a bench. For several minutes, both men were content to quietly watch the activity around them. One little boy was putting his mother in a panic by jumping up on the rim around the fountain and trying to balance himself as he walked around it. The little boy was really quite amusing to Seth and Reuben but not to the young mother, who also had a crying infant in the stroller. Reuben nudged Seth and said, "Let's go help, what do you say?"

"Sure, I guess so. Wouldn't she think we were intruding?"

"Heavens no, son," Reuben replied, getting up and pulling Seth with him.

"Ma'am, I'm Reuben Walker and this here is Doc Bradley. We noticed you kinda have your hands full. Can we help?"

The young woman was almost in tears, and she melted at Reuben's grandfatherly offer. "Oh, would you please?" she asked, reaching out to shake his hand. "I'm Cindi Harrison."

"We'd be most happy to," replied Reuben. "Doc here will catch that monkey of yours. I'll settle this little one down, and you sit on the bench and catch your breath. How does that sound?"

"Wonderful, absolutely wonderful! Thank you both so much," she said with a weary sigh and a face filled with heartfelt appreciation.

Seth rushed over to try to corral the boy who was close to losing his balance and getting a good dunking.

"Hey there, buddy, how about a little help?" Seth called out, reaching for the boy's hand just before he took the inevitable plunge.

"Who are you, mister?" came the reply. With spiked blond hair and happy brown eyes, the boy looked to be about five years old and clearly full of mischief.

"I'm Seth. Who are you?"

"I'm John Jacob Harrison."

"Well now, that's one big name for a little guy."

"I'm not little!" the child howled, jerking his hand from Seth's. "Take it back, mister, I'm not little!"

"Okay, okay, you're not little." Seth recoiled, hands raised protectively. Trying to distract the boy before he erupted again, Seth asked, "Do you go by John or Jacob?"

"My momma always calls me John Jacob, but I think it's cause she's mostly frus-ter-ated with me. My daddy calls me J.J. You can call me that too, if you don't say I'm little anymore."

Seth couldn't help but smile at the determined countenance

staring back at him. "Sure thing, J.J. How about we shake on it like men?" Grinning from ear to ear, J.J. stuck out a chubby and somewhat dirty hand.

"Like mans," he replied in his deepest five-year-old voice.

Taking hold of J.J.'s hand again to help him keep his balance, Seth continued to walk around the fountain with him. It brought back memories of innumerable dreams Seth had as a boy. They clawed their way out of his subconscious. He could see them now. He had never known his dad, had never felt his touch. His fantasy dad was there holding his hand. He felt the warmth, the strength. Poignant vignettes etched on his mind and his heart. They remained as vivid as they were when he was J.J.'s age. Catching a baseball with his dad's oversized glove. His dad's hand on his, showing him how to cast a fishing line. The strong hand of his father on his shoulder the first time he tried to ride a bike minus training wheels. So many dreams, but that's all they were.

"Hey, Mr. Seth, what are you thinkin' about?" J.J. asked, looking into the faraway gaze of the man beside him.

"Nothing much, J.J. Just thinking about when I was a boy like you."

"Am I gonna see you again, Mr. Seth?"

"Sure, big guy, we'll see each other. This is a pretty small town, isn't it?"

Impulsively, Seth lifted J.J. off the concrete rim of the fountain and swung him around and around. The boy's squeals of delight filled the air, joining Reuben's hearty laugh, both transported into a moment of surprise and joy.

Out of the corner of his eye, Seth saw Reuben rocking the baby back and forth, holding it gently on his lap and at the same time, patting the young mother's hand. Reuben's words touched him as Seth heard him say, "I think your little one is finally asleep, ma'am. Are you feelin' better?"

"Yes sir, I am. You're wonderful with children. It must be your quiet manner. Thank you so much, Mr. Walker." She smiled gratefully as she took her sleeping baby and situated him in the stroller.

The two of them walked to the fountain where Seth and the boy were bending over the water to count the coins at the bottom.

"Come on, J.J., it's time to go back to Nana and Poppa's."

"Hey, Mr. Seth, my momma must not be frus-ter-ated anymore. She called me J.J." The three adults laughed as the little boy looked bewildered about what was so funny.

"Momma, can I come back and play with Mr. Seth again. Can I, Momma, pleeease?"

The young mother smiled at her son, running her fingers through his hair. "We'll see, sweetie, we'll see. You just can't know what a blessing you both have been," she said to Reuben and Seth. "We've only lived here a few weeks, and I'm still feeling overwhelmed with an infant and a very active five-year-old son and the move."

"It was our pleasure, Cindi," Reuben replied, gently patting her arm. "Wasn't it, Doc?"

"Yes, yes it was, Mrs. Harrison. And J.J. and I hope we can do this again sometime. Right, J.J.?"

"We sure do, Momma. Mr. Seth and me are mans, aren't we, Mr. Seth?"

"You bet, buddy, we sure are." Seth winked and tousled the boy's spiked hair.

The four waved goodbye, promising to see each other soon.

Seth looked at Reuben and grinned. "I know. You don't have to say it—I will. *I told you so.*" At that both men laughed.

"I was watching you with the little guy, Doc. You're very good with kids. You had him eating out of your hand in no time."

"Thanks, Reuben. I do like kids. I guess I can kind of relax around them. Well, I best be going and get myself settled as much as I can for now anyway. I'm going to the clinic tomorrow and get my office set up. I'll start seeing patients on Monday morning. It's been nice this afternoon, Reuben. I've enjoyed it."

"Me too, Doc. Enjoyed being with you. See you around."

Seth headed back to his car, but Reuben paused before going down the street toward Hank's Hardware.

Reuben watched as Seth strode off to his car and reflected on the new side he had observed in the man and smiled.

"Lord, there's a gentle spirit in Doc. He's just got it tucked down deep inside him. Help him find it more often, Lord, like he did today, and not be afraid to let it show." Closing his eyes momentarily, he added, *"Amen."*

~6~

THE ELEVATOR DOOR OPENED TO A familiar aroma, but today it failed to calm her uneasiness. Escape was only the press of a button away, but her feet propelled her forward. Claire opened the door of New Beginnings Counseling. After signing in, she took a seat and picked up an outdated copy of *Ladies Home Journal*, aimlessly flipping one page after another.

"Claire," the receptionist said, "you may go back now." They exchanged smiles, and Claire walked down the hall toward Meredith Reynolds' office. She made her usual stop at the courtesy desk, fixed herself a cup of peppermint tea, and then knocked on Meredith's door.

"Come in." Claire heard the strong yet comforting reply that had become all too well known to her over the past eighteen months.

"Hello, Meredith. Guess you're kind of surprised to see me again so soon . . ." Claire tried to smile to divert attention from the embarrassing squeak in her voice.

"I am a little surprised but always glad to see you." Meredith waited for her to take a seat in the beautiful upholstered wingback chair that Claire had, over time, claimed as her place.

"You seem nervous," Meredith said as she took the chair across from Claire. "Is everything okay?"

"Well, yes on both counts," Claire responded. "You see, Meredith, I've made a major decision, and I promised Robyn I would talk to you before doing anything." Claire took a long sip of tea hoping for its usual calming effect on her.

"When you're ready, tell me what's on your mind," Meredith said.

Claire's heart pounded, and she felt like a kid caught in some mischief. She was a grown woman and the mother of a five-year-old son for heaven's sake. It's not like she needed permission to make a move. Sitting up a little straighter, she said, "I have decided to move to Mason Falls, Arkansas, where my dad and my grandparents were raised, and well, where my family is from all the way back to my great-great-grandparents who started the town." *Breathe, Claire, breathe*, she told herself.

Although her counselor gave a valiant effort at hiding her surprise, Claire picked up on it immediately. She went on to explain to Meredith what she'd told Robyn about needing a change and the benefits of a small town for Mason. She also stressed the sense of security and stability she'd always experienced in Mason Falls and that she was certain Mason would have the same experience.

Meredith listened intently, her eyes glued on Claire. "If you have no one left there, are you sure you'll still feel that security and stability?" Meredith asked.

"I can't give you a positive answer, but I can say that it has always been a place where I have experienced peace and a sense of belonging." Claire relaxed and the nervousness began to subside. "I do have questions about this, Meredith. It's the most important decision I've made on my own in years. So, I'm listing the house here as a one-year lease to give Mason and me a trial run." She took another sip of her tea while collecting her thoughts.

"I'm not here to ask permission. I promised Robyn I would meet with you, but my mind is made up. It may sound strange, but I'm convinced I'm being drawn back to Mason Falls for a reason. I can't tell you exactly what it is, but I'm as certain of this as anything I've ever done."

The two women sat in silence for several minutes, each with her own thoughts. Meredith broke the silence as she took Claire's hand in hers. "Claire, there are many questions we could go over, and there are some initial concerns I have, but let me say this, I see you making some healthy decisions in this plan. For one, leasing the house and giving yourself a time frame before making a permanent decision. Second, recognizing your need to move on with life, for Mason's sake, yes, but also for yours. You are not an impulsive woman, and if you feel your heart drawn back to your roots, then follow your heart."

Claire could not hold in the emotion any longer. The tears flowed freely, and she felt a cleansing wash over her. The two women promised to keep in touch, assuring each other they were only a phone call away.

Walking out into the sunlight seemed a confirmation to Claire as she left the building. One thing was certain. Her confidence was building about the decision.

Once settled in the soft leather seat in her shiny black BMW, she took out her small notebook and rummaged in her purse for a pen. She was ready to check off the first item on her to-do list. Meet with Meredith. Today was going to be a busy one. The next item of business was to go by the real estate office. She was thankful Paul Lockhurst was a trusted friend and would help her with the details of leasing the house.

On the way to Paul's office, she decided to make the dreaded call to Robyn. Claire knew her decision would be painful for her dearest friend. But her mind was made up, and her new level of confidence enabled her to dial the number.

"Robyn, hi. I wanted you to know I just left Meredith's office. She gave me her blessing on moving to Mason Falls." There was a faint cry on the other end of the line. "Robyn, please support me on this. Please be happy for me and for Mason." Claire's voice cracked as she choked back the tears. "Robyn, say something please."

"I don't know that I can say I'm happy for you right now, Claire. I want to, but it wouldn't be honest. You and Randall and Mason are the only real family I've ever had. Now, it's not just Randall who is gone. I'm losing you and Mason too. Give me some time to process it all. Right now, I can't."

"I love you, Robyn," Claire whispered, clicking off her cell phone. New tears trickled down her cheeks. An overwhelming sense of aloneness welled up inside her, and for the first time in days, she questioned her decision.

A whirlwind of emotions propelled Claire through the following hours. Sadness and fear battled anticipation and confidence, but in the end, her determination won out. The hum of the car engine quieted her thoughts as she sat waiting in the pickup line at Mason's school. It worked out perfectly that Maureen was picking up Billy for a family errand today, so it would just be Mason and her.

The day had ended well except for the nagging ache in her heart for Robyn. She looked at her to do list. She had met with Meredith, called Robyn, worked out the lease details with Paul, and set up a time for the moving company to come give her an estimate. She had two final items on her list. The first was moments away. She was taking Mason to the park to tell him about the move. The last was contacting her dad's good friend, Dr. Angus McQuarry. She would do that after she put her little boy to bed.

Claire felt a warmth come over her, and she had the most profound sensation that Randall was there with her. She could almost hear him say, "Babe, I'm so proud of you." Claire pictured him as she loved him most, his eyes crinkled in a smile, his dimple creasing his left cheek. She reached out, willing him to feel her touch on his face, but only a slight breeze caressed her fingers.

Startled by the click of the door handle, Claire saw Mason's smiling face, a small image of his daddy, peering through the glass.

"Hi, Mommy! You look funny. Are you okay?" His eyes held a trace of concern as he hopped in the car and buckled his seat belt.

"Sure, sweetie, just kind of in a daydream is all. How was your day? Anything fun or interesting happen?" Claire asked, adjusting the rear view mirror a bit and grinning at her little man as they made eye contact.

"Great. Lots of stuff happened. Don't you 'member, Mommy? Today was when we set our butterflies free to go find a new home. It was so cool!" Mason's face glowed with excitement, his hands emphasizing the wonder of it all. "Where do you think they'll live, Mommy? Do you think they'll find a nice place?" Mason's eyes begged for a positive answer.

"I'm sure they will, sweetheart, but let's talk about it in a little while. I thought we would go to the park, okay?" Claire was trying to sound normal, but her heart was beating fast and her thoughts were racing. She couldn't believe how perfect this was. Butterfly day—the perfect way to explain to Mason their upcoming move. They would be going to a new home too, just like his butterfly.

"But don't forget, Mommy."

"I won't, sweetheart, I promise," she said.

The park teemed with moms and children, teenagers, even the elderly, all enjoying the warm, sunny day. Claire and Mason searched for a less crowded area, finally choosing a spot under a young but shady maple tree. She spread an old quilt from her grandmother on the grass while Mason rummaged through the bag of snacks. The sun engulfed them in its warm glow as mother and son munched on apples, cheese sticks, and oatmeal cookies fresh from Early Bird Bakery.

"Sweetie, let's talk about the butterflies," Claire said, pulling him into her lap. She leaned back against the tree, holding her son close while brushing his damp hair off his forehead with her fingers. Mason turned in Claire's lap so he could see her face, and his eyes lit up with childish anticipation. She smiled and gave him a hug.

"Remember when your caterpillar began to build his cocoon?" Claire asked. Mason nodded. "Well," she continued, "he probably thought that cocoon would be his home forever and ever, don't you think?" Once again, her son nodded in agreement.

"He prob'ly thought he would live there years and years and years!" Mason exclaimed.

"I'm sure he did, sweetie, but even though he worked hard and loved his home, we knew he wasn't going to live there forever. It was just a place to live for a little while, right?" Mason's look turned sad.

"But now Mr. Butterfly can make a brand new home anywhere he wants to go. And he can see all the new and different things he could never see as a caterpillar, especially if he stayed inside his cocoon all the time. Sweetie, you and Mommy are going to be like the butterflies. We're going to a new home too." She sat quietly, allowing him time to take it in.

"But how, Mommy? We aren't butterflies. And where would we go? We can't see all the places like they do when they fly away."

Mason crawled out of Claire's lap and sat cross-legged beside her. His eyes held hers with an intensity she had seldom seen in him. She reached out to touch his arm but felt it tense beneath her fingers.

"We're going to Mason Falls where Potch and Honey lived. Remember the stories I've told you about all the wonderful times Mommy had there when I was a little girl?" Claire's voice trembled.

"Uh huh, but I thought you said nobody lives there anymore."

"Well, none of my family is there, but lots of other people live there," she said softly. This was more difficult than she had expected.

"Mommy, I don't think I want to go to that place." Mason's chin quivered and a single tear slid down his cheek.

"I understand, sweetie, I really do. It is a kind of scary idea, even for me, but I'm sure it's what we need to do. Sometimes we have to do something very scary, just like the butterfly breaking out of the cocoon, to discover how wonderful things are on the other side of that scariness." Claire opened her arms, silently pleading for him to fall into her embrace.

The afternoon sun had begun to fade, and there was a hint of a breeze. Claire felt a shiver work its way down her back in the brief moment before Mason leaned over to her and wrapped his arms around her neck. Large tears ran down his cheeks as he sobbed. "I'm scared, Mommy. I've never lived anywhere but here."

"I know, little man, but I'll take care of you in Mason Falls just like I do here. Remember the adventures we had with Daddy? Sometimes you were scared then too, right?" she asked, her tone tender. Mason tilted his head, gazing into his treasured memories when there were the three of them.

"I 'member. Like when we went skiing in that place with the big mountains and snow as high as houses. I was really scared to come down the mountain, wasn't I?"

Claire chuckled, "Yes, you were very scared, but you did it anyway. Why did you go down the mountain, Mason?"

The little boy sat pondering his mother's question. Then a smile crept across his face, and his eyes began to shine with understanding. "Because I was with you and Daddy, and I knew you and Daddy wouldn't let anything hurt me." Mason took her hand in his and squeezed it tightly.

"I love you, Mason," she said. Her heart was overwhelmed with the tenderness she felt for her child.

"I'm still kinda scared, but I'm bigger now. That's why you call me your little man, right? So, I guess it will be okay. We can call it our butterfly adventure." Mason jumped up, pulling his mother up with him. "Let's race to the car, Mommy." Claire grabbed the quilt and snack bag before breaking into a sprint to try to catch the explosion of energy released by her son.

~ ~ ~

She and Mason decided on grilled cheese sandwiches and tomato soup for supper. It had been an emotional day for both of them. Mason accepted bedtime with ease. Soon the house was filled with quiet—something Claire was still struggling to adjust to. Looking around at the hall clock as she left her son's room, she realized it would be 10 p.m. in Arkansas—too late to call Dr. McQuarry tonight. She'd make that her first priority after getting her little guy off to school in the morning. She decided to make it an early night herself. She took a hot shower, then slipped into bed.

~ ~ ~

At the sound of her alarm, Claire hit the button and scrambled out of bed. Slipping into her favorite warm-up suit, she realized it had been a long time since she had felt this energetic. She liked the feeling. She gave her blond hair a swipe with her brush and made a mental note to call for a hair appointment. It was a little early to wake Mason, so she decided to have a cup of tea and think through her day. She crept downstairs to make her tea. The sun streaming through the windows gave promise of a beautiful day.

As the teapot's whistle broke the silence, she glanced at the clock. Six thirty. That meant it was eight thirty in Arkansas. By the time she got Mason ready for school and her neighbor, Maureen, picked him up, it would be about nine forty-five in Mason Falls. She hoped that wouldn't be a bad time to call Dr. McQuarry. Her thoughts for the day began to take form.

It was Wednesday. She needed to call Robyn and see if they could schedule lunch, if not today, then before the weekend. Claire desperately wanted her friend's blessing or at least understanding.

She knew this was not easy for Robyn, and she could not imagine leaving with a barrier between them.

Her conversation with Angus McQuarry weighed on her mind. It would be crucial for any further planning and the timing of her move. The moving company would be here at the end of the week for an estimate, so she needed to have some idea about a date for the move. She would also need to make some decisions about what she would be taking with her.

Claire glanced back at the clock. It was time to get Mason up and ready for school. She headed up the stairs, humming softly. When she opened the door to Mason's room, the room shimmered in the early morning sunlight. How her son could sleep in a room filled with such brilliance she would never understand. Tiptoeing to her child's bed, she saw him curled in the fetal position, clad in his camo pajamas and clutching Po, his worn but well-loved teddy bear. It had been her husband's first gift to his infant son. Po became, with time, her son's best friend, confidant, comforter, and colleague in mischief. Claire smiled as countless snapshots of Mason and Po ran through her mind.

The bed squeaked as she sat down, but there was no movement from Mason. Claire leaned over him and stroked his hair before gently kissing his cheek. "Hey, sleepyhead, it's time to wake up," she crooned. Nothing. "Come on, big guy, we need to get you ready for school." Slowly, Mason opened one eye then the other. He turned and held out his arms to her, and she held him close, relishing the sweetness of the moment. He was growing up too fast.

~ ~ ~

With breakfast over, Claire helped her son with his backpack and opened the door just as Maureen drove up to the curb. She gave her boy a big hug and waved as he jumped into the car and turned to smile at her.

Her thoughts began racing as she closed the door. She was nervous about her call to Dr. McQuarry. She wasn't sure why. Perhaps she feared he would try to discourage her from coming. Maybe the old home place was in total disrepair and would cost too many thousands of dollars to repair. Maybe it wouldn't be worth repairing. Then what?

"Stop it, Claire," she said firmly. She marched to the desk and picked up the note with Dr. McQuarry's office number on it. *Just dial the number. Now,* she told herself.

As the phone began to ring, Claire paced back and forth and chewed on the thumbnail of her free hand. Finally, a warm, very Southern voice answered.

"Mason Falls Medical Clinic. This is Nell Meyers speaking. How may I help you?"

Claire stammered, "This is Claire Mason Westfield in San Francisco. Would it be possible to speak with Dr. McQuarry?"

"Well, Ms. Westfield, I'll go check. Dr. Mac was doing some office surgery, but maybe he is about finished. Do you mind holding a minute?" Nell asked.

"No, that's fine. Thank you so much," Claire said.

Nell tapped on the door only to hear an irritated, "What!" Nell's voice quivered, "Sorry, Dr. Mac, I thought you might be finished. There's a call from San Francisco, a Claire Mason Westfield." She waited anxiously. There must be something wrong. She could count on one hand the number of times in the five years she had worked for him that her employer had barked at her like that.

The door opened a crack. Dr. Mac, usually the picture of quiet confidence, looked harried. "Nell, this will take longer than anticipated. Get Mrs. Westfield's number and tell her I'll call her the minute I'm through. Oh, and, Nell, sorry I snapped at you," Dr. Mac smiled his familiar, gentle smile.

"No problem, sir. I'll tell her right away," Nell said and hurried back to her desk.

"Ms. Westfield, I'm so sorry to keep you on hold. Dr. Mac is in kinda an emergency, and he asked for your phone number. He said he'd call you the minute he's through."

Claire was disappointed but understood. After all, she'd been a physician's wife.

"Thank you, Miss Meyers." She gave her number, and Nell repeated it back to her. After hanging up, Claire decided it would be best if she did something productive until Dr. McQuarry called, otherwise she'd bite off another fingernail.

Over the next half hour, Claire cleaned up the breakfast dishes, put chicken in the crock-pot, and made a grocery list. Just as she started to clean the glass door to the patio, the phone rang.

"Hello, this is Claire Westfield speaking."

"Claire, this is Angus McQuarry returning your call. How are you, my dear? It's been, what, five years or so since we've talked." His voice had a rich smoothness.

"Dr. McQuarry, it's so nice of you to return my call, and it's good to hear your voice again. Yes, it's been five years. I called when Dad died." Claire's throat tightened as she recalled that difficult conversation.

"What can I do for you, Claire? I hope we can visit again soon, but I don't have but a few minutes right now. I hope you understand," Dr. Mac said, his words kind and thoughtful.

"Dr. McQuarry, I want to know if the family home is available or if it has been rented. You see, my son and I are moving back to Mason Falls." Claire's voice trembled at the words.

"Moving back here! That's wonderful, Claire. Mind if I ask about your husband? Is he not coming with you?"

"I'm a widow, Dr. McQuarry. My husband was killed in an automobile accident a year and a half ago." Claire struggled to hold her emotions in check.

"Oh, Claire, I'm so sorry, so very sorry. I didn't know. And yes, the house is available, but I'm sure it will need some work. I know someone who can take a look at it, and I'll get back to you. Do you plan to move soon?"

"The sooner the better. This has been a big decision, and I don't want to wait too long and possibly lose my courage. I have to be honest, Dr. Mac," she said easily, remembering when she had called him that as a child. "I'm sure this is what I need to do, but I'm also a little frightened."

"My dear child, I understand. Let me call Reuben Walker and get him to go over to your family's home and check things out. I'll bet he can get to it today, and I'll call you back this evening. How does that sound?"

"Great. Thank you so much. I'll wait to hear from you."

"Don't worry, dear, it will all work out," Dr. Mac said.

Claire found herself sitting in her solace chair, the one that belonged to her grandfather. She was shaking and chilled. Curling up under her grandmother's afghan, she began to cry but wasn't sure why. The tears subsided as sleep overcame her.

~ ~ ~

When Claire woke, she was startled to find she'd slept most of the morning. She would have to pull herself together to get everything done that she needed to do before her little boy got home from school. Fortunately, he went home with Maureen and her son Billy on Wednesdays so the boys could play. When she picked him up about five o'clock, they would have an early dinner. Thank goodness she had put that chicken in the crock-pot. She didn't usually allow her son to watch television on a school night, but tonight she would make an exception. That way, she and Dr. Mac could discuss the details she needed to know.

Claire busied herself in the kitchen. She made a pan of brownies for dessert. Mason would think this a very special night—brownies and television on a school night. She smiled, picturing the expression on her child's face when she told him.

The rest of the day was a blur. She tried numerous times to reach Robyn but got no response. She would not let her mind even toy with the idea that her best friend would avoid her call.

Claire completed most of what had been on her list for the day. At ten minutes until five, she rushed out the door to drive the short distance to Maureen's. Were it not for the anticipated phone call and the fact that she was exhausted, she would have walked. She and Maureen often met halfway, helping both mothers alleviate a little more of the pent up energy in their active little boys. It would have been a beautiful day to do just that, but Claire felt almost chained to the phone. Why hadn't she thought to give Dr. Mac her cell phone number? She must do that tonight for sure.

~7~

CLAIRE DRUMMED HER FINGERS ON THE table at Barney's Grill, waiting for Robyn to arrive. She had chosen this place for the noise level. Conversations were usually animated and loud. Robyn, while certainly Claire's dearest friend, could be very vocal and opinionated. Claire expected that to be the case today. She sipped her water in an effort to calm the pounding of her heart. She and Robyn had been friends since they started boarding school together. They were more like sisters, and because neither of them had any family left, they'd formed an even stronger bond over the last several years.

Digging around in her purse, Claire found a tissue to swipe at the beads of perspiration dotting her forehead. This was her decision, she reminded herself, and though she longed for Robyn's understanding and blessing, she was confident she was doing the right thing. Startled by dishes crashing to the floor near her, Claire looked up to see the face of a humiliated young server. She said softly, "It's okay, accidents happen."

The girl gave her a small smile and whispered, "Thanks, I needed that."

Claire looked up from the disarray on the floor as Robyn entered the restaurant and was working her way through the crowded tables. Claire waved to get her attention. Robyn's exquisite features, dress, and manner turned the head of every man in Barney's Grill. Claire never ceased to be amazed at the impact her friend had on men.

Robyn bent down and gave Claire a warm hug, "Hey, girl, how's the best friend in the world doing?" she asked. Claire breathed a sigh of relief, thankful Robyn was more herself than she had been during their last phone conversation.

"Just fine but starved. Sit down and let's order."

"My, you must've put in a more intense morning than I did," Robyn grinned, "and mine was unbelievable. Okay, I'll have my favorite shrimp salad with the works, including avocado, and an iced tea. How's that for decision-making?"

Claire laughed and ordered the same from the server who had earlier dropped the tray and now stood waiting to take their order. The small talk centered on Robyn's morning. She was lead attorney in a case that was going sour. Her frustration was evident under her cool demeanor.

When the food arrived, Claire tried to enjoy her salad, but she worried over the timing of this planned conversation. She told herself Robyn had always had an amazing way of dealing with several difficult situations at one time. While she felt bad bringing up the topic of moving when Robyn was having a tough day, she also felt compelled to trust her friend's ability and her own inner conviction. After ordering a slice of key lime pie to split, Claire set her glass of tea down and opened her mouth, hoping the right words would come out.

"Robyn, I want you to know there's an agenda for our time together." Claire knew her friend well enough to know it was far better to approach her by coming right to the point.

"Mason and I will be leaving for Mason Falls a month from now. He will have finished school, and this summer will be a great time for him to adjust and make some friends. The family home needs some work, and I want to be there to oversee the process. It'll also be good getting back into a decorating project." Claire held her friend's steady gaze and went on.

"Robyn, for years we've talked about the two of us making a trip to Mason Falls, but it never seemed to be the right time. Will you go with me, even if it's just for a few days? Then you would have a better understanding of my decision. It would mean so much to me and to Mason."

Claire's shoulders ached from the tension of the moment. She'd expected Robyn to erupt with a deluge of reasons why the entire idea was ridiculous. Her silence sent a cold chill down Claire's spine as she waited. Music blared in the background and numerous conversations and laughter from nearby tables surrounded them, but all Claire heard was her friend's silence.

Robyn rubbed an index finger along the side of her glass of tea. The frown faded, softening her expression, as she said, "Claire, I still disagree with this move, but I will see if I can juggle my schedule for a few days. One question—where will you stay until the house is livable?"

Claire's expression went blank. "I don't know. It wasn't on my list. I—I'll work on that immediately." She saw a sad look cross Robyn's face. "Don't worry, it will be fine. I'll ask Dr. McQuarry, my dad's friend, what he would suggest." The two women finished their pie, an uncomfortable silence hanging heavy between them.

Claire felt relief when the young server approached with the bill. "I'll take that," she said, smiling at the girl. "My treat today, Robyn." She took out her wallet and gave the girl enough for the bill and a nice tip. "You did a really nice job serving us," she said. The look on the girl's face reminded her of how important simple gestures of kindness are to everyone.

When Robyn hugged her before heading back to her office, Claire felt some of the tension between them dissolve.

~ ~ ~

The following few days were a blur of activity as Claire attacked the decisions of what to take, sell, or give to the Goodwill store. In the midst of packing a box of Mason's outgrown clothes to give to a homeless shelter, she heard the phone ring. Initially she decided to ignore it, then abruptly changed her mind. She rushed to pick it up just before it went to voice mail.

"Glad I caught you, Claire. Angus McQuarry here. Listen, I just have a minute . . . on my way to make a house call. Helen and I would like you and Mason to stay with us until the house is at a point you can move in. And Claire, Helen said, 'Angus McQuarry, don't you take no for an answer!' so please say yes, dear, so you don't call down the wrath of a good woman on her poor husband."

Claire could almost see, even after all the years, the piercing gray eyes of this dear man. "Dr. Mac, are you both sure? Mason is an active five year old. I wouldn't want to disturb you and Helen. Also, my friend Robyn is coming for a few days to help me and to see what I'm getting myself into."

"Heavenly days, girl, you can't imagine what filling this old house with young folks would do for my wife!" Mac said with the deep laugh she remembered so well. "Believe me, Claire, the three of you would be a blessing. I'll tell Helen to get ready—the troops are coming. I must go now. Let's talk again soon. Can't wait to meet that little boy. Bet he'll make a great fishing buddy."

Claire hung up with lightness filling her heart. Throwing her arms open wide, she began dancing around the room, swaying to the music playing in the background. "I really do believe Mason and I are supposed to go to Mason Falls. I had forgotten all about calling Dr. Mac and then he calls me. I'm going home. I'm actually going home." Claire laughed as a tear slid down her cheek.

~ ~ ~

Three weeks seemed to evaporate into thin air as Claire continued to finish packing and tie up all the loose ends. She found it hard to believe it was the last week in the home she and Randall and Mason had shared. This would be the difficult part for her, letting go of what had been a place of love and security. But deep inside, Claire knew Randall would be proud of her and give her his blessing.

After she put away the last of the dinner dishes, Claire trudged up the stairs to put Mason to bed. Every inch of her body ached from countless hours of sorting, packing, and distributing items to the numerous organizations for folks in need. At the top of the stairs, Claire stopped abruptly. Mournful sobs coming from her son's room pierced her heart.

Quietly, she opened the door and peered into the packed-up room. Boxes held most of Mason's belongings and were stacked like giant blocks, forming a barricade in places. Her son lay in the fetal position, his sobs causing his little body to heave up and down.

"Mason, sweetheart, what's wrong? Are you hurt or sick?" Claire made her way to the bed and sat down. She rubbed his back tenderly. "There, there, sweetheart, tell me what's wrong."

The child slowly turned onto his back, an anguished look

spreading across his damp cheeks. "Mommy, I don't want to leave Billy or Aunt Robbie or all my other friends." He began to sob again.

Claire reached over and pulled him to her, caressing his wet cheeks. "I know this is very hard for you, Mason. Really I do. It's hard for me too. It's taking all the courage Mommy has to do this. Do you believe that I love you more than anything else?" The boy nodded his head, his eyes wide with yearning to understand.

"Sweetheart, there will be times when you can't understand why I may have to do something that, to you, doesn't feel good. All I can ask, Mason, is that you trust me. Anything I do will be because I love you so much and want what is best for both of us. Can you believe that?"

Mason sat quietly for a few moments running his small hand along Claire's arm. A slight sob escaped now and then. "Mommy, I still don't want to go, but I do want to believe you, 'cause, Mommy, I know you love me a whole lot." He turned his face up to look into Claire's eyes with a sad smile. "I'll be okay, 'cause as much as I want to stay here, I want to be with you even more."

Mother and son embraced in a long hug, stroking each other's back. Claire finally kissed her child, tucked the blanket around him, and watched him settled into sleep before she quietly left his room. She didn't feel nearly as courageous as she had a few moments ago.

~ ~ ~

Those next few days were gone before Claire could catch her breath. Tomorrow was moving day. Sometimes the thought made her skin clammy. Sometimes she just tingled with anticipation. One thing was certain, tomorrow she and Mason would leave their life in San Francisco and begin their adventure just like the butterfly they had talked about a few weeks ago.

Claire reached over to smack the alarm clock when it went off at 5:40. She moaned and threw the blanket over her head. It had been a long night packing up the last essentials.

Head throbbing, she sat up, rubbing her temples with her thumbs as reality sank in. This was moving day. The day her life would change, possibly forever. Crawling out of bed, she made a quick dash to the shower before stripping the sheets off the bed.

There was just enough time to do a load of wash before the movers came. Mason had been eager to sleep in his Buzz Lightyear sleeping bag, so she didn't need to wake him just yet.

Claire dressed in shorts and a tee shirt, grabbed the sheets and towels, and quietly crept downstairs. She desperately needed a cup of tea before starting this day. Holding the load of wash under one arm, she filled the teakettle and turned on the stove.

After starting the wash, she rushed back to the kitchen as the teakettle began to whistle. Pulling a Styrofoam cup out of the bag, she couldn't help but think of her grandmother. She remembered her Honey instructing her as a little girl on the proper way to serve tea. "Claire, drinking tea isn't like drinking coffee. It's more like a ritual. Seems to me, folks who drink coffee can be in too much of a hurry. Serving tea from a china pot and sipping it from a china cup just slows a person down and helps them enjoy the moment. Especially when drinking peppermint tea."

Claire had never forgotten those times with her grandmother. As an only granddaughter, she had inherited Honey's tea service. Soon she would be using it in her grandmother's home. She smiled, thinking how happy that would have made Honey. Catching sight of the clock on the oven, she jumped up. "Sorry, Honey, but this teatime has to be cut short."

Over the next hour, Claire cleaned bathrooms, put the wash in the dryer, and went through her checklist. Now it was time to get Mason up, dressed, and fed. The movers were due at eight o'clock, and Claire was thankful Billy had asked Mason to spend the day with him. It would be a difficult parting for both boys. They had been friends since their toddler years, and her heart ached for the little guys.

Mason was sleeping soundly, curled in his sleeping bag, surrounded by numerous Buzz Lightyear figures and a spaceship. Claire lay down beside her precious little man and stroked his soft hair. Doubts continued to plague her at times like this, and she felt her courage begin to slide from her like a slippery glass before it shattered on the floor.

"No," she mumbled softly. "I won't give in to these doubts. They are not as strong as the conviction that this is the right decision."

With resolve building in every breath, she leaned over and kissed her son's cheek.

"Good morning, sweet boy. It's time to get up." Just like Claire had done earlier, Mason rolled over and moaned. He snuggled deeper into his sleeping bag, denying the day had begun. Claire tousled his hair and tickled him. "Come on, sleepyhead. Billy's waiting for you."

Motivation was instant, and Mason began crawling out of his cocoon much like a butterfly ready to spread its wings.

"Hi ya, Mommy. I'm awake now," he grinned, as he wrapped himself around Claire.

"That's more like it, Tiger. How about doughnuts for breakfast? A special treat today."

"Wow, you mean it, really? Doughnuts?"

"Yes, Tiger, I mean it." Claire hoped this might sweeten what would become a painful day.

While Mason dressed, Claire folded the sleeping bag, stuffed the toys into a backpack, and zipped Mason's suitcase. She took the suitcase and followed Mason and his backpack downstairs.

Claire's cell phone began ringing as Mason finished his second doughnut and drained the last of his apple juice. "Sweetie, go brush your teeth while Mommy gets the phone." He turned and ran up the stairs, counting each one. "One, and two, and three and . . ."

"Hello."

"Claire, it's Maureen. How is the morning going? Is Mason up?"

"Hi, Maureen. Yes, he's up and brushing his teeth. So far it's been fine. He hasn't said anything at this point—just excited to see Billy."

"Billy can't wait much longer. He must have asked me every five minutes for the last hour to call you," Maureen said.

Claire smiled, picturing Billy, so much like her own little guy. "I'll meet you halfway, okay?"

"Great, see you in five."

Claire clicked her phone off. "Mason, Billy's meeting us in five."

Mason came charging down the stairs, his face aglow. "Billy and me get to spend all day at his house, right, Mommy?"

"That's right. I want you to have a great time. I'll check on you later." She struggled to keep her tears from falling. She knew she had to hold things together for his sake.

"Ready, little man?"

"You better believe it," Mason said, his grin filling his face.

~ ~ ~

Returning home, Claire stood in the doorway with an overwhelming sense of loss hitting her. There had been so many happy times in this place, so many precious memories. Wiping a tear from her face, she took a deep breath and told herself that from today forward, she and her son would begin making new memories, lots and lots of them. She saw the moving van pulling up to the house. "Well, it's time to begin," she said with a mixture of sorrow and excitement.

The next several hours flew by. The house, barren of any sign of the lives lived within its walls, gave a hollow echo to Claire's final goodbye. Instinctively, Claire had known seeing the house empty would be one of the hardest things for Mason to deal with, so she and Maureen had agreed that she would pick him up at Billy's. From there, she and Mason would drive to Robyn's and pick her up as they left town.

Claire rarely prayed, but at this moment she bowed her head and said softly, "*Please, God, help my little boy right now. He's giving up all he's ever known. Could You smile on him today?*"

She took her time getting into the car and driving the short distance to get Mason. She had no idea what she would say. She only hoped that if there was a God, He would give her the right words.

Mason and Billy were in the front yard when Claire got to the house. The two boys stood with chubby hands crammed into the pockets of their shorts. Their heads were lowered and silent tears were falling on their cheeks. Claire reached out for Maureen's hand, each fighting to contain her emotions. The two mothers ached not only for their sons' loss but also for their own. Their friendship had grown through the years.

Just when Claire thought her heart would burst with the pain and sadness of the moment, she heard a small voice say, "It's going to be okay, Billy—we will always be best friends." Mason and Billy smiled at each other. Billy gave Mason their secret handshake, then threw his arms around his friend. The boys stood there, neither knowing how to let go.

Claire finally went to her son, knelt down and put her arms around both boys. "It's time to go, sweetheart." She turned to Billy and stroked his hair. "Billy, I promise you, Mason and I will come back before school starts for a visit. How would that be?"

Billy's eyes lit up. "Really, Ms. Westfield? You mean it for sure?"

"Really. I mean for sure, Billy. I want you and Mason to always be friends, and we don't have to let distance come between you guys."

"Thanks, Mommy. You're the bestest mommy ever!" Mason's face glowed with delight. "So, Billy, don't stop working on our treasure dig. Maybe when I come back, you and me will find that treasure."

Claire gave Maureen a long hug then took her son's hand and walked to the car. It was time to pick up Robyn and get on the road. As Claire slipped behind the steering wheel, a thought popped into her head. Silently she said, "*God, maybe You are there. Thank You for the little miracle I just experienced.*"

~8~

DRIVING ACROSS THE COUNTRY WITH A five year old and a friend who rarely sits still proved more challenging than Claire had anticipated. She had heard parents talk about their children asking "Are we there yet" but had never thought much about it until the last couple of days. Now, even the hint of Mason asking those words again shredded what nerves she had left. Robyn wasn't much better. Her high energy, accomplish-the-goal-as-quickly-as-possible mindset resisted long hours in the car.

Claire feared a major meltdown for all of them if they didn't reach Mason Falls tomorrow. She racked her brain for another game to keep Mason occupied, but she came up empty. Then an idea popped into her mind. They hadn't tried singing. While Claire loved music, she had painful memories of any attempt at singing in the presence of the other people, even Robyn. Desperation won out.

"How about singing for a while?" Claire asked. Robyn looked surprised. She was well aware of Claire's feelings about singing in front of others. Years ago in boarding school, Robyn had badgered her to join the chorus. Claire ran through every excuse she could think of, but Robyn, relentless as usual, wouldn't take no for an answer. In the end, Claire finally admitted that she simply could not make herself sing in front of other people. While Robyn never seemed to completely accept the idea that Claire couldn't sing, she slowly relinquished her hope that they would be in chorus together. Claire's glance now told Robyn to tread lightly.

Mason's contagious enthusiasm started them off right. "Can we sing 'Take Me Out to the Ballgame'?" His smile cheered Claire's weariness, and she joined in on a rollicking rendition of the old favorite. By dinnertime, they had created an entire repertoire for future use.

Pulling into the parking lot of a small mom-and-pop café, they all agreed they could eat a horse or whatever else was available. Fortunately, Claire noticed that the menu showed neither horse nor any other unusual creature being served.

Their spirits renewed after enjoying an exceptionally great hamburger, they decided to drive another three or four hours. Robyn insisted on taking the next shift at the wheel. Claire didn't argue. Mason, content with her iPad, soon fell asleep, and Claire reclined her seat, permitting sleep to come unhindered.

Claire awoke to Robyn's nudging. "I found a decent motel, and it's after ten thirty. Ready for a nice soft bed instead of these cramped quarters?"

"Uh huh, sounds wonderful," Claire said.

Robyn took the overnight bags and went to check in. Claire followed, carrying her son.

While Claire tucked Mason into their bed, Robyn cleaned her face then crawled into her pajamas. By the time Claire had gone through the same routine, her bunkmates were snoring.

~ ~ ~

Over breakfast, Claire and Robyn looked at a map while Mason, still sleepy-eyed, watched cartoons on the breakfast room television. They were on the west side of Kansas City, Missouri, and estimated at least a four-hour drive. The navigation in the car would help on that when they plugged in their destination. It had been a lifesaver on the long trip.

"I didn't realize we were getting this close," Claire said. "The end is really in sight."

"And not too soon for me or for Mason," Robyn said. "I'm certainly glad I'm flying back. Maybe I can lead the other passengers in our song repertoire." Both women laughed as Mason turned a questioning stare at them, and then returned to his cartoons.

Knowing the end of the trip wasn't far off put all of them in a better mood for the day ahead. Mason asked, "What is Mason Falls like, Mommy?"

Robyn joined in with a teasing, "Yeah, Mommy, what is Mason Falls like, huh, huh?"

"Okay, you two, you asked for it." Claire grinned at her son in the rear view mirror. "You already know it's a small town, only about three thousand people. There weren't even that many when I used to visit Potch and Honey. It's definitely quaint—like something out of a storybook. Of course, I'm sure it's changed some. After all, I haven't been there in many years."

Claire's thoughts drifted back to a time and place where love and acceptance were the textures of living. Those bygone days stirred warmth in her soul.

"It's difficult to explain my most vivid memories of Mason Falls," she said. "What I remember are the fragrances of wild roses growing on an old wooden fence, jasmine hugging the rock wall around Potch and Honey's home, and the strong scent of pine trees hovering close by. Oh, and how could I ever describe the aroma of Honey's fresh baked pies just waiting for Potch and me to dig into after supper? One of my favorite memories, Mason, is Honey's clothesline."

She looked in the rearview mirror at the questioning look on her son's face. "Many people didn't have clothes dryers back then, so they would hang their clothes outside on a line between two poles. When the sheets or clothes were dry, I would run and put my face right up next to them. I'll never forget that smell. It was like a giant dryer sheet blowing in the breeze, only better because it was the smell of fresh air.

"And the people. No one ever seemed to be in a hurry. They would always have time to stop and talk to you. And they were genuinely interested in what you had to say, even if you were a child."

"Just like you and Aunt Robbie with me, right, Mommy?" Mason's face lit up in his biggest grin.

"Yes, sweetheart, we always have time for our best boy." Claire felt a thrill go through her in knowing her son felt the same love and acceptance. Out of the corner of her eye, she saw the hint of tears brimming under Robyn's dark lashes.

"Another of my favorite memories is walking down a dusty road barefoot. It was wonderful feeling the warm dirt squish between my toes. You will love it, sweetie. And wait until we play in the creek that leads to the waterfall." Claire took a deep breath and chuckled. "And, Mason, I'm going to teach you how to catch a crawdad. You're going to have a blast." The memories sent her heart soaring in ways she hadn't felt in years.

"I can hardly wait to spend this summer with you in Mason Falls." Claire glanced again at her son in the back seat. His eyes danced with delight, and an enormous grin covered his face. "So, Robyn, want to catch crawdads with us?" Claire couldn't help but giggle at the thought.

"You have got to be kidding me!" Robyn's expression threw Claire and Mason into a fit of laughter.

"What?" Robyn looked completely undone. "I didn't bring any-thing to wear for catching whatever those things are you're talking about. I'll just check my email or something. They do have internet, don't they? But no craw daddies or whatever they're called." She sat up straighter, looking her very professional self.

The miles slipped by, broken by a brief lunch, and finally Claire began to recognize scenes from childhood; the rolling hills and gentle creeks, cattle and sheep grazing in the valley pastures, rustic old barns standing where they had stood for decades. Their gray weathered wood catching the sunlight seemed to fill an emptiness in her. Her anticipation mounting, Claire found it hard to contain the intense emotions building inside her. She hadn't realized how much she longed to return to this place until now. And she was almost there. Almost home.

~ ~ ~

Claire slowed the car as they entered the town, taking in sights she hadn't seen in years. Shadows of old memories suddenly shone crystal clear with each familiar sight. Excitement filled her heart. She was ten years old again, coming to spend the summer with her grandparents. Claire wanted to slam on the brakes, park the car, and grab Mason and Robyn by the hand and introduce them to every place she recognized.

"Calm down," she told herself. Everyone was weary from the

long trip and would enjoy a tour more after some rest. She distracted her conflicting emotions by focusing on finding the McQuarrys' house. Her GPS soon had them pulling into their driveway. Their house was just as she had remembered. Charming. Mason clicked his seat harness belt and leaped from the car at the exact moment Claire shut the motor off. Three days confined in a car was all this five year old could take.

"Can I go ring the doorbell, Mommy?" Mason asked, tugging at Claire's door handle.

"Sure, but use your manners when they come to the door." Claire watched her little boy run to the door and couldn't help but think how adorable he was, blond hair shining in the sunlight, as bright and glorious as his almost constant smile.

When Angus and Helen McQuarry opened the door, Claire was taken aback. "They look just the way I remember them," she whispered. She could almost see her dad, standing there beside his longtime friend, smiling at her. Mac and Helen started toward the car, Helen holding Mason's hand. Claire ran into her embrace.

~ ~ ~

Claire lay snuggled next to a sleeping Mason, wrapped in thoughts of the day. She was thankful for a safe trip and even more thankful for the couple who had opened their home to her and her son and welcomed Robyn too. She knew she and Mason would need to make many adjustments, but her confidence about this decision was growing stronger. Lying beside her child, waves of what could only be described as peace washed over her. But there was something else as well, something she couldn't describe but knew with every fiber of her being had played a role in her being here.

As sleep began to overpower her, she thought once more of Robyn's words before they said goodnight.

"You are in good hands, Claire. The McQuarrys are wonderful. Do you think they would adopt me too?" Claire was almost certain she had seen the glimmer of a tear in Robyn's eyes as she hugged her goodnight.

~ ~ ~

Claire awoke early, eager to experience the first day of her new beginning. Convinced Mason and Robyn would sleep another hour or two, she decided to go for a run. Quietly rummaging through her suitcase, she retrieved a pair of shorts, tee shirt, and running shoes. She slipped into her clothes and shoes and pulled her hair into a ponytail. Her son's soft snoring drew her to his side. Claire bent to brush his cheek with a kiss before tiptoeing from the room and down the stairs. The house was silent.

There would be time for reflection while she ran. In the meantime, some warm up stretches would get her ready to run. It dawned on Claire that she had never been here this early in the summer. She hadn't known it would be so cool.

Starting out at a moderate jog, she warmed up quickly. Many long forgotten memories surfaced with each new street she covered. The sleepy town unfolding before her awakened thoughts of a quaint English village she and Randall had visited early in their marriage. The buildings and homes didn't resemble those in Polpero, yet the simplicity and quiet stirred in her a familiar response. "I am glad to be here," she murmured.

Approaching the small town park, Claire stopped short. A sinking feeling struck her heart. An old friend, a giant catalpa tree, had vanished. The tree held vivid memories, and she had hoped to share those with Mason. Generations of children had climbed over the enormous limbs, creating countless adventures in the process. Claire was sorry for Mason and all the children who would never experience those glorious hours of imagination.

Tears stung her eyes as she crossed the street, uttering a silent farewell to that long ago friend. The truth was, she told herself, there would be other changes. Change happens everywhere, even in Mason Falls. Her heart clung to the hope that the changes would be small.

Claire ran with a freedom she barely recognized. Crushing pain had claimed large chunks of her emotions since Randall's death. Rarely did she get through a day without an overwhelming sense of loss. Oh, how she longed to feel Randall's touch again, to see that warm glow in his eyes when he looked at her. But here, surrounded by the tranquility of this place, Claire snatched a glimpse of hope for a new life, and her heart yearned to embrace it.

Turning down Maple Street to head back to the McQuarry house, Claire stopped short in front of a house she recognized. It was a cheerful yellow with white shutters and a bright red door. Claire knew immediately it was Ginny Bingham's home. Claire had always thought of Ginny as her summertime friend. Oh, the adventures they had all those years ago. She would come back later and find out if the Binghams still lived in this house. Checking her watch, she realized she'd better get back before Mason woke up.

The house was still quiet when she arrived but she heard soft murmuring coming from the McQuarry bedroom. Tiptoeing back up the stairs, Claire grabbed some casual clothes and headed for the shower.

~ ~ ~

Breakfast at the McQuarry home was a veritable feast. Claire had never seen her son eat so much, some of which he wouldn't even try for her. There were homemade buttermilk pancakes, bacon and sausage, eggs cooked to order, warmed syrup and homemade peach and strawberry jams. But the real shock for Claire was watching Robyn almost shovel down everything put before her. Robyn, conscientious to a fault, would never eat like this back home. Claire quickly suppressed her smiles.

Laughter and lighthearted conversation filled the sunny kitchen. Mason couldn't get over Dr. Mac and Mrs. Mac having a booth in their kitchen. "It's like we're eating at Dr. and Mrs. Mac's restaurant," he said. His eyes shone with happiness as he sat across from Dr. Mac, fascinated by his fishing tales. Helen charmed Robyn with her gracious manner and genuineness. Claire watched as Robyn's stoic business-like shell began to crack.

After breakfast, they all pitched in to help Helen with the dishes. Before leaving for the office, Dr. Mac motioned for Claire to walk with him to the door.

"Claire, do you want to go to your grandparents' place today?"

"Oh yes, Dr. Mac, I can barely contain my excitement. Will you remind me how to get there? I think I can find it, but just in case. It's been a long time."

"Sure thing. It's not hard. Just wanted you to know that Reuben Walker is the man I hired for you. He works at Hank's Hardware store during the day and goes out to your place after work. Might be a good idea to run by Hank's and talk to Reuben before you go out. How's that sound? And Helen can give you directions to the house before you leave." Dr. Mac smiled and engulfed her in a bear hug.

"Wonderful," she said.

~9~

FRIDAY MORNING FOUND SETH UP AND dressed by daylight. He had plans for the day that would keep him busy. He'd set up a meeting with his real estate agent to check out a couple of rental properties. After that, he was going to get his office organized. Although he didn't have a lot to put in it, he wanted to feel settled before starting on Monday.

Monday. The thought struck him like an avalanche. He was starting his medical practice on Monday. For years, he'd dreamed of this day, denying himself what others considered necessities in order to reach this goal. And now, with all the effort expended over those years, here he was. But the dream had a glitch in it—he should have been in Kansas City.

Seth rubbed his left temple instinctively seeking to ward off an incipient headache. Sure, he wasn't happy about being here instead of seeing his name among those at the Hawthorn Clinic, but he had to face facts. Mason Falls was where he would start the practice of medicine. The smells coming from Mabel's coffee shop lured him back to the present with a mixture of anticipation and apprehension. Tucking in his shirt, he thought about how he could start fresh with Mabel today. Yesterday loomed in his memory as a less than desirable way to start off with a stalwart local citizen, and a stalwart she was.

Mabel Porter was a no-nonsense type and reminded Seth of his fourth grade teacher, Mrs. Imogene Crank. Countless whispers of "Watch out, Crank the Tank is on the move" flooded Seth's mind. Well, he was a man now and towered over Mabel Porter, so he had nothing to fear. He hoped.

Seth walked out of his room and headed to the coffee shop. He was humming to himself, but before he opened the door, he burst into a fiendish fourth grade chuckle as he whispered, "Porter the Snorter is on the move."

He found a table in one corner and sat down. He looked over the menu and quickly found just what he wanted to order. Leaning across the table, Seth picked up a copy of *The Fall Report*, the local newspaper. The headline was astonishing: MASON FALLS' BURIALS ON THE RISE.

The article went on the discuss the aging population and the growing concern that fewer young people were remaining in the town after graduation from high school. Absorbed in the writer's comments, Seth reflected on the effect such a trend would have on a community this size. Several minutes later he had finished reading the entire paper. It certainly didn't compare to the *Kansas City Star*.

Sensing a presence standing next to him, Seth looked up to see none other than the formidable Mrs. Porter glaring down at him.

"Good morning, Mrs. Porter. So nice to see you again," he said with a smile.

"Humph! What do you want to eat?" was her terse reply.

"Let's see. How about your omelet special with biscuits and crisp bacon? I have a lot to do today, and I'm one hungry guy." Seth gave her his most boyish grin but received a scowl in return.

"Humph!" was the only word she spoke as she wheeled around and stormed toward the kitchen.

With a smile, he turned back to his newspaper. Mabel was definitely a replica of Imogene Crank—with a snort. Oh well, he had three years to win her over. It just might be the greatest challenge of his stay in Mason Falls.

Seth turned to the classified section and was amazed at how few listings there were for rental property. Reality struck as he contemplated the possibility of remaining at the Sunset Motel. He shuddered at the thought. A rustling sound interrupted his thoughts.

"Thank you, Mrs. Porter. It smells wonderful," he said to Mabel's receding back. He sighed, but inhaling the aroma of the homemade biscuits, bacon, and an omelet to die for convinced him of one thing—Mabel Porter or someone in the kitchen could cook!

While munching on a slice of bacon, he looked back at the

classifieds. When he glanced up, a number of customers were giving him the once over. He was probably the most recent novelty in town, so he could understand their curiosity. He was sure it wouldn't be long before rumors would fly at the speed of light and maybe, just maybe, some truth as well.

It took great resolve to eat slowly. He slathered warm butter on the biscuits which seemed to melt in his mouth and savored every morsel of the omelet filled with fresh tomatoes, mushrooms, and onions with just a hint of basil. It had been a long time since he was able to enjoy a leisurely breakfast. Yes, he decided, it might be good to slow down and just live in the moment.

A contented sigh escaped Seth's lips as he consumed his last bite of omelet and wiped crumbs of biscuit from his chin. "What a way to start the day," he said to no one in particular. One thing for sure about Mason Falls, a guy wasn't going to lack down-home cooking.

He folded the newspaper neatly for the next customer and left a generous tip that he hoped would take the edge off Mabel's negative impression of him, then headed for the register. On an impulse, he grinned, and gave a generic wave to the other customers. *That felt good*, he thought to himself as he paid the bill and stepped out into a new day.

The morning air was so fresh he couldn't help but take a deep breath and experience the invigorating feeling it gave him. Seth was reminded of those early mornings in high school and college when he was training for cross-country races. Mornings like this made you think you could run forever. He decided right then that he would dig out his running shoes and get back to doing something he loved.

He glanced down at his watch. 7:05. That meant he still had almost two hours before his meeting with Fred Lawson, the real estate agent. Walking the short distance from the coffee shop to #4 at the motel, he realized he needed to retrieve Mr. Lawson's address and phone number from his notes. Afterwards, he'd drive around town to check out his new environment before the meeting.

~ ~ ~

Everywhere he looked as he drove through the quiet streets, he saw that the bright flush of spring's new life had ripened into summer glory as varied as a Monet painting in living color. Parking his car at the corner of Pine and Lincoln, Seth rolled down his window and surveyed the awakening of Mason Falls. The early morning light settled across the tree-lined streets allowing cascading shadows to intercept its rays. His thoughts drifted back to the times he had labored next to Gran in her flowerbeds. The smell of rich, moist earth was as real at this moment as it was so long ago. Those were happy days for him.

Gran taught him to see beauty in the world around him. Each new day was a masterpiece in process to her. She loved her flowers, and she loved art. He was sure that was what brought Monet to mind just now. Gran's admiration of the artist was so much a part of her, he couldn't think of one without the other.

Swallowing the last of the coffee he brought from Mabel's, he permitted himself the leisure of a reflective moment. In some ways, he felt much of the vibrancy of his life had slipped from him as Gran took her final breath. He had never been the same. All he knew to do to ease his grief was throw every ounce of energy into school and work. Being here in Mason Falls for three years didn't fit his goals, but maybe there was some good that could come from his time in this quiet, little town. Just maybe the simple joys of life he'd learned as a boy from a woman he adored would once again be ignited.

With almost an hour left before his meeting, Seth had plenty of time to finish driving through some of the side streets leading off the square. The neighborhoods were coming to life as Seth proceeded on his tour. Moms and dads were getting their day underway and kids were already out playing. Seth smiled. He was going to be busy in the months ahead. There would be lots of coughs, colds, insect bites, and poison ivy, no doubt. One thing was obvious, people in Mason Falls believed in large families.

Waiting for several older children to cross the street at a stop sign, he reached for his notes about Fred Lawson. Lawson Realty was located just one block off the square on the east side.

Seth turned right at the next street, which ushered him onto the square. He took the next right and saw Lawson Realty on the left. Traffic was light and parking ample. He pulled into a spot in front of the office and grabbed a notepad as he got out of the car.

The office door was flung open and a hulk of a man filled the entire doorframe. He was in jeans, a stiffly starched white shirt, a belt with a buckle as big as Seth's hand, and cowboy boots. Seth decided his appearance matched his hearty telephone voice.

"Hey there. You must be Doc Bradley," the man said.

"Yes sir. And you must be Mr. Lawson," Seth said.

"Sure am, but call me Fred. Don't hold much to formality around here. What's your handle, son?" Lawson replied.

"I'm Seth." Shaking hands with the man felt like being crushed by a vice grip.

"Come on in, Seth. We'll have a cup of coffee and get down to business. Right this way." Fred pointed out a chair beside his desk. The coffee was stout with a robust flavor. Seth was impressed.

"Doc, I have to be honest with you. Just like I told you on the phone, there is a mighty short supply of rental property right now. Is there any chance you might be interested in buying a place?"

Seth stared at him, the gaudy blinking lights of the Sunset Motel sign clouding his vision, Mabel Porter's "humph" filling his ears. He tried to clear his throat to make a response but nothing happened. All he could do was sit there and shake his head no.

"Sorry, Doc. I was hoping you might be open to buying a place. There are a couple of properties that might work for you." Lawson tapped his thick fingers on his desk as though willing another property to burst on the scene.

"Well, let's go see what I have, but I have to warn you, it's pretty slim pickin's." Fred's huge frame rose abruptly from his chair, the floor creaking beneath his weight. Seth stood, forcing himself to put one foot in front of the other. What started out as a day with high hopes had deteriorated in a matter of minutes.

Seth followed Fred through the office and out the back door to a pickup truck, a Herculean chariot of modern times, that stood ready to carry them to battle. Fred noticed Seth's surprised look and grinned. "I have to get in some mighty tough country for some of our properties, and I also run a couple hundred head of cattle on my own place. Don't know how I would manage without this monster of a truck. It runs diesel, so it's pretty noisy. You may have to talk up, Doc, if you have any questions." Lawson chuckled and slapped him on the back. Seth almost lost his footing from the impact.

Fred had an easygoing nature that made Seth feel comfortable. He pointed out places of local interest as they drove. There was a beautiful old Victorian home that had served as a hospital during the Civil War, an antique shop that once housed the blacksmith, the first school building in Mason Falls that was now home for the local library, and the county courthouse that had been lovingly restored to much of its former glory after suffering a devastating fire during the Civil War.

Fred drove to the outskirts of town until he came to a neighborhood of rundown older homes. He slowed down as they approached a small, faded green house and maneuvered the monstrous truck into the narrow driveway. The house actually seemed to shrink in size next to the truck.

"Well, Doc, this is the first, and probably the best, of what there is to show you. Like I said earlier, there's not much available in rentals these days. Do you want to see it?"

Seth took a deep breath and agreed to see the inside. Fred tried to point out some positive aspects: small yard to mow, some nice, old trees for shade, house in pretty good shape on the outside, and quiet neighborhood, but it was obvious to Seth that Fred was embarrassed.

"Doc, I've got tell you, the inside is worse than what you've seen out here. It needs a lot of work, and the owner won't do any improvements. Still want to go in?" Fred Lawson, hulk of a man that he was, actually blushed. Seth felt terrible for him and didn't know if it would be better to turn and leave or go in and see for himself. He decided on the latter.

Fumbling in his pocket for the key, Fred retrieved it and opened the weather-beaten door. When they stepped inside, he let Seth take in the impact of his words. "It needs a lot of work."

Seth stood silent, stunned by what he saw. Not only was the place in terrible condition, the stench of urine and smoke was overwhelming. A lot of work didn't begin to describe what the place needed. A controlled fire would be more like it.

"Had enough?" Fred asked.

"Yes, too much actually," Seth replied.

"Still want to see the others?"

"No, if this is the best, I think I've had enough." Seth gave a slight smile. The relief on the other man's face told him it was the right thing to do.

"Doc, I really struggled with whether to keep our appointment, knowing this would be the end result. So, let me tell you why I didn't cancel it." Fred cleared his throat before going on.

"This area is called Swamp Town. You can guess the reason for that name. These houses were built a lot of years ago on the edge of this swampy area. The mosquitos were horrible down here, and no one wanted to live here. It became a low rent area for poor folks. It has stayed that way ever since." Fred took off his cowboy hat and ran a hand through his thick, dark hair. He was graying at the temples but had a ruddy, youthful face and his eyes were kind and thoughtful.

"Not many of the folks of Mason Falls ever have reason to come down here." Fred leaned back against his truck and kicked his heel up on the running board.

"Doc, you could have been here for months before you ever found out about Swamp Town. I have to tell you the folks who live here are kind of a hard bunch to get to know, and they don't cater to doctors. They still believe in folk medicine passed down from their great-grandmother or grandfather. I wanted you to see this place firsthand. I've always had kind of a soft spot in my heart for these people. Guess its cause I came out of sort of a similar background. If I was out of place bringing you here, I want to apologize." Fred stood with his hat in his hands looking more like a repentant ten-year-old boy than a man probably six foot four and solid muscle from years of hard physical labor.

Seth sensed a genuine humility and goodness in this man

and was touched by his concern for the people of Swamp Town. His feelings outweighed his disappointment as he assured Fred he understood.

"Doc, will you be okay at the Sunset until we can come up with something else?"

Seth's heart sank, but he tried to smile as he replied, "Sure, Fred. I have this goal of winning over Mabel Porter. We haven't gotten off to a very good start."

Fred laughed. "Well now, Doc, that's quite a goal for sure. If you win her over, let the rest of us know how you did it."

The ride back to Fred's office was pleasant. A first impression of the man would never do him justice. His physical size was intimidating but small by comparison to the size of his heart.

After leaving Fred's office, Seth drove to the clinic to get his office in order. He had loaded his old red Honda with assorted paraphernalia. He'd never had his own office and was looking forward to this moment. Seth pictured the space as a kind of sanctuary where he could take a few minutes and have a cup of coffee before seeing the next round of patients.

However, the idea of slowing down went against everything he had done for the last twelve years, especially the frenzied pace in the hospital where he trained. It would be a dramatic change. The question was could he make or would he even want such change?

When Seth arrived at the clinic, he noticed the parking lot was nearly full of cars, a good sign. That meant a busy clinic. He parked his car in a vacant space, grabbed two boxes and walked to the back door. He put the boxes down to open the door and kept it ajar with one foot. When he bent down to retrieve the boxes, he was startled at the sound of approaching footsteps. As he glanced up, he found himself staring at a pair of very sturdy legs encased in a pair of knee-high hose rolled down below the hem of the owner's dress. Seth's face flushed crimson as he stood up.

"Howdy do, you must be Doc Bradley," the woman said, her mouth breaking into a wide grin. "I'm Sodie Tucker. I'm the cleanin' lady and all round helper for the clinic. We'll be seein' a lot of each other."

"That's great, Ms. Tucker. It's nice to meet you."

"Now, Doc, surely you've heard by now, we aren't so formal around here as you big city folks. Just call me Sodie, everyone else does. Let me help you with them boxes, Doc."

Sodie grabbed a box, moving down the hall before Seth could argue. He followed feeling a bit awkward since he was carrying the smaller of the two boxes. He'd hoped to slip in the back door as inconspicuously as possible. That didn't happen. Sodie Tucker was announcing his presence to all within earshot.

He cringed as he heard her tell a young woman coming out an exam room, "Look back there. That there is a mighty fine lookin' young doctor come to practice." Sodie waved at Seth, smiling from ear to ear. Seth gave a half-hearted wave while trying not to drop the box and nodded to both women. Where was the proverbial hole he desperately wanted to sink into?

Sodie brushed past the young woman, focused on her mission of getting to his office. Seth hoped it was near. Thankfully, she entered a door on the left, and he could breathe again. Heading back to his car for the next load, he rehearsed scenarios that would convince Sodie he was capable of finishing on his own. Somehow, he couldn't see that happening.

Sure enough, Sodie was already back down the hall and out the door to bring another load from the car. With each trip, she inevitably ran into another patient either coming or going and pointed him out with great relish. Life with Sodie Tucker was going to be interesting to say the least.

After all the boxes and loose items were finally in his office, Sodie announced she had other "b'ness" to attend to and off she went. Seth watched as she hustled down the hall, a tsunami of good intentions, leaving the bewildered young doctor in her wake. Unpacking boxes and concentrating on where to put things helped Seth disengage from his encounter with Sodie and the ensuing embarrassment he'd felt. *Nothing like a little physical labor to put you back on track*, he mused.

The rest of the morning went well since he didn't have a lot of memorabilia to worry with. In comparison to Angus McQuarry's office, his was dull by anyone's standards. He wondered what his office might look like after thirty plus years of practice.

As if on cue, there was a soft tap on his door. "Come in," Seth said, hoping it wasn't Sodie, though he couldn't imagine her tapping softly on anyone's door.

"Good morning, Seth, and welcome to you." Dr. McQuarry entered smiling and holding out his hand.

Hair tousled, coat rumpled, and stethoscope at a skewed angle, Dr. McQuarry would never fit in with the well-dressed, elite physicians at the Hawthorn Clinic. Instead, he was the picture of what they called in residency an LMD—Local MD. *How will I survive the next three years?* Seth thought.

"Good morning, Dr. McQuarry, and thank you."

"Your office looks nice, very professional. Looking forward to getting started on Monday?"

"Yes sir, I am. I can't remember when I've had this much time off. I don't know what to do with my time, especially here in a new place."

Mac's eyes lit up, and he said, "Do you like to fish, Seth?"

"I don't know. I've only gone fishing one time."

"Well then, it's about time you found out. How about going with me tomorrow?"

"Well, sure, I guess so," Seth replied.

"We have some of the best trout fishing in the country right here. I like using a fly rod. It takes some time to get the hang of it, but you'll discover it's really an art form. I have a feeling you'll learn to appreciate it since you love art," Mac said. "I remember what you told me about your grandmother's love of art that she passed on to you. You know, Seth, medicine takes a toll on a man's soul. Years of dealing with people's pain, suffering, and dying weigh mighty heavy at times. You have to find an outlet, something to get your mind and your heart off all the pain. If not, you may end up losing your passion, your heart for medicine.

"Fly fishing has been that outlet for me, so I love sharing it with others. Meet me at the house at six in the morning. Helen will pack up some food and drinks, so even if we don't catch any fish, I promise we'll eat well." He chuckled, heading for the door. "Wear comfortable clothes. I'll have everything else we'll need. I'm really glad you're going, Seth. It will give us a chance to get to know each other better. See you in the morning." He waved and was gone.

Seth wasn't excited about fishing, but McQuarry was right. It would give them the opportunity to get to know each other. Seth knew that would be a positive step for their working relationship.

"Now back to the work at hand," he said, adjusting a new shelf in the bookcase. He thought of Angus McQuarry's rich mahogany bookcases filled with the worn medical books he'd examined while waiting in the man's office, a treasure of medical history wrapped in soft brown leather.

Seth had to admit that his handheld iPad, while containing a wealth of information, couldn't compare to the feel of the one of those old books in his hands. Standing there with Gray's Anatomy transported him to a different era. But he reminded himself that worn old leather may feel great to the touch, but the speed with which he could search out answers on his iPad was the future of medicine. It was an electronic marvel containing more medical information than McQuarry's library a hundred times over. But still, the smooth softness of the leather caressing his fingertips triggered his senses in a way that the hard iPad never could, marvel or not.

He worked without a break for the next two hours. Fortunately, there was already a desk and chair available for him and a rather tired looking loveseat for patients. At some point, it might be a good idea to purchase a couple of nice chairs. He could always take them with him when he finished the three years here. It would definitely cheer things up to have something new in his stark surroundings. Seth gathered the boxes and broke them down for easier carrying but also hoping to escape the helping hands of Sodie Tucker. He was getting hungry and wanted to try out the little café on the square.

He stepped into the hall then stopped cold, boxes crashing at his feet. It was noon on Friday. He would start seeing patients on Monday morning and to his knowledge he had no nurse! He hadn't thought to ask. How dumb was that? No one else mentioned it either. Surely it was just an oversight. Seth rushed toward the front office. Sodie Tucker had best get out of his way. He was on his own mission this time. He felt his face flush and his pulse rate rise. *Stay calm, Bradley*, he told himself.

Turning the corner at the end of the hall, he slammed right into Nell Meyers, knocking her to the floor. Slapping his hand against his forehead and cursing himself under his breath, Seth kneeled to help Nell to her feet.

Both Seth and Nell tried to apologize first, but Seth knew that he was the one at fault. He was in such a panic he wasn't looking where he was going.

"Nell, I'm so sorry. I was so focused on getting an answer to a question that I wasn't paying attention. Are you hurt? Do you need to sit down? Here, let me get you to a chair." Seth was groveling, but he deserved it, he told himself.

Nell shook her head in response to the chair idea but reached out to put her hand against the wall to steady herself. She was visibly shaken yet managed a smile.

"Dr. Bradley, I'm fine, just a little wobbly for the moment. I was on my way to find you. Dr. Mac had to make a quick house call and wanted me to tell you that you'll have a nurse on Monday."

Seth felt as though he needed a chair. He was relieved at the news but disturbed over his thoughtless behavior. Words he hadn't thought of in years tumbled into his mind. "Always put others before yourself," Gran used to tell him. He had been so wrapped up in himself that he'd almost hurt this lovely young woman.

"Thank you, Nell, that's what I was coming to find out. Are you sure you're okay?" Seth asked out of genuine concern.

"Yes, Doctor, I'm fine. Let's go to the kitchen, and I'll tell you about your nurse."

"That would be great. Thank you," Seth said, trying for his own smile.

They sat at a small Formica top table. "The coffee sure is good," Seth said, trying to make small talk.

"You can thank Sodie. I hear you two have met," Nell said. It broke the ice for both of them.

"Oh yes, we've definitely met," Seth replied.

~ 10 ~

Intrigued for days by the name, Seth opened the door of the Singing Dog Café. The place was packed, and he saw no empty tables. Just as he turned to leave, he heard a familiar voice.

"Doc, over here," Reuben called out. He was standing by a table near the back of the room.

Seth hesitated but decided his hunger and the aromas from the kitchen were urging him to stay. He worked his way through a maze of tables and bodies in the crowded room.

"Hello, Mr. Walker, I mean Reuben. Thanks for letting me join you." Seth smiled and took the seat across from the older man.

"No problem, Doc. Glad to see you. How are things going? Are you getting settled in?"

Just then the waitress, an elderly woman who looked as though she could barely walk, approached and took Seth's drink order for iced tea. Seth relaxed as he told Reuben about his morning at the clinic and meeting Sodie Tucker.

Reuben's eyes danced with delight as Seth described retrieving his boxes and finding himself staring at Sodie Tucker's legs with her knee highs rolled down. He thought Reuben might fall off his chair laughing. Seth couldn't help but join in.

The elderly woman had returned with his tea and was waiting to take his order. He gave a quick look at the menu then asked, "What do you recommend, Reuben?"

"Well, everything is mighty fine eatin', but I have a hard time passin' up the Shepherd's Pie when they have it. Isn't that right, Mrs. C? Mrs. C, this is Doc Bradley. He's goin' to be workin' with Dr. Mac." She raised her eyes but still said nothing.

"Sounds good. I'll have the same, ma'am," Seth told her. He

84

feared she was falling asleep on her feet as he spoke. She nodded and shuffled back to the kitchen.

Seth surveyed the crowded room. The clientele was eclectic just like the premises. There were business folks, labor folks, a few mothers with children, and a number of farmers. The room itself was medium sized with a variety of table sizes and shapes. Large windows across the front dispensed an abundance of sunlight, adding to the good-natured atmosphere in the room.

"Is there a story behind the name of this place?" Seth asked.

"Sure is, Doc, and you're about to experience it first-hand. Hap and Madge Carter own this place. Hap's mother is who waited on us. Well, a few years ago, a scrawny little pup started hangin' around their yard. They felt sorry for him, so they kept him.

"Hap's quite a musician and loves to play the harmonica. One night he was playin' that harmonica and that pup started howlin'. Hap got such a kick out of it, he decided to see if he could get that pup to kinda follow along with him. It took him quite some time, but that ol' pup got to lovin' music."

Reuben looked down at his watch. "And in about five minutes you're gonna hear something I bet you've never heard before—an honest to goodness singin' dog."

"You've got to be kidding," Seth said.

"No sir, not kiddin'. Every day at one o'clock, Hap brings ol' Dusty out here, and he sings for the customers. That's why it's called The Singing Dog Café." Reuben leaned back in his chair and laughed at the look on Seth's face. "Yes sir, that's some kinda dog."

Seth looked over Reuben's shoulder and saw the elderly Mrs. Carter shuffle toward them carrying a large tray with their food. The woman's strength for her age amazed him.

"Thank you, Mrs. C," Reuben said with a smile.

"You're more than welcome, Reuben. Got to go. It's about time for Dusty."

"Looks great," Seth said as he took a large bite.

"Don't know if you're a prayin' man or not, but would you mind if I say grace?" Reuben asked.

"Uh, sure, Reuben, that's fine. Sorry." He felt himself blush.

Reuben bowed his head, silent for a moment before he spoke. *"Lord, we want to thank You for this food and for the hands that prepared it. Would you bless Hap, Madge, and Mrs. C as they serve so many of us? And Lord, thank You for Doc and for bringin' him into our lives. In Jesus's name. Amen."*

"Dig in, Doc. It's time for Dusty." Reuben took his own advice.

Hap Carter strode to the front of the café. A large cinnamon colored dog of uncertain heritage walked next to him. Hap cleared his throat. "For those of y'all that don't know, this here is my dog, Dusty. He may not be much to look at, but he sure can sing." Hap took out his harmonica, and Dusty's tail began thumping hard against the floor. Hap blew a few notes then began playing "She'll Be Coming 'Round the Mountain."

Seth, mesmerized by the dog's uncanny ability to keep up with Hap, had to admit Reuben was right. Yes sir, that was some kind of dog. The crowd joined in clapping, stomping their feet and singing. This only made Dusty sing all the louder. Seth couldn't believe how the dog seemed to anticipate when to hold a note or shorten one.

When the song ended, everyone was on their feet clapping and whistling. Hap turned to Dusty and together they took a bow. Seth found himself as enthusiastic as everyone else and patted Dusty as he and Hap walked by the table.

"Gosh, that was unbelievable," he said laughing. And this time he slapped Reuben on the back.

"Told you so," the older man replied with a look of pride. "Well, I best get back to work. I need to try and finish early. Dr. Mac wants me to take a look at the old Mason place. Seems the great-great-granddaughter of our town's founder and her son are moving back here."

"Reuben, I'll get the check. I really would like to do that," Seth said. "I've had a great time, not only hearing Dusty sing but also just being with you. Thanks. And if you don't mind, may I walk with you? I have a question I'd like to ask."

Seth met Reuben outside, and they walked toward the hardware store. He stuffed his hands in his pockets, gathering his thoughts. "I'm struggling with Mabel Porter. For some reason, I seem to have offended her, but I don't know what I've said or done. Can you give me some insight or advice? I get the impression you have a remarkable ability to see beyond the exterior of a person. To be honest, Reuben, I personally find it pretty unnerving sometimes."

"Doc, first of all, thanks for confiding in me. It means a lot. I've hoped ever since I met you that we could build a relationship. I think this may be our first step beyond only being acquaintances.

"We best keep walking. Don't want to be late. And I don't consider myself as having any remarkable or unusual ability. What you may be sensing though is the insight God can give us when we listen for Him. That's real important to me, not to rush ahead of what God may want to say or do through me." Reuben seemed transported to a place deep inside himself for several moments. Seth wondered if it was a peaceful place where the tough questions of life could be unraveled.

"Doc, have you asked yourself what might have caused Mabel to be the way she is?" Seth shook his head no. "You might want to give that some thought. I wish I had time to go into it with you now, but I don't. Think about it, and let's get back on it in a day or so. I've learned over the years that getting to know and appreciate someone like Mabel helps us learn a lot about compassion. Well, here we are. Thanks for lunch, and you take care," he said with his usual friendly clap on Seth's shoulder.

Seth wasn't sure what to make of Reuben's comments about Mabel. Now that Reuben brought up the question of Mabel's past, he did wonder if maybe it wasn't him after all. If that was the case, then what was the issue in her life that he set off every time they saw each other?

~ ~ ~

Crawling out of bed made Seth wonder why he'd agreed to this fishing trip with Dr. Mac. He still couldn't call the man by that name and certainly couldn't call him Angus. He didn't know what to call him.

Seth turned on the coffee pot and headed to the shower. He didn't bother to shave. The fish wouldn't care. The hot water worked wonders on his attitude about the trip, and coffee, he was sure, would make it close to tolerable. Seth pulled on an old pair of faded Levi's and a Kansas City Royal's tee shirt and headed for Old Red.

Slamming the car door shut, he slumped over the steering wheel, chiding himself for agreeing to this trip. "Why didn't I just say thanks, but no thanks?" he grumbled. Seth shoved the gear stick into reverse and headed out. His stomach rumbled, and he realized he'd forgotten to eat anything. Well, it wasn't like he was used to having time for breakfast. He knew he was just in a foul mood.

The streets were quiet with little to no traffic. He eased the car up the slight incline known as Hilltop Road. The first rays of a new day greeted him at the crest of the hill. Again, the wonder of an early summer morning warmed his spirit. Maybe it wasn't such a bad day after all.

When Seth turned into the clinic parking lot, he smiled to see how empty it was. One thing was certain, Dr. Mac had a practice large enough for two doctors. This parking lot was full on weekdays. He wouldn't be sitting around with nothing to do come Monday.

He walked across the wide yard to the McQuarry house. He wasn't sure whether to knock or ring the doorbell. It was still early, and he would hate to wake up Mrs. Mac if she wasn't an early riser. He knocked softly and almost immediately was greeted by Helen McQuarry.

"Come in, Seth." Taking his arm, she led him to the kitchen. "Mac will be right here. He's getting some of the gear from the basement. That should give you just enough time for a cup of coffee and a fresh cinnamon roll. I can't see sending you two off on an empty stomach. Mac has already had his, so you sit right here." Helen gestured toward the booth next to the window. She had flowers on the table and a coffee cup ready for him.

"Thank you. I wasn't expecting to be fed, but I'm not going to turn it down. I'm hungry, and those rolls smell wonderful."

Helen patted his shoulder as she bent over to pour his coffee. "That's good. I do like a man with an appetite," she said as she turned to retrieve two hot rolls from the oven.

Seth relished every morsel of both rolls. He felt like a new man and was ready to take on those fish.

When he thanked Helen, her eyes glowed with delight. "I told you we wanted to see more of you. I hope you believe that, young Dr. Bradley."

Before he knew it, Helen McQuarry was hugging his neck. Though taken off guard, he couldn't help but smile at this lovely woman. And he had to admit it, the hug felt good, really good. He couldn't remember the last time someone had hugged him.

A door off the kitchen squeaked open, followed by heavy footsteps. "There's Mac now," Helen said, shifting her gaze toward the kitchen door.

Seth stood and took his dishes to the sink. "Thanks again for those wonderful rolls."

She nodded and smiled. "You're welcome, Seth. I hope you have a great time."

The tall man stood in the doorway, his arms overflowing with waders, vests, and nets. A floppy hat sat jauntily atop his head. His glasses rested halfway down his nose. Helen chuckled and rushed to rescue her husband. "Angus McQuarry, why didn't you ask for help?" She took a pair of waders and the two fishnets out of his bundle and handed them to Seth.

"I made it, didn't I?" Mac replied, tossing the rest of the items in a pile on the floor. "Mornin', Seth. See you got fed. My girl here loves to make sure nobody goes anywhere hungry. 'Course she doesn't eat enough to keep a bird alive," he said, looking at the slender frame of his wife. His eyes twinkled as he gave Helen's backside a playful pat.

"Dr. McQuarry! May I remind you we have a guest? You two need to be on your way before the fish get tired of waiting for you. And besides, I have things to do myself."

"Can't argue with that can we, Seth? Try these waders on and let's see how they fit." Mac grabbed a pair from the floor and pitched them to the younger man. "Be sure you take your shoes off. These are known as chest waders and have a built-in boot. That way you don't have to get a separate pair of wading boots."

Seth took off his shoes and worked his way into the rubbery garb. He looked from Dr. Mac to Helen for approval but felt foolish standing there in rubber pants up to his chest.

"Hey, it's okay, Seth. Look at it this way. You're the stylish guy—to the fish." Mac's laugh filled the room.

"You stop that, Angus McQuarry. He's never worn anything like those before," Helen said, coming to Seth's aid.

"All right, sweetie, I'll back off," he said with a wink.

Seth crawled out of the waders and put on his shoes. He threw the waders over one arm and grabbed a vest and the fish nets. Mac helped Helen put drinks in the ice chest along with several sandwiches and some apples and oranges. Seth couldn't help but smile as he watched the gangly man with his floppy hat and fishing vest with all kinds of unusual things hanging off of it lean down and plant a huge kiss on the lips of his dainty wife.

For most of the trip to the river, Seth listened as Mac preached the virtues of fly-fishing. The man's passion for his sport rivaled any Seth had observed over the years hanging out in the doctors' lounge. He'd heard men cry like babies when their team lost a game. He'd watched grown men throw temper tantrums when they disagreed with a referee or with each other over a call or play, but there was something different, more intriguing, about Dr. Mac's love of his sport.

He tried to capture the reverence the man described for what he called the art form of fly-fishing. Seth found instead that he was bogged down in the details. Was it a rod and reel or a fishing pole? No, that wasn't it. What had he called it—a fly rod? Dr. Mac said there was a major difference in casting a fly rod versus a rod and reel. And did he really mean it when he said you had to cast like a girl throws a softball? Something about needing to not break your wrist but keeping it straight.

The purring of the engine and the early morning made a deadly combination with all the strange terminologies, and Seth began to yawn. He felt himself drifting into another sphere. The next thing he knew, a hand was shaking his arm.

"Hey there, partner, we're here. Guess I went on a little too long with all the details." Mac rolled down the window and slid out of the Jeep. He stretched his arms and back before moving to the rear of the vehicle and opening the hatch. "This is one of my favorite spots, and we're pretty sure to catch us some nice trout."

"Sounds great," Seth said, trying to cover another yawn.

~ 11 ~

CLAIRE STEPPED INSIDE HANK'S HARDWARE STORE and jumped at the clang of the screen door as it snapped shut. She looked around and noticed an older man with snow-white hair rubbing some kind of oil into an old wooden bin that had a sign that read "Nails."

The man looked up with a smile and said, "Well, good morning, dear lady. Fine new day, isn't it? How may I help you?"

"It is a nice day," she said, smiling back. "You wouldn't happen to be Mr. Walker, would you?"

"Sure am, and you're new in town. You must be Claire Westfield. Dr. Mac said you'd be in town about now. It's a real pleasure to meet you, Miss Claire. How about a cup of coffee or tea? Since it's slow this early in the day, we could visit a bit. I get here pretty early so I can give everything a good once over and keep things looking nice for Hank. I'm due for a break."

"Tea would be nice, Mr. Walker."

"Come on back to the office. Hank doesn't come in for a while and won't mind us visiting in there. And please, call me Reuben, everyone does."

"Okay, Reuben it is, if you'll call me Claire. Is it a deal?" They laughed and shook hands.

Reuben pointed to the only chair indicating Claire should sit there. "Claire, I'm afraid all I can offer in the line of tea is regular Lipton. We don't have any, should I say, more lady-like selections."

"Lipton is perfectly fine. This isn't your typical lady's shopping turf, is it? Tell you what, since we'll be touching base a lot over the next several weeks, I'll bring a box of peppermint tea next time I come." Claire grinned as she accepted the mug offered to her.

"Sure, you could do that. We do have sugar, sweetener, and milk if you use them."

"Just a little sweetener please."

Reuben sat on a stool next to Hank's desk as they made small talk for several minutes.

"Mr. Walker, I mean, Reuben, please give me your assessment of the condition of my grandparents' home."

Reuben stroked his silvery beard as he pondered his response. "Well, the bottom line is there is a lot to be done. But for a house as old as it is, it's in better shape than I thought it would be. Wasn't it your great-grandparents who built it?" Claire nodded. "Seems I've heard they built it about 1905 or so." Claire gave another nod.

"Sorry, these old bones get to aching sometimes when I sit too long. I'll just stand a bit if you don't mind. First, I'd like to mention Sodie Tucker to you. Sometime when you get a chance, you may want to thank her for what she's done for the place. She was your grandparent's friend and their cleaning lady. On her own, she continued to go over every couple of weeks after your grandmother passed on to check on the house. She kept an eye open for any potential problems to let Dr. Mac know.

"Sodie's a real character, if you know what I mean, but she has a heart of gold. And she loved your grandparents." Pouring himself another cup of coffee, he offered Claire another cup of tea.

"No thanks, I'm fine. Thank you for telling me about Ms. Tucker. I am so grateful that someone cared that much for my grandparents. I will definitely get in touch with her. So where do we start, Reuben? What do you see as the most crucial needs?" Claire set her cup down, focusing all her attention on what Reuben was going to say.

"Well, a few years ago Dr. Mac contacted me about doing some work on the place. I had to say no because of a prior commitment that took all my spare time. So, he hired another fella to keep an eye on things and do some repairs." Reuben stared into his coffee cup for a moment.

"Now I'm not here to put down the man that did that work, but he wasn't completely truthful with Dr. Mac about how much he knew when it came to repair work. He left town right after that. So, what I'm gettin' at is some of what he fixed is pretty shabby work. It did help keep the place from gettin' any worse, but we need to go in there and do it right this time.

"I'm goin' to give you several items I think need to be at the top of our list. Then we can get into more detail when we meet this afternoon. First thing is to get the roof replaced. Those shingles are well past their life, and there are several leaks in the roof next to the chimney that will need to be dealt with. Another major issue could be the septic tank, so we need to get it looked at right away.

"I hope I'm not overwhelmin' you, Claire, but I have to be up front with you. The galvanized pipes in the crawl space need to be replaced. They're leakin' like crazy! And the plumbing in the guest bathroom needs to be changed out. It's way too old and leaky to repair. Well, Claire, did I scare you off?"

She could only stare at the man before whispering, "And that's just the beginning?" Taking a deep breath, she said, "No, Reuben, you didn't scare me off. You just gave me a reality check. Thank you."

Reuben agreed to meet her at the old house after he finished at Hank's. "I have to say this before you go, Claire. You've been through an awful lot for someone your age, but you sure have got spunk! I look forward to workin' with you."

~ ~ ~

After Claire left, Reuben whispered, *"Lord, thank You for the time with Claire. She's a charmin' young woman. But she's still hurtin' a lot, isn't she, Lord? Would You help her know You're here for her and that little boy of hers? And that You sure do love them. Help me do a good job on that old house and also be a blessing to Claire. Thank You."* He bowed his head a moment then went to dust mop the store floor.

~ 12 ~

THE MORNING AIR, THICK AND HUMID, hung over him like a heavy coat, weighing him down. Seth reluctantly admitted to himself that he was definitely out of shape. He was determined to complete his goal of running three miles. It used to be so easy. Today, he felt every step. Defeat was not in his vocabulary, but he knew from experience if he pushed too hard, too fast, he would end up injured. Tonight, he would work out a more reasonable plan to rebuild his base mileage.

Seth's thoughts drifted into a review of his first days of practice in Mason Falls. What he had assumed would be boring and routine cases had actually been varied and interesting. He chuckled, thinking back on the first few days. His nurse, Justine Crenshaw, informed him on that first morning, there were no patients for him. He could still see the embarrassed look on her face when she cautiously said, "Dr. Bradley, when they found out you were fresh out of residency, they thought you were just too young. People around here don't like change, especially the older ones. We may have to bide our time and wait for some of the younger folks. I'm sorry, Doctor. It's just the way things are."

He recalled not knowing whether to be angry or relieved. But it didn't take long for the word to reach Dr. Mac, and when it did there was an explosion that rocked the entire clinic.

Seth heard Dr. Mac all the way down the hall telling Nell Meyers to get on that phone and call every one of those people and tell them he said for them to get themselves down here, right now. "And, Nell, if they refuse, tell them they will answer to me. If I didn't have complete confidence in Dr. Bradley, I wouldn't have brought him here. Now get moving, Nell. Seth doesn't want to be sitting around twiddling his thumbs half the morning."

"Yes sir, I'm on it, Dr. Mac," Nell replied and dashed back to her desk.

Seth smiled, picturing Nell and all the energy she exerted as she took charge of her mission—phone in one hand, mouse in the other, scrolling down the appointments for the morning. The ensuing events of the morning raced through his mind at a faster pace than he was running. It wasn't much more than an hour before Justine tapped on his door.

"Dr. Bradley, we have patients waiting to see you," Justine said with a sly smile.

He grinned and propelled himself out of his chair. He grabbed his stethoscope and slipped on his white lab coat. "Well, let's go change some minds," he said, following her out the door.

Over the next two hours he saw the typical coughs, colds, and rashes. Their last patient before noon, though, was one he would never forget as long as he lived. Seth stood at the door of the exam room and studied the file for his next patient. He thought the man's name unusual to say the least—Possum Guthrie. He was seventy-five and in fair health. His complaint was chicken itch. Seth stood there trying to think whether he had ever heard of such a thing. He had enjoyed his study of dermatology and had been convinced he could treat anything that he could see. But he was certain he had never heard of chicken itch. He opened the door, not sure what he might be coming up against.

"Good morning, Mr. Guthrie, it's nice to meet you. I'm Dr. Bradley. You might say I'm the new kid on the block." Possum Guthrie broke into a wheezy laugh. Seth made a mental note that Mr. Guthrie was a heavy smoker.

"Well, sir, that's okay by me, long as you'uns know what yor doin'." Possum smiled a toothless grin.

"You may have me stumped, Mr. Guthrie. I don't think I have ever heard of chicken itch. Can you help me out?"

"Sure I can, Doc. You see, I work over yonder at the chicken processing company. Every now and then, them chickens get to me, and I break out in this here rash. So, I come in and get me some medicine. That's all there is to it."

"Let's have a look at that rash then, okay?" Seth examined the old man and decided a cortisone cream should do the trick. "Mr. Guthrie, I think we have some samples. How about I get you some. I'll be right back."

"Doc, you don't have to call me Mr. Just call me Possum, everybody else does."

"Thank you, Possum, I would be honored. I'll be back in just a minute."

Seth found Justine and asked her to check the sample closet and bring him the cream. Opening the door to the exam room, he was met by Possum's wide, toothless grin once again.

"Possum, my nurse will bring that cream for you in a few minutes. Do you mind my asking how you got those scars on your face? Looks like you had a pretty bad mishap."

"Well, sir, Mr. Doc, I was just a young 'un when one day my daddy comes up to me and says, 'Possum, git them crawdads outta this here yard.'

"Now, I wasn't but maybe thirteen, and there was a dang lot of crawdads in that yard. I wasn't 'bout to ask my daddy how I was supposed to get rid of 'um. I already knew what he'd say. 'Boy, ain't that what you got a brain for?'

"So, Mr. Doc, I come up with a plan. I was gonna burn 'em out. I did some mighty powerful thinkin' on jest how I was gonna do it. Then this idea jest popped into my brain, and it was a doozie!"

Seth took a seat on the exam stool, realizing this tale might take a while.

"Well, sir, I spent all afternoon gittin' my plan together. I walked into town to Johnson's General Store. Back in them days a general store carried jest 'bout anything a body might need. Guess it's why they called it general." Possum smiled his toothless grin before going on.

"I had maybe two dollars I'd been savin' for some time to go toward buyin' me a .22 rifle. But in all my thinkin' that day, I decided it would be worth spendin' that money on what I needed to git rid of them crawdads, 'cause then I would make my daddy proud of me. I didn't know why, but I never thought my daddy liked me much.

"Well, sure 'nough, I was able to git what I needed. I was one happy kid, I'll tell ya."

Possum gazed off as though going back in time to that exact moment, his eyes seeing the replay of it all.

"Mr. Doc, I come into that there yard kinda strutin' like a banty rooster. They's one cocky little bird, I wanna tell ya. And that's jest how I felt!

"You know anything 'bout crawdads, Mr. Doc?"

Seth shook his head no. He had never even seen one. He thought he had heard they looked like a miniature lobster.

"Well sir, our yard was mostly dirt, and them there crawdads had dug these holes all over the yard. There were like these little volcanoes everywhere.

"Now most of us boys back then loved to coon hunt at night. We wore these here carbide lanterns on our hats so we could see but have our hands free for shootin'. That carbide is what give me my big idea to burn them suckers out. The carbide is what I spent my two dollars on at the store.

"Well now, my idea was to drop a piece of carbide in every one of them holes then add a little water to make it gas up. Next I'd drop a li'l match in each one and burn them crawdads to hades.

"Onliest problem was, I didn't know them mounds were all connected by tunnels. I bent over the first hole and lit my match. When I dropped it in, the whole dang yard blew up! I was standin' over that first hole with my mouth hangin' open, and when she blew, it knocked me off my feet, singed my eyebrows off, burnt the roof of my mouth, and burned them places on my face and hands."

Seth sat mesmerized. "What did your daddy say, Possum?"

"Mr. Doc, I was hopin' he was gonna be mighty dern proud of what I'd done." Possum lowered his head, eyes downcast. "But that weren't how it was. He came runnin' out of the house yellin' like a banshee. He hollered, 'What the blazes have ya done, boy? You'un done blowed up this here whole yard. You'un some kinda half-wit?'"

Possum looked up at Seth, pain and sorrow written in every crevice of his rugged face.

"All I wanted ta do was make my daddy proud of me, Mr. Doc.

Guess I was right after all. My daddy never did seem to like me much." Possum Guthrie hung his head once more, the pain of years gone by still in the old man's heart.

Seth stood up hesitantly, then reached out and put his hand on Possum's shoulder. His voice cracked as he said softly, "Mr. Guthrie, I think your daddy missed a real blessing by not realizing what a fine son he had."

The elderly man began to sob as Seth gently patted his shoulder. Slowly Possum Guthrie rose from the exam table, straightening himself as best he could.

"Mr. Doc, I 'pologize for losin' myself. I don't recollect I've ever done that afore. It jest still hurts after all these years. I do thank ya fer yor kind words and fer seein' me. I ain't got much, but I give my word, I'll take care of my bill soon as I can."

"Possum, I'm not worried about that. I can tell that you are an honorable man, and it's been a privilege having you as a patient."

The two men exchanged a handshake before Possum Guthrie, head held high, walked out of the exam room. Justine met them at the door and handed Possum the cream for his chicken itch.

~ ~ ~

Seth still carried a lingering ache for this old man. Possum Guthrie was a rare individual. He possessed nothing of great material worth, but Seth detected a simple outlook on life of great value. He would be wise to learn from a man like Possum Guthrie. Seth smiled about meeting this special patient and slowed his pace, groaning from his aching muscles. He found a good sized tree and leaned his hands against the rough bark, urging his body into a familiar and welcome stretch of his calves. It felt good. His body responded willingly as he alternated from one leg to the other.

On the road again, he estimated he had about a mile left. Easing into his stride, he felt lighter, more refreshed. Running had been an important part of his life since high school. He relished the feel of the breeze on his face, the thrill of exertion as he pushed his body, demanding more and more.

He had set high standards for himself, and they paid off. Not only had running been a stress reliever for him but it had also earned him a cross-country scholarship to college. During the years of his grandmother's fight against cancer, it was the one way he could get relief from the emotional turmoil going on in his heart. Seth accelerated his pace, willing himself to lengthen his stride and reclaim that satisfying sensation of gliding on air.

Running alongside Mason Creek, Seth remembered a question Reuben had asked him. "Don't folks where you come from enjoy the outdoors?" It had angered Seth at the time, something he immediately regretted. Now he realized in all the years of running he had missed the whole point. He had run with focus and purpose, determined to complete his goal. Today he had simply run. He fell short of his goal, but something strange and intoxicating had taken place. He had enjoyed himself. Rarely did he do anything just for pleasure. He had realized long ago that he was a man driven to excel.

In the last hour, he had given himself permission to go easy, and his mind and body relaxed. He actually began looking at his surroundings, seeing Mason Falls with new eyes. He had been so determined that he would dislike his time here, he hadn't allowed himself to see the truth. This was a delightful little town. The place exuded serenity. Church bells occasionally echoed across the valley. He noticed people often stopped a moment to listen. Life here did have a simple and quiet beauty.

While he had every intention of leaving Mason Falls at the end of three years, Seth discovered himself more willing to give the town and the people a chance. If honest with himself, he needed to look at what the place had to offer, not worry about what it lacked.

But rising before him at the top of the hill was the scourge of his existence in this town. The Sunset Motel which meant Mabel Porter. Even if he survived everything else about small town life, could he survive Mabel Porter? That was a question he didn't have an answer for.

Glancing at his watch, he saw there was just enough time to shower and grab a quick breakfast at the coffee shop before heading to the clinic.

~ ~ ~

Seth allowed the pulsating water of the shower to ease the

stiffness in his body. Within minutes he would have to face Mabel's scorn, for what, he still didn't know. He hadn't followed through on Reuben's advice to think about what might have caused her to behave the way she did. Frustrated, Seth turned off the water and stepped out of the shower. Why should he feel guilty? He had only tried to be nice and polite to her. And he sure didn't know her well enough to come up with ideas as to why she became so hopping mad every time she laid eyes on him. While drying off, he came to a decision.

Over the noon hour he would call Fred Lawson to see if just maybe something had become available. If not, maybe he was ready to take the old green house in Swamp Town. Surely, it would be an improvement over living here. For now, he would make his own coffee and grab something at the doughnut shop.

Leaving his room, Seth caught sight of Mabel through the coffee shop window. She looked straight at him while putting a plate of food on a table. He glared back at her, turned sharply and got in his car, slamming the door, mumbling, "What a great way to start the day."

Shoving the car into reverse, he drove off. What he really wanted to do was peel out of there and burn rubber just like some teenage boy would do. One thing was for sure, he had to find a way to get out of Mabel's territory before he exploded.

~ 13 ~

SETH PEERED INTO THE CLINIC KITCHEN, the aroma of strong coffee heavy in the air. Thankfully there was no one there. He grabbed a mug and filled it to the brim. He needed coffee and a few minutes of solitude in his office so he could put Mabel Porter out of his mind and get focused on the day ahead.

A soft tap on the door told him Justine and his patients awaited him. Gulping the last of his coffee, he was ready for his day to begin.

It started with a cantankerous old man itching for a fight, and Seth became the man's first target.

"Good morning, Mr. Stanley. It's nice to meet you. So, how are you feeling today?"

"Not good, otherwise I wouldn't be here." He glared at Seth and his eyes narrowed with suspicion. "You're mighty young to be doctor'n folks, don't you think?" he growled.

"Well, sir, I may seem young to you, but I assure you I've had sufficient training at some great institutions."

"Oh you have, have you? What about life? You think you've seen enough of real life to make you a real doctor?" Gerald Stanley sat rigid, cracking his knuckles. He scowled at Seth, waiting for a reaction.

"I appreciate your concern, Mr. Stanley, but I am a qualified physician, and I hope you will give me the opportunity to prove that to you."

Gerald Stanley puffed out his chest, still scowling, and finally said, "We'll see how you do. Not makin' any promises though."

"I understand, sir. Shall we begin with some questions?" Stanley gave a slight nod.

"How old are you, Mr. Stanley?" Seth barely got the words out of his mouth before Gerald Stanley slid off the exam table. He stood almost nose-to-nose with Seth and shouted, "I'm not payin' some young squirt of a doctor to ask me how old I am. I'm payin' you to help me keep gettin' older." Face red and eyes blazing, he pushed past Seth and threw open the door.

"I'm ninety-one and don't you forget it, boy!"

Baffled, Seth stared as the old man marched down the hall. He had no idea what that was all about. So far, his day on a scale of one to ten was definitely a one. He hated it when things like this happened. He really wanted to help people, but he knew there were times like this that just went with the practice of medicine. He couldn't please everyone even though he tried. The rest of the morning proved fairly normal, seeing several children with allergies or colds, a prostate exam, a cannery worker with a bad cut on his finger, and finally an elderly woman with bronchitis.

At the end of his morning appointments, Seth retreated to the quiet of his office. Rummaging in his desk drawer, he found Fred Lawson's card and dialed the number.

"Lawson Realty, this is Fred."

"Hi, Fred, Seth Bradley here. Just wondered if you had any new leads on rental property?"

"Sorry, Doc, afraid not. About the only thing even sellin' right now is land. I have you at the top of my priority list so the first thing comes up, I'll let you know."

"I understand. Just thought I'd check. Thanks."

"Sure thing."

Seth put the phone down, and his thoughts turned back to Mabel. He wondered what Reuben would do. The question had hardly crossed his mind before he knew the answer. Seth stood up, took off his white coat, and walked out the door.

His thoughts were jumbled as he drove back to the motel. He wasn't sure what he should say, but he knew he needed to do this. The coffee shop closed after the breakfast crowd each day. Seth parked in his place at #4 and walked to the office. He felt drops of perspiration forming on his forehead. He really didn't want to get into a scene like the one with Mr. Stanley. That one had been enough for one day.

Opening the flimsy screen door of the motel office, he saw no one inside. He called out, "Mrs. Porter, are you here?" Seth hoped she wasn't. Just as he turned to leave, Mabel appeared at the door.

"Finishing up at the coffee shop and saw you come in. What do you want?" she asked, stony-faced, her attitude hostile.

Seth crammed his hands into his pockets. He felt like a fourth grader again standing before Imogene Crank. "Mrs. Porter, I came to apologize. I saw you watching me as I left this morning. I'd intended to have breakfast at the coffee shop but started thinking how upset I always seem to make you and changed my mind. I'm going to be frank. I was frustrated. So, when I saw you watching me as I got in my car, it made me angry. That's what I came to apologize for. I don't know what it is I've done or said or what it is about me that upsets you, but I'm sorry. If it would help, I'd check out. The problem is I have nowhere to go." Seth fixed his eyes on Mabel, willing her to say something. She turned and stomped out the door, letting the screen door slam behind her.

Seth stood frozen in place. Taking his hands out of his pockets, he raised a fist and managed to overcome the urge to punch it through the screen. "Well, that was a total bust. So much for trying to do the right thing."

Sometimes he felt his days in Mason Falls were an emotional roller coaster. He either begrudged his time here or experienced a growing fondness for the place and the people. Well, most of the people, he reminded himself. The residency program in Kansas City had never looked as good as it did at this moment.

Later that day after seeing his last patient and completing some dictations, Seth decided to walk over to Hank's and see if he could find Reuben. Reuben had come to mind several times in the last few hours along with a nudging to go talk to him. It was a beautiful afternoon, sunny but not too humid, and there was a hint of a breeze. Seth had to admit that a real perk to being in Mason Falls, at least until he grew a larger patient base, was the freedom Dr. Mac had given him to leave when he was finished. He was beginning to think he could get used to having a little free time.

Walking the few blocks to the square proved to be good for him. Several boys were playing kick ball in an empty lot. When their ball got away from them, Seth caught it and kicked it back. One little guy asked him to play with them. He smiled at the boy and agreed to play for a little while.

A few minutes turned into a half hour of sheer fun. After telling the boys he needed to go see someone, he shook hands with each boy, thanking them for including him in their game. "Hey, guys, could I join you again sometime?" Their answer exploded with shouts and high-fives.

What had started off as a bad day was actually ending on a high note. Maybe he should take Dr. Mac's suggestion to get involved in some way in the community. He had asked Seth if he might consider coaching kids in T-ball or soccer. Seth hadn't thought anymore about it until now. Dr. Mac's reasoning was it would help the community get to know him as a person not just the new doctor in town. An added benefit would be helping him build his practice.

The time with those boys was a good reminder of that but most of all he had thoroughly enjoyed them. He would definitely pursue the possibility of helping out. Probably soccer would fit him better than T-ball. At least he had a little bit of experience with soccer.

Hank's, usually bustling with customers at this time of day, felt almost eerie in the silence as Seth walked through the door. He spotted Hank hunched over the antiquated cash register at the back of the store. Not wanting to startle the proprietor, he called out, "Hi, Hank, guess I caught you closing up."

The man lifted his head, squinting at Seth through his round glasses hanging half way down his nose. "Doc Bradley, that you?"

"Yeah, just wanted to see if Reuben was here," Seth replied.

"Sorry, Doc, I let Reuben leave early. He's taking on a project for the great-great-granddaughter of Mason Falls' founders. She's moving back here from San Francisco to live in the house her great-grandfather built. Can you believe that? Going to be a big change for her. Reuben will be helping her get the old homestead livable. I hear she has a little boy. You could go out to the place and catch Reuben there. I know he wouldn't mind."

"I wouldn't want to be a bother," Seth said, as he turned to leave.

"Doc, there's no such thing as anyone being a bother to Reuben. He has time for everyone." Hank smiled and wrote down directions to the Mason farm. "Here you go. Beware though, Doc, he may put you to work." Both men laughed, knowing the truth in the comment.

"Thanks, Hank. See you around."

Seth walked back to the clinic. Nodding to several familiar faces along the way, he sensed that he was beginning to be accepted. He had to admit it felt good.

Driving to the Mason farm took only a few minutes. A barely visible sign encased by some sort of vine confirmed he was at the right place. Reuben's old truck sat in front of the house, and there was a great ruckus thundering from inside. Convinced Reuben wouldn't hear his approach, Seth honked his car horn. Moments later a very disheveled Mr. Walker stepped out the front door. Seth burst into laughter.

Reuben stood on the porch, hands clutching the straps of his overalls, hair flying in every direction, covered in sawdust. There was a nail clamped securely between his teeth. Seth laughed until his sides hurt. Reuben stared at him, puzzled. Retrieving the nail from his mouth, he looked himself over before puncturing the air with laughter of his own.

"Guess I'm quite the sight to say the least. Just get caught up in what I'm doing and forget to dust myself off." Reuben's grin lit his already jovial face as he gave himself a little shake causing sawdust to fly in the air.

"I didn't mean to laugh, Reuben. You just surprised me. With all the noise in the house, I honked to keep from startling you. Guess you startled me instead."

Reuben motioned for Seth to take a seat on the steps beside him. "How about some sweet tea? I picked some up at the Singin' Dog before coming out here." Reuben pulled a half-gallon jar out of the ice chest nearby. Two Styrofoam cups appeared as if by magic. Reuben noticed Seth's surprised look. "I always bring extras—just in case."

The two of them sat without speaking for several moments,

feeling no need to break the silence. Seth took the last drink of his sweet tea and set his cup on the porch. "I wanted to talk to you about Mabel," he said. "I never got around to trying to figure out what makes her the way she is like you suggested. But today came to a point when I kind of lost it with her." Seth relayed his aggravation with the woman and what transpired over his noon hour. Reuben remained silent but attentive.

"So, I just don't know what else to do. And I'm not sure how much longer I can stay there and deal with her every day. But there's nowhere to go either." Seth shrugged, his turmoil written over his face.

Reuben said nothing for several moments. He reached over and patted Seth's shoulder. "Doc, you did a good thing going back to apologize. A lot of men couldn't or wouldn't do that. Too many think it's a sign of weakness. But I'm here to tell you it's the strongest thing you can do as a man.

"Doc, there may not be any nice neat answers with Mabel. But I'm pretty certain it's not so much about you as it is about something in her past. She's always been very private, doesn't let anyone in close. What you did today, though, Doc, you let the light shine. And when a person does that at some point good will come from it."

Seth stared at the older man, mesmerized. Something in the man seemed to glow as though you could see straight into his heart. The more he was around Reuben Walker, the more intrigued he became. What was it that made him so different from anyone he had ever known?

"Say, Doc, would you mind giving me a hand with something inside?"

Hank was right, Seth thought. "Sure, Reuben, what's up?"

~ ~ ~

After Seth left, Reuben loaded his tools into the tool chest in the back of his truck. It had been a good visit with the younger man. Seth still had his guard up, but Reuben saw a slight crack in the wall around his heart.

"Lord, thank You for this time with my new friend, Doc. Help him continue to let Your light shine into his life. You did a big thing today

between him and Mabel. Would You start tearin' down the walls that are keepin' both of them from experiencin' Your love? Thank You, Lord."

~ 14 ~

THE CRUSHED LOOK ON MASON'S FACE stung Claire's heart. She came very close to backing down and allowing him to accompany her to the farm. But she needed this time alone with Reuben to concentrate on their plan of action.

Kissing the top of his head, she promised that tomorrow afternoon he could go with her. Helen walked in at the perfect moment and rescued Claire.

"How about if you help me make Dr. Mac's favorite cookies, Mason? It would mean a lot to him, and we would have some time to get to know each other better." Helen's soft Southern drawl was like melted butter.

"Well, okay, I guess. What kind of cookies?"

"Oatmeal," Helen said.

"Really? That's my favorite too! Bye, Mommy. Mrs. Mac and me are gonna be busy." He lurched into Claire's arms, giving her a big hug goodbye.

As Claire got into the car, she realized she hadn't told Robyn she was leaving. She considered going back in but remembering her son's ability to manipulate Robyn to do his will, she decided to leave her in Mason's care. If she knew her boy, he would drag Robyn from her computer and have her right in the middle of the cookie making. Claire smiled at the thought of Robyn covered from head to toe in flour, her typical professional persona nowhere to be found.

Claire was enjoying the drive to the farm. She rolled down the window and breathed in the fragrant air. It was honeysuckle. The narrow country road was lined with the vines that were flowering already. She thought back to many summer afternoons when she and Ginny Bingham would walk this road, picking the blossoms then pulling out the stems and sucking in the sweetness. She loved the experience then and wanted to share it with Mason. There was so much from her happy times here she wanted to share with him. She had been sorry to learn from Helen that Ginny and her parents had moved away long ago.

Claire thought about Mason taking Helen's hand as they walked to the kitchen. She hoped that Helen McQuarry might become the grandmother Mason never had. Randall's parents had died in a boating accident while he was in college. Claire's dad died two years after she and Randall married. Six months after her dad's death, her mother, Claudia, left with a man from their country club crowd. Claire did not see her again until Mason was born. But even a new grandson wasn't enough to change her or bring her back, and after a few days, she was gone again. Claire had not seen or heard from her since. A long family history of wall building had been passed down from her mother's great-grandmother. Claire's dad shared some of her mother's family history with Claire shortly before he died. It was his hope it might help Claire better understand her mother.

Her mother grew up in an extremely wealthy, high profile family. Everything was about appearance. Their family was from old money, as she called it. She was the oldest of three children. She had a brother and a sister. Their mother was uninvolved in their upbringing, which she gave over to a nanny.

Claire could still see the pain in her father's eyes when he told her how her mother had cried telling him about being sent off to boarding school at age twelve and how she'd never recovered from the emotional separation from her family. For a brief moment Claire's heart had ached for her mother. She'd known boarding school was a part of her family's legacy, passed down from her mother's great-grandmother, but it didn't remove the sting of rejection inflicted on her at a pivotal time in her own life. Her dad had fought for Claire when her mother decided to send her to the same boarding school, but in the end, he gave in, and Claire was sent away to school. Claire had to admit that she'd never really forgiven her dad for that. What had made Claire so angry with her mother was that she could knowingly choose to inflict on her own daughter the same pain of desertion she had experienced.

Claire pulled the car to the side of the road and wept. The memories of that conversation were etched in her mind and her heart. She had vowed to never send her son away to spend his crucial growing up years with strangers. She and Robyn had both seen what that could do to a child. And that was another reason she wanted Mason to grow up here where she had been so happy, so loved. She wiped her eyes and rummaged in her purse for her lipstick to make herself presentable. She was minutes away from meeting with Reuben.

~ ~ ~

A beat-up green truck was parked in the driveway. Claire pulled in beside it and sat staring at her grandparents' home. Now it was her home. A shiver ran through her. She was actually home. The racket going on inside was almost deafening, but Claire wanted a few minutes to survey the place she hadn't seen in five years. It was a quaint home for rural Arkansas. Claire smiled, remembering her grandparents sharing comments people made about it with her.

Potch, her grandfather, sat in his chair, her chair now, puffing on his pipe. Potch would take a long draw on his pipe then stroke his wiry gray beard before going on. "Some folks would say, 'Harold, that there house that your daddy built looks like some sorta fairy-tale house.'" Potch would slap his leg, throw his head back and roar with laughter. Her grandfather's stories captivated her as a child, fueling her imagination. From then on, Claire always thought of their home as the Hansel and Gretel house.

The house had been built by her great-grandparents in 1905. Her great-grandfather, a bachelor, came home from a trip to St. Louis, a married man. To hear Potch tell the story, his father fell madly in love with a young woman from England. He would not leave until he had convinced her to marry him.

Upon arriving in Mason Falls, they lived with his parents in the original Mason home. Tragedy struck a year later when a fire destroyed the house. Potch told Claire his grandparents, her great-great-grandparents, moved into town but gave the land to Potch's father, Daniel, and his bride Marianne.

Potch said the only thing left of the original house was the rock wall that was built by freed slaves. They kept that wall when they built their own house in 1905, the house that Claire was looking at now.

Claire realized the racket from the house had stopped, and she was stunned by the quietness surrounding her. Taking off her sunglasses, she got out of the car, stuffed the glasses in her shorts pocket, and went up the walk. Stepping onto the porch, Claire was almost overcome by her emotions. She saw Reuben approaching the door.

"Claire, there you are, glad to see you," he said, opening the screen door.

Claire noticed a crestfallen look come over the man's face.

"Reuben, are you all right? Is there something wrong?"

"Oh, just disappointed. I hoped you would bring your little boy. I love children."

"Well, believe me, he wanted to come, but I felt we needed some undistracted time to make our plans. I promised he could come tomorrow. I think you two will hit it off. So, shall we get to work?"

Over the next two hours, Claire and Reuben did a thorough, room-by-room, walk-through. Reuben pointed out numerous issues they would have to address. Because of the age of the house and the fact that her grandparents were not involved with modern technology, they would need to increase the size of the electrical panel to handle today's electronics and add quite a few electrical outlets to meet her needs. Flooring would need to be replaced or refinished throughout the house. At least twelve inches of insulation needed to be blown into the attic, and due to settling, he would need to level the floor in a couple of places.

Claire's head was swimming just from the major issues, which didn't even cover the many minor ones. At the outset, it seemed a daunting task, but the results, she knew, would far outweigh the challenges.

"How about a cold glass of sweet tea? We can take a break out on the porch and set out a plan." Reuben was already to the front door.

"Sounds wonderful. I have to admit I'm pretty overwhelmed."

Reuben opened the door, letting Claire go first. "I know it seems that way, Claire, but a lot of these things can be dealt with in pretty short order." Reuben took out a bandana and wiped his face. They both sat on the top step and took a moment to enjoy their sweet tea.

"How long do you estimate it will take to get the house livable?" Claire asked. "I don't want to become a burden on the McQuarrys, although I think Mason might prefer us staying with them!"

Reuben took out the notepad he had used to jot down notes on what they discussed. Claire looked out over the yard. It needed a lot of work itself. It could be a good project for her and Mason this summer. He loved digging in the dirt, and when they got too hot and dirty, they could walk down to the falls and swim. He would eat that up.

"Claire, we'll basically be at the third week of June when we get started. I have to spend the next several days lining things up with the subcontractors. We are blessed with starting at a time when we typically don't get much rain. But I need to tell you June and July can be iffy in that area. I can be working on the inside, though, even if we get a gully washer.

"I would guess maybe by September the house would be livable. We could make sure the kitchen and bedrooms and at least one bathroom are ready. Would that work?"

"That's fine, Reuben. I know things can get held up, so I'll try to be patient. Hopefully, Dr. Mac and Helen will be patient with having a five year old around."

"I know them and can pretty much assure you they will love every minute. First off, then, is getting in touch with a couple of guys to help me get that roof done."

"I want you to know, Reuben, I'm not afraid of hard work, and if you need me, I can do quite a bit around a house. I'm an interior decorator and believe me, I've done my share of things—even taking down walls and laying wood floors." Claire laughed at the shock that flooded Reuben's face.

"Whoa! I better be on top of my game then."

"That's right, Mister Walker, I'm a woman with a mission. But I promise you I will trust your judgment and not overstep my position."

Claire liked this rugged man. In fact, he fascinated her. His white hair and beard and incredible blue eyes with laugh lines at the edges and his easygoing manner were irresistible. He emanated joy and kindness. But there was something else about him she couldn't quite put her finger on. Whatever it might be, Claire believed it was the essence of the man. She looked forward to getting to know him.

"Reuben, is the same time tomorrow good for you?" Claire asked as they walked to her car. "And I'll bring not only Mason but my best friend, Robyn, who rode out here with us from California. Hope that won't be too distracting."

"That's just fine, Claire. I'll enjoy it. Y'all can do your thing, and I'll try to keep out of the way," he said, opening the car door for her. They waved goodbye, and Claire drove back to town, her mind reeling with ideas for the house.

When she arrived at the McQuarrys', she discovered three very busy people in the kitchen.

"Mommy! You're home!"

"Hi, sweetheart. How's my little man?" she said, hugging him tight.

"I'm so great, Mommy, you wouldn't believe it," Mason said with a huge grin. "Me and Mrs. Mac and Aunt Robbie made those cookies, and now we're makin' dinner. Dr. Mac will be here any minute, and he's bringing another doctor with him." The boy collapsed on the bench. The three women broke into a fit of laughter.

"What?"

"You're just too cute, that's all," Claire bent down and gave him a big kiss.

"Mom, not here!"

Helen and Robyn were anxious to hear all about her afternoon at the house. Claire went over all the details while she worked on the salad. Helen had chicken casserole in the oven and Robyn sliced tomatoes.

"We're having our cookies for dessert, Mommy, but don't say anything about them. They are a surprise for Dr. Mac." Mason glowed with pride.

"Claire, I invited the new doctor who has come to work with Mac for dinner tonight. He's only been here a little over a month, and I think he'd love some 'big city' talk. It's been somewhat hard on him adjusting to small town life. Hope you don't mind," Helen said.

"Of course not, Mrs. Mac. It's fine."

~ 15 ~

"DR. MCQUARRY, DO YOU HAVE A MOMENT? I want to ask you a question."

"I'm pretty swamped right now, but ask away." Dr. Mac leaned against the wall next to an exam room, thumbing at the chart he held.

Seth stared at the Littman stethoscope patched with a piece of duct tape that was slung around the man's neck.

"I was wondering if you could give me a contact person for volunteering to help coach one of the soccer teams. I think your idea about getting involved in the community to help build my practice is right. The other day I ran into some kids playing kickball and joined them for a while. It was a lot of fun."

"Well, well, Dr. Bradley, don't tell me you actually had some fun," Mac teased with a sly grin. "Call Fred Lawson. He's real involved in anything to do with kids. Seth, I'm proud of you. Good decision, Doctor. Got to go, have a patient waiting." With that he opened the exam room door. "Good mornin', Gracie, what seems to be the problem today?"

A sense of satisfaction washed over Seth. He'd made a good decision, and it pleased him that Dr. Mac thought so.

Since his first patient wasn't due for another thirty minutes, he told Justine he'd be in his office on a phone call. This time his call to Fred wouldn't be about rental property. Seth punched in the number for Fred.

"Fred Lawson, here. How may I help you?"

"Fred, Seth Bradley. Glad I caught you."

"Hey, Doc. How you doin'?"

"Oh fine, having a slow morning and wanted to ask you a

question, but it's nothing about houses. Dr. Mac said you would know how I could sign up to volunteer as a coach for kids' soccer. Is that right?" Seth swiveled in his chair to look out the office window.

"Well, yes, Doc, I kinda head up the local recreation program for kids. It's nothin' real formal, but we are tryin' to get some activities going. How did you find out about the soccer teams?"

"Dr. Mac mentioned soccer shortly after I got here. But the other day I happened to run into some boys playing kickball in a lot near the square. I joined them and had a great time. They said they played soccer. So, here I am, at your service." Seth waited for a response, idly tapping a pencil on a prescription pad.

"Doc, you're an answer to prayers for several young moms. You see, we have coaches for the other age groups but none for the five and six year olds. These moms are really wanting to get their kids involved, but all the volunteers wanted older kids. Still interested?" asked Fred.

"Wow, you caught me off guard there, Fred. I guess I was thinking more like ten to twelve year olds. Do you think I can handle the younger ones?" Seth asked.

"I think the better question is, do you want to do it? Kids are kids, Doc. Some just come in smaller sizes."

Stunned, Seth sat there staring out the window. Five and six year olds, man, that's little–like the little guy, J.J., at the square. Seth could still picture the boy, full of energy and ready to take on anything. The thought of that experience and the immediate bond brought back pleasant memories.

"Doc, you still there? Did I scare you off?"

"Fred, you have yourself a coach. Please tell me I'm not crazy."

"You aren't crazy. You're a brave man and soon to be a real hero to at least twelve little guys and girls and their moms! You're going to do great. Hey, have a good day and thanks. I'll be in touch in a couple of days."

Seth sat paralyzed. "What have I done?" he muttered. His mind began reeling from the impact of what he had gotten himself into. He never made snap decisions. What led him to make this one? From the moment he set foot in this town, he felt his world had been rocked, in one way or another, everywhere he turned. But this time he had done it to himself.

It was too late to beg off of this one. Seth was certain Fred was already on the phone with the good news. And besides, there were many things Seth wasn't, but he was a man of his word. Gran had drummed that into him from his earliest years.

The now familiar tap on the door startled him. "Come in, Justine."

"Dr. Bradley, we have a walk-in. They are Dr. Mac's patients, but Kay said he really couldn't fit them in and asked if you would please see them."

"Of course. Do you have them in a room?" Seth asked, thankful for the distraction.

"Yes sir, room three. Their names are Jasper and Opal Mae Hobbs. Dr. Bradley, just to prepare you, they are, well, slow," Justine stammered.

"Slow in what way, Justine?" Seth asked, touched by her desire to speak of them with dignity.

"They are both mentally retarded and live with Opal Mae's mother. The town helps watch out for them, trying to help any way we can."

"Thanks, Justine, I appreciate your concern for them. Let's go see what they need." Relief washed over her face, and she handed him the chart.

Jasper and Opal Mae Hobbs appeared to be in their early twenties. Opal Mae sat in the chair, obviously nervous. Jasper stood protectively beside her, holding her hand.

"Mr. and Mrs. Hobbs, nice to meet you. I'm Dr. Bradley, and this is Justine Crenshaw, my nurse. Just so you know, Dr. Mac is sorry he couldn't see you, but his schedule is really full this morning. Would it be all right if I take care of you today?" Seth smiled, trying to put them at ease.

They looked at each other silently making their decision. Jasper nodded his head.

"Good, thank you both. Now, Jasper would you tell me what seems to be the problem?"

Jasper Hobbs stared wide-eyed at Seth, his face frozen in bewilderment. He opened his mouth to speak, only to stammer incoherently then drop his head in shame.

"Jasper, it's okay. We're here to help you. Sometimes we all have trouble knowing just what to say. Come sit on the exam table. Take a deep breath and try to relax."

"Doc, this is, well, embarassin' to talk about, you know?" Jasper's face turned crimson, matching his red hair. Opal Mae sat glued to the chair staring at clenched hands. They both looked so pitiful Seth couldn't help feeling sorry for them.

"That's okay, Jasper. When you're ready, say what you need to say." Seth patted Jasper's shoulder.

Jasper let out a deep moan. "Aw right, here goes. Me and Opal Mae think she may be gonna have a baby." Jasper peered through child-like eyes at Seth and Justine.

"Well, what was so embarrassing about that?" Seth asked.

"Well, Doc, a couple o' things. Dr. Mac gave us these here pills so Opal Mae wouldn't get this way." His face reddened, "When we, you know, we are . . . and Dr. Mac said to take one of them pills every day for sure. And I did just that. So why is Opal Mae gonna have a baby?"

Seth used every ounce of control he possessed to hold in his laughter. A slight glance at Justine confirmed his suspicion. She was fighting the same battle. Seth carefully opened his mouth willing words, not laughter, to come out. "Jasper, I think you misunderstood Dr. Mac's instructions. You see, it's Opal Mae who should have been taking the pills, not you." Seth sat down on the exam stool and rolled over close to the young couple. "You said there were two things you were embarrassed about. What is the other one?"

Jasper swallowed hard, looking at Opal Mae before speaking. "Doc, I'm sure you're a real smart man, so you prob'ly can tell me and Opal Mae are kinda slow up here," Jasper pointed to his head. "Well, we're a'feared some folks might think we shouldn't be havin' this here baby."

"Jasper, Opal Mae, that will probably be true of some people. Do you know anything about caring for a baby?"

For the first time, Seth saw Opal Mae raise her head. "Opal Mae, do you know how to feed a baby, change its diapers, give it a bath?" She nodded. "What about when a baby gets sick? What would you do?" Jasper started to answer, but Seth raised his hand to stop him. "Do you know what to do, Opal Mae?"

"Yes sir, I would come right down here and bring my baby to ya or Dr. Mac. There's Mr. Allen at the drug store. He knows a lot about what pills to give ya ifin' ya ain't feelin' right." Seth noticed from the corner of his eye Jasper's look of pride.

"That's very good. Now it's very important that you be checked to see how far along you are so that we can have an idea when you and Jasper can expect your baby to get here."

"Yes sir. But what does 'gettin' checked' mean? Will it hurt?" Opal Mae asked, fear clouding her eyes.

"Well, it means that a doctor needs to examine you down below, to check your private parts while feeling your belly."

"You mean like Dr. Mac did before Jasper and me got hitched?"

"Yes, Opal Mae, just like that. Do you want me to do it or make you an appointment with Dr. Mac?"

Jasper interrupted, "Well, Doc, since you are a real doctor, that means you've done it before, don't it?"

"Yes, Jasper, many times. And Justine will be here with me. You can stay in the room too if you want."

Jasper turned to Opal Mae and both nodded their heads in approval.

"Okay, Doc, but I sure don't want to stay, 'cause I get really nervous when doctoring things take place. Opal Mae knows that, don't you, Opal Mae?" With a look of trust enhanced with love, she nodded yes to Jasper. Her look of absolute trust needed no words.

"All right, Jasper and I will step out in the hall. Opal Mae, Justine will pull the curtain to give you some privacy and get you a gown so you can change. Then she will let me know when you are ready. It's going to be okay, Opal Mae." He patted her hand before ushering a very nervous Jasper out the door.

When the procedure was completed and Opal Mae was

dressing, Seth went to rescue Jasper. "It's all over, Jasper. Opal Mae did great. You should be very proud of her."

"Oh, I am, Doc. She don't always look like it, but she's a strong one, my Opal Mae." Jasper rose to his feet nearly knocking Seth over in his hurry to get back down the hall.

"Hey, wait for me," Seth called out.

"Opal Mae, Jasper, everything looks great." Seth beamed as he looked from one to the other. The innocence in their faces touched him deeply. Raising a child wouldn't be easy for them, but he was convinced by the determination he saw in them that they could make it. Bumps along the way, yes, but they could make it.

"Mr. and Mrs. Hobbs, looks like you will be parents in early November. How does that sound?" Seth asked. He reached out to shake hands with Jasper and then Opal Mae. "Congratulations to you both. Justine will spend some time going over a few things with you and setting up Opal Mae's next appointment." Seth patted Opal Mae's hand once more, noticing her lack of nervousness. That was a good sign.

He decided to catch up on some medical journals while he waited for his nine thirty appointment.

~ ~ ~

"Come in, Justine," Seth said, responding to the tap on the door.

"Dr. Bradley, sorry to interrupt you, but thought you might want to know that Opal Mae would like you to do her prenatal care."

"Well, Justine, looks like we're going to have our first baby!"

As Justine turned to leave, she said, "Dr. Bradley, the rapport you built with them touched me. I am very proud to be your nurse." With that she quietly closed the door.

Seth walked to the window, gazing at the patch of brightly colored petunias. Justine's words encouraged him. It made him wonder if she would have been able to say those words if they had been at the clinic in Kansas City. First, would he have even seen a couple like Opal Mae and Jasper? Second, would he have had the unhurried schedule to spend that amount of time with them? Seth looked at his watch. His first official patient was probably checking in, and he felt he had already put in a full morning.

~ 16 ~

OFFICE CHATTER STIRRED HIS CURIOSITY ABOUT the McQuarrys'
house guest, but the invitation to dinner still came as a surprise.
The buzz about the founding family's great-great-granddaughter
returning to Mason Falls was all anyone talked about. Seth tried to
stay clear of office gossip, but he had to admit that the woman being
from San Francisco intrigued him. He found himself wondering if
she too would find it difficult to adjust to a small town.

After seeing his last patient of the day, Seth walked to his office.
His phone beeped and Fred Lawson's name showed up.

"Hi, Fred. Is this rental or soccer news?" Seth inquired.

"Actually some of both. Which do you want first?"

"I guess soccer. Shoot."

"Doc, like I told you before, you're now an official hero. You
have some mighty happy young moms. Every one of them volunteered to do anything they could to help you. I know you're
kinda nervous about this, but you're gonna to do fine. And, Doc, it
wouldn't surprise me one bit if after a couple of weeks some of the
dads begin helping out. I'll bring a list of all the kids and their info
to you tomorrow. I've also got a rulebook for you. Hang in there,
this age group can be a lot of fun."

"Thanks, Fred, all that sounds good. Now on to the rental angle.
I hope it's good news," he said as he went to his desk chair.

"Well, it's interesting for sure. Seems the owner of that green
house in Swamp Town had a change of heart. Says he's willing to
clean up the inside. No painting, but he says you can if you want
to. I took it on myself to tell him that the only way I would even
bring it up to you is if he agreed to a month-by-month rental. And
by golly, Doc, he agreed! Never would've thought the guy would

do it. So, what do you think?"

"Whoa, Fred, I'm not sure. Do you think he can really clean it up enough to make it livable?"

"I'll tell him you and I both have to feel okay with what he does before you'll consider it."

Seth was dubious but decided it was worth a try. "Okay, I'm leaving it in your hands."

"Got it. I'll get back to you when the clean-up starts, and we can keep an eye on progress. See you tomorrow with the soccer information."

Glancing at his watch Seth saw there wasn't time to go to his room and change. Instead he would just have to freshen up here at the office. He brushed his teeth, combed his hair, then surveyed the results and muttered, "Guess that'll have to do."

Dr. Mac had told him to come on over as soon as he closed up, so it was just as well he didn't go back to the motel. Seth locked the back door to the clinic and walked across the wide lawn to the McQuarry home.

As he stood on the front porch waiting for someone to respond to his knock, he wondered how many people were here. It sounded like a party going on inside. A moment later Helen McQuarry opened the door.

"Seth, do come in. I'm so glad you came. I haven't seen nearly enough of you since you got here."

"Thank you for inviting me," he said. "Sounds like you all are having a good time."

"We are and now that you're here, it's going to be even better. Come on and let me introduce you," she said, taking his arm.

"Look, everyone, Seth is here."

"Seth, this is Claire Mason Westfield and her son Mason from San Francisco."

He reached out and shook hands with Claire. "My pleasure, Ms. Westfield. And Mr. Westfield, nice to meet you." Seth grinned and bent down to shake hands with the boy.

"Aw, you can just call me Mason, it's okay," the boy said with the most grown up voice he could muster.

"And Seth Bradley, this is Robyn Hamilton, Claire's dearest friend. She helped Claire drive out here."

"The pleasure is all mine, Ms. Hamilton."

"Nice to meet you, Dr. Bradley, but are we going to be so formal around here? How about we take our cue from Mason? Hi Seth, I'm Robyn, and that's Claire. Isn't that better?"

The women excused themselves to finish dinner preparations and Mac gestured for Seth and Mason to follow him into the den. It was a comfortable room with a beautiful stone fireplace. Helen's taste in decorating was warm and inviting. Seth hoped someday he would have a room like this to come home to.

Mason climbed up in Dr. Mac's lap, clearly a bond had already been established. Seth relaxed in the softness of a deep leather chair. *The only thing they needed*, he mused, *was a pipe to puff on and a dog lying in front of the fireplace.*

When Helen called them to dinner, Mason asked if he could sit next to her.

The meal reminded Seth of the first meal he'd shared with them. Gracious hosts, great food, lots of lively conversation, and a lighthearted atmosphere. What really impressed him tonight was the man, Angus J. McQuarry. He knew Dr. Mac's afternoon at the clinic had been a trying one, yet he was relaxed and enjoying the dinner and the company. Somehow, he'd discovered the secret of leaving work behind him when he came home. One day Seth wanted to know how he achieved it. As he re-engaged with the conversation around him, he noticed how much this fit the picture he carried in his mind of what a family should look like.

"Seth," Mac said, "I have to ask you what's happened about soccer?"

"I actually got a call from Fred before coming here. He's bringing me the list of names tomorrow."

Mac said, "Seth is going to coach a soccer team for five and six year olds. Isn't that great?"

"Did you say five year olds like me, Dr. Mac?" Mason's face lit up. "Could I play, Dr. Seth, could I?"

"Well sure, little man. That would be great."

"Wow, can you all believe that?" Mason shouted. "I've only been here two days, and I'm gonna play soccer with Dr. Seth!" At that everyone broke into laughter.

"What did I say?" The boy looked around the table with a puzzled expression.

"Nothing, sweetie, it's just you are so blasted cute, that's all."

"Thank you, Seth. It will be a wonderful way for him to start meeting some other kids."

"No problem. He'll be a great addition. And, Mason, I'm depending on you to help me out. Okay?" Mason nodded enthusiastically.

Dinner over, Helen and Mason excused themselves to get the dessert. The boy practically sprinted into the kitchen, trying to contain his excitement.

"Dessert must be something mighty special," Mac called out. "Hurry up in there."

Mason came out of the kitchen with Helen following him, his head held high and his eyes beaming. He carried a large platter piled with oatmeal cookies and walked straight to Mac and said, "These are your favorite, Dr. Mac. And they're my favorite too!"

"Well, how about that. Come here, boy." Angus took the platter and set it on the table. He reached out and plopped Mason on his knee. "We better try them first don't you think? Just to make sure they're okay?"

"Oh, they're okay, Dr. Mac. I tried 'em as soon as we took 'em out of the oven!"

~ ~ ~

After thanking the McQuarrys for a wonderful evening and saying good night to Claire, Mason, and Robyn, Seth walked back across the lawn to his car. He had really enjoyed himself, especially the conversation with Claire and Robyn about city life. It felt good to connect with those who could understand why he missed that part of his life. But he had to admit that tonight would remain a fond memory of what life in a small town with family and close friends felt like.

～ **17** ～

CLAIRE HAD JUST FINISHED TUCKING MASON into bed when she heard a soft knock on the door. Robyn motioned her to come into the hall.

"What did you think of the evening?" she asked.

"It was very nice. I enjoyed it. How about you?" Claire said, raising an eyebrow.

"Yeah, me too. It's great about Mason getting to play soccer. It will help him adjust more quickly."

Claire nodded, knowing her friend well enough to sense something else was on her mind. And she was pretty sure she knew exactly what it was.

"Don't even go there, Robyn."

"What do you mean? You don't even know what I'm going to say."

"Oh yes I do. It's about Dr. Bradley, isn't it?"

"Claire, remember when we were kids at boarding school and you'd get like this? What would I tell you?"

Claire crossed her arms and glared at her friend.

"Your dragon eyes are showing, Claire. When you get mad, girl, those green eyes of yours shoot fire like a dragon. Loosen up, girl-friend. It's just like back at school. A new guy would appear and one of us immediately tried to set the other one up with him . . . if we didn't want him ourself." Robyn covered her mouth trying to stifle her laughter.

"Well, you're going to be disappointed," Claire shot back, "but I'm not interested and that's final. He seems nice enough, but I'm not ready for a relationship. And especially with another physician. So cool your jets, okay? Enough said."

"Okay, but you have to admit he's one good looking guy. That

126

brown wavy hair and eyes the color of molasses make me want to check him out if you won't." Robyn giggled. "But not enough to stay in this small town. I'm a big city girl all the way. So, guess you have my permission to go for him . . . when you're ready."

Claire gave a shake of her head. "Good night, Robyn."

"Good night, Claire. Sweet dreams," she said with a teasing grin.

~ ~ ~

Over breakfast Helen told them about the Farmer's Market held at the square every Saturday morning during the summer and fall. While she had a prior commitment, she urged them to go and enjoy the festivities. "Oh, and would you see if someone has the early green peas? We'll have them with supper."

"I don't like peas," Mason scowled.

"Mason! That was not polite," Claire scolded. "You apologize to Mrs. Mac."

The boy ducked his head, then slowly raised his eyes to look at Helen. "I'm sorry, Mrs. Mac."

"I accept your apology, Mason. Have you ever eaten peas fresh from the garden?"

"No," he mumbled.

"They taste so much better fresh, sweetie. And I'll need you to help me get them out of their shells. Will you do that?" Helen said stepping toward him and bending down to his eye level.

"Sure, Mrs. Mac. I can do that." Mason reached out and gave her a big hug.

"Wonderful, we'll sit in the porch swing while we shell them. You'll see that's quite a nice thing for two friends to do together."

~ ~ ~

Claire, Robyn, and Mason all agreed to walk to the square. It was a beautiful morning. White puffy clouds, a clear blue sky, and a breeze made for an enjoyable stroll. The square was alive with music and laughter, colors, and textures.

Claire's thoughts were interrupted by her son pulling her forward. "Come on, Mommy, let's go. Oh, Mommy, look! Look over there!" He pointed toward a small area where four ponies were tethered in a makeshift corral.

"Please, oh please, can I ride one of those?" Mason begged as he dragged Claire closer to the animals.

Robyn grinned at Claire, "Please, Mommy, can I have a ride too?"

"Absolutely not, "Claire said, shaking her finger. "You're far too big!" Both women laughed as they tried to keep up with the excited little boy.

Mason climbed onto a black and white spotted pony. "Look at me, Aunt Robbie, I'm riding a horse!" Robyn waved and threw him a kiss.

"Now that is one happy little guy," she said.

After three turns, each on a different pony, Claire informed her son they needed to move on. His chin quivered for a moment as he crawled off the pony, but after giving its nose a gentle pat, he began looking for the next adventure.

The two women chose a beautiful bouquet of flowers for Helen. Mason was adamant about getting Dr. Mac a small wooden sign that read, 'Hillbilly Fish Finder' with a stick of fake dynamite attached to it.

Each booth displayed an array of unique and sometimes outlandish wares. Mason became infatuated with the sock monkeys, something he'd never seen before. Robyn leaned near Claire and whispered, "Take Mason over to another booth while I buy him a monkey as a going away gift."

It was still too early in the season for many of the fruits and vegetables but when they found the green peas, Mason hand-picked them from the basket they were in. Claire promised herself she would, if at all possible, make this a weekly routine. She could almost taste the delicacies that lay ahead.

"Sweetheart, how about going to the park for a while? It's the same one where I played as a little girl," Claire said.

"Yay! Let's go. Where is it, Mommy?"

"Right over there." Claire pointed across the street. "It's just on the other side of that building. Everything in Mason Falls is close by."

~ ~ ~

While Mason climbed, straddled, or hung from every piece of playground equipment, Claire and Robyn sat at a picnic table sipping freshly squeezed lemonade.

"I'm anxious to see the house," Robyn said, twirling her straw in the paper cup.

"It needs a lot of work. More than I realized. But it'll be good for me to have a project."

"So, you're still convinced this is the right thing for the two of you?"

"I am, Robyn. It'll take some adjusting, and it won't be easy giving up many of the conveniences of city life, but I know it's right." They sat quietly watching the antics of the little boy they both adored.

When his enthusiasm showed signs of winding down, Claire called out, "Mason, it's time to go." Before heading to the McQuarrys' to drop off their purchases, they grabbed some fruit, a loaf of homemade French bread, and a chunk of Gouda cheese.

"I have a surprise for you two," Claire announced on the way back to Helen's. "Since Robyn has to leave tomorrow, I thought we should do this before meeting Mr. Walker at the house."

"Tell me, Mommy, please, please."

"You just have to wait and see—both of you. We'll take the food we just bought, get some sodas, and have a picnic. That's all I'm telling you."

Claire had secretly put towels and swimsuits for each of them in the trunk of her car. The drive to the falls was under ten minutes. The road, however, caused Claire to drive slower than usual. She'd forgotten how rough country roads could be. Following the twists and turns of Piney Top Road, the lush green pastures gave way to the hill country with its massive rock bluffs. She decided not to spoil the surprise by telling Robyn and Mason about the spring-fed creek and the falls below those bluffs. She knew they were getting close when suddenly the road made a sharp turn. All three of them gasped in delight at what they saw. The road narrowed, and the trees meshed high overhead forming a brilliant emerald green canopy.

"It's breathtaking," Robyn said.

"It looks like my storybooks," Mason whispered.

Claire stopped the car. "I have to agree with both of you. It's incredible, like we're going back to a different time."

Mason began to sob.

"Sweetheart, what's wrong?" Claire released her seatbelt and turned to look at the puzzled expression on her son's face.

"Mommy," Mason said in a hushed tone, "will we find Daddy here? Will we, Mommy?"

Her son's question pierced Claire's heart, and she struggled to come up with an answer. She sensed Robyn's desperate attempt to hang onto her emotions.

"Mason, I would love to tell you yes, but the answer is no, sweetheart, we won't find Daddy here. Mommy just meant it looks like a place from a long time ago." Claire reached over the seat and unbuckled her son's seatbelt, then drew him close, stroking his hair. "I'm sorry. I didn't mean to upset you."

"I wish it was true, Mommy. I wish Daddy would walk down this road and say, "Hey, where have you three been? I've been waiting for you." He tried to smile but sadness filled his eyes.

"I know, Mason, that would be wonderful."

Claire pulled the car into a graveled area where a bronze plaque on a stone pillar read *Mason Falls. Discovered by William and Caroline Mason in 1866.* She felt overwhelmed by the realization that she and her son were the fifth and sixth generations to be standing in this place. There was so much she wanted to tell him about his heritage. He was still too young to grasp the significance right now, and she would burst into tears if she tried to explain it. To her relief, Robyn saved the day.

"Hey, Tiger, isn't that cool that the people who found this place were in your family a really long time ago?"

"Yeah, that's really cool. Can we have our picnic, Mommy?"

And just like that normalcy returned, and she could smile. "We sure can, but first let's get some things out of the trunk of the car. We may need them because we're going to go swimming and visit a waterfall!"

Mason danced with happiness. She ran to the rear of the car

and popped the trunk open. They all laughed at the sight of her stash of swimsuits, towels, and sunscreen. Claire and Mason stuffed them in bags while Robyn grabbed the food. Mason, nearly beside himself with excitement, kept urging the women to walk faster.

"That waterfall isn't going anywhere, little man," Claire called out. "Come back here. I don't want you wandering off the trail."

Dense groves of pine trees, oaks, and other trees Claire couldn't remember the names of occasionally gave way to patches of open space. Countless varieties of wild flowers greeted them in a dazzling profusion of color.

"Oh, Claire, it's truly magical. No wonder your ancestors fell in love with this place." Robyn knelt to pluck a bright yellow daisy and stuck it in her dark hair.

"You look beautiful, Aunt Robbie." He bent down and picked a blue cornflower and handed it to Claire. "You wear this one, Mommy," he said handing it to Claire. "You'll be beautiful too."

Claire kneeled to allow her son to place the flower in her hair. He looked from one woman to the other, a pleased smile filling his face.

They continued on the trail as it meandered near the creek, the limestone bluffs protruding from the thick wooded hillside.

"Mommy, what's that noise?" Mason's voice quivered as he ran back to his mother.

"It's the waterfall, sweetie. We're almost there. It's okay, there's nothing to be afraid of." She bent and kissed the top of her son's head. "I promise. Don't be afraid. Let's go!" Still holding his hand, she broke into a fast walk, reminding them to be careful of the rugged terrain.

The sound of rushing water grew louder and Mason clung to his mother's hand. Then, without warning the trail ended and they stood a few yards from nature's masterpiece.

"It's more beautiful than I remembered," Claire said, edging closer. "Tiger, the ground's slick from the water so watch your step." She carefully picked her way to a large flat rock.

"Come on, Robyn, there's room for all of us to sit on this rock. It's a great spot to take in the wonder of this place." She patted a place beside her.

Robyn inched her way cautiously toward the rock. "Don't laugh, you two. I'm a city girl and this kind of thing is definitely out of my comfort zone." Reaching the rock, she eased herself down beside Claire. "Okay, I made it," Robyn said with a great sigh of relief.

Claire and Mason broke into a fit of laughter.

"What?" Robyn asked, trying her best to look her normal, composed self.

"You really don't fit into this lifestyle, do you?" Claire leaned over and gave her friend a big hug.

It wasn't long before Mason announced he was starving. Claire helped Robyn get her footing and pulled her friend up from the rock. Their hair and clothes were damp from the waterfall's misty spray which sent them all into another round of laughter.

"We're really a sight, aren't we?" Claire laughed.

"Speak for yourself," Robyn shot back.

"Aunt Robbie, Mommy's right. You really are a sight. Let's eat! Let's eat!" Mason chanted.

~ ~ ~

After their picnic, Claire led their little group along a narrow trail from the falls until she spied the long rope hanging from a tree.

"There it is!" she shouted, running ahead of the others.

"What are you talking about? We don't see anything," Robyn said, swatting at the gnats swarming around her face.

"It's the swimming hole!" Claire shouted back. She dropped the bag filled with swimsuits, towels, and a child's life jacket. "Come on! It's going to be great!"

Mason ran to his mother, pulling off his tee shirt on the way. "I'm ready, Mommy. I can go in just like I am."

"No, Mason, you'll need your clothes when we leave. Come put on your swimsuit and life jacket. It's not real deep here, but I still want you to wear it."

"Oh, okay." he mumbled, scrunching his face into a scowl as she helped him put on his life jacket.

"Mason, let's have a happy heart. This is a very special place to Mommy. It's not a place to be grumpy. Can you do that?"

"Yes, Mommy, I can. I just don't want to."

"Then you sit over there where I spread out the towel until you do want to." She turned and walked over to Robyn.

"Here, I'll hold up this towel for you to get changed. Then you do the same for me. He won't last long once we get in the water," she whispered to Robyn.

Once changed, Claire ran toward the rope, grabbed it with both hands, and swung out over the creek. Half way across she let go, making a huge splash as she hit the water.

"Awesome," she sputtered as her head bobbed to the surface. "Water's great. You're next, Robyn!"

"Here goes!" Robyn called out, her long legs and fluid motion mimicking the flight of a crane they'd seen by the falls. "You're right, Claire, the water's perfect."

On the bank Mason hopped up and down shouting, "I changed my mind, Mommy. I have a really happy heart . . . and I want to."

"Okay, little man, go for it." Claire gave Robyn a sly smile.

Mason grabbed the rope, stepped back and jumped. "Yippee!" he shouted as he collided with the water. "That was so cool."

~ ~ ~

They collapsed on towels spread in the sun after their swim. To Claire, it seemed time stood still in a place like this. She could picture herself as a young girl in this very spot. She had lain on a towel back then, looking up into the tree tops. Her imagination had flourished in a world all her own.

"Mommy, when are we going to see my new old house?" Mason was sitting cross-legged on his towel, intent on watching a ladybug climb along the twig he was holding.

"Right now. Mommy just forgot about the time. We need to change into our clothes and go see Mr. Walker."

~ ~ ~

Reuben's old green truck sat in the driveway just as it had the day before. The deafening racket of yesterday was replaced with the sound of singing. Claire didn't recognize the melody nor could she make out the words. Mason ran up the steps and hammered on the door. He jumped back in shock when Reuben Walker opened the door. The boy stood rigid, his hand over his mouth.

"Hello there, young sir. You must be Mason Westfield." Reuben stuck out his hand but the boy stood paralyzed. "Are you okay, boy?"

"Are . . . you . . . Santa Claus?" Mason asked.

The man's laugh was loud and deep. "No, Mason," he said.

"Oh," the boy said, a look of disappointment clouding his face. "You sure look like him."

"Well, thank you kindly. I take that as a compliment. Now will you shake hands? How do you do, young Mr. Westfield? I'm Reuben Walker."

Mason stuck out his small hand and returned the man's smile.

"Now who is this fair lady, Claire?"

"This is my dearest friend, Robyn Hamilton. She has to leave tomorrow, and I wanted her to see the house."

Robyn extended her hand to the older man. "So nice to meet you, Mr. Walker."

"And the same to you, Robyn. Please call me Reuben." He gently took her hand. "I feel blessed beyond measure. Now I have three new friends." He ushered them into the house where he'd set the kitchen table with four glasses, a pitcher of tea, and a vase with white peonies.

"Oh, Reuben, how thoughtful. Peonies were Honey's favorite flowers, weren't they?" He nodded with a pleased expression.

After drinking their tea, Claire asked Reuben to take Robyn and Mason on a walk-through. As they approached a medium sized room with a large window, Claire reached out and took Mason's hand. "I think this should be your room, Tiger. It was mine when I would come to stay with Potch and Honey." Giving her son a hug, she took his hand and led him to the window. "Sweetheart, see the bird feeder hanging in that tree? That's the same one that was here when I was your age. I loved watching the birds. Cardinals, bluebirds and goldfinches were my favorites."

"I wanna see those birds, Mommy."

"You will. I'll get some bird seed, and they'll come back."

After the walk-through, they went into the yard, and Mason immediately jumped onto the rock wall.

"Look, everyone! I can balance myself when I walk."

The adults smiled and cheered for a very proud little boy. As they watched him and his antics, Robyn informed Reuben of Claire's many talents. "You're not going to believe how great this place will look when it's finished. Between your remodeling and Claire's decorating ability, this will be a showplace."

After farewells all around, Mason motioned for Claire to lean down so he could whisper something in her ear.

"I like Mr. Reuben a whole lot, even if he isn't Santa Claus.

~ 18 ~

THE QUIET WRAPPED AROUND HER LIKE a cocoon, her thoughts her only companion. Mason had gone for a walk after dinner with Dr. Mac and Helen. Claire offered to do the dishes, encouraging them to go on without her.

She had taken Robyn the day before to catch her plane. Reality struck hard as she waved goodbye to her lifelong friend, and it put her in a melancholy mood. She had needed some time alone to process her feelings.

Claire realized for the first time since this crazy scheme had taken root that she had cut herself off from everyone and everything familiar. She supposed she had understood that in her head, but not in her heart. Now she had to face the facts. An entirely new way of life awaited her. One that she alone had chosen. That choice had impacted the two people she loved most, her son and her best friend.

Thinking back on the morning before, Claire shuddered at the image of her small son telling his Aunt Robbie goodbye. The two of them sat on the sofa, Mason clutching the sock monkey Robyn had given him. The large tears he shed only in the most tender of moments spilled from his eyes.

"I . . . I . . . don't want you to go, Aunt Robbie!" Mason sobbed.

"Neither do I, Tiger." Robyn pulled Mason onto her lap, holding him close while she smoothed away tears. "But, hey, Thanksgiving will be here before we know it. I'm counting on you to have lots of cool things to show me. Will you do that?" asked Robyn as she ruffled his hair. Mason's face crumpled in sadness, but he nodded that he would.

"Okay then, Tiger, we have a date for Thanksgiving!" Robyn popped up from the sofa, lifting Mason up with her.

After numerous hugs and farewells, Claire and Robyn made a dash for the car, knowing full well they would break into tears if they didn't get out of there. The trip to the airport proved somber, their conversation confined to small talk.

Claire, focused on the memory of the painful farewell at the airport, nearly jumped off the sofa at the sound of the doorbell. She hoped it wasn't a patient looking for Dr. Mac. The bell rang again before she would reach the door.

"Dr. Bradley, come in. Dr. Mac isn't here. He and Helen took Mason on a walk."

"I won't stay long," Seth said. "Actually, I came to see you."

"Oh, well, come sit down. May I get you something to drink? There is sweet tea or lemonade."

"Lemonade sounds great."

"I'll be right back. Go ahead and sit down," Claire said.

Moments later she returned with two glasses filled with pink liquid. "Hope you don't mind pink. Helen made it for Mason." She sat down across from him. Claire felt a bit nervous. They sipped the lemonade, neither knowing what to say. Claire broke the silence. "Is your practice going well?" she asked.

He smiled. "Pretty good. I'm seeing more and more patients." He hesitated and then went on. "Because they think I'm too young and don't know enough, a lot of people won't see me." Seth eased back in the chair. "It would probably be the same wherever I started out. I keep telling myself that anyway."

Claire watched him as he spoke. He was about her age, maybe a couple of years younger. He had a quiet, reserved manner about him, and he struck her as someone who might be a poet or philosopher rather than a doctor. But then she barely knew him. Robyn was right about his looks. He was very attractive in an unpretentious way.

She nodded her head in agreement. "Yes, I'm sure that's true. My husband, Randall, experienced similar encounters when he started practice," Claire said.

"Thanks, those are encouraging words I really need to hear right now. This has been a difficult transition, but that's not why I stopped by, so I won't bore you with my frustrations," he said. "I really came by to tell you about the soccer schedule. I tried to call yesterday, but no one answered. Our first practice will be this Thursday at four thirty. Thursday is my afternoon off, so I can meet with the kids earlier. Next week we will go to two practices. The Tuesday practice will be at seven o'clock. I don't think I'll get caught late at the clinic, but you can never tell. You understand about those things though, don't you, Claire?"

"Yes, I do," she replied. "Thanks for making the effort to come by. Mason is so excited."

"I'm getting that way myself. I've never done anything like this before, but I think it will be good for me as well. Oh, I about forgot. We'll practice in the vacant lot across from City Park." Seth stood and handed Claire his glass. "Thanks for the lemonade—pink is good!" he said with a grin.

Standing at the door, Claire waved, a hint of a smile lingering as she watched Seth walk away.

~ ~ ~

Claire felt like kicking herself. She should've waited a couple of days before taking Mason to get his soccer ball. Multiple times each day he asked if it was time for soccer practice. Thursday at four thirty could not come soon enough for either of them. It had been a tough week. Reuben had uncovered a few more things that needed repair. Her phone call to Robyn had been painful for them both and ended in tears, and Claire questioned the whole move. She decided a good run would help get her out of this funky mood. Maybe Helen would keep an eye on Mason for a little while.

Going downstairs, she headed for the kitchen, the most likely place to find them. Her son had attached himself to both the McQuarrys, his obvious need for grandparents being very apparent. Thankfully, they both seemed delighted to fill their respective roles. Sure enough, Helen and Mason were sitting in the kitchen booth in animated conversation when Claire walked in.

"Hi ya, Mommy. Come see what we are coloring. Did you know Mrs. Mac's an artist? She draws pictures and then we color them. Isn't that cool?" Mason's eyes shone with happiness.

Claire walked to the booth and bent to look at her son's art-work. "My, my," she said, rubbing his shoulder. "These are beautiful, Helen. I had no idea you were an artist. You are very, very good."

"Oh, it's just a little something I enjoy doing when I have some extra time," Helen said. "And especially when I can work with such a talented partner." She leaned across the booth and gave Mason's hand a pat. "We're a team, aren't we, Mason?"

"We sure are, Mrs. Mac. I'm learning good, aren't I?"

"Helen, would you mind if I went out for a run? I need to think through some things, and I seem to do that best when I run."

"Well, I'm pretty busy right now—or I should say my partner and I are! Certainly, dear, go ahead. Mason and I need to finish these before dinner. This is probably a good time for a run since it cools down about now. Enjoy yourself."

"Yeah, Mommy, enjoy yourself. Me and Mrs. Mac are hard at work."

Claire bent down and kissed the top of her son's head. "Thank you both. I'll go change."

~ ~ ~

No sooner had she started her run than she knew it was just what she needed. Her frustrations seemed to diminish with each step, and her fears lost their fire. Helen was right. It was the perfect time to be out. The hottest days of summer would be upon them soon. She could well remember sitting on Potch and Honey's front porch swing, rocking back and forth and sipping lemonade. It was a wonderfully unstructured time for her. Nothing like the constant schedule and rules of boarding school. Only during those unhurried days in Mason Falls had Claire understood the sumptuous meaning of childhood. It was here where she could dream and let her imagi-nation be free.

She had reached that sweet spot of her run as she liked to call it where her mind and body seemed to flow in effortless connec-tion. That's what she loved about running—reaching this point of exhilaration. Seemingly out of nowhere, Claire heard someone call her name.

"Claire! Hey, Claire, wait up," the almost familiar voice called.

Glancing over her shoulder she caught sight of Seth running toward her. She eased her pace, allowing him to catch up to her.

"Wow, Mrs. Westfield," he said, his breathing labored, "you set quite a pace."

She slowed, giving him a measured look. "You can join me if you think you can keep up."

"I'm willing to give it a try. You obviously do this on a regular basis," he said, catching his breath.

"Yes, I do. I love to run. It helps me keep my sanity. Especially over the last year. And you?"

"Well, you've already picked up on the fact that I'm a bit out of shape. But I've been a runner since high school. Went to college on a cross country scholarship. But my last year of residency kept me pretty busy, so I had less time to run. Now I'm getting back to it again."

"Good for you. Guess that's one of the perks of starting a new practice—a little more free time, at least in the beginning."

"Yeah, it is, plus there's not much drawing me to go back to my room at the motel."

"You're living in a motel?" Claire asked in surprise.

"I am. But I should be moving into a little house in two to three weeks. Nothing much to look at but more space for sure."

Claire slowed her pace seeing that he was working hard to keep up. "That will be nice. Where's it located?"

"It's a small green house in an area that everyone here calls Swamp Town."

"Um, let me think a minute. Oh, is that across town where . . . how do I say this . . . ?"

"Yes, it is," replied Seth. "It's all that's available right now. But, hey, it'll be fine."

The two continued running in silence for several minutes before Claire said, "That's very admirable, Doctor. You seem to be fitting in here quite well what with coaching a soccer team and choosing to live in Swamp Town. Not everyone would make those choices. I applaud you."

Seth's face turned red. All he could think to say was "Thanks."

Claire changed the subject by bringing up Mason's enthusiasm for soccer practice. "That's one reason I decided to go on this run. He talks of little else, at least around me. Right now, Dr. Bradley, we are both living for Thursday at four thirty." At that they both laughed.

"I need to turn back and rescue Helen from her newest admirer. Mason's fallen head over heels for both the McQuarrys."

"I'll go back with you. Don't think there's much left in me. But one of these days, Claire Westfield, I'm going to take you on the run of your life! You best watch out."

She laughed, "Oh, don't you worry, Doctor, I'll be ready and waiting." They fell into a comfortable silence before parting with a friendly high five.

Seth Bradley was a nice man, Claire decided after they went their separate ways, though a little on the reserved side.

~ 19 ~

SETH HAD LOST COUNT OF HOW many YouTube clips of kids' soccer he had watched, but here he was again, sitting in his office at night doing just that. The Sunset Motel had no internet service, so the clinic was his lifeline to the outside world. There were some really helpful clips. One thing was for sure, if he did rent the green house in Swamp Town, he was getting internet service. Fred had told him the landlord was working on the repairs, but cautioned him not to get his hopes up. "He's not the most reliable landlord in town," Fred warned, "but sometimes he'll surprise you."

After shutting down the computer, Seth straightened some papers on his desk and placed the list of soccer names back in the manila envelope. Fortunately, all but two parents had been at home when he called. Claire Westfield was one of the two not at home when he called, which was why he'd dropped by the McQuarrys' to see her. He had enjoyed the visit and then crossing paths again while they were on their runs. He certainly wasn't thinking of beginning a relationship with anyone while in Mason Falls, but he couldn't deny the truth; she was an unusually attractive woman. *Don't go down that road*, he told himself. *This is a short stop to going in a different direction.*

~ ~ ~

Driving back to the motel, Seth let his thoughts go to Mabel Porter. Things seemed to have settled down some with her, but he faced an issue related to her that could change that. This morning at breakfast when she served him his food, he had noticed something that caught his physician's eye. She typically wore long-sleeved tops, but today she was wearing short sleeves. On her forearm, just below the elbow, was a worrisome dark mole. He was feeling compelled as a physician to mention it to her. Tomorrow, her day off, he needed to find a way to speak with her in private. It would take every ounce of bedside manner he had acquired to handle this one. He hoped he was up to the task.

He tossed and turned all night, thoughts of how to approach Mabel worrying him. There had been ample opportunities during his training to learn to deal with difficult patients. They were just part of a doctor's territory. So why did Mabel Porter seem to bring him to his knees? How could one woman, barely five feet tall, intimidate him this way? There had to be more going on than the obvious clash of their personalities.

Seth finally crawled out of bed. When his feet hit the floor, a realization struck him. This was the first time since coming to Mason Falls that he hadn't gotten a full night's sleep. He had to admit to himself there were some perks to being here. A hot shower and a cup of coffee should also put him in a better mood.

~ ~ ~

Mabel seemed to have vanished into thin air. Seth checked the office and her small house at the end of the property. Nothing. He was the only customer at the motel, so she wasn't cleaning a room. Somehow, he didn't see Mabel as a churchgoer, but maybe he was wrong. Sundays in Mason Falls were pretty quiet. Most people were in one of several churches in town or working in their yards. Taking his coffee with him, Seth drove to the square, bought a newspaper, and settled onto a bench by the fountain. Something as simple as time to sit and read a paper proved to be a rewarding experience these days.

Absorbed by an intriguing account of local politics, Seth jumped at the touch of someone's hand on his shoulder. "Sorry, Doc, didn't mean to startle you," Reuben said. "Mind if I sit down?"

"Not at all. Good to see you, Reuben. Just catching up on some news. I can't remember the last time I did this." Seth smiled at his new friend.

"Kind of peaceful here, especially on a Sunday, isn't it?"

"It sure is. What are you up to today?" asked Seth.

"Just got out of church and thought I'd sit by the fountain a bit. Didn't know I'd get to see you," Reuben said with an easy laugh.

The two talked leisurely about the events of the past week. Seth asked Reuben about the Mason place, sharing that he'd met Claire and her little boy. "He's going to join the soccer team I'm coaching," Seth said.

"That's good of you to take that on. It will mean a lot to those children, especially little Mason. It can be tough moving to a new town."

"Tell me about it," Seth said. "Reuben, I've got a difficult conversation with Mabel facing me today. I didn't sleep much last night, just tossed and turned. It's a medical issue, so I'm not at liberty to give you details. Just wish you would think about me this afternoon. I'm really dreading her reaction."

"Doc, I'll do more than think about you this afternoon—I'll be prayin' for you and for Mabel."

"I have to be honest with you, Reuben. I'm not much on prayer. It's not that I'm opposed to it for others, it's just not something I do."

"Well, Doc, I understand. I've been there myself. Can I ask you a question? Wouldn't it make sense that the Creator would be really interested in anything that affected His creation? We are all His creation, and He cares an awful lot about us. I guess what I'm gettin' at, Doc, is this: I believe God is interested in you and how you tell Mabel about your concern. He's also interested in Mabel and her response, because if it's serious, she needs to hear what you say and follow your advice."

Seth shifted awkwardly on the bench, his eyes riveted on the newspaper in his lap. The air was warm and sticky.

"Doc, you said you're not a prayin' man, and you don't have to be for me to pray for you. Would you mind me doin' that right now?"

"I guess not," Seth murmured, his face flushed.

Reuben nodded, then said softly, "*Lord, You know all about each one of us, and You care about everything that comes our way. You care about Doc here and what he needs to say to Mabel, so give him the words Mabel needs to hear. And Lord, help Doc say them so she will listen. I don't know what the problem is, Lord, and don't need to 'cause You know all about it, but Doc is real concerned. I believe You want to use him to help Mabel. Lord, let the light of Your love shine down on both of them. Thank You."*

Seth opened his eyes to find Reuben's gaze locked on him.

"That wasn't so bad, was it?" the older man asked with genuine interest.

"No, course not. It's simply an unusual experience for me. The only other person who ever prayed for me was my grandmother. A year or so before she died, she got interested in God. I remember her praying, kind of like you did, a time or two." Seth stood up and reached out to shake hands with Reuben. "Thanks, Reuben. I appreciate your concern."

Reuben took Seth's hand in a firm grasp, and said, "It's a privilege, Doc. Our friendship means a lot to me. Let me know how things go."

"I'll do that." Seth headed for his car. He wasn't sure how he felt about what had taken place in the last few minutes. Reuben was sincere in his beliefs, and Seth would honor that. Did it change his own perspective? No. He was still worried about his upcoming conversation with Mabel.

After searching the motel premises once more, Seth trudged to Mabel's house again. A part of him hoped she wouldn't be there, but he pushed those thoughts aside. The woman's life could be in danger. There was no response to his knock on the door. Just as he turned to leave, he heard noise at the back of the house. He followed the sound, and there he discovered an almost comical Mabel Porter. With her back to him, she didn't hear his approach. She was digging in her garden. Her large straw hat looked to have bird feathers stuck in the band and she wore olive green, knee-high rubber boots, baggy pants, and an oversized plaid shirt. She had some kind of apron tied around her middle, weighted down with who knows what. Seth cleared his throat, trying not to startle her.

"What do you want?" Mabel demanded, a ferocious scowl covering her face. "Well, speak up. Can't you see I'm busy?"

"Mrs. Porter, if you could give me a few minutes, I'd like to discuss something with you. It's important."

"You movin' out?" Mabel snapped.

"No, ma'am, not at this time. That isn't what I wanted to talk to you about. Please, could we just sit over there in the lawn chairs for a few minutes?" Seth headed toward a chair, hoping she would follow.

"Aw right, but just a couple of minutes." Mabel brushed past him and plopped her sturdy frame squarely in the chair in the shade.

Seth, already sweating from nervousness, grimaced as he took the chair in the full sun.

"Okay, so what's so blasted important you have to interrupt me on my one day off?" Mabel removed her hat, took out a bandana and wiped her face.

"All I ask," Seth began quietly, "is that you hear me out before you say anything." Her blank stare didn't surprise him, so he just had to hope for the best. Seth found himself hoping what Reuben said in his prayer was the truth. He still wasn't sure he believed any of it, but he needed all the help he could get right now.

"Mrs. Porter, this is difficult for me, because I'm not your personal physician, but I would be neglectful if I didn't speak to you about my concern. When you served me breakfast yesterday, I noticed a worrisome looking mole on your left arm."

"I've had moles all my life. What's the big deal about this one?"

"As a doctor, I've seen lots of moles. Most of them haven't worried me. The one I saw on your arm is unusual, and it does worry me. I think it needs to be evaluated."

"Worries you in what way and what's so unusual about it?"

Seth could feel the tension growing between them, but he was determined to see this through.

"It's unusually dark, and the edges are very irregular. It's different than the other moles I've seen on you."

"So, all this time you've been looking me over like I'm a . . . what do you call it . . . a specimen?"

Seth shot up from his chair, furious, "No ma'am, I would never do that, and I resent your accusation!" Seth paced back and forth trying to get control of himself. She could be so blasted frustrating. It made him want to storm away and forget the whole thing. Instead, he sank into the chair and looked her straight in the eye.

"This is serious stuff I'm trying to tell you. Are you willing to listen or not?" He could see that his outburst had done a number on her, and she actually looked somewhat chagrined. He decided to take advantage of the opportunity before she returned to her usual belligerent self.

"Mrs. Porter, the mole could be cancerous—what we call a malignant melanoma." Seth paused, then asked, "Would you allow me to get a closer look at it?"

"No! And I'm not sure I want any doctor to look at it. But if I did, it wouldn't be some kid who just finished school!"

Biting his tongue, it still took everything in him to control his brewing anger. Seth nodded his head and said, "I understand, but please let me encourage you to see someone. Do you have a regular doctor?"

"No—don't need one. But if I decided to see someone, it would be Dr. Mac. At least he has some experience!"

"He would be a great choice, Mrs. Porter. He's an excellent physician."

"Not that I'm going to, mind you, but if I did, and he tells me the same thing, what do you think he would do?" she asked.

Ah, do I sense a chink in the armor of the formidable Mabel Porter? he wondered.

Seth proceeded, very carefully, to explain as simply as possible what would be involved, starting with a biopsy. He assured her that while serious, and possibly cancerous, it was treatable—even curable if treated early. Seth tried, as gently as possible, to finish by telling her that if proved to be cancer, it would require further treatment.

"More treatment! What's next? Cutting off my whole arm?" Now Mabel was the one jumping out of her chair. She marched back and forth, arms crossed against her chest.

"No, Mrs. Porter, a procedure called a wide margin excision. It's a fancy term for making sure that it is completely removed. It would also determine if further treatment is needed."

"There you go again. 'If more treatment is needed.' Don't you doctors ever know when to quit?" Mabel stomped back to her chair and sat down hard.

"To be honest with you, from my personal perspective, no. We doctors, this one anyway, don't know when to quit. The reason I chose this profession is to do everything in my power to help anyone who needs what I can give them. And I will not quit until there is nothing left to do."

Seth went on to assure Mabel he understood her concern and questions, but he could only say that it all had to be taken one step at a time and not to jump to conclusions.

"It sounds to me like you've already jumped to a conclusion and have me with one foot in the grave," said a more docile Mabel Porter.

"No ma'am, in fact I'm encouraged that if you have it examined and taken care of now, you have a good chance of being cured—assuming you don't delay."

"Well, young man, you've done enough assuming for now, so I'd appreciate you getting back to minding your own business and letting me mind mine." Mabel Porter rose to her feet and without another word, walked back to her garden.

Seth returned to his room and dropped into the old velour chair. Regret swept over him. He had so wanted to help her but instead, he had blown it. He lifted his weary body from the chair. He needed to think, clear his head, and get some honest answers about himself.

He got into Old Red and started the engine. He had no idea where he would go. He just drove. The road curved and suddenly he saw the sign for the waterfall. That would be a great place to go to maybe make some sense out of what had happened and have a little thinking time.

∽ 20 ∽

SETH HAD COMPLETED DICTATION OF HIS notes for the last chart of the morning schedule when Justine had handed him a scribbled message from Fred Lawson. He wanted to meet at the green house at noon if Seth was free.

As he reached the back door, he heard a breathless Nell Meyers call out, "Oh, Dr. Bradley, I have a message for you. It's from Reuben Walker."

"Thank you, Nell, but you didn't need to rush. Next time just leave it on my desk."

"That's okay, Dr. Bradley, I don't mind," she said, handing him the note, "It might be important."

"Well, thanks again. See you this afternoon."

Seth was struck by a gust of hot air when he stepped outside. While Mason Falls sat perched at a slightly higher altitude than the surrounding area, Seth feared summer here didn't catch much slack from the heat. When he reached Old Red, he felt like kicking himself for not lowering the windows that morning. This heat would guzzle the air conditioning.

He arrived early at the house in Swamp Town. Before moving here, he never got anywhere on time, much less early. He realized again how much his life had changed in the last few weeks.

Seth switched on the radio and tapped his fingers on the steering wheel to the beat of an old Alan Jackson number called "Drive." He had never been a fan of country music, but since moving to Mason Falls, the haunting melodies and poignant lyrics reeled him in like a fish on a line. Just as the song ended, Seth caught sight of Reuben's note on the passenger seat and unfolded it. The message he read was simple: *Doc, if you aren't busy after work, meet me at the waterfall. A sweet friend cooked me up enough food to feed two hungry men. Would like to share it with you. Reuben.* Seth stared out the car window, the gentle whoosh of the car's air conditioner the only sound.

Once again Reuben had reached out to him with a thoughtful gesture of friendship. This man was quickly becoming a part of his life. And it felt good. The rumble of Fred's big truck broke the silence.

Seth and Fred looked at the shabby dwelling. It didn't look like much on the outside, but the grass had been cut. The bigger issue was what the inside would look like this time.

Fred said, "Okay, let's see what you think, Doc. I can tell you it's much better than the last time we were here. You ready?" Seth nodded and followed him into the tiny house.

There were definitely improvements since his first visit. The trash and debris were gone, enabling him to get a better idea of what the place could look like with furniture in it. The smells of urine and smoke were diminished, but a tinge of each still hung in the air.

"It's better for sure," Seth said, walking from the living area to the kitchen. He opened the oven door and said, "It's a mess in there."

Fred dug out a small notebook from his pocket to jot down notes. Continuing from room to room, Seth opened closet doors and bathroom cabinets pointing out a few problems. Fortunately, he thought, there was no carpet, only beat up looking linoleum and well-worn wood flooring.

"Fred, ask him if he'll put in some new linoleum. The wood floors I can live with."

"I checked the plumbing. It's all okay. Also checked the crawl space, and for Swamp Town, it was in pretty good shape. A little damp but not bad," Fred said.

"He still won't agree to painting the inside?" Seth asked, looking at the stained walls.

"Says no on that one. But tell you what, Doc, I'll see if he will pay for the paint or at least split the cost with you. If he agrees, you and I can get this place knocked out over a weekend."

"Fred, I can't ask you to spend a weekend painting this place."

"You didn't ask, Doc, I offered. That's what friends and neighbors do for each other, isn't it?"

"Yes, it is . . . and thank you."

"That's small town life for you. We look out for each other. You ready?"

"Yeah, let's go." Seth took one more long look around what potentially could be his new home.

As they were leaving, Fred promised he would talk to the owner that afternoon and call Seth as soon as he had some answers.

~ ~ ~

The afternoon was busier than expected with several work-ins but the pace was comfortable, and he and Justine were beginning to function as a team. She was as good as, if not better than, any nurse he'd worked with in his training. He liked her efficient, professional manner, but it was the woman's kindness and sensitivity toward their patients that won his greatest admiration.

Justine met him outside exam room three as he escorted Cindi Harrison and her energetic young son into the hall. "I'll see you tomorrow at soccer practice, J.J.," Seth said, shaking the boy's hand.

"Us guys do it this way," J.J. shot back, giving him a knuckle punch.

"Okay, big guy," Seth laughed, repeating the parting gesture.

"Cindi, that rash will clear up in no time. Again, it's nothing to worry about, very common in kids around J.J.'s age."

"Justine, do you need to see me?" he asked, waving goodbye to the Harrisons.

"Yes sir, you have a phone call from Mr. Lawson."

"Great, maybe this poor homeless doctor will finally have a place to live. Wish me luck?"

"Of course, Doctor. And it's line two." He slipped into his office and clicked the button.

"Hello, Fred. What's the news?"

"Are you ready to do some painting?" boomed the voice on the other end of the line.

"He agreed? Yeah, I'm ready. I can't believe it. I'm going to actually have my own place. Thanks, man, I appreciate all you've done." He grinned at Justine as she knocked softly and entered. He gave her a thumbs up.

Seth agreed to go pick out the paint color at Hank's. Fred had told him how many gallons to get and to explain to Hank and Reuben to send half the bill to the house owner. Seth was also pleased with the news about an oven replacement.

Fred had cautioned him not to hold his breath on the other items of concern, even though the man had agreed to fix them. "Worse comes to worse, we'll do it ourselves," Fred said. Seth hoped Fred's experience in those areas was a lot more than his own.

Later that day, Justine commented on his cheerfulness and the effect on his patients. "It suits you very well, Doctor," she said with a smile.

After the last patient left, Seth decided to finish his dictation of charts later that evening. Those, he told himself, could be done when it turned dark. Right now, he needed to celebrate, and he was anxious to share his good news with Reuben.

~ 21 ~

HE WAS LOOKING FORWARD TO GOING back to the falls his little town was named for. Then the thought struck him like a brick slamming into his consciousness. Eyeing the deserted turnaround just ahead, he pulled off the road. What had he just called Mason Falls—his little town? Disturbed at the idea he might be developing positive feelings about this place, Seth reminded himself this was a temporary time in his life.

He was beginning to enjoy some of the benefits of a small town and certainly the relationships, but he had to stay true to his plan. He had worked far too long and hard to end up a small town GP. He told himself to keep a clear head and not to let his dreams fade. After all, he could meet great people in a city too. His thoughts put a damper on his spirit, but he was an expert at shoving his feelings into a closet in his mind.

He got back on the road and by the time he turned on the side road that led to the falls, his earlier enthusiasm began to return. The parking area came into sight as did one dilapidated green truck.

Gravel crunched beneath his feet making enough noise, he hoped, to ward off any bears in the area. He thought he was hearing music. It seemed out of place, yet perfectly natural. It had to be Reuben. Was there no end to this man's abilities?

Approaching the clearing that led to the waterfall, Seth spotted the older man sitting on a large rock strumming a guitar. He sang a song Seth didn't recognize. His voice was quite pleasant.

"Hey there, Reuben."

"Doc, I'm so glad you could come," Reuben said with a welcoming smile. He carefully laid the guitar in its case on the rock. "We're in for a real treat, I can tell you. Miss Lilly Hopkins prepared a splendid meal, and she's one of the finest cooks in Mason Falls. Thought this would be an appropriate place to enjoy our good fortune; right here in the middle of the beauty of God's creation. We are blessed men, don't you think?"

Seth nodded in agreement. He still didn't quite know what to expect from Reuben but two things never changed: his contagious joy in life and his love for those around him. At Reuben's urging, Seth walked to the waterfall for a closer look. The roar of the rushing water had a quieting effect Seth hadn't anticipated. He supposed it must be much like the crashing of waves against the seashore, although he'd never experienced that sound either.

He sat down on a fallen tree limb near the water's edge and picked up a handful of small pebbles. He tossed a few, one at a time, across the water. Funny, he thought, he couldn't remember ever having done this simple act before.

"Hey, Doc," Reuben called. "Are you ready to eat?" We can fix our plates and sit over there on that rock. It's still a good view of the falls. And believe it or not, the best part of the day is just ahead."

The men sat on the rock trying to balance their plates and eat delicious fried chicken at the same time. Reuben was right. Miss Lilly Hopkins had done herself proud. This was one fine meal. Her fried chicken reminded Seth of the way Gran had cooked hers. Miss Lilly's feast included potato salad and green beans cooked long and slow then placed in a Thermos to keep warm. She had sent homemade rolls, fresh strawberries, and peach cobbler. Reuben had his jug of sweet tea to finish out the menu. Neither he nor Reuben felt the need to talk. Enjoying the food and one another's presence filled the space just right.

After a time, Seth said to the man he now thought of as a friend, "I'm going to rent the house in Swamp Town. It's not much to look at, but it will do for now, and at least I'll have my own place."

"That's mighty fine, Doc. You can make a real impact on the lives of those folks who will be your neighbors. There's never been a professional person live there. Most people don't go down there except maybe at Thanksgiving or Christmas to drop off some food or gifts for the children.

"Beware though, some folks may give you a hard time about it; not think it proper for a man of your standin' to be livin' there." Reuben locked eyes with Seth and his words were slow and pointed. "I want you to know it's the finest thing I've heard of in a very long time. I, for one, am proud to call you my friend."

"Thanks, Reuben, that means a lot." Wanting to change the subject, Seth said. "I have a question for you." The older man smiled, giving him the go ahead.

"What is the name of that song that you were playing when I got here?"

"It's an old hymn called "This Is My Father's World." Want to hear it?"

Seth nodded.

Reaching behind him, Reuben plucked the guitar from its case. He strummed a few chords, adjusted one of the strings and started to play. He hummed softly at first and then began to sing the words:

"This is my Father's world,
And to my listening ears
All nature sings, and round me rings
The music of the spheres.
This is my Father's world;
I rest me in the thought
Of rocks and trees, of skies and seas;
His hand the wonders wrought.
This is my Father's world;
He shines in all that's fair;
In the rustling grass I hear him pass;
He speaks to me everywhere.
This is my Father's world,
From shining courts above,
The Beloved One, His only Son,
Came a pledge of deathless love."

Reuben continued playing the melody and said, "Remember how I told you earlier the best part of the day was still ahead? Well, it's here, Doc, right now. Look across the creek and toward the falls."

Seth turned to see what Reuben was looking at.

"It's like God opened a vat of liquid gold," Reuben said, his eyes filled with delight, "then He poured it down this hillside in celebration of His goodness. The light that shines on us and fills even the shadows and dark places of our hearts is just like God's love, Doc . . . when we are open to it.

"That's why I love to play that old hymn when I'm here. This really is my Father's world, and if I look around, I can see Him everywhere. Do you feel His presence, Doc?" Reuben asked, his words hushed and filled with awe.

The silence hung heavy between them.

Seth's emotions clashed inside of him. He was pretty sure he knew the answer his friend wanted to hear, but it wouldn't be truthful if he agreed with him.

Well, Seth thought, *I've always tried to be honest, even when it wasn't the comfortable thing to do. Guess I'm not going to change now. I just don't want to hurt Reuben, he's been so kind to me. But here goes.*

"Reuben, the sunset is beautiful, breathtaking even, but I guess my answer to your question has to be no. I can't say I actually feel like God is right here with us. I'm sure you wanted a different answer, but I'm just being truthful. I know you mean well, Reuben, and I get the impression God is important to you. But to be honest, when I've really needed God, He didn't show up." Seth looked across the creek bank, captivated by the light. "I'm not saying He isn't real. He's just never been real to me."

Seth glanced at Reuben to catch a glimpse of his reaction. His friend's piercing blue eyes were fixed on him as though the man could see into his innermost being. Seth lowered his eyes and kicked at the pebbles near his feet. He had a knot in his stomach and a lump in his throat. Just when he thought he couldn't take the silence any longer, Reuben spoke.

"Seth," he said softly, calling him by name for the first time, "I appreciate your honesty. You're right on about God being an important part of my life. Actually, He is my life. I see so much of me as a young man in you, Seth. There was a time when I felt just like you do about God. I didn't think He knew I existed. One of these days I'll tell you my story.

"Your friendship has come to mean a lot to me, and I hope we can always be open and honest with each other. For now, I'll just say that God has always been there for us, but we're the ones who aren't willing to give Him permission to reach out to us—usually because of pride.

"I've always liked this line from Elizabeth Barrett Browning: 'Earth is crammed with heaven and every bush afire with God but only he who sees takes off his shoes.' There comes a time, Seth, when each of us needs to 'take off our shoes.'"

Uncomfortable didn't even come close to describing how Seth felt at that moment. He wished he was on call and his phone would ring, but only the sounds of nature broke the solitude.

"Doc," came Reuben's gentle words, "are we okay, you and me?"

Seth raised his eyes and said, "Of course, Reuben, but talking about God is an uncomfortable topic for me. Just so you know."

"Understood. But, Doc, I need you to understand that talking about God is very much a part of who I am. And when I talk about Him, I'm not trying to preach to you. I'm just being me." Reuben reached over and patted Seth on the shoulder. "Okay?"

"Okay." Seth stood and stretched. "Man, that rock is hard!"

"You ought to be my age, then you would really know how hard it is. Guess we better pack up and get going. Thanks for coming," said Reuben.

"Hey, thank you for asking me. It was good. Thanks for being my friend, Reuben."

The two men packed up empty containers. They had polished off all the food. Reuben put his guitar in its case, and they headed toward the parking area.

～ 22 ～

Rising anticipation filled Seth's thoughts. Thursday was finally here, and a few hours from now he'd be staring into the eyes of twelve energetic five and six year olds. He'd gotten up early so he could load his gear into Old Red before going to the clinic.

Fred had promised to bring the goals to the field that afternoon and also help him mark off the grid. Seth had already picked up a couple of extra soccer balls and several orange cones to use to teach the kids how to dribble, so he threw them in the trunk.

He decided to walk over to Mabel's coffee shop and grab some breakfast. The place, jam-packed as usual, buzzed with the early morning crowd's chatter. Several patients waved or tipped their hats as Seth entered. It gave him a sense of belonging, and he realized he was beginning to enjoy it.

"Hey, Doc, come on over and join us," a voice boomed. Seth searched for the voice's face, then saw George Meyers stand and motion to him. He was at one of the larger tables with several other men. Seth jostled his way through the crowd.

"Hey thanks, George. It's great to see you.

"No problem, Doc, we have an extra chair—just for you! Let me introduce you to these guys. These are my sons, Calvin, Billy, and James. Say hey to the Doc, boys," George said with obvious pride.

Seth reached out to shake Billy's hand first. "Nice to meet the husband of the lovely Nell Meyers. Your wife is quite special, Billy. She's the heart of the clinic. I know you must be very proud of her."

"Thanks, Doc. I'm mighty proud of her, for sure."

Before Seth could complete the round of introductions and handshakes, he saw Mabel headed his way. He felt the tension in his body as he wondered how she would react to him. He prepared for the onslaught.

"You want the regular, Bradley?"

Seth, dumbfounded, said, "Yes, please, Mrs. Porter. Thank you." Watching her march back to the kitchen, Seth plopped down in his chair. Had she really used his name?

"Looks like you may be making progress with Mabel, Doc. The town grapevine has it she's not too fond of you." George snickered and his sons nodded in agreement. "What did you do to her anyway, if you don't mind me askin'?"

Seth said, "I moved here."

At that, the entire table burst out laughing, and George slapped him on the back. "Welcome to Mabel's world, Doc."

A few minutes later, Mabel bustled over and set a plate filled with an omelet, bacon, and biscuits in front of Seth with one hand and poured his coffee with her other. "Enjoy," she mumbled and walked off. The aroma from the steaming plate of food triggered Seth's taste buds. He grabbed his fork and proceeded to devour the best tasting breakfast he'd had since coming to Mason Falls.

After leaving the coffee shop, he drove toward the office, wondering the entire way what had happened with Mabel. If he got a chance, he'd ask Dr. Mac about it. Maybe she'd gone in to see him after all. Most of his attention, however, was focused on rehearsing his strategy for the upcoming soccer practice. On Thursdays, there was usually a drug rep who would bring lunch to the office and talk to them about one of the newer medications. He decided to grab a quick lunch with the rep, listen to his presentation, then go back to his office to replay some kids' soccer videos on YouTube. He couldn't believe how nervous he felt but also how excited he was about getting started.

~ ~ ~

Seth pulled up to the clinic and walked to the back door. As he reached out to open it, the door gave way and Sodie Tucker crashed into him. She was carrying a large trash bag while trying to balance two good sized boxes.

Seth found himself lying on his back with Sodie on top of him, trash and boxes everywhere. Their faces almost touching, Seth could only imagine what they must look like. "Sodie, I can't breathe. I need you . . . to roll over." Shock distorted the woman's face.

Out of nowhere Dr. Mac appeared and helped Sodie get to her feet. "Looks like you two had a bit of a tumble!" Mac said, trying not to laugh.

Sodie started crying. "I'm so embarrassed. I've never done nothin' like that before." Her sobs became stronger as Seth struggled to his feet, brushing pieces of trash from his clothes.

Mac patted Sodie's shoulder. "There, there, Sodie. It's okay, these things just happen." Giving Seth his cue to join in, Mac added, "Don't they, Dr. Bradley?"

"Uh, yes, sure they do. It was just an accident, Sodie. We're both okay, that's what's important." He could tell Dr. Mac wanted to burst out laughing but knew better than to do it.

"Now then, we'll all three clean this up and start all over." Mac patted Sodie again and winked at Seth. "Won't we, Dr. Bradley?"

"Yes sir," Seth nodded. "We sure will."

Sodie Tucker, shaken by the fall and cringing with humiliation, reluctantly accepted help from Seth and Dr. Mac. She drew the line when they attempted to take the gathered trash and boxes to the receptacle. "You two have more important b'ness to take care of. This is my b'ness," she said as she hurried off with her arms full.

"What a way to start your day," Mac chuckled. "It was all I could do to keep from laughing out loud."

"I could tell." Seth grinned and said, "Me, I think I was in shock."

The morning schedule was pleasantly busy. Once again, he reminded himself how fortunate he was to have Justine Crenshaw as his nurse. They were indeed working together as smoothly as a well-oiled machine. Sometimes he was convinced she could read his mind. The highlight of the morning turned out to be an appointment with Opal Mae and Jasper Hobbs. She looked healthy and happy, just like a soon-to-be mother should look. Seth was pleased to see how Jasper had stepped up to the responsibility of making sure Opal Mae got plenty of exercise and was eating right. He congratulated them both on a job well done.

Seth finished seeing his last patient just before noon. Heading to the small kitchen, he met the drug rep bringing in what looked to be a substantial amount of food and offered to help carry part of the load. His stomach growled in spite of his breakfast at Mabel's.

After lunch, it was soccer YouTube videos.

~ ~ ~

Seth and Fred met at the vacant lot at three o'clock. Both had changed into shorts, tee shirts, and athletic shoes. They measured and chalked the grid area and set up two goals. Seth decided Fred's excitement over the whole thing might even outweigh his own. The man talked non-stop about all the potential this had not only for these twelve kids but for many more in the future.

"Have you thought of a team name, Doc?"

"No, thought I'd let the kids come up with the name," Seth answered.

"Um, that might not work, Doc. These are little kids, and you're going to get twelve different answers and probably hurt feelings if their name doesn't win," Fred said.

"Hadn't thought of that, but you're right. Have any ideas?" Seth waited, watching Fred's face go through multiple contortions with the enormity of the decision. When Seth had all but given up, Fred snapped his fingers.

"The Beavers. It's perfect. One thing I can promise you, Doc, they are going to be busy as little beavers!" Fred slapped Seth on the shoulder, grinning from ear to ear.

"The Beavers it is. I like it. Good job, Fred."

"If you'll get sizes and decide on a color, I'll get the shirts in Maysville and take them to the place where we get the older kids' uniforms done."

"Sounds good. Thanks, Fred. Are you going to stick around?" Seth hoped his friend would say yes.

"Nope, this is your deal, and the kids and the moms need to see you as the one in charge right from the git-go," Fred said and winked at Seth. "You'll do just fine."

"Thanks, but I'm getting a little nervous."

Fred grinned, "Doc, just remember you're a lot bigger than

those kids, and they don't know anything about soccer." Fred laughed as he waved and headed toward his truck.

Seth looked at his watch. Four fifteen. He was at countdown. He had discovered long ago the best policy for the jitters was to keep busy. The one thing he had left to do was get the ice chest. He walked across the field to get the chest out of Old Red. The water bottles had been a last-minute decision, but he congratulated himself for thinking of it.

Just as he set the ice chest down, Seth saw a number of cars pull in the parking lot. *Okay, here we go. I can do this*, he thought. He watched numerous moms and their children climb out of cars, but his attention was drawn to a particular young woman who had walked, not driven, to the field. Her son bounced from one side of her to the other, his excitement straining to be unleashed. Claire crossed the field with effortless grace. Her hair glistened in the sunlight, and Seth found himself breathing faster as she waved at him.

Mason must have gotten the okay to run ahead. Before Seth knew what happened, the boy had tackled him and almost brought him to his knees.

"Hi ya, Dr. Seth!"

"Hi yourself, buddy. You ready to play some soccer?"

"Oh yeah! I've been ready for a really long time!" Mason said, a huge grin stretching across his face.

Seth smiled at Claire as she approached. "Hi, I think we have a boy who's kind of excited."

"That, Dr. Bradley, is an understatement to say the least," Claire said as she tousled her son's hair.

"Well, we'll see if we can work off some of that energy. Glad you're here," Seth said. "Both of you."

As the mothers began to gather nearby, Seth excused himself to greet the others. Once the introductions were complete, he asked the moms to take a seat at one side. He had noticed they all came prepared with either a blanket or a lawn chair. Almost all of them had one or more little ones in tow as well. He sure wished Fred had agreed to stay.

Seth sensed immediately the need to be short and sweet with

any introductory thoughts.

"So, everyone, you are now members of the very first soccer team for five and six year olds. Want to know your team name?" A deafening chorus of "Yeahs" exploded from the kids in front of him.

"Well, your team is the Beavers! And you may know that beavers are very busy and energetic animals. They are also very hard-working. Do you think you can be like the beavers?" Seth laughed as one by one, led by J. J. Harrison; each child jumped up and chanted "Beavers. . . Beavers . . . Beavers."

"Okay, grab your soccer balls, and let's get started."

Kids of all shapes and sizes, boys and girls, crowded around Seth.

"Everyone, listen up so you'll know what to do," Seth began. The noise level was ear-piercing. He made a mental note to purchase a whistle ASAP. For now, he let out a "Quiet!" and held his hands above his head.

"Now, that's better. First thing is to get good and loose, so here's what to do. Mason, you and J.J. get everyone in a line. Then when I give the signal, all of you are going to run down the field to the goal in that direction," said Seth, pointing to his left. When you get there, run down the field to the other goal. You're going to do that three times. Understand?"

"Okay, Dr. Seth," said Mason, "but who's J.J.?"

"That's me." J.J. strutted toward Mason.

When everyone was lined up, Seth raised his hand and shouted, "Everyone, ready . . . set. . . GO! In a flurry of motion, twelve children sprinted for the goal. Seth congratulated each child with a high five as they finished the first exercise. "Great job, guys. Now this next one is like a game. It's called, I can do, can you? So here goes. I can skip, can you?" Seth felt totally foolish, but he skipped a short distance from the kids. "Now it's your turn." Twelve smiling faces zeroed in on him as the children skipped toward him. "You guys are doing so good." Seth patted or tousled each head. They proceeded through somersaults, one-legged hops, and jumping jacks.

"Now we're all warmed up and ready to have fun," Seth said. He asked the kids to sit on the ground so he could explain the next part of their practice. Within a couple of minutes, several were sprawled out inspecting the grass or a teammate's shoes, or their own nose. He could sense he was losing them . . . better get them up and moving again.

Out of the corner of his eye, Seth saw Claire walking toward him. "Coach," she said, her smile warm and encouraging, "excuse me, but maybe I could help you with these next drills."

Seth's gut reaction was to walk straight over to her and hug her, but instead he said, "Thanks, that'd be great."

Claire smiled at him. "Divide and conquer works really well with this age group."

"I believe you're right about that. This is definitely out of my comfort zone." Seth wiped his forehead.

"Hey, you're doing great. They really took to you. It's just their lack of attention span—not you. So, what can I do?"

Seth got the kids on their feet while giving a quick overview of the next drill, which was learning to dribble. Having someone else to help with the very busy Beavers made a huge difference, and his appreciation for Claire Westfield escalated that afternoon.

While the kids drank their water at the end of practice, Seth spent time with the moms going over details. He wrote down shirt sizes, reminded them about sunscreen, and asked for any questions. He was thrilled when they all eagerly offered to set up a schedule for bringing drinks and snacks.

Seth made sure he told each child what a good job they'd done and that he looked forward to them being at Tuesday's practice. He looked around to thank Claire again, but she and Mason were gone. A wave of disappointment rushed over him, taking him by surprise. He gathered up the practice cones, extra soccer balls, and ice chest, dumping them in the trunk of his car. Fred had promised to come by and pick up the goals later.

Seth sat in his car with the windows rolled down and stared at nothing. Two questions rolled over and over in his mind. Where had the thoughts about Claire came from, and how could twelve little kids drain a grown man in one hour? He knew one thing for certain. He had a whole new appreciation for mothers of young children.

~ 23 ~

CLAIRE'S ALARM JOLTED HER TO CONSCIOUSNESS. She had set it the night before to go off half an hour earlier than usual, which at the time seemed like a good idea. Rubbing her eyes with one hand and slamming the off button with the other, she couldn't remember for the life of her why it seemed necessary.

Easing herself into a sitting position, she waited for her brain to engage. Then it came like a splash of cold water, propelling her to her feet. She wanted to get her run over before Seth Bradley started his.

Claire was thankful Helen had suggested moving Mason into the other spare room after Robyn left. The privacy and not having to be concerned about waking him gave her a bit more freedom. She slipped into her clothes, pulled her hair into a ponytail, grabbed her shoes, and quietly picked her way down the stairs. Claire sat on the front porch steps to put on her shoes and mull over her reason for avoiding Seth. *He is a very nice man and great with the kids at soccer. If he wasn't quite so uptight otherwise,* Claire mused, *he could be a lot of fun to be with.*

There were those thoughts again, and she was not ready for them or for any kind of a relationship. That's why she would find a new route to run. It had dawned on her last night after soccer practice that she and Seth were seeing each other several times a week between running and soccer. Of course, there was nothing to it, and that's the way she wanted it to stay. *Right?*

Claire jumped from the steps, hoping to put the whole thing from her mind. She decided to focus on the new route. Maybe if she ran in the opposite direction, toward that new housing development, she would miss him. She started out at an easy jog, allowing plenty of time to warm up. The slower pace, though, gave her more time to think. And like it or not, those thoughts turned more and more to the question occupying her mind . . . could she fall in love again?

Not once in the nearly two years since losing Randall had Claire entertained any fantasy of finding love again. And she certainly never imagined the idea would surface here in a small town in Arkansas. If anything, coming here may have been her way of running away from the possibility.

She decided analyzing the situation just might uncover what was going on. Claire increased her pace. She hoped it would help her think more clearly. That was one of the reasons she loved to run. So many major decisions had become crystal clear as she hit the pavement, more than she could count. While she tried her best, this run ended not with clarity but confusion. Claire walked the last block to the McQuarry house to cool down. She felt discouraged but reminded herself that sometimes, especially in matters of the heart, dissecting an issue didn't always bring a quick answer.

As she walked up the front steps of the house, Claire realized that maybe she was making something out of nothing. Seth was becoming a friend, and she would leave it at that. The smell of bacon frying filled her senses and sounds of her son's giggles and Dr. Mac's deep, rich voice came from the kitchen when she stepped into the house.

After breakfast, Claire threw on a pair of old shorts she used to work out in and met Mason at the car. They had been here a little over two months, and she and Mason were settling into somewhat of a routine. Claire loved the days when he accompanied her to the farm. They worked in the yard clearing out the overgrown flowerbeds, raking leaves, and carrying other debris to a burn pile Reuben had set up.

Mason could hardly wait for the day they would have the bonfire Reuben promised. Her son chattered constantly about how huge it would be. "The biggest bonfire ever," he would say over and over again. She hoped it wouldn't be as large as in Mason's make believe world.

Today was Saturday, so Reuben would be at the house all day. On these days, they would take an hour off for lunch, sharing what each had brought as they sat either on the front porch or on a blanket under one of the huge old trees. Mason was captivated by Reuben's stories, his eyes wide and full of wonder. Sometimes Claire wasn't sure he was breathing as he sat in such awe of Reuben Walker. When lunch was over, Reuben would give Mason a nature lesson. Claire watched and listened as this dear man gave of himself and his knowledge to her son. Reuben opened Mason's eyes to a world unknown to him before coming to Mason Falls. Today as she listened, she brushed away a few tears. Warm memories from her childhood of Potch telling her stories surfaced as she watched Reuben and Mason.

"Now, young man, here is something really important for you to remember," Reuben said, pointing to a blue jay landing nearby. "This is a lesson I learned," Reuben continued, "when I was, oh, maybe ten years old. And I learned it the hard way. So, listen up, okay?" Mason's expression turned serious.

"Well, sir, my daddy told me from my earliest days, 'Son, never kill something unless you intend to eat it. If you kill a critter just for sport, you're goin' to have to eat it.' Guess I didn't really believe him, 'cause one day me and my buddy were out in the backyard. Now our backyard was pretty big since we lived in the country. Well, sir, we each had our .22 and saw this blue jay flying around. We didn't much like those birds. They were always squawking and stealing other birds' eggs.

"So, me and my buddy looked around real good to make sure nobody was watching us, and I raised my gun, and pow! I shot that bird dead."

Mason stared, wide-eyed. "What happened then, Mr. Reuben?"

"I'll tell you, son. I turned around, and there was Mama standing at the kitchen window. She pointed for me to come to the house. Right then I knew, sure as anything, what I had to do. I reached down, picked up that dang blue jay and headed to the back porch. Me and my friend plucked that bird naked and walked inside straight to the fireplace. It was fall, so Mama always had a fire going.

I got a clothes hanger, opened it up and stuck that ol' jay on it and started cookin' it right then and there."

Mason popped up from where he sat and paced back and forth. "Did you eat that ol' bird, Mr. Reuben, did you?"

"I sure did, boy, yes indeed. My friend and I told my mama it was the best eatin' we'd ever had. But then we ran outside and puked our guts out." Reuben threw back his head, roaring with laughter. Claire laughed until her sides hurt while Mason rolled around on the ground howling like a dog.

Reuben turned more serious. "I knew I'd done wrong and chose to disobey my daddy, but what I learned a long time later was that every creature is made by God, and its life is precious to Him. He gives us birds and animals and fish to enjoy and to eat if we're hungry and need food. But He also expects us to respect them and their right to exist." Reuben watched Mason, who sat Indian style in front of him taking in Reuben's serious tone.

"Mr. Reuben, I think you were wrong to kill that ol' jay and your daddy and God were right. If I ever have me a gun, I'm goin' to try real hard not to kill me an ol' jay."

"Mason Westfield, you learn well, son, very well." Reuben picked the boy up and twirled him around and around in a circle. Mason's shrieks of laughter filled the air. Claire put a hand over her heart, knowing she would treasure this moment forever.

~ ~ ~

It had been a full day. Claire glanced in the rear view mirror at her son who snored softly in his car seat. She smiled at her little man. He tried so hard to be a big guy, but he was still just a little boy.

Her thoughts turned to Reuben's good news as they said good-bye. "We're at a good place for you to start some painting if you want," he had told her. She was ecstatic. Reuben was a true marvel at what he had been able to accomplish. The weather had also been good, and most things had proceeded with little difficulty. She could hardly wait for morning.

At dinner that night, Helen and Dr. Mac asked if Mason could spend Wednesday with them. Helen thought Mason would enjoy going with her to a class for kids his age that she was teaching at her church, and Dr. Mac wanted to take him fishing after lunch since he was off on Wednesday afternoons. It seemed a perfect fit for all of them. Claire could really knock out some serious painting with a full day to herself.

After helping with the dinner dishes, Claire and Mason said goodnight to the McQuarrys. Mason, going from one to the other, crawled into their laps and smothered them with hugs and kisses. The three of them were becoming increasingly close, filling the empty places in each heart.

"Mommy, aren't you glad we came here and get to stay with Dr. and Mrs. Mac?" Mason asked, his eyes reflecting the growing love he had for the couple.

"Yes, I am, sweetie. They have been wonderful to us," Claire said, tucking the covers around her child.

"And Mommy, aren't you glad Dr. Seth is our friend? I sure do like him. He's the bestest coach I ever had."

Claire hesitated, trying to collect her thoughts.

"You do like Dr. Seth, don't you, Mommy?" asked Mason, an anxious look on his face. "He's a really nice man, and I know he likes you 'cause sometimes he looks at you the way Daddy used to do."

Claire's words caught in her throat. "I do like Dr. Seth. You're right, he is a nice man, and I'm glad you like him as your coach. But, Mason, we hardly know him. I . . . I think you're mistaken about how he looks at me the way Daddy did," Claire said. "Now, that's enough talking. You have a big day tomorrow, so you need to go to sleep." Claire leaned over and kissed her son's small face, taking in the scent of shampoo and shower gel. "Sleep well, sweetheart. I love you so much."

Mason reached out for a hug. "I love you too, Mommy."

Claire couldn't get to her room fast enough. Every nerve in her body seemed on high alert. Why in the world would Mason think about how Seth looked at her, especially in the way he had described? Then, out of nowhere, it struck Claire. Mason missed his dad's presence in his life. He was a little boy who longed for what he'd lost. Seth's kindness and encouragement to him reminded

Mason of what it had been like to have a father in his life. Her heart ached for her son. Was the timing of his comment about Seth and her own questions earlier that morning more than coincidence? She wasn't sure how to deal with any of this.

~ ~ ~

Wednesday morning Claire got her run in once again without seeing Seth. She grabbed a quick shower, made sure Mason was up and getting dressed, and went to help Helen with breakfast.

Once the dishes were done, everyone headed out at the same time. Mason asked, "Now what are we going to do, Mrs. Mac?" They waved goodbye to Claire as he took Helen's hand. Claire stood by her car and waved back, watching them until they were out of sight.

She was excited as she got into her car. She couldn't believe she could actually start painting. She wanted to do Mason's room first. She hoped it would help him begin to think of the place as his new home. She had chosen her color scheme a month ago, looking forward to the day she would put a paint-loaded roller to the walls. Mason's room would be Revere Pewter by Benjamin Moore. It was a light gray, and Claire considered it boyishly masculine. Reuben wouldn't arrive right away, but Claire didn't mind working alone, and today she especially needed some alone time. Her heart continued to reel from not only her own questions from yesterday but also from those of her son.

Her painting equipment awaited her in the tool shed Potch had built one summer during her visit. She had always loved the shed. Most of all she loved the pungent smells of motor oil, grass shavings clinging to the lawn mower, bags of fertilizer, and gasoline cans. Claire had spent two days cleaning out the shed and reorganizing the shelves to hold her own supplies—new cans of paint, paint rollers, brushes and pans, her favorite ladder, and the set of "lady's tools" as Randall had called them. They had been a gift from Randall and Mason one Mother's Day. All of the tools were pink, including a hard hat which Randall had insisted she wear when climbing around on her ladder.

Overcome by the memories that day, Claire had found herself sitting cross-legged in the middle of the raw dirt floor, tears streaming down her face. But now she reminded herself that today was to be a happy day—a step forward not backward.

Light flooded the space. Her grandmother had insisted on large paned windows not only in their house but also in the tool shed. Honey's natural instinct for beauty didn't stop short of even a tool shed. Claire couldn't help but smile remembering her tiny grandmother looking up at Potch, tall and handsome, and shaking her finger at him. He picked her up, much as Reuben had done with Mason the other day, and twirled her around and around. Honey had pounded her small fists into his shoulders, commanding him to put her down while Claire ran in circles around them laughing in delight.

Even now, after all these years, it was a magical moment tucked safely away in her heart. These were the kind of memories she wanted for Mason. And so far, Mason Falls and the people here were helping create the experiences that would one day be his memories.

Claire gathered what she needed to start painting and headed for the house. First thing on the agenda was to get the room taped off. She planned on having Mason's room done and ready for a second coat of paint by noon. One thing Claire knew she had down to an art form was painting rooms. She loved the entire process but especially seeing the results. Watching a room change before her eyes as she rolled a new color onto lifeless walls never ceased to give her a thrill.

As an interior decorator, Claire had made it part of her service to do some of the actual painting, usually a main room or unique area of the home for her clients. This was the way she connected to the project and was able to capture the right ambience for those who lived there. Right on schedule, she took a break at noon to sit under a huge tree and eat a pear and a cup of Key lime flavored yogurt. Satisfaction flooded her. The room looked great, and at the rate Reuben was going, they might get to move in before school started.

Claire decided that tonight after Mason went to bed, she would order the comforter and rug she'd found a few nights ago on IKEA. They would perfect for his room. She smiled, picturing the finished look, boyish but tasteful. Claire could hug Helen for being quite a techie for a woman her age. She must have used her feminine wiles on Mac to get a computer and internet service in her study.

Mac, on the other hand, according to Helen, left anything related to computers and the internet to Nell Meyers at the office. Seth had mentioned on one of their runs how thankful he was for internet service at the office since there was none at the motel. That meant he had to do anything online at the office—even watching his YouTube videos on kids' soccer. They had laughed about all the adjustments they were making from big city life to small town life. It was difficult for both of them to understand how the people here didn't consider technology a common necessity. Since that day, though, Claire found herself wondering if just maybe that was a good thing.

By the time Reuben arrived that afternoon, Claire had administered a second coat of paint to Mason's room and taped off her room and both downstairs bathrooms. They sat on the porch and sipped cold lemonade while making small talk before going over plans for the afternoon agenda. Reuben, so easy to talk to, had become a dear and trusted friend. He reminded her of what Potch had been for her so many years ago. Someone to share her heart with. Someone who listened from the depth of his soul.

~ 24 ~

ANOTHER THURSDAY HAD ROLLED AROUND, AND while Seth looked forward to a short day at the clinic, he felt moody and in a funk. He hated waking up this way. He was convinced his thoughts the night before were the cause.

Two things had weighed heavily on his mind, things he didn't really want to admit to himself. First, he was lonely and second, Claire Westfield was avoiding him. For the life of him, he didn't know why or what he might have said or done. If he could get up the courage, he was going to ask her out for coffee after soccer practice to talk about what happened. He was pretty sure she didn't want any kind of relationship, but neither did he. *Did he?* Couldn't they just be friends? They had more in common than either had originally realized. Seth suspected she needed a friend just as much as he did.

After a quick shower, he dressed and walked to Mabel's. With one thing and another he hadn't been there in a while though at least things had been improving on that front. She still tended to be aloof but way better than before.

~ ~ ~

The morning proved to be uneventful—coughs, colds, lots of poison ivy and chigger bites. The one troublesome exam was a seven-year old boy with possible Rocky Mountain spotted fever. The history proved classic: mother discovers tick on child, child develops rash and flu-like symptoms and achy joints. Seth ordered a blood test and started the boy on an antibiotic while they waited on the test results.

This was drug rep day, so Seth moseyed into the clinic kitchen to grab a bite to eat and listen to the newest spiel on medications.

Surprised to see Mac there this early, he took a chair across from him at the table.

"Your patient load must have been pretty light, sir, you don't usually get here this early," Seth said.

"Not really light, just the kind that don't take much time, medically, but still need that extra bit of personal attention."

"That reminds me. If you don't mind me asking, has Mabel Porter been in to see you lately?"

"Let's step into your office for a minute, Seth," Mac said and got up from the table. "Folks may appear in here any moment. I've been meaning to catch you up about this, but I've been awful busy of late.

Dr. Mac closed the office door and leaned against it. "Yes, she came in. I think it was a couple of days after your talk. Oh my, I have to tell you, though, she was mad as all get out with you! Said you needed to mind your own dern business and leave other people alone. She was on a tirade for sure. Apparently, you did a real number on her. That was a gutsy thing you did—confronting Mabel. She isn't the easiest person to be around, is she?" Seth nodded in agreement.

"Your courage and concern paid off, Dr. Bradley. Your actions are probably responsible for saving the woman's life. I told her so in no uncertain terms. Our time went pretty well. It took her a while before she would admit to a long-time fear of cancer. She didn't go into details, but I suspect she lost someone close to her from the disease. It may shed light on her dislike for doctors.

"I did a thorough exam and told her I agreed with you. She was definitely frightened but wouldn't make an immediate decision. I came on pretty strong with her about not waiting too long. She called me the next day and agreed to the surgery. I'll give you a full copy of my chart notes. We did the procedure the next day. I did an excisional biopsy and extended the biopsy to the underlying subcutaneous tissue.

"As expected, the pathologist confirmed it was a malignant melanoma, but the good news was that it appeared to be completely excised with the margins clear. I arranged for a surgeon to perform a wide margin excision without needing a skin graft just to ensure no cancer was left behind.

"The surgeon paid you quite a compliment before releasing Mabel. He told her that she was very fortunate and that she needed to thank you because you saved her life."

Seth put his head in his hands, a huge sense of relief flooding over him. Mabel Porter was the most exasperating woman he had ever known, but he felt truly thankful for her good news.

"Seth," Dr. Mac said softly, "Mabel was very appreciative and relieved, even breaking into tears when she heard the results. She wanted me to thank you. Before she left, she said that in her own way and own time, she would thank you herself. I want you to know how proud I am of you. You're going to be a fine physician.

"Speaking of fine things, Dr. Bradley, you and I need to spend some time together. It's been a while. Let's go fishing tomorrow evening. I'll have Helen fix us a picnic. You won't be sorry."

Seth had planned to do some cleaning at the green house since he was moving in on Saturday. "Sounds good," he said instead, feeling a little glow from Mac's words and the good news about Mabel Porter.

"Come on, let's go back to the kitchen. Say, how's soccer coming along?"

"Really good actually. The kids are pumped up and ready to go every practice. I only wish I had half their energy." Both men laughed and agreed. "The moms have been great about bringing water and snacks. And Claire has helped me a lot in keeping the kids focused."

"Well, if the rest of those kids feel about it like Mason does, I can assure you you've been a success. Good job, Seth," Mac said.

"Thanks, sir, that means a lot."

~ ~ ~

After leaving the clinic, Seth changed clothes and headed to the green house. He could get at least three hours of work in before soccer. That would make up for not going to the house tomorrow night.

~ ~ ~

Soccer practice turned out to be fast and furious, but Seth was determined to catch Claire before she got away. During the water break when everyone else was busy visiting with the kids or each other, Seth walked over to Claire. His heart was pounding, and he felt sixteen again. He hoped he didn't make an absolute fool of himself.

Claire said, "Hello, Coach. What's up?"

Seth adjusted his Royals ball cap and said, "I wonder if you might be up for coffee or something after you get Mason home. I have something I'd like to talk to you about."

Seth sensed her hesitancy but felt relief when she agreed.

"I can't stay long, Seth. I like to help Helen with dinner. She's been so good to us, it's the least I can do."

"Hey, no problem, I understand. How about The Singing Dog? It will be too early for the usual dinner crowd, so it should be more on the quiet side," he said.

"Sounds good. I'll just walk over since it's so close. See you in umm . . . say fifteen minutes after practice is over." Claire's smile seemed a little forced.

~ ~ ~

Soccer practice ended well with the kids happy at their progress. Seth began to pack the gear in the trunk of Old Red. He drove the short distance to the square. He had been right. Things were quiet at the café. Now if he could just not botch the next phase. He sat at a booth in a quiet corner, tapping his foot against the concrete floor waiting for Claire. He had never considered himself the nervous type, but today he'd just shot a hole through his self-image. After all the verbiage about confidence and taking control of the situation handed to him in med school and residency, all he could do was keep tapping his foot.

He stood as Claire entered the café and waved to her. She seemed a little stiff, he thought, as she made her way across the room. She gave him a slight smile and slid into the booth. They both ordered iced tea.

Seth decided he'd get right to the point after Hap brought their drinks. In the meantime, they did what came easy. They talked about soccer practice.

Stirring his tea, Seth took on the gorilla in the room. "Claire, I know you're uncomfortable about our meeting. Believe me when I say, no more than I am. I guess it's always best to just get to the point, so here goes. Have I said or done something that has offended you? It dawned on me the other day that after running together pretty often, I haven't met up with you in a while." He hesitated, hoping she would pick up from there. But for what seemed like several minutes, they were both silent.

"Seth, you're right about this being uncomfortable. I had no idea what was on your mind when you asked to meet, so you know what happens. You go through all kinds of scenarios. I'm going to be honest with you. I have been avoiding you. I've been running a different route." Claire played with the straw in her glass. "In answer to your question, no, you haven't offended me in any way. And I need to apologize to you for taking the cowardly way out. I realized how often we were seeing each other, and it frightened me. I . . . I just don't think I'm ready to move forward right now. Please, please don't think it's you. I enjoyed our runs, and I love helping you at practice." Claire reached for his hand.

His first instinct made him want to rush to her side and take her in his arms. She looked so vulnerable, so in need of comfort. Instead he held her hand in his, willing her to look at him. "Claire," he said, "I know you are still in a very difficult place. I just want to be friends. I think we're both a little on the lonely side. I know I am. Can't we simply enjoy each other's company at this point?"

She raised her head, her hair falling across one shoulder. "Yes, Seth, we can be friends. I would like that."

Seth slowly removed his hand, silently thanking Reuben's God for the answer he had hoped for. Before leaving, they agreed to resume their running routine.

"Would you like me to drive you back?"

"No thanks, I'd rather walk. It will give me some time to unwind. Hope you understand."

"Of course I do. See you tomorrow morning?"

"Sure, same time, same place. See you then. And Seth, thanks for being willing to get us to talk this out."

He watched her make her way across the square and toward the McQuarry house. Meeting had been the right thing to do. It restored a growing friendship.

Stepping back to let some of the dinner crowd in, he decided he might as well stay and snatch some dinner himself. He walked back to the booth they had shared and pulled a menu from behind the napkin holder. He knew immediately what he would order. Steak. It would be a kind of double celebration for being courageous enough to talk to Claire and for his move this weekend.

Mrs. C appeared out of nowhere to take his order. "What do you want to eat?" she said.

"I'll have a large T-bone, medium rare, with fries and another iced tea please."

"Boy, you can't eat a large," she said, peering down at him through thick glasses. "Fact is, you can't even eat a medium. I'll bring you a small, and you may have trouble with that," she said before tromping back to the kitchen.

Seth watched her go. What was it with some of these people? Or was it just that he brought out the worst in them? He couldn't help but wonder if Mrs. C and Mabel Porter were related.

Trying to pass the time, he grabbed his phone and punched the home button. Maybe he could catch up on some email. He went to his account but no signal. Out of habit he'd done what used to be very normal. But no Wi-Fi. Instead, he stared at his hands, checked out the new arrivals coming in for dinner, and recounted his time earlier with Claire.

Out of the corner of his eye, he saw Mrs. C hobble toward him. How she managed to carry a tray loaded with food amazed him.

"Here you go. I'm takin' bets in the kitchen as to whether you can eat all this," she said before she hobbled away. Seth stared at the piece of meat in front of him. By gosh, she just might be right. The thing hung off the edges of the plate!

His valiant effort to finish the hunk of meat ended in defeat. Mrs. C had been right after all. When he saw her at a nearby table, he motioned he was ready for the bill. She looked at his plate and grinned.

"I know, Mrs. C, you win the bet." Before he could say more, she leaned over and patted his shoulder.

"Yes sir, I sure did, but you ate much better than I expected. Proud of you, boy." She laughed and handed him the check.

~ ~ ~

Seth awoke the next morning still feeling full from the meal the night before. He opted for just coffee at the office, no breakfast. Gathering up a change of clothes for his fishing date with Mac, he showered and shaved. His thoughts turned to tomorrow and his move. He was so ready to have his own space, not to mention the pleasure of being surrounded by his own furniture, especially the antiques he inherited from Gran. Seth found himself whistling as he walked out the door. Even the thought of finishing charts didn't change his feeling of well-being.

~ ~ ~

Sitting at his desk, he reflected on his time with Possum Guthrie, replaying their recent conversation in his mind. It had started when Seth mentioned he was going to be a neighbor to Possum. The old man broke down and wept. Swiping at his tears, then blowing his nose, Possum said, "You'un would do that . . . live in Swamp Town?"

"Well, sure, Possum, I don't see why not. Besides, knowing you're down the street from me is plenty of reason to live there."

"That's mighty kind to say, Mr. Doc. But it's just us plain folks, poor folks livin' there. We got no education, no good jobs. We're just workin' people."

Possum's emotion had set off his hacking cough. Seth had jumped off his exam stool to pat the old man's back a few times. He had stepped to the door and called Justine to bring a glass of water. Once Possum had calmed down, Seth said, "Possum, listen to me. You are a fine man and an honorable man. You are more than a patient to me, you are my friend. I will count it a privilege to live near you and all those in Swamp Town. Education and great jobs don't make a man who he is. That's a lesson my grandmother taught me over and over again, and I believe she was right."

The old man had struggled to his feet, hat in one hand and the other extended to Seth. Seth replayed Possum's words. "Mr. Doc, it pleases me greatly to be yor friend, it surely does. We'll make you'un welcome in Swamp Town. My word on that."

Reflecting on those moments, Seth touched something deep in the core of who he wanted to be. Something was happening to him. He was seeing a side of himself he didn't even know he had. Sure, he was a doctor because he wanted to take care of people, but something else was going on, and he couldn't quite define it. Maybe he would bring it up to Mac while they were fishing. He stacked the charts on his desk for Justine and went to change clothes.

A cooler front had blown in the night before and Seth sucked in the fresh air as he walked from the parking lot to the house. The evening held promise of good things to come. He felt himself relax, free for a time to enjoy the unforced rhythms of life, and he congratulated himself for doing the cleaning at the green house yesterday. His charts were up to date and nothing hung over his head to break the spell of the moment. It felt good.

Helen answered on the second ring of the doorbell. She was her usual smiling self. Seth was struck once again how she seemed to light up from the inside out the same way Reuben did.

"Well, there you are, Seth dear, come in." Helen gave him a warm hug and ushered him to the kitchen. By now, Seth understood it to be the hub of the house. It was a wonderful room filled with rich and tantalizing aromas. Large windows framed the ancient trees that studded the back lawn. And the booth, where meals were eaten or conversation shared over coffee or iced tea, offered experiences of family and life itself. In his mind, it had become a living Norman Rockwell painting capturing the love and generosity of simple pleasures.

Heavy stomping on the back porch announced Mac's entrance into the kitchen. He was a mixture of refined Southern gentleman and rugged outdoorsman. Angus McQuarry's uniqueness continued to amaze Seth, and he wondered what snippets of the man he would discover that evening.

"Hey there, Seth, we're packed and ready to go." The man's anticipation lit up the room. "Come here, woman, and wish me luck." Mac took two long steps, picked up Helen and planted a kiss on her that spoke volumes about his feelings. "Now, I can catch me some fish!" he said, grinning at her.

~ ~ ~

Standing knee deep in the creek, clad in his waders, Seth thought of his initial reaction to the idea of fishing. It had never been something he would've chosen to do. But here, on this evening, he couldn't think of anywhere he would rather be. More and more he could understand why Mac found it so relaxing. But what struck Seth most was the sense of reward, even if he didn't catch a single fish.

Drawing in his line, he pondered the notion, then cast the line to the far side of the creek. Outside of his running, he'd never done much in the way of outdoor recreation. He had no father to teach him those things. And while Gran had done her best, she worked full time, and they lived in a city. As Seth reflected on those years, he realized his personality also gravitated more to books and art. For him, running and helping Gran with her flower beds had seemed enough. That, he admitted to himself, was no longer true.

The surrounding beauty and quiet spoke to a newly discovered place inside him, somewhere he had never allowed himself to go. Out of nowhere a question Reuben had asked him charged through his thoughts. *"Can't you just feel God's presence all around you, Doc?"* Remembering his answer brought a twinge of shame. It had been instant, flat, and with no real thought to it. Is this what Reuben had tried to get him to embrace? As though a light came on in his thinking, Seth grasped meaning behind Reuben's question. It was about stopping long enough to permit the place and the moment to capture the wonder all around him.

Seth wandered along the creek, casting his line in the long, graceful motions Mac had taught him. The man was right. Fly fishing was an art form, and he had grown to enjoy it from that first fishing trip.

Hearing a whistle, he turned to look downstream where he had been. Mac waved, gesturing for Seth to come back.

"Don't know about you," he said, pointing to his stomach, "but this old guy is gettin' hungry."

Seth laughed. "Thought you'd never bring it up. Me too." The two of them laid down their rods, walking awkwardly in the cumbersome waders. Mac had told Seth early on it was too much trouble to climb in and out of them.

The two men rummaged through the ice chest with great enthusiasm. "My gal has outdone herself this time," Mac said. "And I'm telling you, Seth, that's an accomplishment."

Seth often wondered how Helen could stay so slim when she cooked the way she did. He had been the grateful recipient of dinner invitations or a meal prepared for him to take back to the motel many times.

They moved the ice chest in front of a fallen tree trunk and sat down to enjoy the fruit of her labor and love. It was a feast of homemade ham salad, deviled eggs, homemade bread, and her famous fried pies, some chocolate and some peach. There seemed to be no need for conversation; the food and the evening filled the space around them.

After they'd each finished some of the fried pies, Seth decided to bring up the topic he'd wanted to discuss with Mac for some time. "Sir, would you mind if we talk a little business? It seems there's never time at the office, and I've wanted to ask you something for a while now."

Mac poured coffee from a thermos for Seth and himself. "Fire away, son."

"It's about electronic medical records. Why do you not use them?"

"Well," Mac said, "why should I? You tell me." He smiled as he tossed the question back into Seth's court.

"Okay. First is the area of immediate availability of data."

"Let me interrupt you a minute, if I might and ask you a question." Seth nodded to go ahead.

"How does all the data get into the electronic records?"

"The MD enters it," Seth said.

"When does he do that?" Mac asked slowly with his piercing gaze.

"Well, sir, at the time of the patient encounter and then later, after all the patients have been seen."

"Seems rather time consuming to me," Mac said, scratching his chin. "And Seth, something else. I prefer spending time with my patient, not with a machine. I know our training has been quite different in many ways. There's a lot of new technology and many discoveries out there. I'm not opposed to that, but let me say this. From my perspective, we are losing a lot when it comes to patient care.

"I was trained to lay hands on my patients, to evaluate their condition, not just with the use of technology and tests, but through knowing and caring for them as individuals." After a long moment he said, "I just don't think I'll get that same feeling of empathy by laying my hands on a machine."

"I appreciate what you just said, sir, and it's a valid and commendable position. Before I came here, if I had heard you say that, I would have chalked it up to you being the typical local medical doctor. An LMD, you know?" Seth stirred the small rocks in front of him with a twig, considering Mac's words. "But since I've been here, I've learned a lot from you and how you practice. You've helped me become more personally interested in my patients. And I must say it turns the practice of medicine into more than a job."

"You're so right, young doctor; it turns it into a calling!" Mac stretched out his legs and took a long drink of coffee. "Seth, when I decided to bring you on, I knew we were going to have our differences. I've been in practice close to forty years. You've just completed your training. I was even prepared for us to clash, if you know what I mean, but we really haven't." Both men laughed at the truth of the comment.

"I made the decision that besides needing your help, I wanted to pour into you what I had gained in experience. So, the basis of my decision came down to this. I am here to help you in your becoming. What I mean by that is helping you learn the art of medicine. That, my boy, is what keeps your calling alive and vibrant."

Mac hesitated, a faraway look in his gray eyes. "Seth, when you were awarded your MD on graduation from medical school, you became a doctor. As you develop your skills and combine the science of medicine with the art of medicine, you will continue in your becoming. You will become a physician, not just a doctor.

A gentle breeze had kicked up, stirring the water. Seth watched a blue heron in an effortless glide skim the water's surface and come up with a fish. The muffled sound of an owl's whoo whoo drew his eyes to the tree tops. He had yet to see one of the elusive creatures, but the call was perfect music for the moment.

Seth worked his way to a standing position. The waders, now dry, felt like a suit of armor. He caught a glimpse of Mac in a similar act of contortion as he struggled to his feet and extended a hand.

"Thanks for this talk, sir. It's given me a lot to think about."

"You're a good man, Seth Bradley, and I'm proud to have you with me. Let's try and learn from each other, okay?"

Seth nodded in agreement. "And thanks for teaching me to fly fish. I'm getting hooked big time." At that both men broke out laughing.

"That's a good one, Seth," Mac said, slapping him on the back.

~ ~ ~

Mac eased the old Jeep Cherokee into the driveway. Mason looked up from kicking his soccer ball and charged toward them. "Hi ya, Dr. Mac and Dr. Seth. Did you catch any fish?" Both men gave a sad shake of their heads.

"But we had a really good time," Seth said, giving Mason a knuckle punch.

"Aw, fishing's no fun if you don't catch fish," Mason's mouth drooped, and he slammed his foot into the ball sending it clear across the yard.

"Hey, big guy, can you kick the ball that way when we play our game?"

Mason, still pouting, shrugged. "Guess so. But I was wantin' to watch you all clean those fish. I bet if I'd been there, I would've caught me lots of big ol' fish," Mason said, stretching his arms wide.

"I'll bet you would have, buddy," Seth said, looking up to see Claire walking toward them.

"They didn't catch any fish, Mommy, and they said they had a good time. Can you believe that?" Mason said and then ran out to get his ball.

Claire smiled at the two in a knowing way. "Can you imagine

that? A child's thinking is a wonder to behold." Dr. Mac laughed and headed toward the house.

"Tomorrow is moving day," she said, smiling at Seth. "Are you ready?"

"Oh yeah, I can hardly wait. The moving van should get to Mason Falls around eight. Since I don't have that much stuff, they put it in last on the truck so they can unload me easily before they go to their next location."

"I'd like to help, Seth. It's kind of my area of expertise, you know. And I promise, I'm not a pushy decorator."

"Are you sure? I mean it's not much of a place. Pretty shabby actually." Seth stuffed his hands in his pockets.

"Yes, I'm sure, Seth. We'll have it looking great. You said you had some of your grandmother's things. It'll be fun. You'll see."

He looked at her and grinned. "Okay, thanks." *She is so beautiful,* he thought. Her hair glistened in the evening light, and her eyes nearly took his breath away. He tried to convince himself to back off the thoughts. They were just friends. That's what they had agreed to. It was going to take some gut-wrenching determination to keep that agreement.

Before leaving, Seth went to find Helen and give her a hug and big thank you for the wonderful meal.

Driving back to the Sunset Motel, Seth's thoughts ran through his time in Mason Falls. He had to admit it was not what he'd expected in many ways. His goals were still the same, but if he was truthful with himself, he would have to say there were some real changes going on inside him. For one thing he was surprised how well it had gone when he had let Mabel know he'd be moving into a house soon. He surprised himself even more when he told her he still expected to come to the coffee shop often, and he would look forward to seeing her there. She just looked at him and nodded her head before walking back into the kitchen. But she hadn't acted mad at him.

~ 25 ~

MASON, WORN OUT FROM STAYING UP late to catch lightning bugs the night before, snored softly as Claire peeked in at him. Helen had encouraged her to let him sleep in and go on over to help Seth before it got too hot.

She smiled thinking of Helen bustling around downstairs baking cookies and making sandwiches "for any folks who might stop by and help out Seth," she told Claire. "Bachelors don't tend to think of those things, so it's up to us women to help them out."

Not sure if Seth had air conditioning in his small house, Claire had dressed in her most comfortable shorts and a sleeveless tee shirt. She itched with excitement at the prospect of decorating again. A project, large or small, sparked her adrenaline. She loved to take whatever she was given to work with and bring about beauty and harmony. Today might be her biggest test. She had no idea how much, how little, or what she would be working with. She crept down the stairs with a whispered, "Bring it on. I'm ready."

Claire and Helen placed the cooler and a basket filled with goodies in Claire's car. "Thanks, Helen. He's going to be so surprised. You're amazing!" She hugged the older woman, slid into the driver's seat, and waved goodbye.

Helen's directions to Swamp Town were simple, and within minutes Claire turned onto Olive Street. A large moving van sat parked in front of a small green house. She pulled up in front of the house next door, cracked her window, and put her windshield sun shade in place. Carrying the basket and her tool bag, she headed to the house. It was a relief to see the guys with the moving van hadn't started unloading. If she could get a quick look inside the empty house, it would give her a better feel for how to attack the project.

Claire stepped onto the sagging front porch and heard voices inside. She scanned the front entrance for a doorbell but found nothing. "Hello . . . Seth?" she called. "It's Claire." Movement on the other side of the screen door caught her attention. "Come on in." Seth strode toward the door and opened it for her.

"Gosh, I never expected you to get here this early," he said. "Here, let me take your basket."

"No big deal," she said with a wave of her hand, while plowing through her thoughts of how Robyn had described his eyes. Then it hit her. Eyes the color of molasses were Robyn's words. Claire felt the heat rising in her cheeks at Seth's questioning stare before the rush of words poured out of her mouth.

"I wanted a chance to see the place empty. Kind of like an artist with a blank canvas before she starts sketching. I would like to ask a favor, though. Helen sent a cooler full of drinks and sandwiches if you wouldn't mind retrieving it from my car."

Seth set the basket off to one side and stepped aside for her to go ahead of him.

"Helen was determined to feed you and anyone who happened to be here helping you."

"She's some kind of lady, isn't she?" he said as they walked out to her car.

"Yes, she's wonderful. Have you noticed her uncanny ability to sense a void in your life and how she unconsciously pours herself into that empty space?"

Seth leaned against Claire's car. "Hmmm, you're right. She's like . . . a female version of Reuben. Know what I mean?" Claire nodded.

"I've never met anyone like those two," he said, swatting at a gnat. "This may sound strange, but I'm intrigued by their outlook on life and at the same time kind of uneasy, especially with Reuben. He asks some really probing questions."

Claire laughed. "Yeah, like my counselor back in San Francisco, no beating around the bush. But it doesn't offend me. You can tell how much they care about you."

"True. Guess that's why I keep going back for more."

Claire watched him rub his chin and noticed the hint of stubble that accented his chiseled jaw line. This casual, slightly scruffy look was out of character for him, but she found it very appealing.

Seth ran his hand under the bill of his Royals cap. "Hey, it's getting hot out here. Let's get the cooler into the house."

Claire clicked the button on her car key, and Seth hoisted the cooler from the back seat and started up the sidewalk.

"There must be enough in this thing for a small army. I owe Helen a big thank you!" he said with a laugh. "Are you ready to see what you're getting yourself into with the house?"

"I'm always ready for a challenge," she shot back, holding the door open to let him get the bulky cooler inside. They unloaded the drinks and sandwiches, nearly filling the fridge.

The tiny kitchen became an obstacle course where they kept bumping into each other as they tried to get all the food and snacks from Helen unpacked. When they both reached for a fallen pack of paper plates that Helen had tucked in, they knocked heads so sharply they both saw stars. Seth reached out to support Claire, and they both started laughing.

They heard a knock at the door, then Fred Lawson along with the movers and a collection of others peered into the kitchen to see what the laughter was all about. Seth and Claire were rubbing their foreheads where their heads had collided.

"Would you introduce me to your friends, Dr. Bradley?" Claire gave each one her most engaging smile.

Seth proceeded with the introductions of the people he knew, after casting a thank you smile in Claire's direction.

Possum Gutherie's introduction of the others led to lavish praise of his good friend, "Mr. Doc," setting Seth's cheeks aflame. "Mr. Doc, you'un are goin' to be eatin' mighty fine for quite a while. These here ladies are some of the finest cooks there is." Possum's toothless grin spread across his weathered face. One by one, the women approached Seth, presenting him with an assortment of casseroles, salads, and desserts.

"Ladies, I . . . I don't know what to say, except thank you so much. You must know how much a home-cooked meal means to a bachelor."

Each woman responded with a shy smile before wedging herself into the kitchen, forcing Seth and Claire into the eating area.

Claire leaned over and whispered to Seth, "Let them do their thing. This is where they can shine." He nodded with a grateful look.

Claire appreciated Seth remembering she wanted a walk-through of the house before the furniture was brought in. He asked the men to get ready to start unloading but to wait until he gave them the okay before beginning. Seth and Claire went room to room, Claire making mental notes of approximate room size and location of closet doors and windows.

The house was small and plain—nothing unique. She hoped Seth had a few interesting pieces of furniture or even pictures. If not, she would introduce him to the flea markets she'd discovered where untold treasures could be found.

"Do you mind if I organize the troops?" Claire asked as she and Seth went to give the okay to their helpers.

"No, not at all. I'll just play the role of the assistant to the boss," he said with a deep bow.

"Good," Claire said with a little jab to his arm. "That's how I like it."

Standing on the porch, Seth asked the men to listen up. He thanked them for their help and explained that Claire was going to be in charge of placing the furniture and other items, then he motioned for her to take over.

"Guys, thanks from me too. I offered to help Seth arrange things. It's what I do as a decorator. If we use a plan, it makes things easier for all of us." Claire proceeded to give directives for all boxes to be stacked in the carport until the furniture was in the house. Claire would be at the front door to direct them on which piece went to which room. She was surprised by each man's willingness to follow her directions. That didn't always happen.

The initial pieces brought to the porch made her stomach lurch. Flea markets, here we come ran through her brain. Then she spied a piece coming off the truck and let out a squeal of pure joy. Running down the steps, she shouted for Seth to come quickly.

He hurried toward her, alarm written all over his face. "Claire, what's wrong? Are you okay?"

"Yes, I'm more than okay! You didn't tell me you had something this beautiful!" She stopped short. "Please, please tell me this gorgeous chest is yours."

"Hmm, maybe I could try to sneak it into the house before anyone noticed, you think?" he teased.

"Seth Bradley, you stop it!" she said and smacked him on the shoulder.

"It's mine, Claire. My grandmother gave me that chest . . . and that," he said pointing to the beautiful antique table and chairs the men were bringing to the edge of the truck. "And if I'm not mistaken, there's more to come," he called out to Claire who had sprinted toward the truck.

"You're surprised, aren't you?" She nodded, gently running her hand over the table. "It's incredible," she said. "Someone has taken wonderful care of these pieces."

Seth puffed out his chest. "That would be me," he said with obvious satisfaction. "Gran trained me well on 'the loving care of family heirlooms.' She made me polish these pieces every week with lemon oil. They were a priority. Until I had to store them the last few months, it's been a part of my routine for as long as I can remember."

Claire patted his arm. "You've done a great job and it's paid off, because they look to be in great shape."

A large man in a jumpsuit with the moving company logo blazoned across his chest ambled up to Seth. "Excuse me, sir. Are you ready for us to unload these last few pieces?"

"Yeah, sure. Sorry, we kind of got sidetracked."

"I can understand why," the man grinned at Claire then back at Seth.

Flustered, Seth suggested Claire decide which pieces she wanted them to take first.

Claire's excitement continued to grow at the sight of a Lincoln rocker, an exquisite library table, and a beautiful old sleigh bed. This was going to be fun. She could hardly wait to get started. Instructing the movers to start with the bed frame, Claire explained her plan to move items into the back rooms first as that made it easier to maneuver. The men seemed impressed, agreeing it made a lot of sense.

A few hours later, Claire, hands on hips, stood at the front door taking in the transformation of the small, plain house. It wasn't finished, to be sure, but what she saw pleased her.

Rumblings from the front porch turned out to be the neighbor ladies. Each woman was clad in a unique apron and armed with a basket of plates, cups, napkins, or utensils. Claire stared in amazement as each of them entered, giving her a silent nod before marching toward the tiny kitchen, their mission clear—feeding their troops! After the fiasco she and Seth had endured in the small space, she had no idea how five women could work in there. Less than twenty minutes later, the women had worked their magic even down to bringing a quilt to cover Seth's table.

Possum Gutherie had convinced the movers they needed to eat before heading to their next destination. Claire counted a total of fifteen people, and they all managed to work around each other, filling their plates and getting something to drink. The men moved out to the porch to sit on a step or lean against one of the spindly posts supporting the tin roof.

Claire insisted the women make a plate and sit with her at the table. Their hesitancy saddened her. Gentle nudging paid great dividends, though, and by the time Claire helped clear the table, she felt she'd been given a special gift, getting each woman to tell something about herself and her family.

Her effort to help with the dishes wasn't successful. The women put the dishes off limits to Claire. "Miss Claire, you'uns have better things to do than these here dishes. You'uns go on and help that fine, young doctor," instructed Pearl Henry, unquestionably the group's leader.

Claire started for the door but stopped midway, did an about face, and said to Pearl, "Thank you for making Seth and me feel so welcome." Claire's hug clearly startled Pearl, who for the first time that day was at a loss for words. Claire made her way to each woman, thanking them and giving hugs. As she turned to leave, she noticed tears in their eyes.

Outside Claire found Seth rummaging through boxes in the carport. Looking up as she approached, he greeted her with a smile. "How are things inside?"

"Good. I think I just discovered where the old phrase 'the salt of the earth' came from. Those women have such a sense of community. They have so little materially, but they have such big hearts."

Seth stood from where he had been squatting next to an open box. He moved next to her and cautiously put his arm around her shoulder. Claire's first instinct was to withdraw. Her second found her leaning into his embrace. It had been two years since she had felt the strength of a man's comfort. She realized she had forgotten how sweet it could feel.

A moment later Seth eased back and gently wiped a tear from her cheek. "You want to know something?" Seth ran a hand over his face, scratching at the beard stubble. "Sometimes I wish, I mean it would be nice if it didn't seem unmanly to show more emotion."

Claire looked at him. "Seth Bradley, where did you hear that? Showing your emotions isn't unmanly. As a woman, I can tell you I personally think it is one of the most courageous things a man can do."

In an effort to change the focus, Claire asked, "So what's in the boxes? Anything that might aid me in working my magic?"

"Actually, there are several items I think you might find helpful. Want to help me get them out?"

"Treasure hunting is my favorite activity! Let's get to it."

Seth dug deep into the box and drew out a large rectangular object wrapped in heavy brown paper. "See what you think of this."

Like a child at Christmas, Claire ripped off the paper. Her eyes widened followed by an astonished gasp. "Seth, it's beautiful!" She sat cross legged on the driveway drinking in the details of the painting before her. "Where did you get it, and who is the artist?"

He kneeled beside her. "I got it from my grandmother. She was the artist. There are several more in those boxes." He gestured toward the half circle of cardboard containers behind him. "Let's get these boxes inside before unwrapping any more paintings; this heat and humidity can really affect them."

Claire carried the unwrapped painting as Seth manhandled the first box into the house. Minutes later the living area had paintings of various sizes stacked on or against every piece of furniture. Exhilarated by countless discoveries, Claire lost all track of time until Seth took her arm and pointed to the time on her watch. "You have done enough, Claire. It's time for you to go check on that little tiger of yours."

Her hand flew to her mouth. "Oh my goodness, Helen is probably worn out. Mason doesn't know what slow down means."

Seth laughed, "Oh, I wonder where he got that trait."

"Watch it there, Doctor, or you may lose your decorator." Claire nudged his arm while stuffing a wisp of hair behind her ear. "I do need to go, but tell me truthfully, does what we've done make the place feel like home to you?"

"More than I ever imagined. I had no expectations that this house could look so good but you literally have transformed it. Thank you."

"I loved doing it, Seth. You've been truly blessed to have inherited such incredible pieces, not to mention your grandmother's paintings. They will make your rooms look wonderful when they are hung."

"I agree and I'll get on that soon as I can," Seth said.

"This has been so much fun for me. Thank you for letting me help. See you at the soccer game tomorrow. Do you think they're ready?"

"Let's just say we'll find out tomorrow. Go get some rest, and thanks again so much! I can hardly wait to sleep in my own bed tonight."

~ 26 ~

SETH'S EXPECTATIONS OF A GOOD NIGHT'S rest in his own bed vanished as he lay watching the clock move from one minute to the next. At one a.m., he slid out of bed and wandered into the kitchen. He wasn't really hungry, but hey, weren't you supposed to check out the stash in the fridge on a night like this? That's how it was done in the movies or on TV anyway.

Remembering Gran's favorite snack, Seth poured a glass of milk and crumbled a large piece of leftover cornbread into the glass. He picked up a spoon and a napkin and padded over to the table and replayed some of the thoughts that had disturbed his sleep. He fought admitting to himself that today had rocked his carefully laid out plans. But the scent of Claire's shampoo still clung to his senses. Her closeness as he had held her that brief moment turned his heart upside down, and he could do nothing to change it.

"This was not supposed to happen," he cried out, banging his fist on the table. The nearly empty glass fell to the floor before Seth could catch it. "Great, now look what I've done!" He grabbed his napkin to blot up the bit of milk that had spilled.

Staring at the damp spot on the floor, he found himself powerless to move from his knees. Buried emotions arose, bringing back haunting memories of the past. Fear of emotional commitment hovered like a dark shadow over his life. Except for Gran, he had allowed only one other person to capture his heart. He met Angie in the fall of his sophomore year in college. They were chemistry partners. Though they both were gifted scholastically, Angie was full of life and fun while he was reserved and quiet.

Despite their differences, they had become a team of sorts, in

195

class and out of class. Seth ran his hands through his hair, the memories chaining him down.

Convinced he'd found the love of his life, Seth put aside his deep fear of commitment, giving his heart completely into the care of his beautiful chemistry partner. Toward the end of the school year, he had discovered Gran was in far worse condition than she had been telling him. After a trip home to check on her, he returned to campus devastated by her prognosis. In desperate need of comfort, he turned to the one person he thought would understand. She, however, was too enamored with college life, fun, and the idea of love to recognize Seth's pain and need.

Angie brushed away everything that wasn't lighthearted or intellectually challenging. For all her beauty and intelligence, she lacked what Seth had needed most, compassion and empathy. Instead, the love of his life chided him for his unmanly emotions, stressing his need to get a grip on them and keep his mind on school.

His heart still ached at the memories of that time in his life. He wondered if at some point he would be able to share them with Claire, which also raised the question if he could ever fully give his heart away again. The memory of Angie always led him further back in time to his deepest issue of commitment. He had never shared this part of his history with anyone. Only Gran knew the extent of the pain he'd suffered.

As a young boy, he often wondered why other children had a mom and a dad and he only had Gran. He'd lost his grandpa three years earlier. He had asked Gran many times if he too had parents, and she would tell him of course he did. They just lived someplace else. That answer satisfied him for several years, but there came a time when he wanted, actually demanded, the whole story.

It was a cold night in late autumn. The logs in the fireplace gave a warm glow to the living room. He loved this time of year and congratulated himself for having hauled the firewood into the garage. On this particular night, Gran had said he was old enough to build the fire himself. It was a proud moment for him. He sensed maybe he was moving from childhood to manhood, and that was why he brought up the subject of his parents. He was determined to get the whole story out of Gran once and for all.

"Oh, Seth, do we have to go there again?"

"Yes, Gran, we do. I do. There has to be stuff you aren't telling me. Parents don't just 'not live here.' I'm old enough to know why my mom and dad live somewhere else."

"It isn't a pretty story, Seth. Are you certain you're ready to hear it?"

Seth pictured himself sitting cross-legged with his back against the hearth, the heat from the fire comforting him when he said he was ready.

"Your mom, Lila, was our only child. She was the apple of your granddad's eye. He loved making her happy, seeing her light up with delight when he would get home from work. I could tell from the beginning that I would have to be the one to discipline Lila. Your grandad just couldn't do it. She was a joy to be around most of the time as a small child, but when she got her mind set on something, she wouldn't let it go."

Remembering the sadness he'd seen on his grandmother's face and the struggle it was for her to continue, the story never failed to touch him. He could still see her sad face as she clutched her sweater tighter around herself.

"Lila's will and stubborn pride grew stronger the older she got. She broke your granddad's heart, and mine, time and time again. But we were determined not to give up on her. Seth, do you want me to go on?"

"Yes," he replied. "I want you to tell me all of it."

"Lila was very artistic and received an art scholarship to a small but prestigious art school in New York City. She was thrilled. We were frantic with worry. The worry that first crossed my mind was if New York City would be right for Lila. In the beginning she seemed somewhat overwhelmed with her new environment, and we thought that might be a good thing for her not being the one in control. But true to form, by the end of her first semester, she was back to her old ways."

Gran sat for several minutes, Seth remembered, before she

tried to go on. The pain on her face broke his heart. He wanted to spare her from suffering, but he needed to know what happened. The thoughts of his grandmother's valiant attempt to make what she had to say as easy on him as possible still brought tears to his eyes.

"Seth," she said, her voice barely a whisper, "your mother married a much older man who was an artist. When he found out she was pregnant, he ran off, leaving her alone and destitute. Her pride kept her from telling us about any of this. When you were born, to her credit, she tried to take care of you the best she could. In the end, though, her selfishness and stubborn ways won out.

"When you were about eighteen months old, Lila came to see us. You can imagine our shock when she stood at the door holding you, the grandson we didn't know we had. Over the next two days she never once told us anything that had happened, even when your granddad tried to get her to talk to him.

"Finally, on the evening of the second day, she told us the full story. The morning of the third day I went to get the two of you up for breakfast and found a note taped to her door. I remember the words like it was yesterday. It said, *Dad and Mom, I can't do this parent thing. I'm leaving Baby with you. I just can't become who I want to be and take care of the little guy. Hope you understand and can forgive me.*" We never saw her again.

~ ~ ~

Seth again sat cross-legged on the floor, just as he had the night he heard those words. He wondered if there would ever come a time when he could let go of the pain of knowing neither of his parents wanted him or thought he was worth fighting for. He was pretty sure this was the major component in his insecurity about getting into a serious relationship. The other question that nagged him was would he react to having a child in the same way as his parents had? After all, his mother hadn't even given him a name. She had simply referred to him as Baby. Thinking back, this may have been the most devastating part of the sad story he had asked Gran to tell him.

Seth untangled his legs from his sitting position on the floor and stood to stretch his aching muscles. It was the middle of the night, but sleep eluded him. Opening the back door, he walked out on the porch and gazed up into the night sky. The multitude of stars took his breath away.

For so many years his entire focus in life had been work and reaching his goals. He was beginning to realize that he had become addicted to them. And he now knew why. They had acted as pain-killers in his life. They gave his life purpose and meaning, even though it was a very lonely existence.

He couldn't remember when he'd allowed himself time to look up into the night sky and drink in the beauty and grandeur surrounding him. A strange thought came over him. It seemed the lights of heaven were shining down on him. Shining just for him. He wondered where that thought could have come from, but it seemed so real he couldn't shake it. He had a strong sense of being wrapped in a loving embrace. "This is a Reuben moment," he said, giving himself a little shake.

Seth went back into his house. It was now three a.m., and he realized the soccer game would be at ten. He knew he needed to get some rest to be at his best for his team. He turned out the lights and made his way back to bed. Sleep did not come. There was the last piece of the puzzle of his life to be dealt with, like it or not.

The creaking sound of Gran's rocker echoed in his memory, back and forth, over and over again. Seth lay there staring at nothing, knowing he had to give the story its closure.

That night Gran had asked him if he wanted some hot chocolate. He shook his head no, just wanting her to finish the story. She made herself a cup of tea then returned to her chair by the fireplace.

"Gran," Seth remembered asking, "How do you know what happened next if you never saw my mom again?" Seth could still feel the hot tears on his face.

Gran's rocking slowed and her eyes welled with tears. She set her tea cup on the small table beside her rocker and said, "It was a day in early spring. I remember because you and I were digging in the garden, getting the ground ready to plant. It was a day when I thought all was well with the world. I hadn't thought that in a long time. You were six at the time and would start school in the fall. Oh, how full of energy and excitement you were at that age! It was good medicine for me, made me see the world from a better perspective.

"And then I heard the phone ring. Your granddad had gone to run some errands, so I went to take the call. There was a man's voice that I didn't recognize, and I started to hang up. He seemed to sense that and rushed to ask if I was Lila's mother. I stood frozen, unable to move or respond for what seemed a long time but was only a few moments.

"He introduced himself as Harry Meeks, Lila's husband. He went on to tell me he owned a bookstore in New York City, and he and Lila had been married almost two years. I'll never forget his next words.

"'Mrs. Bradley,' he said, 'I have bad news to tell you. Lila passed away two weeks ago. It was only yesterday that I discovered this phone number while going through some of her things. I know you hadn't been in touch for a long time, but it seemed the right thing to do to let you know. I'm so sorry. She was way too young to die that way. The doctors said it was a ruptured brain aneurysm. She never knew it happened. She was fine one minute and gone the next.'

"The man was very kind, Seth, and seemed to truly care for Lila and that gave your granddad and me comfort that she hadn't been alone."

Gran had begun to sob. Something Seth had never seen her do. As a 10-year-old boy, he had struggled with how to respond, but he finally moved to her side and began stroking her hair. He could almost hear his words now. "Don't cry, Gran, I'm here. I'll always be here for you. Please don't cry."

The weight of his memories sucked his spirit dry, and weariness enveloped him like a thick cocoon. He gave way to long awaited sleep.

~ ~ ~

The beep of his alarm woke him with a jolt. Pulling the pillow over his head, he tried to ignore the sound but to no avail. As he reached over to hit the button, he came fully awake. Today was Saturday, and the soccer game would take place in less than two hours.

Seth jumped out of bed but catapulted back into its safety when his bare feet landed on something cold and slimy. He peered down to stare at multiple slimy creatures that looked like short, oversized worms.

Spying one side of the floor free of the ugly things, he carefully put his feet down, tiptoed to where he had left his loafers and checked inside each one before slipping them on. A plan of sorts formed in his mind as he made his way to the kitchen. He'd get a roll of paper towels and a bucket and pick up the things. He'd take them to the furthest part of the backyard and, after the soccer game, look for Possum to find out what these things were and how to get rid of them. He didn't consider himself squeamish, but he was a city boy, and this kind of thing made his skin crawl. Right now he had to get a move on to get ready and have everything set up for the match.

While catching a quick shower to get himself moving, he thought of how hard the kids had worked at practice on Thursday. He felt as proud of them as if they were his own. They had come a long way over the last several weeks, much further than he had imagined in the beginning. Mason and J.J. turned out to be quite the little athletes, very competitive, especially with each other. Seth chuckled thinking of the two boys trying to show off and running head on into each other. Today should prove very interesting.

He dressed in a pair of khaki shorts and the new team tee shirt before going to pop a bagel in the toaster and turn on the coffee pot. The kids would be so excited when they saw the shirts. They had turned out far better than Seth expected.

After taking the box of shirts and soccer balls to the car, he sat down to eat his bagel. Coffee was his greatest need. The long night had taken its toll, but all in all, he felt better than expected. Of course that probably had to do with the adrenalin rush because of the game. It reminded him of those mornings years ago when he prepared to compete in cross country events.

Chugging down the last of his coffee, he made a second cup to go then headed for the car. It had taken the proverbial act of congress to get the coach from the nearby town of Hudson to agree to play the Beavers, and now the day was here.

Seth was under no illusions about the upcoming game. His kids were definitely outmatched. That headed the list of reasons the Hudson coach struggled with agreeing to the game. But Seth won the battle, and he hoped he knew his kids well enough to know they would make an impressive effort. They deserved the chance, after all their hard work, to experience the thrill of actually playing against another team.

Seth sipped his coffee as he drove to the field, his thoughts filled with scenes of that first practice. Most of the kids didn't even know what a soccer ball was, much less how to play the game. The changes in the last several weeks amazed him. He found himself constantly astounded not only by how quickly children can learn new skills, but more than that, they were not intimidated with this adventure.

Finishing off his coffee, he threw the cup in the trash bag. Then for some reason it dawned on him how much he had changed in this whole adventure. The kids were actually teaching him. He felt more relaxed than he had in years. What he was seeing through these little people spoke volumes about living freely, not being afraid to make mistakes but to learn from them. Their sense of wonder, joy, and enthusiasm was contagious. He was their coach, but the Beavers were impacting his life in a way he never would have imagined. He hoped his kids would play well today and have fun.

Seth maneuvered Old Red into a parking space next to Fred's huge truck. Getting out of the Honda, he had to laugh at the sight of the two vehicles sitting side by side. It duplicated how Fred towered over him. His friend waved and shouted a welcome from where he was getting the goals in place. "Big day, Doc!"

"Sure is, Fred," Seth called back, dragging the bag of balls with one hand and balancing the box of shirts with the other. "Have to admit I'm kind of nervous."

"Aw, don't worry, Doc. The kids will have fun no matter the outcome." Fred's generous smile covered his face. "And speaking of the kids, here they come."

Sure enough, kids were piling out of several cars and charging toward them shouting "Beavers, Beavers, here come the Beavers!" He dropped the gear and the box of shirts, ready to be tackled.

Four pairs of hands took his legs out from under him amid howls of victory. "We gotcha, Coach! Do you give up? You gotta say uncle, 'member?" Seth struggled to get out from under his attackers but not hard enough to win. He knew their trophy was one word. With bodies sprawled all over him, he let out a loud holler . . . "Uncle!"

Shouts of glee filled the air as boys pushed and shoved each other off of Seth. Getting to his feet, he knuckle punched each kid with a "You win, you're too much for me. Now let's go get ready for some soccer!"

Once all the team members were accounted for, Seth sat on the ground with his kids. Several were vying for places on his right and on his left. He finally chose one girl and one boy to sit beside him.

"Okay, everybody, listen up." Seth's breathing increased when he saw Claire smiling at him. Trying to regain his focus, he nodded in her direction. "This is our big day. You guys have come a long way, haven't you?"

"Yeah!" resounded the eager reply.

"And what have I told you at every practice that we are going to do?"

In unison all twelve Beavers shouted, "Have fun and learn soccer!"

"And have we had fun?"

"Yeah! Lots of fun!"

"Okay, well, that's what we're going to do today. But guess what? We're going to do it wearing our official Beaver team shirts!"

Happy shouts filled the air. Kids and parents danced around Seth like he had given them a gold medal as he handed each kid a shirt.

"All right, put on your shirt, and let's go have some fun and warm up." Seth threw out several balls, and the Beavers took to the field.

While the Beavers practiced their dribble and ball control exercises, Seth strode over to introduce himself to the coach of the other team. They were known as the Hornets and lived up to their name.

Most of the players were larger than the biggest kid the Beavers had on their team. Not only was their size against Seth's kids, they literally seemed to swarm the entire field.

Making his way to the coach, Seth began to question his decision to play them. It looked like the story he had once heard of a little kid named David going up against a giant. He seemed to remember the story was in the Bible, but he wasn't sure. If he wasn't mistaken, he thought the kid defeated the giant. Maybe there was a measure of hope to take from that.

Seth introduced himself to Coach Hoyt. He was a bulky man who obviously worked out a lot. His handshake nearly brought Seth to his knees, but he fought the pain, determined to stand up for his kids.

"You still sure you and those kids want to take us on, Coach?" The glint in his eyes told Seth this man was not used to losing.

"Yes, Coach Hoyt, we are. My kids may not be as big or as seasoned as the Hornets, but I can tell you they play with all their heart. And, Coach, they have fun. Isn't that what the game is all about at their age?" Seth stretched himself to his full six feet two inches as he thrust out his hand again. "Let's have fun in a great game and keep in mind that is the whole purpose. Nice to meet you." Seth walked away to gather his kids.

Claire met Seth before he got to the kids. "Is everything okay? It looked like you two were in a standoff of some kind."

"Yeah, he is major serious about the game. You would think he has high school kids instead of five and six year olds. I hope this wasn't a mistake, Claire. I sure don't want our kids to get hurt. If Hoyt pushes too hard, and it looks like that could happen, I'll forfeit the game."

Reaching out to take his hand in hers, Claire said, "Seth Bradley, the Beavers are fortunate to have you as their coach. And as a mother of one of those kids, I want you to know just how much your concern means to me."

Seth felt that now familiar blush color his cheeks.

"Why, Dr. Bradley, I believe you are blushing! Come on, let's get those busy Beavers ready to show just who they are." Claire grabbed his hand drawing him back toward their sideline.

Seth noticed the crowd on their side growing with parents, grandparents, people from the clinic, patients, Mac and Helen, Reuben, and so many he didn't even know. One thing for sure, he thought, the Beavers' support team put the Hornets' support to shame.

The Hornets blasted onto the field, pumping their arms and shouting, "We are the Hornets! We are the Hornets!" Seth looked at the faces of his kids, fear written on each one—even J.J.'s and Mason's.

"Now look, kids, I want you to remember this is a game, and it's meant to be fun. You're going to do great. And no matter what happens, I will be proud of you. We don't play to keep score at your age. We play to learn the game and have fun. Now, who are we?"

The silence hung heavy in their air. "Who are we?" Seth asked again. He could see several chins quiver before he heard J.J. shout, "We're the Beavers!" With that, kids, parents, and all the others who had come began clapping and stomping their feet.

"Come on, Beavers, we've got a game to play!" Mason yelled at the top of his lungs. Seth pointed to the first round of kids to play and sent them out.

~ ~ ~

The game was over, and the outcome was clear even though no official score was kept. The Hornets had scored more goals. The teams lined up to shake hands. When Hoyt reached Seth, the man's smirk and muffled "told you so" sent a rush of anger through Seth he hadn't felt in a long time. The man's behavior and arrogance was opposite of everything Seth believed about the purpose of kids playing sports. Hoyt had berated his kids for every error, bringing a few to tears. Seth couldn't believe the parents didn't rise up against him, unless they too wanted to win no matter the cost. Most of all, he felt sorry for those kids.

Everyone had left, and Fred was putting the goals in his truck when Seth heard someone come up behind him. He turned and there was Claire smiling at him.

"Tough loss huh, Coach?"

"It was, but not really because we lost. I thought our kids did great. I was so proud of them. It was really hard to watch the kind of example Hoyt demonstrated to his kids. Win at any cost. It made me so angry to think someone could treat little kids like he did."

"I could tell it was getting to you. And I agree with everything you've said. So, Coach Bradley, would you go have coffee with me? Please say yes. I've never asked a man on a date before. I think I would feel really humiliated if you turned me down."

"I think that coffee with you might be just what the doctor would order, Claire Westfield."

~ 27 ~

When the McQuarrys offered to take Mason home with them and let Claire stay and visit with the other parents, she settled on her plan. Today had been hard on her. Helping out at the kids' practices was fine. There were no dads there. But today was different. She was the only one without a husband.

It brought back memories of San Francisco and how she had found herself adrift from her full and productive life after Randall's death. She had felt out of place without him. She didn't want to do the things she used to do. It had been awkward for her friends. They had not known what to do with her.

She thought she had moved beyond those feelings, but today they all came rushing back. The urgency of wanting to run away, to pretend she wasn't alone, that she wasn't a widow. Reality smacked her in the face reminding her she was the odd one out.

The McQuarrys' offer had seemed perfect timing. Now sitting there with Seth, drinking her latte, guilt sucked the anticipated joy out of her. Was she using him for her own benefit or had she truly wanted to be with him?

"Hey, Claire, where are you? You look like you're miles away." Seth's voice broke the silence, bringing her back to the moment. She tried to smile, but it didn't seem genuine. Should she confess her reason for asking him to come?

"Seth, I want to apologize. When I asked you for coffee, I thought it was because I had some news to share with you, but I was just thinking maybe my asking you to have coffee with me was, in a way, using you. I'm so sorry. I can assure you it wasn't intentional." His confused look unnerved her.

She tried to explain what she had experienced at the game and why she questioned her motive in asking him out. "I feel terrible, Seth. I understand if you want to get up and leave," she said.

"Claire, our growing friendship over these last few weeks means a lot to me, and I hope you feel the same. I can only imagine what you have been through. Please know that I understand why you might question your motive, but I don't. Now, I for one want to enjoy being asked on a date by a beautiful woman who is also a good friend."

"Thanks, Seth," Claire said with a small laugh. "And your friendship is becoming important to me too. Here's the news I wanted to tell you. Mason and I are flying out to San Francisco for a couple of weeks before school starts. I promised him we would go for a visit, and he's really been missing his friend Billy. They grew up together, so it's been quite an adjustment for him."

Comfortable conversation about the trip eased Claire's bruised emotions. The man she first thought reserved, even cold, had revealed a different side of himself over the last few weeks. A side she thought he may have just discovered himself. Their morning runs were the starting point, but working with him at soccer practice had moved them to a new level.

~ ~ ~

Claire found herself comparing Seth to Randall. Seth's chosen profession fit him though he was very different in personality from Randall. Her husband, though kind and often thoughtful, lived for the practice of medicine. She had loved Randall completely and had accepted their way of life and his deep commitment to his work as the norm for a doctor's family. Of late though, a troubling thought caught her off guard at odd moments. Had their way of life really been the norm or might there have been something different? In her time of grief, she had promised herself never again to fall in love with a physician. And that led to the next troubling thought . . . but Seth's low laugh startled her back to reality.

"A penny for your thoughts," he said, his eyes twinkling. "I'm beginning to feel like a dud as a date."

"Oh, Seth, please forgive me again. I promise it's not you. It's me. To be honest, I think the upcoming trip has caused me to become easily distracted. I have so much that needs to be done here on the house, but I made a promise to Mason."

"Well, if you want me to help Reuben while you're gone, I'd be happy to run errands or whatever. These long days of daylight find me looking for something to do when I'm not on call."

"That's really sweet of you, Seth. You're sure you wouldn't mind? I know Reuben would appreciate any help you could give him, although he would never admit he needs it. I have worried about him working in this heat."

"Well, spending time with Reuben has been one of the best things, and one of the most challenging things, about being in Mason Falls. You know, every time I'm with him I feel I come away a better person. I can't quite put my finger on what it is, but I think it has to do with who he is on the inside." Seth scrunched his face in a funny grimace.

Claire covered her mouth to hide her laugh. "That's the first time I've seen you do anything that qualified as silly. You really do have a fun side to you, Seth. And I like it. Thanks for helping me get out of my 'woe is me' mood. Will you have coffee with me again sometime when I'm not so rattled?" Claire felt herself flush as she studied the man smiling back at her.

"I will look forward to it. How about soon after you get back from your trip?" he asked.

~ ~ ~

Mixed feelings about the trip to San Francisco weighed on Claire over the next week. She relished the idea of time with Robyn. She couldn't remember when they had been apart this long. Their friendship had been a stabilizing factor in both their lives for almost as long as either could remember.

Claire's struggle surfaced from several nagging questions she couldn't resolve. The one tugging at her the most was how this trip would affect Mason. She also wondered if being back in what had been her comfort zone for so many years would remind her of all the pain and uncertainties when her life changed. And, trying to be honest with herself, she had to question what effect it would have on this delicate new life she was building in Mason Falls.

If those weren't sufficient worries, one more question loomed with growing intensity in the deepest recesses of her heart. She had not allowed herself to even consider opening the door to that solitary place. Until now. But could she even find the key if she wanted to?

~ ~ ~

The day had arrived. Excitement charged through the house in the form of one five-year-old boy. "Mommy, come on, it's time to go. Mrs. Mac said so. B'sides I've already packed my suitcase three times, and you're still on just one. And, Mommy, Billy is wait'n for me."

Claire giggled at the accent her once very cosmopolitan little guy had developed over the last few months. His friends, and hers, in San Francisco would be shocked. He definitely had the beginnings of a Southern drawl.

"I'm on my way downstairs now, sweetie."

"Mommy, come on." The door bell sounded over Mason's shouting. "I'll get it, Mrs. Mac," he said, running to open the door. "Hi ya, Dr. Seth. We're going to San Francisco to see Billy and Aunt Robbie. If my Mom will ever get down here."

Claire was dragging a suitcase and a carry-on bag. "Seth, hi, what's up?"

Seth handed her one red rose and grabbed both bags. "I know they may not let you get on the plane with this but I, uh, just wanted you to know I'll miss you."

"Me too, Dr. Seth? You will miss me, won't you? But don't worry, me and Mommy will be back soon." Mason's missing tooth accentuated his disarming grin.

Seth picked him up and heaved him into the air. "Of course, I'll miss you too, buddy. But you have a great time with Billy and tell me all about it when you get back." Seth set Mason down, and Helen headed the child toward the car.

"I do hope you both have a wonderful visit, Claire. I just wanted to run over and say bye and, well, let you know it won't be the same around here with you gone."

Claire's hand trembled as she laid it on Seth's arm. "Thank you, it was very thoughtful of you to drop everything and come by. And for the rose. It's just beautiful."

"Claire," he said, then hesitated, "I really will miss you."

"Mom!" Mason shouted. "We need to go!"

"I'm coming, Mason! Goodbye, Seth, see you in two weeks."

"Right, two weeks. Reuben and I will make you proud, so don't worry about the house." Seth followed Claire out the door, bags in hand. He stowed them in the trunk and said, "Patients waiting, better get back to work."

~ ~ ~

The hour and a half drive to the Branson airport seemed to take no time at all. Claire hadn't realized how close this part of Arkansas and Missouri were to each other. She and her dad had always driven to Mason Falls when she was a child, but they had never come this way. Her grandparents had both died before the airport was opened. Claire and Helen caught up on some of the local happenings while Mason counted hawks in the passing trees.

His excitement about starting school grew each day. He had come up with the hawk idea on his own, explaining to Claire that "I sure do want to count real good before going to school."

~ ~ ~

Mason and Claire both gave Helen a big hug before getting caught up in the security line. Mason turned to give Helen a final wave and big smile.

"I sure do love Dr. and Mrs. Mac. Don't you, Mommy?"

"Yes, Mason, I do. They are very special people and have made us part of their family. We are very fortunate."

"And, Mommy, don't forget Dr. Seth. We love him too, don't we?" Mason's eyes shone with childish innocence.

A huge lump formed in Claire's throat as she searched for a reply, but the gate call spared her for the moment. "That's us, Tiger, we need to go."

As the line moved, Claire said a silent thank you to God. That was the second time she had thought God may have actually been there for her. She wondered if He really cared about something as small as an answer to a little boy's heartfelt question. When they got back from the trip, Claire thought she might ask Reuben about it. She was sure he would know. Reuben seemed to be in close communication with God.

Claire hadn't been sure how Mason would do on the long flight, but to her pleasant surprise, he handled it like a pro. She had brought along an assortment of snacks, a couple of activity books, his three favorite Rescue Heroes, and a DS game she only let him use at times like this. Fortunately, their connections were all on time and before they knew it, they had landed at the San Francisco Airport. By the time they made it to baggage claim, a beaming Robyn was searching the crowd for them. Mason spotted her first and broke into a run to get to her.

"Aunt Robbie!" Mason yelled, dropping his backpack and hurling himself into her outstretched arms. Tears flowing, Robyn, dressed in a sophisticated designer suit, sat on the floor cradling Mason in her lap.

Claire stood silently soaking in the tenderness of the moment, her own tears slipping down her cheeks.

"Aunt Robbie," Mason whispered, "I think maybe Mommy would like a hug too." Mason crawled out of Robyn's lap while giving her his hand to help her up. He took her hand and led her to Claire. Now one small boy became the bystander to a long-awaited reunion between two people he loved with all his heart.

Mason entertained Claire and Robyn with one story after another on the ride to Robyn's condo. Robyn, on the other hand, teased Mason about his Southern accent.

"I can't believe how much you've grown, Tiger. What are they feeding you down there? Turnip greens?" she asked, glancing in the rear view mirror and grinning at him.

"Oh, Aunt Robbie, we don't eat those things. Mrs. Mac is a great cook, and Mommy helps her a lot. We eat lots of stuff out of our garden. And you know what? I help Mrs. Mac work in that garden and bring in all kinds of stuff when it's ready to pick."

"He really has been a great help to Helen, and she loves every minute of it," Claire said, reaching back to give Mason's knee a pat.

"So what else have you been doing, Tiger? Having any fun or just working?"

"I've been really busy, Aunt Robbie. There's lots to do there. Dr. Seth is my soccer coach, and we practice two times each week. I've made a new friend. His name is J.J., and he's really cool. And I have another new friend too."

What's his name, Tiger?"

"Jesus. Do you know him, Aunt Robbie?"

Claire felt as shocked as Robyn looked. "Uh, when did you meet him, Mason?" Robyn asked.

"Oh, when I went to that school at Mrs. Mac's church. He's really special and you know what?" Mason's eyes sparkled as he looked at Claire then at Robyn.

"No, what, sweetheart?" Claire asked, glancing at Robyn who stared straight ahead.

"He wants to be your best friend too. Isn't that great?"

Robyn stole a quick look at Claire that begged for an answer to her silent *what do I say?* Claire could only mouth, "I don't know."

"Mom, I bet Billy would like to know Jesus too. Then we can all be best friends! Wouldn't that be so cool?"

"Well, let's talk about it a little more before you tell Billy about Jesus, okay?"

Mason's confused look tugged at Claire's heart, but she needed to find out just what her son had been hearing before he became the next Billy Graham. They were coming into familiar territory, and Mason's excitement of seeing places he recognized distracted him for the time being.

"Can we go swimmin' in your pool, Aunt Robbie? I'm gettin' pretty good at swimmin'," he said proudly. "You'll be real surprised."

"I'm sure I will, Tiger. Will you race me?"

"You better watch out, Aunt Robbie. I can almost beat Mommy sometimes."

Robyn turned left onto Jarrod Avenue with Mason's squeal of delight filling the car.

"We're here, Mommy. Look! It's over there. I sure am glad we came to see you, Aunt Robbie. Mommy and me have missed you a whole lot. Haven't we, Mommy?"

"Yes, little man, we have, a whole lot for sure."

Robyn had orchestrated their first afternoon perfectly. She left directions for her housekeeper to prepare something for dinner that could easily be heated up when they decided to eat. Claire breathed a sigh of relief when Robyn told them they would eat in tonight. It would have been a disaster to take Mason out to eat after the long plane ride. This way they could all unwind at the pool, especially one very energetic little boy.

The pool, as Claire had expected, proved the right choice for Mason. He and Robyn raced back and forth until neither of them could do one more lap. After a few laps of her own, Claire was content to watch the two of them.

Robyn sat in a lounge chair next to Claire while Mason sprawled out on a fluffy beach towel. Catching up on the news of one another's lives soon became boring for Mason, who finally got up and began searching the bushes to see how many different kinds of insects he could find.

By seven o'clock San Francisco time, a very tired little boy asked if he could go to bed. Claire and Robyn tried to smother their chuckles, but a bleary-eyed Mason caught them. "What's so funny?" he yawned.

"Oh just that Aunt Robbie and I have never heard you ask to go to bed!" Claire leaned over and kissed him soundly on the cheek. "Come on, Tiger, let's get you tucked in. It's been a very long day."

"It has been a long day," he said, yawning again and reaching up to give Robyn a hug. "I'm sure glad we're here, Aunt Robbie. See you in the morning." Robyn hugged him close, kissing the top of his head. "Night, sweetheart, I sure have missed you. Go get some rest."

Claire and Robyn talked almost nonstop until Robyn noticed Claire's dazed look. "Hey, girl, you need to get to bed, you're worn out. We have two glorious weeks to catch up on everything." Claire nodded in agreement.

"Do you realize," Robyn asked in a stunned whisper, "I've never taken a two-week vacation? See how important you are to me? Of course, I may get a little edgy, so just tell me if I get into my lawyer mode."

"It's a deal. And, Robyn, thank you for taking time off. I know you're busy, and it's hard for you not to be working."

"You know me too well, girlfriend! But believe me when I say I'm really looking forward to this. Get some sleep, you," she said, giving Claire a hug.

~ ~ ~

Claire woke up at eight-thirty central time the next morning amazed that her son was still curled in a ball next to her. The trip had taken more out of him than she expected. Quietly slipping out of bed, she grabbed the robe Robyn had put out for her and tiptoed out of the room. Making her way to the kitchen, she filled the tea kettle half full of water and turned on the burner. She stood nearby waiting for the water to boil. True to form, Robyn had placed a small jar of peppermint tea leaves, a diffuser, and a delicate china cup on the counter next to the cooktop.

When the water began to boil, she grabbed it before it began to whistle, retaining the quietness of the moment. She cherished moments like this. Wrapped in Robyn's soft robe, she padded over to a chair by the window.

It felt strange to be back here in the city she had called home for so many years. She had to admit it unnerved her a little. How would she respond to seeing the old familiar places—and people? And more importantly, how would Mason react?

Claire drank her tea, her thoughts drifting to memories of the past; memories of Randall and their life together, their home, and their friends. She had been happy then . . . hadn't she?

Draining her cup, she walked to the window, staring out at the cluster of condos. It was so different, so very different, from what she would see back in Mason Falls. She couldn't help but wonder if this trip would change her decision about living in a small town in Arkansas. Would the past have the power to crush the fragile hope of the present?

~ 28 ~

THE ACHE SETH FELT FROM CLAIRE's absence hung over him like a dark cloud. He stared into his cup of coffee, now cold, the chatter of Mabel's early morning crowd only a dull throb around him. He was grateful for a busy schedule. His patient load had been unusually heavy these past few days, days with no word from Claire. As long as he stayed busy, thoughts of her smile, her touch, her scent didn't attack him. But the other moments played havoc with his heart.

A couple of days ago he'd come close to talking to Mac or Reuben about his feelings, but in the end, he had pushed those thoughts aside. He told himself it was no big deal, she was only going to be gone two weeks. But what if she decided to stay?

A familiar 'humph' broke his thoughts. Mabel Porter was looking down at him, his plate of eggs and bacon in her hand.

"You look like some sick old coon hound, boy. What's got you down? Missin' your lady friend?"

Shocked to think it might be that obvious, Seth hurled a vehement "No!" back at her, his tone sharper than he meant it to be. Guilt flooded him immediately. He had been rude and just outright lied, and he knew it.

Mabel set his plate down in front of him. "Not what folks in town are sayin'. You're in a small town now, boy, and folks here see things real clear. But if you want to go on lying to yourself and others that's your business." Mabel stomped back to the kitchen.

There had actually been a truce of sorts between them since her conversation with Mac and undergoing the surgery on her arm. Seth hoped he had not messed it up just because he was out of sorts with Claire away and didn't want to admit it.

After he wolfed down his breakfast and his now cold coffee, he

216

grabbed his ticket, laid a tip on the table, and headed toward the register. Mabel was running the thing. At that point, all he wanted was to get out of there.

To his surprise, she told him there was no charge. When he asked who paid for it, she just said, "Don't worry about it. I said it's taken care of." All Seth could think to do was tell her to thank the person for him. As he was leaving, a sudden thought came to him. Maybe Mabel herself paid the tab as a peace offering. He hadn't noticed anyone in the café who might have wanted to do him a favor. *Now that would be a true turn of events*, he mused and walked into a day filled with sunshine.

~ ~ ~

Seth had just slipped on his white coat when Justine appeared at his open office door. "Good morning, Doctor. Are you ready for a full day? Our schedule is back to back appointments."

"Just what I like. Justine, I'd like to ask you a quick question first."

"What can I help you with?" she replied.

"You've been here most of your life, so I assume you know Mabel Porter pretty well." Justine nodded. "Have you ever seen or heard of the woman having a chink in that armor she shields herself in?"

"No sir, I haven't, and you know how small towns are about gossip." She gave Seth a calculating look. "Do you know of any?"

"First of all, I am definitely learning all about small town gossip. I just got a big dose of it for breakfast! Second, I may have just experienced a small chink in Ms. Porter's armor. Not for sure but the more I think about it, I may have seen a small miracle. But that's all I can say right now. Let's get to work."

~ ~ ~

By lunch, Seth and Justine had seen eighteen patients. He never ceased to be amazed by some of the people he met or the conditions he took care of. This morning proved no different.

He smiled as he thought about the lady with a very unusual name. She introduced herself as Freelove Benson. He had almost choked, but she rescued him just in time.

"It's okay, Doc. I know my name does things to people the first time they hear it. I can thank my parents for that. They were really big in the hippie movement, and you can figure out the rest, can't you?" she said, a knowing smile curling the corners of her mouth.

Then there was the old man from Swamp Town. He said, "My wife was one a them women who brung you'uns food when you'uns moved in. She done told me then and there if that there man can come live on our street, ya sure can get over yor fear of goin' ta see him as a doc. Well, sir, I guess she was pretty much right. So here I am. Name's Willie Tuckett. Pleased to meet you'uns."

"And I'm pleased to meet you as well, Mr. Tuckett."

"Aw, Doc, I don't stand on that formal talk. I'm just Willie."

"Okay, Willie, what brought you in, other than Mrs. Tuckett?"

"That's a good one, Doc, and that's the only reason I come ta see you'uns. Hopin' ta get her off my case." Willie's raspy cough shook his entire body. "She keeps worrin' about this cough I've been havin' for quite some time. She also keeps tellin' me I'm not eatin' right, and I'm more tired than usual. Guess that's about it."

"Well, how about I check you out and see what we come up with, okay?"

"Sure, Doc. Then maybe she'll leave me alone."

Seth wasn't surprised by the results of his thorough exam. They only confirmed his initial suspicions based on the man's gaunt look, shortness of breath, and other symptoms he had described.

"Willie, I want to do some tests and get to the bottom of what's going on. Are you okay with that?" The old man tried taking a deep breath before answering but suffered from a wheezing episode. Once he caught his breath, he mumbled a barely audible yes.

Justine took a shaken Mr. Tuckett down the hall for lab work and a chest X-ray. If the results came back abnormal, which Seth was convinced would be the case, he would call the hospital in Granville to order a pulmonary function study and a CT scan of the man's chest.

Willie's crusty nature made Seth chuckle even now. He remembered some of his older professors in med school describe men like Willie as an "old salt." And it fit Willie Tuckett to perfection. It was obvious from the beginning while taking Willie's history and especially after listening to his chest that he would have to talk to him about smoking.

Seth had just come out of another patient's exam room when he heard Willie's wheezy approach. The exertion of walking back from the lab proved to Seth the need to call the hospital and order the pulmonary function study and CT scan.

Justine gently helped the exhausted man into the chair in the exam room and went to get him a glass of water.

"Now, Willie, how much do you smoke a day?"

"I feared you'uns was goin' ta bring that up. I smoke more'n I should and I know that, but, Doc, I'm gettin' on up there in age, and I like ta smoke," he said in quick raspy gulps, gripping the chair arms with what strength he had left. "Smokin's one of the few pleasures I have."

"I can understand that, Willie, but you're in real trouble physically. There are some things we can try to help you quit."

"Are you'uns talkin' about medicine? No sir, I ain't takin' that stuff!" He began coughing and wheezing again.

"Hold on there, Willie," Seth said and rolled his stool over to the old man. "It's okay, take a deep breath now and try to relax."

Willie sucked in air, but the color drained from his face. Justine rushed from the room and returned with a cold compress.

Seth continued to sit close by until the attack ended. Willie's face showed his exhaustion. "Are you afraid of medication, Willie?" Seth asked gently.

There was no response for a moment, then the old man, shoulders slumped, raised watery eyes filled with defeat and said, "Doc, in answer to yor question, yes, I am afeard of gettin' hooked on them drugs. See, a long time ago, I had a purty bad drinkin' problem. When I come ta see that I had to quit or I weren't goin' to make it, I just up and done it cold turkey.

"I'm no educated man like you'uns but I've been with this ol' body for goin' on eighty-five years, and I figure I've learned a thing or two 'bout its workin's. If I got hooked on alcohol makes sense ta me I could just as easy get hooked on drugs. So, bottom line is

Willie Tuckett ain't takin' none of that stuff. Hope you'uns can see where I'm a comin' from."

The old man's strength of character broke through the walls of exhaustion and fear that only moments before had crippled his body and spirit. Seth vowed never to forget the gift Willie Tuckett of Swamp Town had given him that day—a look at the inner man.

Willie went on to tell Seth that if it came to quitting smoking, he would do it cold turkey. After finally agreeing to have the tests done, Seth asked Justine to do a pulse oximetry test using Willie's index finger. As suspected, it confirmed him being low on oxygen. Seth explained to Willie how that was contributing not only to his shortness of breath but also to his tiredness, especially with any exertion. He then took some extra time to explain the use and benefits of using oxygen, and Willie agreed to try it. Seth emphasized to him the danger of smoking and using oxygen at the same time and was pleased when Willie assured him he understood.

When Willie left, Seth told Justine to cover for him. He couldn't get to his office fast enough, nearly breaking into a sprint. Shutting the door behind him, he took refuge in his desk chair and sat cradling his head in his hands. He had never been the emotional type and almost prided himself in his aloofness. In his mind, it made a lot of sense, protecting him from getting too involved in the lives of others. He had always rationalized that made him a better physician, because he could keep an open mind.

But right now, at this moment, everything he'd believed was crumbling. His heart seemed to have awakened to the lie he had lived, crying out for him to look for truth. What was the truth he needed to come to grips with? Folding his arms on the desk, he laid his head down, letting the quiet wrap itself around him.

One truth he needed to accept swept over him immediately and that was how much he was beginning to care for the people of Mason Falls. People like Reuben and the McQuarrys and Fred Lawson had touched his life and offered unconditional friendship. Patients like Willie, Possum, Jasper and Opal Mae had put their trust in him.

And then there were Claire and Mason. The truth was now

clear, both in his mind and in his heart. They had breathed life and joy into him. Because of them he had begun to understand another truth about himself. He was lonely, and he needed something, someone, more than he needed prestige and money. As he raised his head, a final truth struck him like the blow of a hammer. In the deepest parts of him, he was empty.

Seth had to reach down for the energy and will to finish seeing patients while his heart longed to get to a quiet place and process this new realization. He called on the willpower of all his long years of training and putting the needs of his patients ahead of his own. Thankfully the afternoon schedule was even busier than that morning, giving him little time to think about what had transpired earlier.

But in a fleeting moment of mid-afternoon calm, a plan had come out of nowhere. After work he would run by The Singing Dog, grab a couple of sandwiches and a drink, and head for the waterfall. What better place to contemplate the events of the morning than where Mason Falls began.

～ 29 ～

BEFORE HE REALIZED IT, THE DAY was over and freedom beckoned, but conflicting emotions crept into his mind as he walked to The Singing Dog. On one hand, he felt anticipation for some solitude. Then just as quickly it turned to apprehension. Being totally honest with himself would challenge him in ways he wasn't sure he was ready for.

Things were slow at the café, and Seth was in and out in minutes. Next on his agenda, a quick dash by his house to change into shorts and a tee shirt before heading to the Falls. Punching the radio dial, Seth hoped to distract himself from his nagging thoughts. He couldn't help but grin when the country channel popped up. It continued to surprise him how much he gravitated to this kind of music. The soulful sounds of the singer searching for some heartfelt need made for the perfect fit with his own melancholy.

One of his favorite songs pounded out the last chorus as he turned into the deserted parking area for the Falls. Tapping to the beat on his steering wheel, the music cushioned the ragged edge of his emotions. Seth grabbed his food and pulled on his Royals cap.

In town it was hot and muggy, but here under the canopy of trees lining the path, the air was cool and smelled of honeysuckle and wild roses. His shoulders relaxed as he breathed in the sweet aroma. This had been the best plan he'd had in days.

A bluebird fluttered by him, looking to be on a mission of its own. *How simple the bird's life*, he thought. *No longings or fears, no questions about life or tough decisions to make, just looking for the next worm or bug. Is that what I'm looking for? A life free of responsibility?*

Seth puzzled over these thoughts as he walked through the

beauty of the forest. Had he been living but not conscious of what was around him? Living life under anesthesia? Maybe that's why he felt empty.

The thunderous roar of the falls stopped him mid-stride. The majesty of the sound overpowered everything around it. Seth suddenly realized, even before seeing the water cascading over the bluff, how small it made him feel. The emptiness inside him grew. He wanted to go back the way he came, but some force pushed him forward. Chills ran down the back of his neck, and his breathing came in short spurts. What was going on? His heart beat faster, and try as he might to run toward his car, he kept moving closer and closer to the falls.

Seth's medical opinion of his condition was crystal clear. He was having a panic attack. But why? He'd never had one before, so why now? Still, he was compelled to put one foot in front of the other, moving forward, not turning back.

Then he saw it. Mason Falls. The overwhelming beauty and power of it struck him to his core. What was different today? He'd been here several times over the last few months, and nothing like this had happened. Without knowing how or why, Seth suddenly found himself on his knees in the dirt, tears streaming down his face, sobs shaking his body. Was he going crazy? What was happening to him?

At the gentle touch of a hand on his shoulder, Seth squeezed his eyes shut, fearing what he might see if he opened them.

"Seth," came a soft familiar voice. "Open your eyes, son, it's okay."

When he could open his eyes, there was Reuben standing beside him. Before Seth knew what happened, Reuben kneeled down, wrapping an arm around him. The two of them remained that way for what seemed forever to Seth.

"How about we go to our log over there? These old knees are about to give out. Then, when you're ready, you and I can have a long-awaited talk." Reuben's hand felt heavy on Seth's shoulder as the older man braced himself to stand up.

Reuben seemed in no hurry to get Seth to talk, and Seth

appreciated his thoughtfulness. It would be hard trying to put into words what had happened much less what he was feeling.

While trying to find a way to ease into the conversation, Seth noticed his sack of food lying on the ground. "I'm hungry, how about you? A little food helps a person open up and talk, don't you think?" He tried to laugh, but the hollow sound fell short.

Seth and Reuben sat side by side on the log. He thought of the first time he met Reuben here. Miss Lilly had loaded Reuben down with a cooler full of food, and Reuben had wanted to share it with him. He thought too of the old song Reuben had been singing when he arrived. Seth had asked him about it, and he'd told Seth it was an old hymn about God's greatness and majesty in the creation around them.

Seth stared at the waterfall and thought of the few words he remembered of the song. *This is my Father world . . . in the rustling grass I hear Him pass, He speaks to me everywhere.* So was that song saying something about God speaking to a person through the things of nature?

Seth picked up a pebble and threw it in the creek, giving himself a moment to get up the nerve to ask the man beside him some perplexing questions.

"Reuben, I'm ready to talk, and I have some questions. First, why are you here right now? Sometimes it's like you appear out of nowhere."

"Whoa there, Seth! You're making it seem kind of spooky, don't you think?" Reuben's throaty chuckle helped Seth relax.

"Well, sometimes that's exactly how I would describe it to tell you the truth. And Claire thinks so too."

"Rest assured, my young friend, there is nothing out of the ordinary about me. But I will tell you that there are times when I do sense God leading me to a certain place at a certain time. You see, I've been walking with Him a lot of years. And I try to live my life listening to Him. Now I'm not saying He speaks out loud to me, but it's kind of like a great marriage. People who love each other deeply and want to know and please each other begin to know in their spirits what the other person is thinking or wants from them. Does that make sense?

"I guess I understand what you're saying, but I've sure never experienced it. You're saying God can guide someone to a certain place at a certain time if that's where He wants them to be?"

"Yes, if that person has a relationship with Him and is sensitive to His guidance." Reuben stroked his beard, then said, "Or if it's part of His plan in drawing someone to Himself."

Seth raised his eyes from where he'd been scratching at some rocks with a stick, and his gaze returned to the waterfall.

"Remember that song you were singing the first time we met out here? The one about your father's world. I was thinking earlier about it when we came to sit on this log. It said something about hearing God in the 'rustling grass, and He speaks to me everywhere.' Do you think," Seth hesitated, "I may have been hearing Him speaking to me from the Falls?"

The silence wrapped itself around them like an embrace. There seemed no need for a hurried response.

"God's ways are far beyond my understanding, Seth, but I can tell you this. The purpose of His creation is to show His glory. And if we stop long enough to recognize His creation for the glory it is and for who He is, then we may very well find ourselves on our knees in the dirt . . . just like I found you."

Reuben's tone became hushed as he stared at the rushing water. "Could He or did He use the power and majesty of the falls to speak to you? I can't say for certain, but did He make you aware of His presence? I would say yes. God's presence surrounds us everywhere. The question is are we willing to acknowledge that He's there?"

The pounding in Seth's heart shook him to his core. If he had listened through a stethoscope to that thudding in one of his patients, he would have immediately called an ambulance. But one thing was very clear to him; this pounding was no physical problem.

Dropping the stick he'd been toying with, Seth held his hands between his knees. His pounding heart smothered the sound of the waterfall. Hot tears streamed down his face, tears that had been shut up in his heart his entire life. Reuben's hand lay once again on his shoulder, bringing a measure of comfort.

Seth heard the cries of his heart, but it was as though he heard them from far away. In his mind, he was walking down a path much like the one he had walked to get here. But this one was different, more beautiful than anything he had ever seen, and he was a child again.

He pictured someone in the distance who seemed to beckon him. Was it his father, the man he'd never known? Would he recognize his father? Would his father recognize him? He felt afraid and hesitant, but a moment later he knew there was nothing to be afraid of. The one who called to him loved him. How could he not respond to the love that poured over him? But he didn't know how.

Slowly opening his eyes, Seth said, "I've been all alone for a long time, and today, earlier, I saw how empty my life is, how lonely I am. Reuben, how do I find the peace and joy you have?" He brushed a hand across his face to wipe away his tears.

"Is it okay with you if I read something out of the Bible?" Reuben asked quietly. Seth nodded, and the older man took a worn book out of his backpack that lay at his feet.

"This comes from the book of Isaiah, and I think it fits with what we talked about earlier. 'Look up into the heavens. Who created all the stars? He brings them out one after another, calling each by name. And He counts them to see that none are lost or have strayed away.'

"A verse in the book of Romans puts it this way, 'From the time the world was created, people have seen the earth and sky and all God made. They can clearly see His invisible qualities—His eternal power and divine nature. So, they have no excuse whatsoever for not knowing God.'

"My dear young friend, I read these verses to you as a way to introduce you to my best friend. His name is Jesus, and He created this world. He not only created every star and gave it a name, He created you! If He cares about where each star is and doesn't want them to be lost or stray away, can you imagine how precious you are to Him?"

Reuben looked up into the sky, a smile lighting up his face. Turning back to Seth he reached out and patted his arm. "There is no question in my mind, Seth Bradley, that God has been working on your heart today. In your own way you acknowledged His presence and your need, and He reached out to you.

"When we come to the end of ourselves and admit, like you did, that we are empty and we need Him, we will always find Him faithful. Jesus Himself put it this way, 'For God so loved the world that He gave His one and only Son, that whoever believes in Him shall not perish but have eternal life.'

"You said you wanted the peace and joy I have. Well, son, it all comes from Him. All you have to do is to thank Him for forgiving your sins, all those things that in the depth of your heart you know were wrong. And to accept the truth that Jesus is the Son of God and came here to die for you and for your sins. It's a free gift, Seth, but you have to reach out and accept it. If that's what you want to do, just tell God in your own words. And remember, He is your Heavenly Father, and He loved you enough to let His son die for you."

Seth sat for several minutes, heart pounding, hands sweating, and more tears trickling down his face. Sliding off the log, he once again found himself on his knees. His voice shaking, the words tumbled from his heart, all the hurt, the anger, the bitterness, the loneliness, and finally his rejection of Jesus for not sparing Gran's life.

"*God, I've kept You at a distance my entire life. I thought You didn't care, and that I didn't need You. But today You showed me how wrong I have been and how much I do need You. Please forgive me for all the times I turned my back on You. I'm so sorry. Thank You for sending Jesus to save me. And God, thank You for showing me You have always been the father I've needed and longed for. I want to accept the gift You have offered, Jesus dying for me so I could know You.*"

Seth's heart continued to pound, but there was something different now. Instead of fear and anxiety, the pounding was more like huge waves of joy and peace flooding his soul. And each wave carried away part of the burdens he'd lugged around in his heart for so many years. He knew, as sure as anything he had ever experienced in his life, the truth of what had just taken place. He was free! He felt clean and new, as though he'd just been born, born to a whole new life!

~ 30 ~

Days evaporated like the early morning fog. Claire couldn't believe the first week of their time in San Francisco was half over. The weather had been unusually glorious with mild temperatures and only an occasional shower.

Mason and Billy hadn't skipped a beat in their friendship. Both boys picked up where they left off, digging holes in Billy's backyard to reach China and the buried treasure they were convinced they would find. Sammy, the gerbil Mason had given Billy before leaving, was fat and happy, making for a second positive reunion.

Claire and Robyn were enjoying relaxing by the pool or lazing on Robyn's deck, but Mason was begging to spend time at Billy's again this morning. Claire called Maureen, who assured her she'd love to have Mason come over and to bring him right away.

Robyn pitched Claire her car keys and said she would check up on some emails while Claire ran Mason over to Billy's house. "But be sure and pick up a couple of iced mochas on your way back," she shouted as Claire and Mason headed out the door.

~ ~ ~

Returning to the townhouse, Claire elbowed the doorbell while balancing the mochas to keep from spilling them and tried to keep her purse from sliding down her arm at the same time. Only moments before certain disaster struck, Robyn opened the door.

"Whew! I thought you'd never get here. My hands feel frozen," Claire gasped, "and I couldn't get the key."

Robyn cackled at the sight meeting her at the door.

"Just take your drink, okay?" Claire half snarled.

"Sorry, but if you could see yourself, you would laugh too. Come

229

on out to the deck. I was reading the paper, waiting on you to get back."

While they were enjoying their iced drinks on the deck, Robyn's list of questions was unending, fitting her lawyer mindset perfectly. Claire filled her in on the details of the renovation and what a great job Reuben was doing and reported happily that the house should be ready to move into in less than a month. Claire knew Robyn was itching to ask about Seth but so far had controlled herself. She decided to let Robyn make the first move, because, in all honesty, she hadn't really wanted to talk about him. The questions rattling around in her mind, much less her heart, sent her into a tailspin every time she thought of him.

Later that morning, Claire called Maureen to see if she and Robyn could pick up Billy and Mason and take the boys to lunch at the pier and to see the antique boats. Maureen's response was a quick yes. She had just gotten a call about some papers she had to go over at the bank. It would be so much easier without a five-year-old boy in tow. The boys happily explored the pier and made up tall tales about adventures on the old boats until exhaustion quieted them. Claire thought it was a perfect afternoon for all four of them.

~ ~ ~

Claire awoke early the next morning, made herself a cup of tea and headed to the deck. Grabbing a cozy throw off the sofa, she quietly opened the door and curled up on the loveseat.

She needed to change the direction of her thoughts and maybe taking in the cool morning air would help. If not, then a hot shower might do the trick.

It was more unnerving coming back here than she had anticipated. She had been so focused on how her son would handle it, she had neglected her own possible reaction. She loved the feel of this particular kind of San Francisco early morning. It reminded her of all those early runs she would go on when Randall had been at the hospital all night and then stayed home a little longer than usual the next morning, giving her the opportunity to go for a run before Mason got up.

If her husband was still in bed when she woke up at six, she had learned it gave her about forty-five minutes to hit the pavement. If an emergency came up, he would know to call her cell phone, and she could be back before he would be ready to leave. Claire felt a tiny tear trickle down her cheek. She did still miss him.

Making a snap decision, she decided to leave Robyn a note and go for a twenty-minute run nearby. That would help get rid of some of this anxiousness she was beginning to feel.

~ ~ ~

Exhausted from the hills and humidity, Claire walked the last half block to cool down. The run had been just what she'd needed. Her head felt clearer and her emotions had settled down. She felt ready for the new day.

Opening the door to the townhouse, Mason's wailing assaulted her. Robyn, visibly shaken, sat on the sofa trying to comfort a very distraught little boy.

"What in the world is wrong?" Claire shouted, running to grab her child. "Robyn, what happened?"

"He woke up before I did and couldn't find you. He panicked, Claire. I've tried to calm him down, and I read your note to him, but nothing seemed to help." Robyn burst into tears as she handed Mason to his mother.

"It's not your fault, Robyn; it's mine. I never should have tried to go before he was awake." Claire sat on the floor at Robyn's feet and pulled her son onto her lap. Holding Mason close against her, she whispered quiet words of comfort in his ear while kissing his cheek and stroking his back.

As her son's sobs began to diminish, Claire reached up and patted Robyn's trembling hand, assuring her it was okay, and they could talk about it later.

"Hey, Tiger, how about if we go run you a nice warm bath and maybe Aunt Robbie will make us some breakfast?" Claire noticed a look of relief and approval in Robyn's expression. She knew this had taken a toll on her friend as well.

When Mason nodded yes, Robyn jumped up and headed to the kitchen. "I'll make your favorite, Tiger, pancakes and sausage.

Even I can make that!" Robyn's nervous chuckle told Claire just how shaken her friend had been.

Once her son was soaking in the tub and seemed more relaxed, Claire gently asked, "Sweetheart, can you tell me why you got so upset? Aunt Robbie said she read you my note so you would know where I was." Mason's haunted look sent a shiver down Claire's spine.

Eyes brimming with tears gazed up at her. "I . . . I thought you had gone away like Daddy did. When I woke up that day you told me he had gone away and couldn't come back." The tears streamed down his small face, and he reached out to hold her.

"Oh, Mason, I'm so very sorry to have scared you like that. I would have never gone out if I had any idea you might think I wouldn't come back." Claire pulled a towel around him and sat on the toilet seat holding her little boy as he cried.

The feel of her child's damp hair against her cheek was sweet. She longed to say just the right words to him. How do you discuss life and death with a five year old? Her heart ached for him. He was still so young, too young, to have to try and understand something so complex.

"Sweetheart, Mommy doesn't have the answer to why Daddy had to die. I don't understand it myself. But, Mason, remember it was an accident, something that wasn't supposed to happen, but it did. That doesn't mean you have to worry that every time Mommy leaves you, I won't come back because there was an accident." Claire's words sounded so hollow, even to herself. Would they help her child at all?

"Mommy," Mason said, his voice quivering, "is it kind of like when I go get a glass of milk out of the 'fridgerator and I'm being real careful, but it slips and I drop it by accident?" The innocence and simplicity of a child's thoughts never ceased to amaze Claire. Maybe it was a beginning that would help him process all the deeper issues later; for now, it seemed sufficient.

Taking her son's sweet face between her hands, she kissed the tip of his nose. "Yes, kind of like that. I love you, sweetie." Mason snuggled closer.

"Sweetheart, will you promise Mommy something?" Claire hugged him tighter. "Will you come talk to me any time those scary thoughts creep back in your mind?" Claire twirled a strand of her son's hair between her fingers. "Did you know I have those thoughts sometimes too? The things I can't understand or things that hurt so bad . . . like losing Daddy?"

"You do, Mommy? But you're a big person. I didn't think grown people got scared. I'm sorry you get scared, Mommy, but I'll be here to take care of you. Okay?" Mason gently touched his mother's cheek before planting a kiss there.

"Let's get you dressed and go try out Aunt Robbie's breakfast, okay, Tiger?"

"Yeah," Mason grinned and slapped his mom a high-five.

After breakfast, Claire told Mason he could watch cartoons while she and Robyn got dressed and made plans for the day. It also gave her the opportunity to check up on Robyn and see how she was doing after the traumatic morning.

"Claire, I felt so totally helpless to comfort him or help him understand you were coming back," Robyn said, putting on the last of her makeup. "He looked so pitiful and so frightened. My heart was breaking for him, but nothing seemed to help."

"It wasn't you or your fault. It was me. I made a poor decision, and I learned something that just hadn't registered until now. He's been distracted from what took place here while we've been in Arkansas. His days have been filled with all the things every little boy should get to experience. He has fallen head over heels for the McQuarrys and Reuben and," she hesitated, "Seth, I uh, mean Dr. Bradley."

"Oh, so it's Seth now, is it? I wondered when you would mention him." Robyn gave Claire that knowing look and swatted her with a pillow.

"We're just becoming friends, that's all. He is a good running partner, really challenges me. I'm doing my best times. And he's Mason's soccer coach. I told you that in one of our phone calls."

"And you forgot to mention how gorgeous he is. And I could see how he looked at you, even that first night we met him. So be honest, girl, there must be some kind of chemistry brewing, even if it is in Arkansas! In fact, I imagine things move even faster down there when it comes to romance!" Robyn's eyes sparkled with mischief. "Come on, Claire, admit it. There's something happening right?"

Claire used every ounce of self-control to keep from smiling, but it failed. "Okay, I'll be honest with you. He is very nice, and I do enjoy his company. We had coffee after Mason's last soccer game. And yes, we were alone! And if you must know, I'm the one who asked him out! But it doesn't mean anything. We're just friends, that's all."

"Well glory be, girlfriend. I'm impressed. And by the way, don't give me that 'we're just friends' bit. I know you almost better than you know yourself, and I see something more than what you're willing to admit."

Since they'd been friends most of their lives, Claire knew Robyn well enough to know when to let it go. There was no use trying to convince her otherwise at this point. And like it or not, she knew Robyn had uncovered a significant part of the truth. Seth Bradley might be becoming a little more than just a friend. But she couldn't admit it to herself, much less to Robyn.

"I think it's time to turn this conversation from me to you! How many men have you left in the dust lately, hearts bleeding and egos wounded? Come on now, 'girlfriend,'" Claire mimicked, "be honest. Or is there someone who just might be making you sit up and take notice?"

"Mommy . . . Mommy!" shouted Mason from the living room, "The show's over. When can we go get Billy?"

"Right now, Tiger. We're ready. Turn off the TV, okay? You," she said, pointing to Robyn, "are off the hook for now, but we will pick this conversation up later."

~ ~ ~

Returning to Robyn's, tired but happy after another full day of fun, all three agreed that pizza delivered to their door was the way to go for dinner. Mason sprawled out on the living room floor with the Legos Robyn kept for him, while they plopped into comfortable chairs and scanned the latest magazines on the coffee table.

Flipping through the pages of *Better Homes & Gardens*, Claire did a mental replay of their day. Smells and sounds that had once been so normal but had faded in her memory since leaving here seemed vibrant and familiar again. She smiled remembering the pungent smell on the pier at Fisherman's Wharf; the sea air stinging her nose and the woeful barks of the sea lions cavorting or basking in the sun near the docks filling her ears. The boys watched entranced as what seemed to be hundreds of the creatures played within feet of them.

Claire had savored her Vietnamese noodle salad at the café in the California Academy of Science. It had been one of her favorites when she and Randall had brought Mason there. More memories had washed through her heart that day, touching wounds still open after all this time. Claire realized she had considered that this trip might be difficult for Mason and even herself, but she might not have realized how many memories would be dredged up.

She had to keep her focus on all the positive things going on around her and not dwell on the past. The loss she and Mason had experienced would always be a part of their lives. But she had to see to it that the dark times didn't define either of them. They had to move past those days and discover what lay ahead.

Thinking back on their day, she smiled as she pictured the boys and their enthusiasm about everything they had done. The rain forest at the Academy had wowed the boys and eating ice cream at the original Swenson's Ice Cream on Hyde and Union was quite a treat. But what kept them talking nonstop, even on the trolley ride back to the parking garage, was the aquarium, the highlight of that adventure being Shark Week. Claire and Robyn had stifled their laughter at the constant chatter of the boys and how the stories and size of the sharks continued to grow with each telling. By the time they returned to Mason Falls, her son's stories to the McQuarrys, Reuben, and Seth would be the things fairy tales are made of.

A surprising twinge of homesickness ran through Claire's thoughts. She had to admit it. While this visit was wonderful, this was no longer home. Home was a small, rather quaint town in the hills of Arkansas. And most of all, it was not the town but the people who made it home.

~ 31 ~

SETH STRETCHED, KICKED OFF THE SHEET, and hopped out of bed only to be reminded once again he wasn't alone. Jumping back on the bed, he pulled yet another squishy creature from his foot.

It was Saturday, and he was determined that if he got nothing else done today, he would track down Possum Gutherie and find out how to rid himself of these disgusting critters. Leaning over to the end of the bed, he retrieved the slippers he had been keeping there so he could get past the slime that greeted him each morning. Winding his way through what he now referred to as his room-mates, he headed to the kitchen to put on the coffee. After he found Possum, he would go out to Claire's and help Reuben.

Things were taking shape at her house, and he knew she'd be pleased by the progress. Reuben's craftsmanship amazed Seth. His skill and eye for detail transformed everything the man touched. Seth loved being a physician and knew that was where he belonged, but the time spent with his friend had opened the door to unexpected pleasure in learning how to work with his hands.

Reuben was a born teacher and mentor, and every day Seth spent with him had enriched his life in countless ways. He was not only learning the beauty of working with wood but at the same time Reuben often used these times to teach him about his new faith in God. And he began to feel a profound connection to Jesus through working with the wood. After all, his Savior was a carpenter too.

It took Seth half the morning to run down Possum. He found him at what neighbors had told him was Possum's favorite fishing hole. It wasn't that far away, but Seth kept getting lost on all the dirt roads and his GPS proved no help in the middle of nowhere. He actually impressed himself by finally finding the place. He wished he'd had a camera to catch the expression on his friend's face when he walked up behind him.

"Hey there, Possum."

Possum was kneeling down digging around in his tackle box and nearly fell over at the sound of Seth's greeting.

"Mr. Doc! What in the world are you'uns doing out here?"

"Oh, just wandering around looking for one of my favorite patients," Seth said, with a wide grin.

"Well, sir, yor prob'ly the last person on this here earth this ol' man would have 'spected ta see. But come on over and set for a spell now that you'uns are here." Possum brushed off a place for both of them on a large rock nearby.

The two men watched birds flutter by or stop to drink at the edge of the stream. Neither felt compelled to speak. Seth had begun to realize how comforting the silence between friends could be. He had never thought of that before. In the past, he'd always felt silence was awkward, and he tried to fill it with what he considered "fluff talk." The kind of talk that had no real meaning to it.

One of the qualities most people in this small town seemed to have was patience. They weren't in a hurry to do things or to talk just for the sake of talking, and he found this very refreshing, a far change from what he was used to.

"So, other than feelin' the need of my company, what brings you'uns out here? It's shore not the easiest place ta find," Possum asked, taking his worn hat off and scratching his thinning hair. "Must be mighty dern important, I'd say."

Seth chuckled, then became serious. "It is extremely important. Actually, it's a life or death matter, and you are the one I need to help me."

"Well then, what's the problem?" Possum grinned at him.

Seth began to explain his dilemma with the slimy creatures that invaded his room at some point during the night or early morning. Possum laughed was so hard he nearly fell off the rock they were sitting on. After catching his breath, he turned to Seth and tried to speak, but jerked his hat off instead and began slapping his leg with it.

"I'm sorry, Mr. Doc, I don't mean no disrespect. It's just pictur'n you'uns dancing around those slugs ever mornin' cracks me up!" The old man dug a blue bandana out of his pocket, wiped his eyes, then blew his nose. "Yor really a city boy, ain't ya?"

"No question about that, Possum. I never knew those things even existed until I moved into my house. Now, how do I get rid of them?"

"Well, sir, onliest way I know of is to get yourself a large size box of Morton salt and pour a thin line all the way 'round your bed ever night afore you get in it. Then when them slimy things come crawlin' out durin' the night and cross that line, zap! No more slugs. They done shriveled up! My mama did that ever night I grew up, yes, sir, she shore did." Possum's toothless grin spread the width of his face.

"Well . . . okay. Sounds simple enough, but I was hoping to get rid of them permanently."

"Well, sir, you'uns would need to talk to one of them terminators to pro'bly do that. I'm thinkin' that's a whole lot of salt you could buy."

Seth nodded in agreement while making his plan to call an exterminator the minute he got home. The two men talked of fishing and what was new in Possum's garden for a while, then Seth thanked his friend for the advice and for the promised tomatoes and radishes that would be delivered later that day.

~ ~ ~

After leaving Possum, Seth headed back to town. He'd forgotten to put his work gloves in the car, and he would need them to help Reuben. When he got to the house, he grabbed a couple of bottles of water, his Royals hat, and the gloves. He flipped through the phone book to find an exterminator. "Yes," he said, pumping his hand as he read the ad: Johnson's Pest Control, we take on anything! Give us a call and be pest free.

Seth punched in the number and waited for someone to pick up. "You have reached Johnson Pest Control. We are closed on Saturday and Sunday. Thank you for your call. Please call back Monday. We are open from 8:00 a.m. until 5:00 p.m. Have a wonderful and safe weekend. And God bless you."

He should have known better. "So, guess I better get some salt and see if Possum knows what he's talking about," Seth mumbled. He could stop on the way to Claire's, otherwise the store might be closed when he got through helping Reuben. Sometimes small town businesses felt closing early seemed more important than waiting around to take a chance that one more customer might happen by.

~ ~ ~

Anticipation built in Seth as he approached the Mason place. He always enjoyed his time with Reuben, but in the days since he'd given his heart to Jesus, he couldn't get enough time with the man. He felt like a sponge soaking up everything Reuben had to say, but Reuben didn't preach at him, he simply shared his life experiences of walking with his Friend.

Seth's breathing increased as he pulled up in front of Claire's house. How he would love to see her walk out on the porch and wave at him. And Mason. He had missed that little guy. Only one more week and they would be back. Back where they belonged.

The buzzing of a saw inside the house told him Reuben was hard at work. It was time for him to lend a hand to the man who had done so much for him. Dust swirled through the main living area like a stunted tornado. Seth dug into his back pocket to retrieve a surgical mask he had brought for such a situation and pulled it over his nose and mouth. Reuben gave a quick nod to acknowledge Seth's presence but continued sawing what Seth learned was a piece of crown molding.

A few moments later Reuben shut off the saw and took out a handkerchief and wiped his forehead. "Whew! And to think we're actually having kind of a cool spell. Sure glad of that! I'm ready for a break. Let's go sit out on the porch."

The older man poured two glasses of lemonade, and they went to take what had become their regular places on the porch, Reuben in the rocking chair and Seth in the porch swing.

"How's your day been, Doc?" The chair made a clacking sound on the wooden porch, and somehow seemed to stay in sync with the squeaking of the swing. Seth had discovered these to be welcoming sounds. They seemed to speak of unhurried companionship.

He filled his friend in on the time with Possum and his slug dilemma. Reuben confirmed Possum's remedy as valid but agreed with Seth's decision to call the pest control people.

"I want you to know how much it means to me that you're taking your vacation time to help me refinish the floors next week," Reuben said after taking a swallow of lemonade. "It's a pretty big job, even for the two of us. But together I think we can have it done by the time our lady gets home. I know she's getting mighty anxious to move in." Reuben went on to tell Seth he had rented two professional sanders with the dust bags attached. He said they would suck up most of the excess dust, but it would be advisable to wear a mask.

"That was the last piece of crown molding to cut, so let's see if we can get what's left up today, okay? Then I'll get all the air vents and fireplaces covered with plastic. If you don't mind doing some vacuuming before we call it a day that would get us good and ready for a fast start Monday morning."

"Sounds good to me. Things sure are taking shape around here. I'm trying to picture what it will look like once Claire does her thing. She transformed that old house I'm living in. It really feels like home."

"Glad to hear that, Seth. You're fitting in real nice around here, if you didn't know it. And even if you didn't want to in the beginning," Reuben said, sincerity shining in his eyes.

The two worked without a break for the next several hours. Seth pounded his mentor with question after question about Jesus and God and his newfound faith. Reuben never seemed to tire of the unending questions. Seth was struck with the way the man talked about Jesus as his friend and how close a relationship they seemed to have. It was all so personal. It didn't sound like what he had always thought religion was supposed to be like.

Seth brought that up to Reuben, who laid down the section of crown molding he was getting ready to put up and smiled. "It's not meant to be a religion, Seth. It's meant to be a relationship. Son, now that you know how much God loves you, you are His child, and He is your Father, you can come to Him with anything and know without a doubt that He loves you and wants the very best for you. No matter what may come, you can trust that God's heart beats for you.

Seth muttered a "thanks" and came up with a reason to go check on something. He didn't want to break down and cry like a baby in front of Reuben. Not only had he been told that God considered Himself Seth's father, but Reuben—a man he'd come to care about deeply—referred to Seth as "son" in what seemed a more personal way. He hadn't experienced this much emotion since Gran had died. But now it was wrapped in love and peace, not despair and hopelessness. He realized these new feelings were opening his heart once more to a willingness to love and be loved.

~ ~ ~

When the alarm went off the next morning, Seth reached over and gave it a smack. His mind fuzzy, he wondered why he set the blasted thing for a Sunday morning. Sunday! He had asked Reuben if he could go to church with him, that's why!

Without thinking, he hopped out of bed, feeling the coolness of the wood floor beneath his feet. Something was wrong. What was it? Then he burst out laughing. The salt had worked! He had not squished any slimy creatures. He looked down. No creatures.

The ring of salt, however had numerous gaps. Aha, they must be where a slug had tried to get through. They must have shriveled up just like Possum said they would. What a great way to start his day!

~ ~ ~

Seth found the church tucked back in a grove of beautiful trees. The trees must have been there for many years judging by the size of them. The scene before him looked like a Norman Rockwell painting of an idyllic rural town. And that was a pretty accurate description of Mason Falls as far as he was concerned.

His nervousness held him glued to the seat in Old Red. He had never been inside a church before. Even when Gran died, her service had been at the funeral home. He regretted that now. She had deserved a church for her service. But he had taken his anger and the pain of losing her out on God. How foolish he'd been. How alone he had felt. Unbuckling his seat belt, he opened the car door to what he believed to be a new chapter in his life.

Walking up the sidewalk, he spied Reuben standing near one of the large trees talking to a young couple. As he got closer, he recognized J.J. and his family. Well, at least now he knew more than one person here. When his soccer player saw him, he let out a screech and ran toward Seth, shouting, "Look, everyone, it's my coach! Hey, Coach," he yelled, launching himself at Seth. "I didn't know you come here!"

Seth picked up the boy and tossed him in the air, caught him, set him down, and tousled his hair. "Hey there yourself, J.J. Actually, this is my first time here."

"Come on, Coach, and say hi to my folks."

The two walked over to join Cindi and John Harrison and Reuben.

Feeling more comfortable, Seth began letting his guard down. Maybe he would fit in here after all. He hadn't known what to expect but so far so good.

~ ~ ~

Walking out into the bright sunlight after the service, there were two distinct things on Seth's mind. His heart was full to overflowing and his stomach growled with emptiness. Before he had the opportunity to say his goodbyes, Cindi asked him and Reuben to share lunch with them. His first thought was to decline, but he sensed it would do no good, so he heard himself accepting her gracious offer.

~ ~ ~

Driving home in that contented state of satisfaction after a huge meal, Seth convinced himself to take his mentor's advice. "God meant Sundays for thinking about Him and resting. We've thought about Him, now it's time to rest." Seth found himself ready for a nap on that Sunday afternoon.

~ ~ ~

The next morning Seth hummed to himself in the shower, thinking of the day ahead. How long had it been since he'd actually had a vacation? He couldn't remember that he'd ever had one. Then a picture popped into his mind of one summer when he was maybe ten or eleven. Gran had scraped together enough money to take him camping at a nearby lake. She'd borrowed a neighbor's tent and reserved the best campsite. Gran had surprised him with an inexpensive fishing pole and laid down the challenge for him to provide fish for supper that night. It was a good thing she'd stashed supplies in the cooler. His two average-size bream didn't make a meal, but it was the beginning of a few very special days.

~ ~ ~

Seth had been shocked when Mac had asked him if he'd signed up for vacation days yet. His reply had been, "No sir, I wasn't expecting any." He could still visualize Mac's response. The lanky man unfolded himself from his desk chair and stood to his full six feet four inches. He had laid a hand on each of Seth's shoulders and said, "Dr. Bradley, you not only deserve vacation time, you have more than earned it. Vacation time makes for a much better employee. Aren't you accustomed to taking time off?" he asked, scrunching his bushy eyebrows.

Seth had come to know this expression well over the last months. If you tried to argue your case, you would inevitably come out the loser. Angus J. McQuarry's mind was already made up.

"Sir, in answer to your question, no, I'm not accustomed to taking vacation time. I can't remember ever doing so."

"Lord of mercy, man," Dr. Mac had stormed, "then it's high time you do. This is an order. You go straight to Nell and sign up for a time right now."

Seth had wheeled around and half run to the front desk. *What in the world would he do with a vacation?* He hadn't known when he chose a week that it would coincide with Claire being gone and Reuben needing some help. He was sure Mac wouldn't consider it a vacation, but for Seth it was turning out just fine.

He threw on cargo shorts and a tee shirt, an old pair of tennis shoes and his ball cap. The cap had seen far better days for sure, but it had become an extension of him when he did have free time. Heading out the door, a mug of coffee in one hand and two face-together pieces of peanut butter toast in the other, he looked forward to the day ahead, despite the hard work he would be doing.

~ ~ ~

Seth was thankful Reuben had asked him to simply watch while the older man sanded a small room at the back of the house first. This way, Reuben told him, he could demonstrate the technique and potential hazards. The plan his friend laid out for the day seemed simple and straightforward, but by midmorning, Seth equated the physical effort to running a marathon with a hundred pound barbell strapped to his shoulders.

The industrial sanders themselves were large and cumbersome, although he hated to think what it would be like sanding by hand or with a lesser model. They stayed at the back of the house working their way toward the front.

By noon both men were ravenous and in much need of a break. The constant buzzing of the sanders echoed in Seth's ears. The dust escaping the sander bags swarmed around them. Seth breathed a relived sigh when Reuben tapped him on the shoulder and signaled him to stop.

The two men retrieved their lunches from the refrigerator and headed outdoors. The coolest spot looked to be under the ancient oak tree to the side of the house. A slight breeze ruffled their hair and cooled their sweaty skin. They had opted to leave the air conditioning off and taped the vents so any excess dust wouldn't work its way into the ductwork. They would still have vacuuming at the end of the day, but overall Reuben had said it was the best way to go.

Seth had the weird sensation of his body still vibrating to the pulsing motion of the sander even though he was sitting in a lawn chair. He had bitten into his sandwich when he realized Reuben had bowed his head and begun to pray. Seth stopped chewing, his cheeks flushed in embarrassment. All this was still so new to him that he felt he took three steps back to one forward most of the time.

The man sitting across from him patiently led by example, allowing Seth to begin his new journey in the same way a parent lives out what they want their child to internalize. Seth bowed his head and soaked in his friend's words of thanks.

~ ~ ~

What had been a long and grueling day ended with a deep sense of satisfaction. Reuben beamed with pride at what they had accomplished, giving Seth a good natured slap on the back and praising him for a job well done. Tomorrow they would stain the floors, which sounded like the easiest part of the process to Seth. The polyurethane would be the most time consuming, but Reuben seemed convinced the two of them would finish by Saturday. Claire and Mason would return sometime Sunday.

As the two men walked to their vehicles, Reuben motioned for Seth to follow him to his truck. "I have something for you," Reuben said with a smile.

Seth raised his eyebrows in a questioning look then followed his friend to the old truck. Reuben leaned in through the open window and retrieved a plastic shopping bag. "I've had a hard time getting over to Granville with all that's going on here but finally got there last evening. For some strange reason, the owners choose to stay open late on Monday night."

Seth accepted the flimsy plastic bag, surprised by the weight of whatever was inside. He glanced at Reuben who grinned and waited for him to open the bag. The box Seth withdrew held a Bible. Glancing at Reuben, he was encouraged to open the box. Stunned by the rich brown leather, Seth ran his hand over the cover. But when he saw Dr. Seth Bradley imprinted in gold letters across the bottom right corner, tears formed in his eyes. His voice cracked as he tried to thank his friend. The next thing Seth knew Reuben had him in a bear hug, and a sob escaped Seth. He realized now how very much he had needed a man like Reuben Walker in his life. A man who could show him the father love of God.

～ 32 ～

THE SHRILL SCREAM STARTLED CLAIRE, WHO was dozing on the sofa. She jumped up, instantly awake.

"Mommy, Mommy, come quick, it's going to get me!" wailed Mason.

Thrusting open the door to the spare bedroom, Claire rushed to her son's side. Mason was crouching on the floor in the corner, terror etched on his face.

Catapulting himself into her arms, he buried his head against her chest.

"There, sweetheart, I'm right here. There's nothing to be afraid of." She hugged him closer, smoothing his hair, trying to calm his fears. Several minutes passed before little gasps replaced his sobs. Claire continued stroking her son's hair and dabbing away his tears with the edge of her blouse. She and Mason were alone as Robyn had an unexpected evening work meeting come up. Mother and child remained on the floor, gaining comfort from one another. His steady, more normal heartbeat gave Claire the cue it would be okay to ask what had frightened him.

"Mason, sweetie, what frightened you?" She sat totally still not wanting to change her position for fear it would disturb the sense of security they had achieved. Just when she wasn't sure she could stay in that position much longer, she felt Mason's body relax giving them both the opportunity to settle into a more comfortable position.

A tiny, trembling voice whispered, "It's a giant spider on my wall. See it, Mommy?" He pointed a shaky finger at the wall then hid his face against her once again. She turned to see where he was pointing and felt her little boy raise his head and peer over her shoulder at the same time.

It did look just like a giant spider! No wonder it had seemed so scary. It took her a moment to realize it was the shadow of the bedside lamp's harp. When the lamp was on in the dark room, it cast an ominous pattern on the wall. Claire took the time to show Mason exactly what he had seen by having him look inside the lamp and then turn it on and off several times so he would believe the pattern came from the lamp. After staying with him until he went back to sleep, Claire replayed the entire routine in her mind.

It had still been a little light outside when Claire had tucked her son into bed. The exhausted little boy had fallen asleep almost immediately. Since there was no nightlight, Claire had flicked the bedside lamp on to its lowest setting and left the room. This had been the same routine every night with the exception that tonight her son had awakened before daylight.

Claire found her phone and sent Robyn a text. "Need you to pick up a night light before coming home. Will explain later."

Claire's nerves had been on edge for the last few days. She was beginning to think this trip had been a mistake, not only for her son but for her. The enjoyment of the familiar surroundings she had felt the first few days after arriving was giving away to something else as the days went by. Her emotions were on high alert most of the time. This newest episode with the lamp escalated the tension.

Mason loved playing at Billy's house, but each time she picked him up, she had seen a troubled look cloud his face. She had tried to talk to him about his feelings but more and more he ignored her questions. Convinced it had something to do with seeing their old house down the street from Billy's and all the memories it brought back, she had started inviting Billy to come to Robyn's. Maureen had been great and assured Claire she understood. It did seem to help some.

Robyn had agreed to take Mason to a matinee the next afternoon so Claire could see her counselor, Meredith Reynolds. She'd been such a help to Claire in those early days of grief, Claire hoped Meredith could give her some insight to help her son. As Claire drove to the New Beginnings Counseling building, she had the strangest impression that she needed to talk to Reuben Walker as soon as she got back to Mason Falls. Why would she think of

Reuben now? Dear as he had become to her and to Mason, her need was to see a counselor, not a carpenter. Trying not to start analyzing herself, she brushed the thought aside.

Stepping through the door to New Beginnings caught Claire in a time warp. Her senses responded immediately to the aroma of what she knew to be a lemon grass candle, the faint sound of music, and the all too familiar frigid blast of cold air. She had never understood why the place maintained such a cold temperature, but maybe it kept the patients' emotions under control. That was the only answer she could come up with. If it had been warmer and cozier, Claire was pretty certain she would have lost all sense of control on numerous occasions.

After glancing through the *Art and Architecture* and *National Geographic* magazines, she finally heard her name called. Claire found herself slipping back into the routine of countless former visits, smiling at the receptionist, opening the door to the inner sanctum hallway, stopping to make a cup of peppermint tea, and finally tapping on the door marked Meredith Reynolds, Ph.D.

Meredith stood up as Claire walked in and came out from behind her desk. "Claire, my dear, dear Claire. How are you?" The woman's genuine pleasure was written across her face. She wrapped her arms around Claire, giving her an affectionate hug.

"Come sit," Meredith said, pointing to the chair her patient had always chosen in the past.

"Now, before we get started on why you're here today, please tell me about your new place and how things are going. I've thought of you so often, Claire."

Claire smiled and eased back into her chair, taking a sip of tea as she did so. Knowing Meredith's time was limited, she gave her a short version of the past few months. "I'm only here a couple more days, Meredith, and some things have been happening with Mason that concern me. I wanted to get some input from you before we head back." Meredith nodded for her to go ahead and fill in the details.

Claire began with her son having sad expressions on his face when they would leave Billy's house, but he didn't seem ready to talk about what was troubling him.

Then there was the episode when she had gone for the run, and he had panicked thinking she wouldn't come back. She relayed the numerous times since they had been back that Mason, for no obvious reason, had a look of deep sadness. Claire described the spider incident, confessing it hadn't concerned her nearly as much as the others. Meredith listened intently as Claire told her the way she'd been able to explain it to him and seemed to weigh each example as Claire poured out her concern.

"Last of all," Claire murmured, "I feel like all this is my fault for bringing us back here. That it was too soon. He had been doing so well in Mason Falls. But I had made him a promise to do this before school started. Now I feel like I've reopened all the old wounds." Claire jerked several tissues from the box on the side table and slumped back in the chair.

Meredith looked down at her clasped hands resting on her desk, obviously deep in thought. When she raised her head, her eyes brimmed with understanding. "In all honesty, Claire, you probably are right regarding your visit. Perhaps more time away would have been a better plan. But that's over and done with and can't be changed. So, let's talk about the now and what's down the road."

Tears slipped uncontrolled down Claire's face, her mother's heart breaking for her child. Meredith, not seeming to be in any rush, gave her time to regain her composure. Meredith stood and stared out the window of her office for a few moments, choosing her next words carefully.

"Let me begin by saying that more than likely, considering Mason's age, he believed that by coming back to San Francisco he would find Randall. Children his age tend to think death is temporary. They can also look at it more as a separation than a final state. The things you've described are very common in a child his age. Often the fact that they can't express in words the struggle and pain they're experiencing leads to what you're seeing in Mason right now. While you still lived here, Mason probably assumed that one day he would find his daddy again. Then when you moved to Arkansas, he got distracted by all the new people and experiences.

"Here is a suggestion on what you might do before you leave town. You might consider taking him to the cemetery and opening a conversation about what happens when a person dies. Be very honest with him explaining that his daddy will never come back because his body, his heart, and his mind no longer work. That is what it means when a person dies."

Claire felt herself go rigid. Her own body seemed to stop functioning except for her mind. It replayed the phone call from the hospital like she was hearing it for the first time. She felt the weight of reality as she relived the sensation of her heart not wanting to take the next beat. Her hands once again balled into fists, and she trembled with pain and rage.

Meredith moved from where she stood by the window, laying her hand on Claire's shoulder. "It never really goes away, does it?" she asked softly. Claire shook her head in agreement. "It hasn't gone away for Mason either. And he was so young at the time he may just now be dealing with some of his questions.

"I would suggest the two of you sit by Randall's grave and you begin sharing some of your own sadness and pain. Let him know it's been hard for you being back here and knowing Randall can't be with the two of you. Tell him it's okay to feel bad and to miss his daddy. Don't try not to cry because he may need to see it's all right to show how sad he feels. Then the two of you might just sit and share stories of special times and memories. Help him know it's always good to remember the things he loved about his father.

"Keep me posted on how things go, and if you need to call or email me, don't hesitate. You may be half way across the country, but I'm always here for you, Claire. You've become very special to me."

Claire asked a few more questions then made her way out to her car. She would have just enough time to get to the theater before the matinee was over. Everything Meredith had said made sense to her, but she had to admit she wasn't looking forward to following through on a trip to the cemetery. She hadn't thought of it until now, but perhaps not going had been a way of coping for her. She was feeling guilty about this but still was not sure she could handle opening her own wounds. From what Meredith had said though, maybe that's exactly what both she and Mason needed to do. And they needed to do it together.

There were two days left before they returned home. Claire gasped. This was the second time since she had been here that she had referred to Mason Falls as home. Had she really made the transition that quickly? A slight smile creased her face. *Yes,* she thought. Yes, unbelievable as it seemed, her heart and her life had transitioned from Northern California to a small town in Arkansas. "I'm ready to go home!" Claire said and burst out laughing.

She would continue the healing process for her and for Mason tomorrow morning and go to say goodbye to Randall. He would forever be part of their lives, but it was time for a new beginning. In her heart she knew Randall would be happy for them and encourage them to live their lives with his blessing.

~ ~ ~

After their time at the cemetery the next morning, which had gone much better than she'd anticipated, Claire had dropped Mason off at Billy's house for one last play date. Reflecting on the conversation, sitting by Randall's grave had definitely been the right thing to do. She and her son had opened their hearts to one another. They had laughed and cried, mourned and remembered the man who meant so much to both of them.

Today would be a full day. She needed to go by and meet with Paul Stevens, her Realtor, about leasing the house for another year. She and Robyn had a lunch date planned with several of their friends and afterwards, the two of them were treating themselves to a massage and pedicure. She smiled at the day ahead.

When Claire and Robyn got to Billy's house to pick up Mason, Maureen ushered them into the kitchen for a glass of iced tea. The day had turned warm and humid and the cool drink tasted good. The three of them sat at the table, and Maureen filled them in on the boys' antics of the day.

"This one is best of all," Maureen said. "Where kids come up with some of this stuff amazes me. The boys had been out in the yard most of the day, but it was getting so humid I told them they had to come inside to play. They went to Billy's room and a few minutes later I heard Billy screaming. Before I could make it to his room, here they both came running down the hall, huge crocodile tears streaming down their faces." Maureen stopped to turn and make sure the boys weren't nearby.

"They were both trying to carry Sammy the gerbil at the same time. Billy jerked away from Mason and ran to me, crying even harder.

"I took one look at Sammy, and there was no question the little thing was in full rigor mortis. I wanted to try and comfort them and all I could think to say was, 'Well, you know there are little boys and little girls in heaven.' They both nodded. 'Well, maybe they needed a gerbil to play with,' I said. Without either one looking at the other, in unison they said, 'What do the kids in heaven want with a dead gerbil?'"

The three women stared at each other then broke out laughing! Claire wasn't sure how she would have dealt with that scene yesterday if she had been in Maureen's place. But after what she considered a healing time at the cemetery, it seemed to be the natural response from two very normal little boys. There was so much to learn when you looked at life, yes, even death, through the eyes of a child.

～ 33 ～

Every inch of Seth's body ached, but he wouldn't trade one minute of the past week. He and Reuben had worked from daylight till dark every day. At the end of the week, Reuben put an arm around Seth's shoulders as they were admiring their finished product. "We did good, my young friend, very good! I think our lady's going to be very pleased."

Reuben motioned for Seth to follow him to the porch. The older man took off his old hat and ran a hand through his hair before urging Seth to take a seat on the step. Reuben sat down beside him. An awkward silence filled the space between them. When Seth looked at his friend, Reuben looked sad. Seth froze, not knowing how to respond.

"I want to tell you something, Seth. Many years ago, I married the love of my life. When she became pregnant, we were thrilled. We both wanted children so much. It was an answer to our prayers. But in the end, I . . . I . . . lost Lois and the baby . . . a son, in childbirth." Removing the ever present bandana from his hip pocket, Reuben wiped away tears.

Haltingly Reuben said, "Seth, I want you to know how much our time together has meant to me. But more than anything that if my son had," Reuben fought to get the words out, "grown up, I would want him to be just like you. In one way you are my son, Seth, my son in the faith. And I'm very thankful our lives have intertwined."

Seth's own tears fell freely and without shame. Reuben moved beside him drawing Seth's head to his own shoulder. "Let it go, son, just let it all go. I understand your pain, and I know what it's like to keep it all locked up inside you. It can destroy you, Seth. Don't let it. Remember, God loves you. And Seth, I love you too."

They sat quietly, each with their own thoughts of loss and heartache.

"I've never told anyone but my grandmother I love them. I thought there was someone once, but I never said the words," Seth whispered. "But I've come to love you too, Reuben." The older man sniffed as he brushed at his eyes with his bandana once again.

"That sure means a lot to me, Seth, an awful lot." Reuben grabbed the porch railing easing himself up from the step. "Well, now that we've got that all settled," Reuben said with his familiar smile once again returning to his face, "let's go eat. I'm starved and I'm sure you are too. How does The Singing Dog Café sound?"

"Perfect," Seth said, "and I'm going to shock Mrs. C and eat one of those big steaks!"

~ ~ ~

The following Monday morning started like a whirlwind. By mid-morning, Seth and Justine were both working overtime to keep their composure and patience intact. For whatever reason, it seemed they were deluged with either cranky patients or bizarre requests. For Seth, the one that really got to him was Mr. Elmer Sanders.

"Mr. Sanders, I'm sorry, but I don't understand what you're asking me." The man made no sense. He just kept talking about his tulips.

"Well, it's like this, Doc. I come in 'cause I haven't had a checkup in a really long time. So, I figured I should come in and see if you can do one of them tube tests where you stick that tube up your rear end and look for tulips."

Seth struck his professor pose and bit his thumbnail till he thought it might bleed, trying not to laugh. He got enough control to breathe before he looked at his patient and asked, "Do you mean polyps, Mr. Sanders?"

"Maybe. I knew it were somethin' like tulips. So, can you do that tube thing for me?"

"I would be happy to do your checkup, but you need to see a specialist to do the actual procedure. It's called a colonoscopy, which I'm not trained to do."

"Is he a real doctor like you are?"

Frustration with the man melted immediately. Seth had a feeling Mr. Sanders' compliment would stay with him for a very long time.

"Yes sir, he is a real doctor, and I will personally talk to him about you. His name is Dr. Hanson. I'll have his office call you to schedule an appointment."

Seth's next patient turned out to be Opal Mae Hobbs who was scheduled for a checkup.

"Opal Mae, Jasper, so good to see you." Seth and Jasper shook hands while Opal Mae turned several shades of red.

"So how is our little momma doing?" Seth patted Opal Mae's shoulder when she stood and motioned for her to sit back down. "You look healthy and happy, Opal Mae, the picture of what a soon-to-be new mother should look like." Seth hoped his words would help her relax, but nervousness etched every inch of her face.

He took it slow and easy, asking questions related to her diet, rest, and prenatal vitamins. He went on to ask her if she felt the baby moving on a regular basis. After seeing the young woman begin to breathe more normally, he brought up the next part of the exam.

"Now, Opal Mae, I'm going to have Justine come in while we do the vaginal exam. That's when I get to check the baby."

Opal Mae's eyes were riveted on Jasper, begging him not to leave her, but she didn't want to say a word.

"If it will make it easier for you, Opal Mae, Jasper can stay with us," Seth explained.

"Now, Opal Mae, it's gonna be okay. The doc has to do what he has to do. You know I'll be close by, and Miss Justine will be right here with you too." Jasper reached out and gently caressed Opal Mae's cheek to comfort her.

Seth excused himself while Opal Mae changed into the exam gown. When Justine came to get him, she said having Jasper stay for that part was definitely the right decision. Opal Mae seemed more relaxed having him nearby.

Seth found himself saying a prayer, asking God to help his patient not be frightened and to trust him as her doctor. He realized how anxious he'd been as his own tension began to disappear.

After completing the exam, Seth helped his patient sit up. "Opal Mae, Justine and I will step out while you get dressed then I'll come back and tell you the results. You did really well today. I'm proud of you."

A few minutes later, after looking in on a child with a cold and sore throat, Seth and Jasper returned to Opal Mae. "Well now, Opal Mae, your exam shows an active baby, and everything seems very normal. I would like you to get something called an ultrasound. We do this with all our mommas-to-be. Do you know what an ultrasound is?" Jasper and Opal Mae looked confused.

"It's a very easy test to see how the baby is developing. They rub some gel on your tummy, Opal Mae, and then swish a kind of camera over it. This can tell us if everything is fine or if there is something we need to check on. Personally, I think it will be a good report.

"Then here's the exciting part. It will take a picture of your baby and you can actually see if it's a boy or girl. And you get to take the picture home! How does that sound?"

Seth had never seen such a joyous expression on any woman's face as he did at that moment. Opal Mae jumped out of the chair and hugged him for all she was worth!

"We can really see our baby?" she asked.

'You sure can. He or she may even be sucking its thumb. I've seen that happen many times. So, you're okay with having the test?"

"Oh yes, Doc, we're okay! I've never been happier, 'cept when Jasper here asked me to marry him," she said and grasped her husband's hand.

"Okay, then, we'll get you scheduled for an ultrasound at your next visit."

Watching them walk down the hall hand in hand, Seth turned to Justine. "That made my day, how about you?"

"I couldn't agree more, Doctor."

～ 34 ～

Seat 4B was occupied by one very tired little boy. Claire reached over to try to adjust her son's head to a more comfortable position for him. The last two weeks had been nonstop, and Claire felt the same exhaustion she'd seen in her son's face. She found herself anxious to get back to the slower pace of life in Mason Falls.

Granted, there would be plenty to do when she got there. A text from Seth confirmed that the floors were finished. That meant she could start moving into the house. She really appreciated all the work Reuben and Seth had done while she and Mason were away. She wasn't sure what to think about Seth taking his vacation time and spending it doing physical labor that he would not accept payment for. And why did Mason have to gravitate to him?

Claire had to admit several times while they were in San Francisco she had found herself missing Seth. Those were private thoughts she wasn't ready to share with anyone. She closed the airline magazine she was scanning for a second time, and after a very clumsy attempt to get comfortable, a sweet drowsiness washed over her.

～ ～ ～

Mason's excitement at seeing the McQuarrys as they entered the terminal tugged at Claire's heart. He'd never known what it was like to see grandparents since both of Randall's parents and Claire's father had died at an early age and Claire's mother seemed to have no interest in either her daughter or her grandson.

"Hi ya, Dr. Mac and Mrs. Mac!" Mason shouted, catapulting into Mac's outstretched arms.

"Hi yourself, bucko," Mac fired back. "It's about time you two got back home! You better give this beautiful lady who came with me a big hug, or I'll have to sleep on the couch and settle for canned soup for supper! You know, Mason," Mac said, "I think we need to get some ice cream before we start home." Mason's reaction left little doubt about the decision.

Once they started the drive home, Mason's constant chatter, full of tales of his adventures with Billy, entertained the McQuarrys and Claire, making the trip seem half of the actual drive time.

Mac parked at the back entrance of the house and signaled for Mason to open the door for Claire. Walking around the car, Mac opened Helen's door, adding a gallant bow. Mason was definitely getting lessons in Southern chivalry. *Not such a bad thing*, Claire thought. She took her son's extended hand to help her out of the car.

Walking arm in arm into the house with Claire, Helen whispered that Mac would keep Mason occupied if she wanted to go see what Reuben and Seth had gotten done at her house. Claire hugged her. "How did you know?"

"Oh, not so hard to guess. If it was me, I wouldn't be able to get there fast enough. Anyway, I think Mac would like a certain little boy's help gathering some things from the garden. I'll get supper under way. Just go and enjoy some alone time."

Claire hugged Helen and ran upstairs to change into a pair of shorts and get her car keys. The difference in temperature here and in San Francisco was dramatic. But as Claire ran out the door, the weather seemed perfect. She was home.

Mason and Mac were deep in conversation about what needed harvesting in the garden, but Claire wasn't taking any chances. She didn't want any repeats of what happened when she went on that run and he didn't know where she'd gone.

"Mason, sweetie, I'm going to go out to the house and see what Mr. Reuben did while we were gone. I won't be gone long."

"Okay, Mommy. Me and Dr. Mac are goin' to be real busy." Mason's grin lit up his face as he waved to Claire.

Before getting into the car, Claire turned back to see Mason take Mac's hand as the two walked to the far end of the garden. Such a simple gesture, but to Claire it spoke of hope and healing for the most important person in her life.

On the drive to her grandparents' place, now hers, thoughts of Seth floated through her mind. Did he know she was back? Would he want to see her? "For heaven's sake, girl," she said aloud. "You're acting like a teenager."

She turned on music to distract herself, but every song brought up a memory of something Seth Bradley had said or done. She finally gave up and turned it off. This was getting her nowhere.

The entrance to her new home would appear after the next curve in the road. Anticipation grew as she took the curve. There it was. The stone columns with a small sign that read *Mason*, stood like sentinels guarding the entrance. Nothing on the outside of the house had changed, but the anticipation growing inside Claire surprised her. For the first time she believed this was home.

Almost reverently, Claire got out of the car. Hugging her arms to her chest, she walked slowly toward the house. The only sounds were those of chirping birds flitting through the old trees surrounding her house. She hesitated, drinking in the simple beauty of the place, not just the house but the fragrances of lilac and jasmine teasing her. Walking up the steps, her hands caressed the smoothness of the old oak handrails, stirring memories of the days of childhood.

She dug the key out of her shorts pocket and slid it into the lock. She took a deep breath and opened the door. Standing motionless, tears stinging her eyes, Claire stared in disbelief at the sight before her. As an interior decorator, she had worked with some of the best flooring craftsmen and companies in San Francisco but never had she seen such beauty as what she saw in front of her.

She'd hoped she was doing the right thing in asking Reuben to refinish the floors but had to admit to some reservations about the outcome. Taking off her shoes, Claire made tentative steps across the floor, at one point kneeling to inspect the floor up close. "These are gorgeous!" she shouted. Twirling around and around across the large empty room, she felt like a young girl again, laughing as she hadn't done in what seemed like years. Her laughter grew as she rushed from one room to another. "What a homecoming!" Claire shouted, thankful no one could hear her talking to herself.

There were moments, she decided, when certain things needed

to be said aloud whether anyone else was around or not. And this was one of those moments when outright joy shouldn't be contained or bottled up inside. It needed, no, it demanded, to be set free.

On the drive back to the McQuarrys, Claire thought she might explode if she didn't get to tell Reuben what a wonderful job he'd done. She pounded the steering wheel, frustrated for leaving her cell phone at Mac and Helen's. It was a stupid thing to do. What if Mason had needed her?

~ ~ ~

Mason's dirt smudged face greeted her as Claire got out of the car. "Hi, Mommy, wait till you see all the good stuff Dr. Mac and me got from the garden. Mrs. Mac says we're goin' to have a feast tonight!"

Claire hugged her son. He was probably feeling the same kind of joy she had just experienced.

"Wonderful, Tiger! I'm sure it will be even better because you picked it." Claire brushed the hair back from Mason's face and gave him a kiss, reminding herself to put a haircut for him on her to do list.

"Don't forget Dr. Mac. He picked the most. And Mommy, us mans don't like to be kissed outside."

"Oh, really? Interesting. I seem to remember your daddy liked to get my kisses most anywhere. I'll try and keep your request in mind. But you need to know that mommies pretty much can kiss their boys whenever they want to. I think it may even be a law." Claire did her best to bottle up the giggles building inside her.

"Oh, Mommy!" Mason said and ran back to the garden.

Claire went to find Helen to make sure it was okay to try to call Reuben before helping in the kitchen. Assured there was no hurry, she ran upstairs and dug around for her phone, discovering it on the bed under her travel clothes. There was a short message from Robyn wanting to know if they had arrived safely. Claire called her friend's number. No answer. She sent a text letting Robyn know they were here and that she'd call back later.

There was no answer at Reuben's house. Reuben was one of those rare people who felt no need to enter the age of technology.

She would just have to wait to share her excitement with him.

She hurried downstairs to help Helen, who was at the oven checking something that smelled enticing.

"What are you making, Helen? It smells wonderful!" Claire walked over and peered into the oven.

The older woman's smile lit up her face. "Oh, nothing exotic, I can assure you. It's called consommé rice. Just something I've been fixing since Mac and I first married."

"Do you share the recipe?" Claire asked, inhaling the aroma once more.

"Well, that depends," Helen said. "Maybe, if someone had an adorable little boy, and I could be his adopted grandmother."

"Done," Claire said without hesitation. "Actually, I think that the little guy has already claimed you and Mac for his own."

~ 35 ~

SETH COULD HAVE KISSED HELEN MCQUARRY when she invited him to dinner. He knew Claire and Mason had just returned from San Francisco but felt awkward about calling too soon after their return. Helen turned out to be the angel Seth needed to open the door.

Hot water pulsated across his shoulders, relaxing the tension after a long and challenging day at the clinic. He wrapped a towel around himself, stepped out of the shower, and looked in the mirror. He needed to shave but knew there wasn't time; besides, didn't women these days like a guy with a day-old beard?

Scrounging around in his closet for what to wear struck a moment of déjà vu from the years of teenage narcissism. "Get a grip, Bradley, they've only been gone two weeks." Jerking a dark blue polo shirt off the hanger, he pulled it over his head, found a pair of khaki slacks, and slipped into his Sperry loafers. Running a comb through his hair, he took one last look in the mirror and headed out the door.

The short drive across town to the McQuarrys' heaped more tension on him than the entire day at the clinic. Waiting at a stop light, Seth caught a glimpse of himself in the rear view mirror. "Man, you've got it bad, don't you?" he muttered.

Seth drove to the parking area at the back of the house. He noticed Mason dangling his feet over the edge of the porch swing, pushing it back and forth. Mason's head shot up at the sound of the car. He charged down the back porch steps shouting, "Dr. Seth is here, everybody!" Leaning down to hug the boy, Seth got tackled around the knees, throwing the two of them to the ground. Going for the most ticklish spots on his attacker, Seth gave his opponent no mercy. Screaming and laughter echoed across the yard. Three startled faces peered through the screen door. Seth scrambled to his feet, trying to brush the grass off his slacks while holding the energetic almost six year old at arm's length.

The boy's attempts to grab Seth's knees again left him only one solution. Reaching down with one swoop of his arm, he seized Mason around the waist, threw him wiggling and giggling over his shoulder, and marched over to the rest of the welcoming committee.

Stopping in front of Claire, he bowed low, sweeping his free arm in front of him. "Madame, I believe this rascal belongs to you." He plunked the boy down on the ground between them and stood gazing on the face he had wanted to see for two long weeks.

Claire's smile completely filled the lonely places of his heart.

"Welcome home, Claire," his voice sounded like a tongue-tied fourteen year old to him. He hoped it didn't sound like that to her.

"Thank you, Seth, we're glad to be back. And I want to thank you so much for what you did at the house. The floors are wonderful, more beautiful than I imagined. I don't know how to express what it means to me. You taking your vacation time to help Reuben; it was such a gift, and thank you seems so little in return." Claire lifted a hand to wipe at the hint of tears filling her eyes.

"Hey, what are friends for? It taught me a great new skill. Thank you for the opportunity," he said. Heat creeping up his face confirmed his blushing. Somebody save me, his pride pleaded. The familiar rattle of what he knew would be an ancient green pick-up truck did just that.

"Mommy, it's Mr. Reuben!" Mason tore across the yard waving both hands in the air. "Mr. Reuben, you came!" Jumping up and down, Mason backed up long enough for his friend to park and climb out of the truck.

Reuben held out his arms to catch all fifty-five pounds of one squirming boy. Mason's joy rang out as Reuben threw him in the air then heaved the boy onto his back and trotted toward the group. Easing his feisty load to the ground, Reuben wiped his forehead with a white handkerchief. "Welcome home, Miss Claire. We sure have missed the two of you. Haven't we, Seth?" He gave a sly smile to Helen before nodding at Seth.

Seth felt his face burst into a full blown blush. Wait till he got Reuben alone. He had some words for the man he thought was his friend.

Claire gave Reuben a big hug and words spilled out thanking him for all he had done. Claire stepped back from Reuben and said, "You clean up nicely, Mr. Walker. No jeans, work shirt, or bandana. Don't let the local widows see you like this. You'll have more casseroles than you could eat in a month!" When Claire winked at Seth, he captured the moment like a photo, downloading it straight to his heart.

Helen's meal rated at the top of Seth's list, right with Gran's. Fresh vegetables from her garden, an incredibly delicious rice dish, cornbread, ham, and her famous peach pie settled nicely in a bachelor's stomach.

Helen had an aristocratic look but down to earth manner about her, the epitome of past generations of Southern graciousness. But to Seth it was her quiet spirit and love for others that set her apart; in her presence everyone knew they were special.

Like one boisterous, happy family, everyone helped clear the table and do the dishes. Seeing Dr. Angus J. McQuarry in one of his wife's aprons was a sight Seth would never forget!

When they adjourned to the back porch, sitting wherever they found a vacant spot, sipping iced tea with a sprig of fresh mint, the peace and contentment Seth experienced overwhelmed him. In a moment of quiet, Helen said, "Why don't you two young folks go for a nice walk? The three of us older folks have some catching up to do with our special boy. Helen's eyes twinkled. "Go on now," she said, with a wave of her hand.

Seth gave Claire a questioning look and jumped to his feet. Everything in him wanted to hug Helen's neck but instead he said, "There is a nice breeze and after that incredible meal, I need a walk. Sounds okay to me, how about you?" he said to Claire.

Claire grinned and stood up, "You're right about working off some of that wonderful meal. I'm stuffed. Is that okay with you, Mason?"

"Yeah—I mean, yes, ma'am, Mommy. I've got all kinds of stuff to tell them. Bye, Mommy. Bye, Dr. Seth."

Seth stood back as Claire walked down the steps. The breeze transformed the sweltering day into a pleasant evening. The sweet scent from Helen's beloved roses teased him. From what Seth could tell, they were in for a beautiful sunset. The perfect time for a walk.

An easy silence hung between them; neither compelled to make conversation. Seth admired that in Claire. She could be clever and funny, serious and business like, but this side of her fit with him to perfection. As the sky exploded in orange and yellow with tinges of pink and violet, he heard Claire gasp.

"Oh, Seth, it's magnificent, isn't it?"

He nodded, thinking how much she resembled her child with the look of wonder and awe on her face. Without thinking, he placed his hand on her shoulder as they watched the beauty of the setting sun.

"It's God's masterpiece." His tone hushed almost reverent. "He paints a new canvas each day just for us—if we have eyes to see it." Seth froze. Those words came out of nowhere. Stunned, he glanced at Claire to see her reaction. Her surprised look matched his own. The silence fell between them once again, but this time it felt heavy.

"Seth, I didn't know that you are religious," she said, questions written in her eyes.

He searched for an answer. Then he remembered something Reuben had told him. "I don't think of myself as a religious person, Claire. And to be totally honest with you, this is all new to me." Seth's heart beat faster with every thought. How could he explain what had happened to him? He still didn't completely understand it himself.

"There's been a change in my life, I guess more accurately, in my heart. While you've been gone, I came to a place when I knew I was alone and empty." He hesitated. "I haven't told this to anyone, so I'm not quite sure how to express it. I just knew I needed something or someone bigger than myself. The bottom line is I came to understand that the emptiness and loneliness I felt was God showing me I needed the love He wanted to give me. Reuben introduced me to his best friend, Jesus.

"He also helped me understand that knowing Jesus is about

a relationship with Him, not about religion." Seth crammed his hands in his pockets and stared once again at the sunset. He caught the smell of smoke, probably from someone grilling in their backyard. "I don't know what else to say, Claire, except I'm not the man I was when you left. There is peace that seems to be filling up the holes in my heart."

Claire stared at him but with a distance in her gaze.

~ ~ ~

Seth's thoughts battered him like an angry sea attacks a small boat. Sleep failed him. He crawled out of bed, resigned to a long night. Pulling on a tee shirt, he padded barefoot to the kitchen for a glass of water and made his way to the back porch. He eased himself into the Adirondack chair, a gift to himself. Someday he hoped there would be a need for a second chair.

Looking into the night sky made him feel small and helpless. But Reuben said God had created and knew every star in the universe. And just like the stars, He knew every person ever created.

Claire's look when he told her about accepting Jesus haunted him. It was the wall between him and sleep. He gripped the chair arm and said into the night sky, "What now, God? I thought You were here for me. Don't you realize I love this woman?" Resting his elbows on his knees, Seth lowered his head into his hands. Would God make him choose between Him and Claire? His new relationship with God wasn't ready for this kind of question.

Somewhere in the back of his mind a picture began to form. Eyes closed, head still resting in his hands, he saw an image take shape. His breath came in spurts as the image became clearer and clearer. Seth recognized himself bending over an exam table. There was a woman on the table getting ready to give birth. He could almost hear the screams as he saw her push hard, rest, then push again. He was reaching for the baby's head, encouraging the mother to push again one more time. He could almost feel the slippery, little head ease into his hands followed by the small torso and the legs. He saw himself double clamp the cord and cut it.

The child's loud, spontaneous cry shouted its claim to take hold of life. The baby didn't know what life would look like or what lay ahead. But when the mother cradled the child in her arms, it grasped her finger, reaching out to the one who had given it life.

"God, I'm like that baby, aren't I? I'm so small in this new life You've given me, and I don't know anything except that You love me and will take care of me. God, I'm going to choose to trust You with Claire. Would You please show her You love her too?"

～ 36 ～

SETH'S BOMBSHELL LAST NIGHT ABOUT HAVING some kind of experience with Jesus made Claire cringe. What was it with these people around here? Before coming back to Mason Falls, she hadn't heard anyone talk about Jesus in years. This had been on her mind all day. Mac and Helen had taken Mason for a walk, giving her some needed alone time to think.

Sadness had filled her when she heard Seth trying to explain the phenomenon he had experienced. Thoughts of him and their growing friendship occurred more often than she wanted to admit. But this was like walking into murky water having no idea what was there and where to step next.

Why did he have to get religious on her? What was it he said? She gave the porch swing a strong push making the chains squeak as it swayed back and forth. Relationship not religion. That was it! How in the world did Seth think he could have a relationship with someone who had lived over two thousand years ago?

She knew Helen and Reuben believed the same thing. She wasn't sure about Mac. If he did, he wasn't as open about it. And even Mason talked about Jesus as his friend. Was she the only one who could see the truth? Or was she the only one who couldn't?

The grudge she held against God for letting Randall die still churned deep inside her. She wasn't ready to let go of it. In a bizarre way, it gave her something to cling to. The creaking of the swing mirrored Claire's mood. She had to put up her guard once again she told himself. Her emotions were still too fragile to get involved with someone, especially now that Seth was on some kind of spiritual journey.

Stopping the swing with her foot, she walked into the kitchen and jotted a note to Mac and Helen telling them she was going to her grandparents' house for a little while. She'd be back in time to put Mason to bed.

She drove slowly out to the farm, windows rolled down so she could breathe in the cool evening air. Only days from now she and Mason would move into the place where her memories could again become reality. The tree-lined drive to the house had intrigued Claire as a little girl. A mysterious awe wrapped her in anticipation as each tree seemed to whisper its own secrets. To this day, the drive still captured her imagination as she pictured herself entering into a storybook world.

She parked at the side of the house and sat for several minutes trying to clear Seth from her thoughts. She had hoped coming here would change her mood and help her put him out of her mind. Claire opened the car door and stepped out just as the sun's curtain call for the day flamed into a brilliant orangey red. Sitting on the top step of the front porch, she hugged her legs to her chest. Memories of doing the same thing as a child with Potch and Honey engulfed her. She felt like that child again, back in her safe place where she had always felt loved and cherished.

Watching the vivid colors begin to fade, thoughts of Seth swept over her. His words played in her mind. "It's God's masterpiece. He paints a new canvas each day just for us if we have eyes to see it." It was a beautiful thought. But if God could paint sunsets, why couldn't He keep Randall from being killed?

She wasn't sure she'd ever have an answer. It was probably too late anyway. She had given up on God that night she cried out to Him and Randall still died. God had probably given up on her too.

Claire pulled the house key out of her short's pocket and unlocked the front door. Standing in the large front room, she made herself picture where she would put her furniture. She didn't want to think about those painful memories or about God right now.

The original stone fireplace made a magnificent focal point. She knew without hesitation that her grandfather's chair would be placed near the fireplace. Memories of sitting in his lap and listening to stories warmed her heart. It would be a nice tradition to pass on to Mason. She envisioned cold winter evenings, a glowing fire, hot chocolate, and her son curled up in her lap in that chair. As she took a last walk through the house, she made mental notes of ideas for furniture placement.

Pausing at the front door, Claire took one last look at the main room. What memories would Mason carry with him from this place? Would his be as wonderful as those she carried in her heart all these years? She longed for him to experience the love, joy, and peace that once filled these rooms. She glanced around the now empty space. This home, perched on the precipice of a new beginning for her and for Mason, would birth only what those living here put into it.

As Claire started down the steps, she realized she had never stopped to ask herself how her grandparents and great grandparents had filled this wonderful old home with all the qualities that made it so special, so memorable. She took her time driving back to town. Whatever it took, she would uncover the answer for how her grandparents had made their house a home whose influence lingered even now. She would also tackle Seth's comments and try to make some sense of them.

It must have been the excitement of being back in Mason Falls, Claire decided. Mason had returned from his walk with the McQuarrys wired up, sleep the last thing on his mind. After making him take a long, warm bath, he finally fell asleep while Claire read *Huckleberry Finn* to him. Exhaustion from a busy day claimed her moments later. She crawled into bed early, relishing the feel of cool sheets. Expecting to fall asleep immediately, Claire found her thoughts racing through her day instead.

When sleep refused to come, she got up and went to sit on the window seat. The cozy nook looked out on the side yard. Large oak trees graced the space and the cooing sound of doves filtered through the window. She felt herself relax. The full moon and dusting of stars across the sky captivated her. Staring out the window, she felt more like a teenage girl than a grown woman with a child.

The thoughts about Seth, and God, and her grandparents continued to drift through her mind. She must find a resolution to each one. Crawling back into bed, Claire let go of her questions, allowing sleep to take over.

～ 37 ～

THE STEEP INCLINE OF THE STREET took every ounce of reserve energy Claire had left. Sucking in cool fall air to expand her lungs, she leaned forward, pumping her arms to help propel her up the final yards of the hill. Her quads ached from the five strenuous miles she'd already run. The top of the hill couldn't come soon enough. Her body screamed at her, begging for mercy. *No wonder this is known as Heart Attack Hill,* she thought, straining to reach the crest ahead of her.

With a final push of pure determination, she reached the top and ran in place a few minutes before collapsing to her knees in the grass along the edge of the street. She wiped the sweat from her face and neck with the washcloth she'd tucked into the waistband of her running tights and sat on the curb, pulling her knees up to her chest and lowering her head on them. Heavy sobs erupted, shaking her weary body. She was spent, mind, body, heart. No reserve left.

The two months since their return from San Francisco had been a mixed bag of good and bad. She never knew from one week to the next what she'd be handed. She worried about how Mason was adjusting to first grade and if he was making friends. When a breeze rustled her hair and caressed her face, Claire felt herself began to calm. Her eyes were drawn to the luminous white clouds filling the sky like the meringue on her grandmother's lemon pies. As she watched the clouds drift across the cobalt blue sky, she focused on the fall beauty of the Ozark Mountains she had come to love. A sense of peace emanated from them. They'd been standing there for thousands of years like giant warriors protecting the small town nestled at their feet.

They made her feel small and very needy. Her emotions were a mass of confusion and emptiness weighing her down. A conversation she and Robyn had in San Francisco played through her mind.

"Claire, have you made any friends since you moved there?" Robyn had asked.

She'd hesitated before answering her closest friend with her excuses. "I've been so busy with the house. No time. But Cindi Harrison and I see each other when we trade off Mason and J.J. And I see Karen Simpson once in a while."

She remembered how she'd prickled at Robyn's probing question and replaying the rest of her curt reply sent a shiver through her heart. "The thing is, friendships take time and effort. And to be honest, right now I have little of either one to give." Picturing the look on Robyn's face made her cringe, and the sting of her friend's response hurt even now.

"That's not a healthy way to look at things, girl. If you're planning to live there, then do it. Live. Don't hide behind work. Don't just exist."

Claire had shot back, "Whoa, who's talking about working too much? You wrote the book on that one!"

Robyn had glared at her, the heat of battle filling her eyes. "We're not talking about me," she'd snapped.

"Well, maybe we should," Claire had volleyed back, watching as her friend weighed her response. Robyn's skill at rebuttal was notorious in the court room.

Claire remembered clenching her teeth, waiting for the onslaught. But Robyn had jumped up and stormed toward the kitchen. "Want some coffee or tea?" Half way there she'd turned and said, "Do you really want to end up like me, Claire? You're right, my work is my life. But it doesn't give the kind of satisfaction I get from my relationship with you and Mason. You're my only family, and I can tell you family trumps work every time in the dividends it pays. Don't follow in my footsteps and close yourself off from others. The effort you put into cultivating friendships is a time-consuming thing, but think where we would be if we hadn't worked at our friendship."

Claire had walked out on the deck and bent over the railing. A slight wind had muffled the sounds of conversation coming from the pool area below. She hadn't wanted to deal with her dearest friend's questions but in the end, she had agreed to try and reach out and make new friends.

Sitting there on the curb, physically and emotionally exhausted, Claire realized she'd failed to live up to the promise she'd made Robyn that day. She'd meant to make an effort, but she'd gotten so busy with the house, the days evaporated into weeks. Why did she feel threatened by the idea? She didn't have an answer, but she needed to move beyond whatever was holding her back.

Her anticipation and excitement about moving into her grandparent's home had filled her thoughts over the last few weeks. She'd worked long hours getting things just the way she wanted them. Trying not to be prideful, Claire still had to admit she'd turned the old house into a showplace. She hoped her grandparents would be pleased.

It was good to be settled in their home, but since Mason had started school, she'd struggled with too much time on her hands. And instead of following through on her promise to Robyn, she'd inadvertently gotten caught up in trying to fill the empty hours with tweaking every space in the house. Now she realized that was easier for her than establishing new relationships.

Looking at her watch she couldn't believe how long she'd been sitting there on the curb. She jumped up, did a few stretches, then began her run back home. Running almost always helped clear her mind. The thud of her feet on the pavement brought a cadence to her thoughts. But what she felt now was emptiness. Empty hours. Empty spaces. Empty hope. Empty dreams.

Coming to an abrupt stop, she bent over, lowering her head while resting her arms on her legs. That was it. She was empty. It was affecting every area of her life. All the tweaking of details in her house to bring perfection wouldn't fill that void.

Her eyes filled with tears. Where was the answer? Who could she turn to? She had isolated not only herself but her child. Regret tugged at her. She'd been so focused on what helped her cope with change that she'd neglected to see her child's needs. Claire's feet pounded against the pavement once again. She pushed herself as a sort of penance for all the lost moments.

Running for all she was worth to get home, another realization struck her. After first moving into their new home, Claire had worked at being intentional on keeping her and Mason both in touch with the McQuarrys, Reuben, and Seth. She and Mason had invited all of them for a celebration dinner in honor of all their help and the growing friendship between the six of them. But over the last few weeks, Claire now realized, days would go by when they had no contact. Mason was in school, and Claire kept working on the house. It was now obvious to her that her son was grieving the loss of those he'd grown close to. The sadness began to turn into outbursts of anger over almost anything.

Claire had taken Mason by the McQuarrys' house after picking him up from school a few times. But Mac had usually been at the clinic. While Helen insisted that they take Mason over to the clinic for a quick visit, it just wasn't the same. Her little man missed the personal interaction of going fishing, planting, and then harvesting in the garden.

They saw even less of Reuben and Seth. Both men were busy and while they tried to meet up at times, it was hit-or-miss depending on Seth's schedule or where Reuben might be working. She didn't blame them in any way. There was edginess in her relationship with Seth. It too was her fault. She'd backed off when he tried to pursue her. Robyn's comment shouted at her, "If you're planning to live there, then do it! Live. Not just exist."

The three men had become an important part of Mason's life. They helped fill the void for a little boy without a dad, and he missed them. And she had to admit, she missed them too. She understood the adult perspective of busy days and long hours on the job, but her child simply wanted the familiar routine he'd become accustomed to.

Mason had been an easy child to raise until having to face all that came from Randall's death. She knew the adjustments were hard on him, and she tried her best to be sympathetic.

Just the other day they'd gotten into a big argument over

nothing in particular, and he'd yelled at her and run out the door. She'd stared after him in total shock. This wasn't the little boy she'd known. Looking everywhere for him and on the verge of panic, she walked to the back yard. Moving across the yard, she caught sight of one of his legs dangling from the limb of a large old maple tree. It had taken her several minutes to coax him down.

She knew she would never forget the look in his eyes as he ran into her arms. In his gaze she saw the remnant of anger but most of all she saw loneliness and confusion. She'd led him to the back porch, and they'd sat down on the top step. When he raised his head to look at her this time, she saw shame in his eyes.

"Mommy, I'm sorry for being so mad at you. Sometimes I just feel really mad, and I don't even know why."

Caressing his face, she'd brushed his hair away from his eyes and whispered, "Thank you, sweetheart, for being sorry. I don't like for us to be upset with each other. We've had a lot of things change in our lives, haven't we?" Mason had nodded. "I know it's hard to understand why that happens. Just always remember how much I love you and that Mommy is trying really hard to figure things out." Her son had thrown himself into her lap, wrapping his arms around her neck and bursting into tears.

Thinking back on that day and others like it, Claire began to gain some clarity about their situation. The potential for emotional mine fields was everywhere. To guide him through this, she had to get proactive. Now. Not tomorrow or next week. Right now.

~ 38 ~

Seth sat at his desk updating Possum Gutherie's chart. The ring of his cell phone startled him, but it was the caller's name on the screen that was a real jolt. Punching accept he said, "Hey there, Chad. What a surprise!"

"Thought it might be, ol' buddy," came the cheerful response. "So, man, how are you doing down there in the boondocks?"

Seth drew in a deep breath. Chad Peters was a nice guy, a little bit of a show off, but the two of them had worked together a lot in residency. Seth guessed he could be called a friend of sorts.

"Actually, I'm doing okay. Better than I thought, to be honest. It's different, and I mean a lot different. But it's got its interesting and challenging side too. How about you? All going okay at the Hawthorn Clinic?" Seth's gut wrenched as he asked that question. A big part of him didn't want to hear Chad's response.

"Man, I wish you were here. We're going ninety to nothing, in full gear, day in and day out. But that's not what I called about."

Seth sat straighter in his chair, taking a swig of his now warm Diet Coke.

"Listen, I overheard a conversation that might interest you." Chad hesitated before he said, "Oh heck, maybe I shouldn't be telling you this, but I'm going to anyway. Seth, I heard Hawthorn, the younger, mention your name the other day. He was in the break room with someone else, but I'm not sure who. When I heard them talking, I didn't go in. Hawthorn was talking about an opening that would be coming up in the future. Guess one of the older docs is planning to retire. Well, he told the other person that they'd been hashing over possible candidates to contact, but so far, they didn't see a good fit. The other guy, or gal, mumbled something I couldn't

278

hear and then Hawthorn said that reminded him of a guy they'd offered a position when he completed his residency and that he would have been great only there was one problem. He had a three year loan commitment to pay off. His name was Seth Bradley. He went to some small town in Arkansas. What a waste. He was one of the sharpest guys we've ever interviewed. Then Hawthorn said— and this is why I called you—that he thought he would talk to his dad and see about calling this man just to check things out, see if he was still interested because the timing would work pretty well for us and for him.

"So, what do you think, old buddy? Sound interesting?"

Seth's thoughts were bouncing all over the place. "I'm stunned, Chad, not sure what to say. I figured I'd lost my chance when I moved to Arkansas."

"Well, don't give up, okay? Listen, I've got a big date tonight so I need to run. Hang in there, man. I'll keep you posted if I hear anything more."

"Yeah, that would be great, Chad. Thanks. It means a lot to me that you called." Seth tapped the phone off and stared out the window of his office. His heart pounded as he ran his hand back and forth across his face. Could this really happen? Could everything he'd planned and hoped for still become a reality?

He needed to go for a run and process this news. He would get back to Possum's chart afterwards. He needed to clear his head after Chad Peters' bombshell. He didn't want to be distracted while evaluating a patient's chart, especially a friend like Possum Gutherie.

~ ~ ~

The run was grueling but Seth had wanted it to be. Stopping to catch his breath, he bent over and grabbed his knees. He had pushed himself hard and was sweating profusely, but it was just what he needed.

Chad's phone call tore a hole in the veil of contentment he had allowed himself to feel. This one connection with his former world opened the wound of disappointment once again. The Hawthorn Clinic's reputation for being a state of the art medical facility overshadowed every other clinic in Kansas City. The physicians who were asked to join this group came with the highest recommendations. The list of names engraved on the plaque inside the front door read like the Who's Who list of medicine for the city. The clinic also prided itself in offering more disciplines of medicine in one building than any other clinic in the state.

An overwhelming thought rushed though Seth. Couldn't the Hawthorn Clinic benefit from what he'd learned from Dr. Mac? But most of all from what he'd learned from Jesus, the greatest healer of all time? Seth had noticed great detail had been given to creating as warm and comfortable an environment as possible in the McQuarry Clinic. He'd never asked, but he got the distinct impression that Helen and Nell were responsible. Each exam room had simple but welcoming touches to help soothe the raw nerves or apprehension many of the patients experienced while waiting to see the doctor.

The question was could he or maybe more critically, would he be willing to erase the shadow of Hawthorn Clinic that loomed large so he could get back to the contentment he had gained during his time in Mason Falls?

～ 39 ～

After dropping Mason at school, Claire stopped by the local market to do her grocery shopping. Today was the day Robyn would be here. Getting out of the car everything in her wanted to do the victory dance her son let loose that morning when she told him about Robyn.

"Wait till you get home before dancing," she muttered. "Mason Falls may not be ready for that kind of public display."

At the top of her grocery list she had all the ingredients for her famous spaghetti sauce. Memories of past times flooded her thoughts, and a sting of sadness made her wince. Wrapping her sweater closer she marched herself through her past and into Murphey's Market.

Claire was well known among her San Francisco friends for her shopping expertise. They commented often about her organized lists and her ability to get through them in half the time it would take them. Energized by the memory of those comments, she tackled her list in record time, eager to get home and put the groceries away. A project awaited her she intended to finish before Robyn arrived.

~ ~ ~

Glancing at her watch sometime later, it seemed the day had evaporated into thin air. She had just enough time to get to the school before the bell rang. Gathering up the finished project, she placed it back in the box. The pick-up line at Bryant Elementary School was bumper to bumper when Claire got there, but it gave her time to jot a few notes in her reminder app.

She still had several things to do before Robyn arrived.

For over a month she'd been planning how to make this a very special Thanksgiving, their first in Potch and Honey's home. She wanted this to be a celebration of the four generations that had given thanks under the same roof. Claire had invited the McQuarrys, Reuben, and Seth to join them. Each of them had helped make it possible. And now those preparations were almost complete. Exhaustion was outweighed only by the happiness she felt. How she would have loved for her grandparents to be here. Maybe in some way they were. If there was a heaven, could Potch and Honey look down at her? The thought intrigued her.

~ ~ ~

Robyn would be arriving at the airport later in the afternoon. Against all of Claire's objections, as usual, her attorney friend had won the argument. Robyn would rent a car and drive to Claire's house. Claire could hear her now.

"I will not have you and Mason driving an hour and a half to get me. You've worked yourself silly getting everything ready. I know that for certain because I know you. So just face the facts. I am perfectly capable of driving myself. And that, dear Claire, is final!"

She couldn't help but smile as she thought of her friend. They were such opposites but closer than most sisters. She missed Robyn something terrible. Claire still had trouble believing Robyn had taken off an entire week to be with them this holiday. There were so many things she wanted to talk to her about. This visit was coming at the perfect time.

~ ~ ~

The long lines of children began to emerge from the red brick building. And like every other mother in the row of cars, she began to scan the crowd for that very special face. Claire's eyes lit up when she saw him. He looked happy and very much a part of the group. She grabbed these good moments and held them tight.

Mason and the boy beside him were trying to pull the straps on the backpacks of the girls in front of them, then pretend to be focused on something in the sky when the girls turned around. The same scene, in one version or another, had taken place in countless school yards for generations, but it was the normalcy of it that made her smile.

Coming at last to the loading section of the line, she hit the unlock button on the arm rest just as Mason ran up to the car door.

"Hi, sweetie, how was your day?" Claire asked, glancing in the rear view mirror.

"Oh, it was okay. But you know what would make it a whole lot better, Mom?" A mischievous grin lit up his face. "To stop at Sonic."

Claire made a right turn out of the school property and headed toward the drive-in. She would normally pull into one of the stalls so Mason could call in their order. But today, she explained, they needed to use the drive-through. Disappointment faded from his face when his drink appeared almost like magic.

By the time she pulled into their driveway they were both almost finished with their drinks. "We sure do like cherry limeades, don't we, Mom?" Mason grinned, taking one final slurp.

Claire still couldn't get used to the more grown up sound of Mom. She'd known it would happen; she just hadn't wanted it to happen so soon. "We sure do." She reached over to stroke his cheek as they walked up the sidewalk.

"Mom, that's for little kids. I'm in school now!"

"Young man, you may be in school but you are not too big yet for me to show you I love you. So, don't forget it."

"Aw, dang it. But not in front of the other kids, okay?"

"Mason Westfield, what did I tell you about talking like that?"

"The other kids say it all the time. Why can't I?"

"Because I'm your mother, and I don't like to hear you talk that way."

"Well, okay. Then I'll only say it at school."

"Listen very carefully. I do not want you talking that way no matter where you are. Is that clear?"

"Well, I think you're being mean, and I don't like that!"

Claire sucked in a deep breath, silently counting to ten. "You know what, I think you need to go to your room and don't come down until I come to get you. Now go."

Mason charged up the stairs and slammed the door to his room.

"What in the world has gotten into him?" she muttered under her breath. "Did something happen at school he doesn't want to talk about? Well, whatever it is, that boy needs some time to think about his behavior."

Claire spent the next half hour trying to finish some details for dinner but her mind was focused on the little boy upstairs. Deciding enough time had elapsed for him to cool down, she made her way upstairs. She tapped on the door before going in. Mason lay on his bed with his face to the wall.

"Sweetheart, there's not much time before Aunt Robbie gets here. Let's talk and make up, okay?" She moved toward the bed and sat down next to her child. She felt him tighten up under her hand as she stroked his back.

"Mason, what happened downstairs wasn't like you. Did something go on at school today?" His body trembled as he turned toward her with a look of hurt and confusion.

"Some of the kids, they made fun of me. At recess they ran around calling me names." Tears trickled down his cheeks as he threw himself into Claire's arms. Holding him close she let him cry until only sobs shook his small body.

"I'm sorry, sweetheart," Claire said, running her fingers through his hair. "I know how bad that can hurt. Do you want to tell me what they were saying?"

He clung to her for several minutes until the sobs began to ease. "They called me that city boy who has no daddy." Tears rose up once again, spilling down his face.

"Oh, sweetheart, I know how much that must've hurt. And it hurts me too."

Claire held her son, gently rocking back and forth. "Some people don't think about how hurtful their words can be, sweetie. But you and I know you do have a daddy. He isn't with us anymore in person, but he's always with us in our hearts and in our thoughts."

"Yeah, but I still feel sad, and it made me really mad too. Mommy, I'm sorry I talked mean to you." Mason reached up and ran a finger under Claire's eyelashes where tears had gathered.

"I know you are but thanks for telling me. Why don't you go down to the living room and watch for Robyn while I check on dinner." Claire gave him a big hug.

"I love you, Mommy," he said, giving her a quick kiss before he ran downstairs to watch for his Aunt Robbie.

~ ~ ~

Having lost track of how many times she had checked the spaghetti sauce, Claire stirred the simmering concoction one more time. Mason's happy shout came from the front room.

"She's here! Mommy, hurry! Aunt Robbie is here!"

Claire heard a thud as she ran into the living room and caught a glimpse of her son jumping off the sofa and tearing out the front door.

Following suit, she ran after him nearly missing the top step in her excitement. Mason made a flying leap into Robyn's outstretched arms.

"Look at you! Mason Westfield, you've grown so much! Gosh, I've missed you, Tiger. Give me a hug, you rascal." Robyn's gaze caught Claire's as both took in the moment.

Mason took Robyn's hand and led her to his mother. The two women embraced and tears fell freely.

"Come on, Aunt Robbie. You've gotta see the house. Mom fixed it up really good. You're gonna like it."

"I'm sure I will, Tiger. Your mom is one talented lady."

After a complete tour of the house, Claire made their favorite peppermint tea and sliced a pound cake. Robyn and Mason were sitting cross-legged in front of the living room fireplace when she brought in the tray.

Robyn started to get up but Claire motioned for her to stay put. "We love to sit right where you are and have our tea, don't we, sweetheart?" Her son's head bobbed in agreement.

~ ~ ~

The evening passed in a blur, each trying to catch up on all that had happened over the last several months. After dinner the only place they all wanted to be was in front of the glowing fire.

Later that night Claire took her tired little man upstairs and tucked him in bed. She and Robyn knew the evening was just beginning for them.

When Claire came back downstairs, Robyn was curled up in a chair near the fire with a fleecy throw around her.

"I saved your grandmother's afghan and your granddad's chair for you, girlfriend. It must seem surreal to be using those right here in their home. Did you ever imagine that happening?"

"Never! To be honest, it's still feels a little weird. But I also wouldn't trade these months for anything. I, well, I feel like this place is helping us heal emotionally." Claire gave a half laugh. "Of course, we still have a way to go."

"Let's change into our pj's," Robyn said, "and meet back at the fireplace for girl talk."

By the time Claire returned, her friend was already curled up near the fire. Claire put another log on the grate, bringing the fire to life again.

"I have to say I could get used to this." Robyn stretched her legs then curled them under the throw. "Gas logs just can't compete with the real thing."

"It's always been one of my fondest memories from the few times Dad brought me here at Thanksgiving or Christmas. And now Mason actually gets to enjoy all this on a regular basis." Claire snuggled deeper into Potch's chair.

In the early hours of the new day, Claire and Robyn admitted defeat and tiptoed to their rooms.

∼ 40 ∼

IT HAD BEEN A FULL DAY of happy preparations and one special adventure, at least for Robyn, lay ahead. Claire could hardly wait to see the look on her friend's face when she would tell Robyn and Mason they were going to cook hot dogs in the living room fireplace for supper. A slight giggle escaped her at the thought of Robyn's expression.

Just as she expected, Robyn looked at Claire like she'd lost her mind but Mason jumped up, grabbing them both by a hand in a mad rush to the living room. Her son's eyes glowed with delight when they walked in. While Robyn and Mason had been sharing time in his room, Claire made all the preparations. She had a fire going and a card table covered in burlap set up. An arrangement of fall's colored leaves in an old pewter pitcher graced the little table. There were hot dogs and buns, chips, and a plate of veggies with a bowl of dipping sauce.

Claire had rolled in her grandmother's tea cart to hold the drinks and the makings for S'mores. Mason's eyes grew huge at the sight of the Graham crackers, Hershey candy bars, and marshmallows.

"Mom, this is awesome! You're the best mom in the whole world! Isn't she, Aunt Robbie?"

Robyn's valiant attempt to cover her shock worked on the boy but not on Claire. Mason noticed the hot dog roasting sticks and ran to the hearth. Grinning from ear to ear, he jammed a hot dog on the stick and stuck it in the fire.

Claire motioned Robyn aside. In a whisper she said, "I know this may be hard for you. It is totally out of your comfort zone. Just try it for his sake. "

Shaking her head in disbelief Robyn picked up a stick. "This is the ultimate test of our friendship, you know that, right?"

Claire's laugh filled the room as she gave her friend a huge hug. "You're the best!"

~ ~ ~

After the women finished cleaning up in the kitchen, Claire went to get Mason ready for bed. "Tell Aunt Robbie good night, Tiger. It's way past your bed time."

"I'm not tired, Mom. And I wanna finish my Lego spaceship," he muttered. Lowering his head, he added another piece to his project.

"Tired or not, you are going to bed, young man. And I'll accept an apology when you have changed your attitude."

Mason glared at her while breaking the Legos apart and pitching them in the plastic carrying case. "Fine, there. No more spaceship!" Picking up the case he ran up the stairs and slammed the door.

"Well now," Robyn said with a startled laugh. "Is that the little guy I've known his whole life or is it some other kid?"

Claire shook her head in frustration. "Some of both. Most of the time he's the boy he's always been. Then without any understandable reason he becomes—I hate to say it, a tiger, but not the Tiger we know and love. I'll be back in a few minutes. I need to try and resolve this."

~ ~ ~

"Sorry it took so long. But I needed to work through the attitude issue with him. Our Tiger is down for the night," Claire said, padding across the room in her pj's, robe, and slippers. "Can you handle another late night?"

"Let's not stay up quite as late," Robyn said with a grin. "Tomorrow's a big day.

"Thanks, that's my feeling too."

"Oh, and I hate to admit this but those hot dogs were pretty good. The S'mores, now they were awesome. It sure brought back some memories, didn't it?"

"Let's sit in front of the fireplace. It's so cozy here."

"Does this room make you think of the earlier generations who have done just what we're doing right now?" Robyn asked.

Claire smiled as she placed logs on the fireplace grate.

After running through their typical list of topics dealing with Robyn's legal cases, new restaurant discoveries, and most current romantic involvement, the conversation lulled for a moment.

"You mentioned this place seems to be helping the two of you heal emotionally," Robyn said, "but that you still have a way to go. Talk to me about that."

"I thought we decided on a shorter night," Claire said, getting up to stoke the fire.

"It's been months since we've been able to sit and talk together. I want to know not only how you say you two are doing, I want to see it in your eyes and on your face. You're my dearest friend. You and that little guy upstairs are the most important people in my life. Besides it's still early. So, get to it, girl."

"Robyn, I'm not sure I'm up for this," Claire said as she put another log on the fire. "There's a lot I've never shared with you, or even with Meredith in all the counseling sessions. It's still so painful—too many regrets, too much guilt." Claire shook her head while choking back the tears and sucked in a deep, agonized breath.

"Hey," Robyn leaned forward, "look at me. I understand. We've walked most of this road together, haven't we?" She stood and gazed at the fire.

When she faced Claire, tears glistened in her eyes. "Do you actually think I would judge you? My word, I'm the last person who could lay blame on anyone else. But sometimes," Robyn hesitated, "all that pain needs to be opened and let out, girlfriend, like a doctor lancing a boil. I have to tell you . . . I've sensed for a long time you were carrying a heavy load and that it's not just the grief. I'm not going to force you, but maybe it's time to get rid of the guilt so you can let go of the past."

Claire stood up. "If I'm going to spill my guts and my deepest secrets, we're going to do it over another cup of tea." Her voice wavered only a little.

Returning with two mugs, she handed one to her friend before curling up in her chair. Words failed to come immediately, and the silence wrapped itself around them like a cocoon.

"This guilt claws at me for having these thoughts. It makes me feel like I'm being," Claire hung her head, dragging her fingers through her hair, "well, like I'm being disrespectful of Randall," she sobbed, her body trembling as she struggled for control.

Robyn left her mug and sat on the floor in front of her friend. "It's just me, the friend you've shared countless secrets with for years." She stroked Claire's knee. "You know you can trust me. This isn't about knowing your secrets, it's about you starting a new life."

Claire stared out the window looking into the darkness. An owl called its lonely "Whoo, Whoo." Her thoughts were like swirling leaves, floating, not knowing where they would end up. And her heart was still raw with the pain of regret.

"Robyn, Randall was a very good man and a wonderful father to Mason. When he was around. I knew he loved me too. But—this is so hard to put into words," Claire said with a deep sigh. "I never seemed to be as important to him as he was to me."

A heavy silence hung between them as she gathered her courage to go on. "All our friends, and I believe that included you, thought we had a storybook marriage. And in many ways, we did."

Claire stood and paced back and forth in front of the fire, rubbing her hands together. Turning toward Robyn, her voice just above a whisper, she said, "But I knew in the secret place of my heart I could never compete with the practice of medicine."

She sat down, propping her elbows on her thighs and resting her head in her cupped hands. Tears ran down her cheeks as she choked out her final confession.

"Robyn," she said, raising her head to look into the dark eyes of her life-long friend, "what I've already told you and what I'm about to tell you doesn't change my love for Randall or how much I still miss him. But you asked me to get it all out so I can heal. Do you still want me to tell you the rest?" Robyn gave her a small nod.

"Because I was too ashamed, I've never told you that the night of the accident Randall and I had a terrible argument. I had yelled at my husband and then he was dead. That's part of the guilt I feel.

That night Randall called to tell me he would have to cancel the date night we'd planned. I yelled at him. I said, 'Randall, not again! I feel more like a widow than a wife!' Little did I know that just a few hours later that would be all too true. I shouted into the phone, 'It never fails! I'm fed up with playing second fiddle to broken bones,' then I slammed the phone down. I shoved a kitchen chair under the table and stormed around the room looking for anything else I could shove, jab, or whack. I was out of control angry.

"There were times I almost hated my husband's chosen profession. I've never said it out loud, even to myself, until now. It sounds so awful, so selfish. I mean the people he operated on and watched over were people in pain, and Randall didn't plan for them to get hurt and need him."

Staring at the fire, Claire tried to gain enough strength to go on. Everything she had said sounded terrible in her mind and hearing each word out loud sliced her heart. She wanted to look into her friend's eyes but looked at her sock-covered feet instead. "I know all this is awful for you to hear, Robyn, but if I'm going to do this, I might as well do it all.

"In those days before the accident, I asked myself why my pain didn't count. Granted it wasn't physical like broken bones and all the other physical pains, but it was real pain for me.

I asked myself a lot why we had to spend his free time going to parties and events. It was Randall who wanted to go and then nine times out of ten, I had to show up alone or else we were late arriving. It embarrassed me to no end, but of course, people always said they understood because Randall's work was important."

Claire went to stoke the fire again. The distraction gave her time to collect the energy to go on. "I know it seems trite and childish, but I just wanted Randall's personal time to be for Mason and me."

Wrapping her arms around herself she tried to gain control. "Pretty ugly picture of your best friend, huh?" She had no sooner said the words than Robyn embraced her.

"Just let it all out, Claire. Let it all go. I've seen your tears before."

~ ~ ~

When Claire was all talked out and emotionally drained,

Robyn held her until their tears dried and then guided her to her bedroom with the gentle instruction to let the pain flow away and to get some rest.

A downside to this wonderful old house was an elusive draft that had escaped even the thorough search by Reuben Walker. Collapsing into bed, Claire pulled the flannel sheet and down comforter up to her neck. Her head pounded, her heart ached, and her body screamed for rest.

Lying there alone, Claire reached out by instinct to touch the side of the bed where Randall would have slept. She drew his pillow up next to her face, hoping for a whiff of his Bay Rum aftershave. Disappointment met her instead. She would have to dab some on the pillow case in the morning.

"I wish I had gotten the chance to tell you I was sorry for yelling at you, Randall." Feeling sleep flood her consciousness she whispered, "I will always love you."

~ 41 ~

Claire hadn't slept well. Too many things on her mind, she told herself. This was the big day and she wanted it to be a day everyone would remember. Hopping out of bed, she eased into her slippers and robe and headed downstairs.

The cold air in the garage stung her face as she rushed to the stack of wood in the far corner. What nicer way to start Thanksgiving Day than to have a warm fire going. She smiled as she thought of the day ahead.

She and Mason had made so many changes since moving to Mason Falls. They'd had their share of sadness, but this was a time to celebrate all there was to be thankful for. Stacking the logs on the grate, she turned on the gas jet and lit the fire. It was only seven o'clock, and the house was silent except for the crackling sounds coming from the wood in the fireplace. Especially after the difficult conversation with Robyn and a restless night, Claire cherished this quiet moment.

She poured herself a cup of coffee and headed for her chair. She rarely drank the stuff at home, but Robyn preferred it to tea in the morning, and right now it tasted quite good to her. She thought of the special friends who would share this day in her home. Each person had been an integral part of helping her start this new life.

The McQuarrys had welcomed them into their home and treated them as family. Helen and Dr. Mac had poured their lives into them, giving them stability and support during this time of change.

Reuben had been priceless in his knowledge, guidance, and hard work in getting the house restored. The relationship he and Dr. Mac had built with Mason had given her son two new grandfather figures.

Robyn, always the faithful friend, had given love and acceptance, even in moments of hard truth. She was Claire's rock.

And what about Seth? She hesitated, trying to gather her thoughts about him. Sipping her coffee, she gazed into the dancing fire. Could she be totally honest with herself when it came to him? If she was completely truthful, she had to admit she felt attracted to the man. He was kind and thoughtful. A little stiff socially, but making some headway. And Mason adored him as a coach and as a friend.

The truth was clear if she'd admit it. She was afraid to let herself move forward in their relationship. He had hinted several times that he'd like to see more of her. But her immediate reaction had been to put him off. Maybe today her heart would allow her to open the door, just a crack, to give him a chance.

Claire had gone into her organized, professional mode before Robyn had arrived. Now she was glad. Many of the more time-consuming things that needed to be done were finished, like setting the long rustic plank table in the dining room and making the cornbread for the dressing. She loved having a low-key morning and not feeling rushed. That was something to be thankful for.

When she got up to pour another cup of coffee, her eyes fell on an item she'd recently discovered in her grandmother's old trunk. Reuben had brought the trunk over a couple of days ago. In all the work of getting the house in shape, he said he'd completely forgotten the storage shed her grandparents had rented. He told her there weren't too many things stored there, but he'd felt sure she would like to have the trunk. Thrilled, she asked Reuben to put it in her bedroom.

That night she'd looked through some of the items. There wasn't much in the trunk, but she was drawn to two things. One she knew immediately she would give to Robyn. The other thing that caught her eye had been a leather bound book that turned out to be Honey's Bible. A vivid image of herself as a girl splashed across her mind. She was spending her vacation time with her grandparents. It was after dinner and the dishes were done. They were playing Cribbage, a game her grandparents learned while visiting a friend in England.

After their game was over, she had gotten a book to read while Potch and Honey read to each other from their large leather books.

Claire never really understood a lot of what they would read aloud, but they always finished by reading a story out of one of their books just for her. She liked those. She remembered how she would sit on the floor near the hearth as they read. Some of the stories made her smile and some made her sad. Potch and Honey talked a lot about the man named Jesus. He was a friend of theirs they would tell her. She smiled enjoying warm memories of such simple things as watching her grandparents fall asleep in their chairs, their Bibles open in their laps.

She poured her coffee and picked up the book on her way back to her chair. She rubbed her hand over the well-worn leather, silky smooth from age and use. Claire flipped through some of the pages. When her own name jumped out at her she stopped. There beside a couple of verses Honey had written, "praying for Claire." A chill ran through her as she read the words on the page. "Your Word is a lamp to my feet and a light to my path."

It felt eerie, as though her grandmother was right there speaking to her as she had when Claire was a child in this house. She stared again at the verse with her name beside it, trying to understand what it meant. Then it dawned on her. Potch and Honey had always talked about the Bible as God's Word and it being like a letter where God shared the things He wanted people to know about Him.

She had to admit it would have been nice to have someone much wiser than herself guiding her through the countless dark moments she had experienced. And she knew there were still plenty of struggles and questions to come.

But the big issue was where had God been when she needed Him most? Maybe someday she would find the answer. Maybe, she thought, it might be in this book. Her grandmother was a very intelligent woman. Claire couldn't imagine her believing in a storybook God. This book must be what helped guide Honey. Could it also help her? Hearing footsteps coming down the stairs, she stuck the Bible back on the shelf for a later time.

A still sleepy, tousle-haired Mason appeared in the doorway. "Is it Thanksgiving yet, Mommy?" he said yawning.

"It sure is. Come here, you." Claire opened her arms. "I need to snuggle with my special boy." Claire took his hand, leading him to her chair. When he crawled up in her lap, she wrapped the afghan around them and held him close. He was growing so fast. His legs hung almost to the floor now as she held him. And he was losing some of his little boy look. Times like this would be gone before she knew it.

"Mom," he said in a hushed tone, "I'm glad we moved here. I miss Daddy and Billy, and Aunt Robbie when she isn't with us, but I sure like this place."

As he snuggled closer, Claire kissed the top of his head, breathing in the familiar scent of Johnson baby shampoo. That too would change in the coming days.

"Me too, sweetheart."

"Do you miss Daddy?" Mason turned his head to look into Claire's eyes.

What a strange question, she thought. "Well of course I do, sweetie. Why would you ask that?"

"Just wonderin'. I'm hungry. What's for breakfast?" Mason said, jumping up from Claire's lap. He moved to stand by the fire. "Mom, it's so cool having a fireplace like this. It feels like the olden days, huh?"

Claire laughed, kissed him on the forehead, and went to make him some pancakes. Yes, it was like the olden days, and she loved that.

~ ~ ~

The day was a perfect mix of being slow paced and hurried. The morning seemed to go on forever but by noon the pace starting picking up fast. Claire hustled to get the turkey ready to put in the roaster and put the dressing together. She commandeered Robyn and Mason to peel potatoes and crumble up the cornbread, which came close to being a bad move. When Robyn and Mason started flicking the crumbled pieces at each other, Claire moved into the role of general of the kitchen.

By the time their guests began arriving, everything was going smoothly, all disasters averted. Now they could relax for a while and enjoy the rest of day together. Watching everyone together, Claire realized they looked very much like any large happy family with three generations represented.

"Claire, may I speak to you a moment?" Mac said in his deep gravelly voice. Claire wiped her hands on a dish towel and followed him to the far side of the kitchen.

"What's up, Dr. Mac?"

"I had an idea of something that might be fun to do," his eyes glowed with mischief. "Don't know if you noticed that I put something in your fridge. Well, I bought some oysters at the fish place in Granville yesterday. How about we give a challenge to everybody to see who will eat a raw oyster? Some folks probably like them, but the fun will be getting those who've never tried one to do it."

"Why, Angus McQuarry, you're quite the prankster, aren't you?" Claire grinned at him. "You really want to see if Mason and Seth will do it, don't you? My kitchen is yours. But if anyone throws up, that's yours as well!"

Claire followed Mac into the living room where he announced there was an order of business that needed to be addressed in the kitchen. Everyone trooped to the kitchen behind him.

"It has come to my attention," Mac said in his deepest voice, "that some you have missed out on one of life's greatest culinary experiences." His steel grey eyes zeroed in on each person, especially Mason. "We are here today to remedy that situation. I am laying down a challenge like the knights of old to each one of you." Mason's eyes grew larger with every word.

"It will be known," Mac paused for effect, "as the McQuarry Oyster Challenge. If you succeed or at least try to do the challenge, you will be knighted as Lady or Lord of the McQuarry Oyster Challenge.

A hush fell over the room. All eyes glanced at the little boy who stood in awe.

"Prepare yourselves for the challenge." Mac disappeared and

returned wearing a paper crown, a towel around his shoulders, and a wooden spoon in hand to anoint the participants. The adults were doing their best to keep their laughter under control and watch Mason's expression at the same time.

"Who will show the greatest bravery by going first?" Mac stood arrow straight with not the hint of a smile crossing his face. Helen McQuarry stepped forward to Mac's surprise.

"I accept the challenge," Helen said. Cheers and applause broke out.

Mac leaned down and in a low voice said, "Are you sure about this? You've never eaten an oyster in your whole life."

"Then it's time I do! But maybe I should do it over the sink." Laughter filled the room as she strode over to the sink. "I'm ready as I'll ever be. Let's do this!"

Stunned, Mac stuck a fork into a plastic container and brought out a large grayish blob. "Do you want a cracker to help it go down?"

"I do not! Let's get it done!"

Shouts of "Helen, Helen, Helen" erupted from all those watching. Leaning over the sink, she lifted the gooey thing to her mouth, closed her eyes, and swallowed. When she turned around, the entire group applauded again.

Standing before her husband, she grinned as he anointed her Lady Helen McQuarry of the Order of the McQuarry Oyster Challenge. Mac beamed with pride and picked up his wife, swinging her in circles until she begged to be put down.

Reuben went next. With one huge gulp his oyster was down. He slapped Mason a high five. Claire got the thing up to her mouth then the smell got to her, and she ran to the bathroom.

Mason poked Seth in the ribs, urging him to be next. "I will if you will," he told Seth. Taking a deep breath, Seth rubbed his hand back and forth across his face then nodded okay to Mason.

Then shouts began. "Seth, Seth, Seth!"

"Come on, Dr. Seth, you can do it!" Mason shouted, running up to him. Seth grinned at the boy, took one gulp then promptly threw up in the sink. Mac handed him some paper towels.

"Sorry to let you down, buddy. It's your turn. Come on, show us how it's done," Seth said. Chants filled the room. "Mason, Mason, Mason!"

Mac brought a kitchen stool to the sink and Mason took one hesitant step after the other. Looking at the slimy glob, he started to back down then looked at Seth. "This is for you, Dr. Seth."

Amid continued chanting of his name, he grabbed the fork and pulled the oyster off with his teeth. He chewed twice and swallowed. The room erupted. Mason stepped off the stool, pumped both arms in the air proudly. Seth lifted him on his shoulders and carried him around in a victory march. Then he put Mason down in front of Mac who knighted the boy Lord Mason Westfield of the Order of the McQuarry Oyster Challenge.

The surprise of the night was Robyn's refusal to take the challenge. In all their years as friends, Claire had never seen Robyn back down from anything.

The women returned to their preparations and the men moved into the living room. The noise level from the wrestling match between Seth and Mason got so loud, Claire went to ask the men and boy to go outside for a while.

"I'll get my soccer ball, and we can play kick ball!" Mason hollered.

After grabbing the ball, Mason jumped off the porch steps and threw himself on a large pile of colored leaves. He pitched the ball to Seth but continued to roll around, throwing the leaves in the air and trying to catch them before they hit the ground.

"You know what I need?" he asked no one in particular. "I need me a good dog! He'd really like playing in these leaves with me."

The three men looked at each other and all smiled knowing they were thinking the same thing—a good dog for Mason.

In the kitchen, Helen was showing Robyn how to make mashed potatoes. "Are you sure we need to put that much butter in these things?" Robyn, the quintessential health food guru was at the point of hyperventilating. "And regular milk? Helen, we may all die of heart attacks before dessert!"

Helen simply patted her on the shoulder assuring her people had eaten like this for eons, so one day would not kill any of them.

"You keep slowly adding the milk and scraping along the edge of the mixing bowl, sweetie. I need to have Mason help me with something. We won't be but a minute." Helen wiped her hands on a towel and headed to the back door.

Robyn gave Claire a helpless look and scraped the whirling bowl of her biggest nightmare. Rich, calorie-loaded food!

Returning to the kitchen, Helen said "I sent the men folks and Mason to wash up. They said they'd behave themselves while we finish.

She walked over to Robyn and looked in the mixing bowl. "Now just look at what a wonderful job you did on those potatoes, Robyn, not a lump in them. Claire, come see what this friend of yours has done."

Claire went to take a look, giving her friend a wink as she stood gazing at the fluffy mound. "This is truly amazing. Robyn Hamilton, I do believe you might be able to cook real food after all! Let's call the guys. It looks like we're ready."

As everyone was entering the dining room, Mason started hopping up and down, excitement overtaking him. "Look what me and Mrs. Mac made everybody! They're called place cards, and they have your name on them and that tells you where to sit. And I picked out the places too. Do y'all like the turkeys we made?"

They all proclaimed these were indeed the best paper turkeys they'd ever seen and began searching for their names. Seth's face turned bright red when he found himself sitting between Claire and Mason.

The adults knew exactly why Mason had chosen that placement. Claire's face burned, but she gave a quirky "kids will be kids" smile around the table.

Her son, however, glowed with pride for his accomplished plan.

They all stood around the table admiring the rustic elegance Claire had created. Claire asked Reuben to say a prayer of thankfulness before they sat down to eat. She knew her grandparents would want that.

Conversation flowed easily as food was passed and stories shared. Laughter and, yes, love filled the room creating a happy atmosphere.

After dessert was served, Claire tapped her glass. "I would like to say a few words if you don't mind." She looked around the table. "The hope I had for this day has come true. It's even exceeded my expectations. And that's due to each one of you.

"I wanted this first Thanksgiving in our new-old home to honor my grandparents, Harold and Ruby Mason, or as I called them, Potch and Honey. We did that today." Claire rubbed her hands together to keep them from trembling. "On this Thanksgiving Day, I am thankful beyond words for each and every one of you." A hush fell among them.

Mason stood and said, "Me and Mom have been sad a long time, but since we came here, we've smiled and laughed a lot more. I think my daddy would be very happy about today, so I'm thankful we get to be a family—a family of friends."

Claire swiped at her tears as her son hugged her. She was pretty certain there wasn't a dry eye in the room.

One by one each person around the table shared something they were thankful for.

~ ~ ~

Claire came downstairs from tucking her son in for the night and saw Robyn looking out the back porch window.

"I made hot chocolate earlier, Robyn. Are you up for taking it out to the porch swing?"

"Sure. I'll get the jackets and a down throw if you'll get me a mug of that stuff."

The night air stung their faces but the hot liquid warmed their insides. Neither spoke as they pushed the swing back and forth taking tentative sips from their mugs. A full moon enhanced the beauty of the star-filled night. Claire nudged her friend and pointed to the meadow past the old rock wall. Edging out of the trees was a buck, followed after a few moments by three females.

Robyn's hand flew up to cover her mouth to squelch her excitement. Staring at the magnificent buck, she shook her head in awe. "He's so regal," she whispered to Claire.

Claire nodded and watched as the animals moved gracefully across the meadow, the buck stopping often to assess their security.

Feeling her friend's hand on her arm, Claire turned to see tears glistening in Robyn's eyes.

"As much as I miss you two, this is a very good place for you both. I just wish it wasn't so far away."

"Thanks," Claire said, in a hushed tone, "I needed to hear that from you." The two sat watching nature's gift, feeling thankful once again.

~ ~ ~

After saying good night, Robyn opened the door to her room and switched on the light. There on the bed lay an exquisitely wrapped gift she recognized in an instant as the handiwork of her dearest friend. Feeling like a child at Christmas, she ran to the bed and sat down. She cradled the rectangular box on her lap for several minutes, wanting to open it yet hesitant to tear away the beauty and love with which it had been prepared. Running her hand over it one last time, she began to take away the ribbon then the paper.

She carefully folded the paper and the ribbon and put them aside. When she opened the box, Robyn gasped at the beautiful embroidery work. She discovered it covered the top of a photograph album. She read the inscription from Claire.

To my dearest Robyn with whom I have shared life,

I recently found this piece of embroidery Honey had done specifically for you in an old trunk of hers. She loved you, Robyn, because you were so important to me.

In trying to decide how to give it to you, I came up with the idea of making this a gift from Honey and from me. So, turn the pages and walk back in time with me. We were quite a pair (as these photos will remind you).

With all my love,
Claire

Robyn sat cross-legged on the bed, turning page after page of photos, reliving wonderful times of school days and after she and Claire had together. Trying to keep her tears off the pages, she held one end of her bed sheet close to her face. One page after another brought back memories of two lonely little girls cast away by parents too busy to be involved in their lives. Clinging to the album, she snuggled into the warm bed, finding satisfaction in knowing she hadn't been totally alone or unloved.

∽ 42 ∽

"WANT TO EXPERIENCE SOME SMALL TOWN life?" Claire said, brushing a lock of her hair behind her ear. "Helen called and said they'd love to have Mason for the morning. There's something she wants him to help her with. She'll give him lunch so you and I can do the girl thing."

"You know me, I'm always ready for an adventure!" Robyn raised her arms above her head, palms outspread in a victorious pose. "But I can't quite get my head around there being much to do in such a little town." Taking a last drink of coffee, she hopped up from her chair. "So, what's on our agenda?"

"Let's just say it will be like nothing you've ever done before." Claire's eyes sparkled as she put their dishes in the dishwasher.

"Well then, what's the attire for this glorious adventure?" Robyn asked as they left the kitchen.

Stopping midway up the stairs Claire turned and grinned at her fashion conscious friend. "Jeans and a sweater! And if you don't have them, I'll loan you one of each."

"You've got to be kidding! We're going to be going around town dressed like teenagers?" Robyn froze, staring at Claire, in horror. "Girlfriend, please tell me you're kidding. And besides, I don't own a pair of jeans and never plan to."

"Well, it's a good thing we're the same size then because that's what you're wearing today." Claire turned to go to her room as she said, "I'll pick out a really nice pair for you and a warm sweater to go with them. Oh, and wear tennis shoes if you brought them. If not, I'll supply those too."

Claire and Mason stood by the front door waiting for Robyn. Hearing footsteps, they both turned to see a very unhappy, big city attorney march down the stairs in borrowed jeans, a cable knit sweater, and her friend's tennis shoes.

"Aunt Robbie, you're wearing jeans!" Mason's face lit up in a grin. "I've never seen you in jeans before," he said with total innocence.

"That's right, Tiger, and you'll never see me in them again." Robyn shot back, scowling at Claire.

~ ~ ~

After dropping Mason at Helen's, they drove to the edge of town and pulled up at Mabel's Café. Claire tried not to laugh when she saw the expression on her friend's face.

"Don't worry, the food's really good. Just that down-home Arkansas cooking."

"You are pushing the limit. It looks like what they call a greasy spoon café. Is it safe?"

After assuring Robyn she had not only survived eating at Mabel's but even enjoyed the food, they walked in and found a booth.

"If a short, stout woman with the brightest red hair you can imagine waits on us, that's Mabel. Be very nice. She could eat your lunch in a court room." Claire grinned at the look of faint trepidation in her friend's eyes.

Robyn scanned the premises and the patrons getting a feel for what she might be up against. There were burly men in plaid flannel shirts and denim overalls. They all wore grungy ball caps. Claire watched as her friend stared down even the boldest of the men who gawked at them. Robyn could make grown men cringe in the court room, and she transferred that ability to Mabel's customers. The thought of watching Robyn take on Mabel made Claire smile. That would be something she wouldn't want to miss.

"So, what'd you two want to eat?" They both looked into the glaring eyes of the red-haired woman before them.

After they ordered, Robyn, accustomed to working through a busy schedule, wanted to know details of their day. Claire simply smiled, reminding her she was now on Southern time. No need to rush. Just enjoy the moment. Her expression was classic Robyn when she was not the one in control.

~ ~ ~

Breathing in the cool morning air as they left Mabel's stirred Claire's runner instincts. But after the large breakfast they had eaten now wasn't the time to run. Robyn had eaten every bit of her breakfast with relish after the first heavenly bite of her omelet. A walk would be the perfect answer for both of them and a great way to help Robyn get a feel for the town.

It had been a late fall and many of the trees remained a blaze of color. There was a faint smoky smell from someone nearby burning leaves. The sky, a glorious blue, held not a hint of clouds, and busy little squirrels ran back and forth, diligent workers preparing for winter. Claire pointed out some of the historic homes to Robyn, sharing stories passed from generation to generation. Her favorite had always been the large house taking the entire corner of Maple and Pine Street.

The original owners, Potch had told her, were from Lunenburg, Nova Scotia. They wanted their house to be a replica of their former home. Lunenburg was a fishing village and most of the men worked on fishing boats. Because of that, someone had developed a unique architectural feature known as the Lunenburg Bump. The Bump, an enlarged dormer with windows on all three sides, jutted out from the second story of the house, allowing wives and mothers to watch for boats coming into the harbor.

Memories of the woman in Mason Falls standing in the bump in front of her home flooded Claire's thoughts. It had always been a haunting scene to her. What or who was the woman waiting for?

Glancing at Robyn on their return to the car, Claire noticed the wistful look cross her face. "You okay?"

"Of course. I'm always okay, aren't I?" came the strained reply.

"Actually, no you aren't. You just make everyone think you are."

"All right, guess it's my turn to confess, huh? I was thinking this hole in the wall town is not so bad. Don't think I could ever live here but visiting is kind of refreshing. Helps a person slow down and smell the roses, as the saying goes. Only no roses right now. Guess I better come back in spring."

"That's a great idea. Can I hold you to it?" The look in Robyn's eyes needed no words.

"Okay then, let's move on to a totally new experience for you. This will give you endless stories to tell your city folk friends. And they'll be convinced I've lost my mind."

Driving to the opposite side of town, Claire pulled up to a long grey metal building. A huge sign proclaimed *Bygone Flea Market*.

"I am not going in that place!" Robyn said, crossing her arms. "Surely you don't go in a place like that. The name alone creeps me out. It sounds so dirty. Do you touch the stuff in there?"

"You'd be surprised by the things in my house that came from here or other places like it. This one is my favorite. It's really fun. Trust me. So, let's go junkin'!" Claire hopped out of the car and walked to the front and waited.

Robyn didn't move. Her arms still crossed, she gave Claire a stubborn frown.

Knowing her friend all too well, she decided to go on in and let Robyn stew for a while. Her curiosity would win out in time. Waving a cheery goodbye, Claire turned and walked through the apple green door.

Twenty minutes later, Claire was about to concede she had lost when she spied a hesitant Robyn walking through the door. Deciding it would be better to ignore her, Claire continued sifting through a stack of antique lace tablecloths. She was spreading one out on the table to check for stains when she felt movement behind her. Deciding not to make the first move, she focused hard on the small stain on one side of the cloth.

"That looks really old. Is it?" Robyn sidled up next to Claire. "Seems to be in good condition."

"It does. Think I'll get it. It's a great price."

"Sorry I acted like a spoiled brat. Forgive me?" Robyn reached out and hugged Claire.

"Sure, no problem. Ready to shop?"

~ ~ ~

Every aisle brought a new gift of nostalgia. Claire noticed within a short time an obvious softening in her friend's attitude.

"Look, Claire, remember when we had those same Madame Alexander dolls? Weren't we about ten?" Before she could answer,

Robyn squealed, "Oh my gosh, come here." Claire rushed to where Robyn danced in a circle.

"You are never going to believe what I just found! Proudly pulling a book from behind her back, her face beaming, she held a copy of *Anne of Green Gables* in front of her.

"You can get that at any book store," Claire said.

"Not a first edition, you can't." She opened the book to show Claire. "I'm buying this. It's only three dollars. Someone didn't know what they had." Excited by her find she tugged at Claire's arm. "Come on, who knows what's down the aisle."

After nearly an hour and a half of being dragged through the aisles, Claire was convinced she had created a junkaholic. But she hadn't seen Robyn this relaxed in years. It was worth every minute. Claire followed along behind, carrying Robyn's treasures until her arms were aching. "How about I take all this and have them hold it for us up front?" Robyn gave a slight nod but clearly her attention was focused on the next find.

Returning by a different aisle, Claire stopped dead in her tracks. *This is perfect,* she thought. *Talk about memories, she's going to freak out.*

When she reached Robyn, she took her hand and said, "Follow me now!" Returning to the next aisle over, Claire led her to a booth loaded with old hats, scarves, vintage clothing, and a fox stole like her grandmother used to wear.

"Let's play dress up! I've already asked the lady up front, and she said just be careful."

Digging through clothes of different decades of fashion filled their imaginations of days gone by.

"What about this?" Claire asked, slinking around the small booth in a Roaring Twenties outfit with matching hat.

"Oh, dahling, I love it. So chic. You can do the Charleston, can't you?" They laughed till their sides hurt. "Let me get a photo." Robyn pulled out her phone and snapped a shot of Claire in a dance move.

"Okay, it's your turn. Find something really sophisticated."

A few moments later Robyn presented herself in a large Audrey Hepburn hat and tight fitting dress. Claire grabbed her phone and took the shot; careful to include the protruding hint of Robyn's jeans hanging below the hem line.

An older man making his way toward their booth stared wide-eyed at the two. Robyn slunk toward him like a model on a runway and gave him her most engaging smile.

"You are just the man we need, dear sir. Would you be so very kind and take a picture of my friend and me?" The man stood soldier stiff nodding his head. Robyn showed him how to take the picture with her iPhone.

After taking shots of several poses, they thanked him and turned to go back to the booth. The man said, "Uh, ladies, can I ask you a question?"

Always the one to take the lead, Robyn replied, "Well, of course, dear man."

His face turned a deep red. "I was just, uh, wonderin'," he paused, ducking his head for a moment, "are y'all in the movie business?"

Claire bit her lip so hard she was afraid it might bleed. Robyn took the question like the attorney she was—head on. "My goodness, you are quite astute, aren't you? Let's just leave that for you to answer. I'm sure you will come to a good conclusion." Robyn gave him a wink and her most convincing smile.

When they were certain he was out of ear shot, they broke out laughing. "How could you do that and keep a straight face? Poor guy. I think he actually believes we're movie stars."

"Poor guy nothing, girl, we just made his day! He'll be bragging all over town he met two movie stars."

"Yeah, and what if I see him again? Remember, I live here, you don't."

"Oh, lighten up a little, Claire. If you see him again, swear him to secrecy or insinuate it's me not you."

Claire could only shake her head like so many times in the past. She never knew what to expect when she was with Robyn.

Once in the car she said, "So, seems like you had a good time after all."

"You know, I have to admit I did. When we first got there, I really thought you'd gone off the deep end, but it was a lot of fun. All but the smell."

"Too dusty?"

"No, I got over that okay. But the place smelled like cat pee!"

Claire turned to face her. "How do you know what cat pee smells like? You don't have a cat and never did."

"That's true, but I still say that's what it smelled like."

～ 43 ～

CLAIRE AND ROBYN BOTH AROSE EARLY to have some time together before Robyn had to leave for the airport. Wanting that alone time, they had left Mason sleeping.

Claire had coffee and two sweet rolls ready for them to attack. Taking the first bite, Robyn said, "Helen's?"

"Of course! Aren't they delicious?"

"Delicious doesn't even begin to describe them! Girl, I've tasted sweet rolls from almost every bakery in San Francisco and none come even close. Why do you think that is?"

"I already know. It's her secret ingredient."

"Really? Do you know what it is?"

"I sure do. It's called *love*."

Enjoying her last bite, Robyn turned to Claire, a concerned look on her face. "Claire, my dearest friend, on coming here my wish had been that you and Mason would be ready to return to San Francisco. But after this special week, I am convinced you are both happy and content here in your new home and community. You and I are true soul-sisters and will always be, for no distance will ever separate that." The look on both faces confirmed the commitment made years before. Holding one another in a long-held hug sealed a promise never to be broken.

Climbing the stairs, they quietly entered the room of one little boy obviously deep in dreamland. Sitting on opposite sides of his bed, together they tussled his hair awakening their precious "Tiger."

Sleepy eyes opening, he threw arms around both of them. "Mommy, Aunt Robbie. I sure do love you!"

Finally released from what seemed a never-ending hug, Claire said, "We love you too, Tiger, but you need to get dressed and come downstairs because Aunt Robbie is getting ready to go back to San Francisco."

"Don't leave, Aunt Robbie. Can't you stay longer?"

"I wish I could, sweetie, but it's time. So, you get dressed and come downstairs. I need your muscles to help me load my car. Can you do that?"

Raising both arms and flexing small biceps, he said, "You bet! I'm getting lots of muscles. See?"

~ ~ ~

Standing on the porch, arms wrapped around one another, Claire and Robyn watched with pride as one little boy made three trips to Robyn's rental car to carry two suitcases and one carry-on bag.

Running back to the porch, his words spoke volumes. "See, Aunt Robbie, I'm pretty strong!"

"You are strong indeed, Tiger," Robyn said, engulfing him in one last hug. "Okay if I kiss you on the cheek?"

"Sure thing! Men like kisses, don't we, Mom?"

Bringing Claire into the embrace, Robyn whispered, "One last hug, girlfriend. I love you."

"Love you back," Claire said, the words baptized by tears falling on Robyn's shoulder.

Hand in hand, the three walked to Robyn's car. She quickly loaded her bags in the trunk. Mason opened her door and bowed as he waved her to the seat. "See, Aunt Robbie, Dr. Mac is teaching me how to be a gentleman."

Before Robyn could close her door, Claire leaned in giving her best friend one final hug. "Call me as soon as you get home."

"Will do, love you." Closing the door, Robyn started the car and drove away, giving them a tearful wave.

Returning the wave, Claire whispered, "I'll miss you."

～ 44 ～

A DECISION HAD NIGGLED AT HER for days. Like walking into cobwebs, it clung to her thoughts. Plucking her phone from her pocket she dialed Reuben's number as she watched Mason's school bus drive away. There was no answer. He must've already left for work.

The cold air hit her face, and she stepped up her pace back to the house. She loved the morning walk with her son to the bus stop. There was a sweetness to these moments she would always cherish. Still somewhat groggy from sleep, he didn't try to cover up his tender side.

But they were still on a rocky path. Most days were normal. Then out of nowhere came the tantrum. She had become more and more convinced he was reacting to the loss of the men in his life. Another major adjustment for him. This wasn't how things were supposed to be. She'd thought when they got into the house everything would settle down. Those first two or three weeks she felt they'd achieved it. And the special time at Thanksgiving had been wonderful, but then the days went back to routine, and the tantrums escalated. Claire's hands trembled as she raked them through her hair.

She took the stairs two at a time to her bedroom. Grabbing for her hairbrush, she knocked over the picture of Randall she kept on the dresser. Picking up the frame, Claire brushed her fingers across the image of her husband's face. "Why aren't you here? My life is falling apart," she screamed, slamming the photo face down, breaking the glass as she crumpled onto the floor. "Why didn't you get someone else to take call and not go to the hospital that night?" Flinging her hairbrush across the room, she hugged her knees to her chest and sobbed.

"Your son needs you! I need you! Don't you see? You left us. You left us alone." A wave of nausea rushed over her, and she ran to the bathroom. She splashed cold water on her face and stared at her image in the mirror as she began to calm down.

The reflection showed someone she barely recognized. A woman on the verge of desperation. A chill ran through her body. She needed someone to talk to. And she knew that person was Reuben Walker. Something was drawing her to him. She had to find him.

Picking up the brush from where she'd thrown it, she ran it through her hair. Another glance at her pale face in the dresser mirror told her she needed to make a little more effort. When she reached for her lipstick, she saw Randall's picture still face down. She lifted it and looked into the eyes she knew so well, disfigured now by the broken glass. She whispered, "I'm sorry, but I have to go." She applied her lipstick and, decision made, went downstairs to gather her purse and keys to go ask Reuben for help.

This would be the day she'd become proactive about their lives. She refused to allow grief to suffocate them any longer. In the days since Robyn left, Claire had given their conversations a lot of thought. She thought of the guilt she had shared with Robyn and of Robyn's gentle but firm encouragement to move on with her life. Maybe it was the guilt she had kept buried so deep for so long that had kept her from really being able to release her pain and move forward.

Thinking about all this hadn't been easy. It hung over her making her deal with the truth. She knew it was time for her and her son to stop living in the past. She and Mason had said their goodbyes to Randall at the cemetery. But that did not tell her what their future would look like. She still had no idea, but for her child's sake she had to try. For now she had to find Reuben. It seemed to her that he could help her find that new direction. She decided to try the hardware store first.

~ ~ ~

Walking into Hank's Hardware never failed to transform the present into a time machine to the past. She had come to love the faint, musty smell of aged wood, the creaking floors, and the sound of the screen door slamming. She felt like a child again clutching her grandfather's hand and staring wide-eyed at the head of a buck whose blank gaze followed her every move. These days it was the deer head from Hank's taxidermy work that hung in that spot.

"Welcome, Miss Claire," came the quiet voice of the proprietor. "What can I do for you today?"

"Hello, Hank. Actually, I was wondering if Reuben was here."

"No, he isn't, ma'am. He's on a job, but you're welcome to run him down. He's repairing a fence row at the Martin place out on Deer Holler Road. Their name is on the mailbox, and their house has a brand new, bright red tin roof."

"Thanks, Hank, and say hi to Karen for me. I've missed seeing her with all the holiday preparations going on. I'd love for her to come out one day soon. Tell her I'll call."

Hank gave her a shy grin. "She'd like that very much. I'll let her know."

~ ~ ~

Claire had never been on Deer Holler Road. Pot holes seemed to make up most of the road. Some were so deep she wondered if the car would make it out of them. Breathing a sigh of relief when she saw the bright red roof up ahead, she steered the car into the driveway. Reuben's old green truck was the only vehicle around. As she got out of the car, she spied him down the fence row.

Claire honked the car horn a couple of times to alert him to her presence.

Reuben shielded his eyes from the sun's glare and squinted to see who was there. The moment he recognized her, he waved and came to greet her in long, quick strides. Wiping his brow with his bandana, he put out his hand, but Claire gave him a big hug instead.

"Well, you just made this day special, young lady. What a wonderful surprise. Let's go sit. I'm due for a break."

Inhaling the cold air, Claire snuggled deeper into her jacket and stuffed her hands into her pockets.

"How about some coffee? If I'd known you were coming, I would've put tea in this thermos." Reuben chuckled as he motioned to a bench looking out over the pasture.

"I hope this doesn't mess up your work schedule, Reuben, but I really need to talk to you if you can spare the time," Claire said, accepting the cup offered to her.

"No, no, I'm not on any set time frame, and I did need a break. Not as young and tough as I used to be." His eyes sparkled as he winked at her.

"Reuben, I'm concerned about Mason. I'm convinced he's missing all the interaction he's had with you, Mac, and Seth over these past months." Claire took a sip of the hot liquid, allowing it to warm her from the cold air. "It's been another big adjustment, and he's not handling it well. I never know from one day to the next what to expect from him. One minute he's the same happy little guy he used to be, and the next thing I know," she paused, "he's a little tyrant." Heavy sobs shook her body, and she hid her face in her hands.

Reuben slid an arm around her shoulders to comfort her. "Let it out, Claire," he said, his voice tender. "Tears can help bring healing."

When the sobs subsided, she turned to Reuben. "That's where Mason is, Reuben, and that doesn't even take into account what's going on with me. Oh, Reuben, some days I think I'm turning into a basket case. I see every fleck of dirt or dust on the floors and attack them with a vengeance. And I can't seem to stop rearranging the furniture. I'm scared I'm going to fall to pieces."

Never one to rush in with words or comments, Reuben gazed at the blue hills beyond the valley stretching before them. "That little guy's had a rough road to walk. And so has his mother," he said, patting her shoulder. "I'll help in any way I can, Claire. The two of you have become very special to me. I think of you as family. What are your thoughts? Anything specific you want me to do?"

Claire hadn't analyzed what she would like each of the men to do, but catching a glimpse of the fence row and Reuben's gloves draped on one of the posts, an idea popped in her head. "I hadn't thought of this until just now, Reuben, but you have so many wonderful practical skills. Would you teach some of those things to Mason? And Mac loves taking him fishing and having him help in the garden."

"And what about our young doctor?" A slow smile crept across Reuben's face.

Claire rubbed her forehead. "That's my dilemma. Mason is crazy about Seth. I just don't want him to get the wrong idea or have expectations that may never work out."

Reuben stood and motioned her to follow him to his truck. "Are you up to a little fence building?"

Claire stared at him. "I've never built a fence." Her startled expression made Reuben laugh.

"Well, Ms. Westfield, a lady as talented as you should have no problem pounding a few nails. We'll continue this conversation while we work. But come spring I'll give you a real challenge. You and I can repair that old rock wall around your house."

"You know me too well, Reuben Walker. You know I can never turn down a challenge. You're on. Give me a hammer!"

Reaching his truck and opening a large tool box, he gave her a hammer and a can of nails and said, "Hard work helps solve a lot of problems, doesn't it?"

She nodded and said, "Let's get to it."

Reuben reached for his work gloves and passed them to Claire. "Can't have a lovely lady getting blisters." When Claire tried to refuse, Reuben waved a hand at her and bent to pick up a plank. Taking the hint, she slid her hands into the gloves. The leather was well-worn from years of hard work. Turning her palms up she stared at the finger tips. Several were worn through the leather, merely gaping holes staring back at her. She instinctively lifted them to her face catching the smell of sweat, oil, and grime. Instead of recoiling from it, she inhaled it again. The gloves were loose on her hands, reminding her of their owner's size.

Who was Reuben Walker, this man whose large hands had worn through leather? She thought of the countless times he'd pat her arm or hand. His hands were rough from the work he did, but his touch was always gentle.

~ ~ ~

Claire's arms ached as they heaved another plank between

the next two posts and then pounded the nails into it. The work stretched her physically but also energized her. As the tension in her arms eased, she looked at the man working at the next fence post. What was his story?

"Reuben, you've learned quite a bit about me in the time we've spent together, but I know hardly anything about you—with the exception of what a wonderful man you are." She laughed as she watched his face turn bright red.

"Why, Mr. Walker, I think I embarrassed you! I didn't mean to, but what I said is the truth. Were you just born wonderful? Would you tell me your story, Reuben? I want to understand what makes a man like you tick. You seem to have such a great outlook on life. And people are instantly drawn to you. Mason and I certainly were."

Leaning down, he took a nail from the can, stuck it between his teeth and then picked up another plank. "It's a long story, Claire, and most of it is not very pretty."

"Reuben, I know 'not very pretty,' believe me. If you don't want to tell me that's fine. I understand."

Claire grabbed her own nail and picked up the other end of the plank. In unison they attacked the posts, the sound of hammers against wood echoing in the stillness.

"I was a troubled boy who became a troubled young man." Reuben stuck another nail in the plank and pounded it in. "My father worked odd jobs when he was sober. My mother did the best she could to nurture me, but holding down two jobs left her with little time or energy."

Reuben sighed before going on. "My parents died when I was twelve years old. My dad was drunk and ran off the road, killing them both. I was home alone when the police came and told me they were dead."

Claire gasped. "Oh, Reuben, how terrible. I'm so sorry."

"It was terrible, but it just kept getting worse." Reuben's gaze drifted toward the hills beyond them as though drawing him back in time. "None of my extended family wanted me," he said so softly Claire almost missed it. "I got sent to an orphanage near St. Louis. That's where I lived until I ran away when I was sixteen."

They reached for another rail at the same time. The air had grown colder, and Claire zipped her jacket up to her neck to break its sting. Their teamwork improved with each new section of the fence. Claire looked over her shoulder, amazed at their progress.

"Weren't you frightened? Where were you planning to go?"

"I had a plan, one I'd thought about for some time." He struck a nail into the wood with one powerful blow.

"At the orphanage everyone, even the little ones had a job. Mine was to help the man in charge of the yard crew. I was a good sized kid for my age and really strong."

They worked in silence for some time, each drifting into their own thoughts. *Why couldn't life be as simple as hammering nails into these fence posts?* Claire wondered. Only the sound of the hammers broke the quiet. After completing several sections, Claire asked, "Where did you plan to go?"

Reuben rubbed his hand over his beard, once again deep in thoughts of the past. "The man I worked with was quite a talker. He went on and on about how one day he was goin' to Steubenville, Ohio, and get himself one of those good jobs at the steel mill. He also talked about 'ridin' the rails' to get there. I couldn't figure out why he never pursued it. So that became my plan. I'd do what he only talked about doin'. By that time the orphanage was feeling like a prison."

What had been only a chilly breeze had turned into a biting wind. Reuben looked over at Claire. Even the determined look plastered on her face couldn't conceal how cold she was.

"I think it's time we wrap this up for today. Don't want to lose you to frostbite," he said and reached out and took her hammer. "You are some kind of great help, young lady, I must say." Reuben smiled as he put an arm around her. "Let's get you into your car and get the heater going."

Claire nodded, welcoming the thought of heat. Once in her car with the heater turned to high, she saw Reuben coming with two more mugs of coffee. She motioned him to get in the passenger seat.

"What are you doing for dinner?" she asked, clinging to the mug for extra warmth. "Mason's having a sleepover at J.J.'s tonight.

How about coming to my place for some leftovers?"

"Sounds wonderful, but I don't want to be an imposition. You worked really hard this afternoon."

"Reuben Walker, let's get one thing straight. You will never be an imposition! Now that's settled. I made some of my grandmother's hash yesterday. All I have to do is warm it up. Besides, you have to finish your story. Don't think I'm going to let you get out of it."

~ 45 ~

CLAIRE WARMED THE HASH AND PUT some yeast rolls in the oven while Reuben built a fire in the fireplace. Both had agreed that in front of the fireplace was the place to eat on this cold night.

As Reuben stoked the fire, he hummed a tune that sounded familiar to Claire. "What song are you humming?"

"Didn't even realize I was doing it out loud," he said. "Can't seem to help myself when I'm in this place. It was your grandparents' favorite hymn. We spent many a time right here talking, singing, praying. Guess it just seemed a natural thing to do."

"What's the name of it? It sounds familiar."

Standing by the fire and rubbing his hands together, the look in Reuben's eyes seemed to transport him back to another time.

"Reuben? Are you okay?"

"Sorry about that. Just so many memories. Your grandparents were special people, Claire. They meant the world to me. I still miss them; especially when I'm in this house. The hymn is "Great is Thy Faithfulness.""

"Would you sing it for me? The rolls have several minutes yet. Oh, and wait, I'll be right back." Running into her study, she retrieved Potch's guitar and handed it to Reuben. "Seth told me you play." Claire curled up in the chair next to the hearth and waited.

Reuben spent some time tuning the guitar, his face reflecting mixed emotions. His eyes filled with tears as he began to play and sing

"Great is Thy faithfulness, O God my Father,
There is no shadow of turning with Thee;
Thou changest not, Thy compassions, they fail not.

321

As Thou hast been Thou forever wilt be.
Great is Thy faithfulness!
Great is Thy faithfulness!
Morning by morning new mercies I see;
All I have needed Thy hand hath provided.
Great is Thy faithfulness,
Lord, unto me.
Pardon for sin. And a peace that endureth,
Thine own dear presence to cheer and to guide;
Strength for today and bright hope for tomorrow,
Blessings all mine, with ten thousand beside."

They sat in comfortable silence, each with their own thoughts. When the timer for the rolls broke the quiet, Claire stood and moved to get them. As she walked by her guest, she bent down and kissed the top of his head. "I remember the song. Thank you." He took her hand and held it for a long moment.

The conversation as they ate focused on Mason and ways Reuben could interact with him. Later, as Claire added scoops of ice cream on warm brownies, Reuben brought up the idea of a dog. When he recounted the scene at Thanksgiving of Mason jumping into a pile of leaves and proclaiming that he needed a good dog, they both laughed. Reuben told how he, Mac, and Seth had looked at each other at the same time in silent agreement.

"Do you really think a dog could help?" Claire asked, uncertainty creasing her brow.

"In all honesty, I do." Reuben savored a spoonful of brownie and ice cream. "This is wonderful, Claire! I rarely give myself permission to eat sweets. Now I remember why—my love of them! Ah, Mason and a dog. There are many wonderful ways a dog can help all of us. I know because I experienced this help in some of my darkest days. Do you still want to hear the rest of my story?" When Claire nodded, he stared into the fire seeming to draw the memories from the flames.

"So how did you end up in Mason Falls?" Claire asked.

"Well, after two years of cleanin' bathrooms at one of those steel mills the guy had talked about, I was ready for a change. When the war in Vietnam started, I decided that was my ticket to a better life. It scared me to no end thinkin' about going off to war, but life so far hadn't offered much either. I signed up at the recruiter's office. When I started boot camp, my life took a turn for the better. That's where I met George Meyers. He was the biggest guy I'd ever seen and our friendship was one of those that seemed meant to be." He paused. "Probably like yours and Robyn's."

Claire scooted to the edge of her chair, hanging on every word. She'd never heard this gentle man say this much, but even more unbelievable, he was sharing his life story with her.

Reuben finished off his tea and moved to stand by the fireplace. The glow of the embers reflected in his eyes.

"George talked about Arkansas and his family all the time. I was fascinated by his stories and the closeness of his family. When he insisted I come here with him when we finished our stint in Vietnam, it was difficult, actually make that impossible, to say no.

"He had told me so much about his family I felt I already knew them. So, I decided it would be a great way to transition back into civilian life. Going to Arkansas would give me time to come up with a plan for the future.

"What I didn't count on was fallin' in love with this small town and its people. One person in particular played a major role in my decision to stay. I fell in love with George's sister Lois the moment I saw her. The more I got to know her, the more convinced I was we were made for each other."

Claire moved to stand next to him by the fire. The comfort of its warmth calling to her. "I wish I'd known her, Reuben. She must have been a wonderful woman." He nodded, his eyes filling with tears as he turned toward the fire.

"Lois was life itself to me. We were married six months after I met her. We both wanted a large family. Me because I'd never had one and Lois because that was all she'd ever known." Claire was mesmerized by the man she now realized she'd never really known.

"The happiest moment of my life," Reuben said, "was the night she told me she was pregnant. We'd been tryin' for three years. That night we sat by a fire, much like this one, and talked of all that was ahead. We pictured a house full of rambunctious children and thought of names for each one."

Claire returned to her chair to hear the story of Reuben and Lois Walker. There was no sound except the crackle of the fire, and she found herself holding her breath.

"You're a parent so you understand," Reuben said, his voice cracking, "how anxious you are when it's time for that little one to enter this world. Like any soon-to-be father, I spent those hours at the hospital drinkin' coffee and pacin' the floor. When the doctor emerged looking grim and shaken, I knew the news would be bad. It was worse than I could have imagined as the doctor told me they lost not only Lois but our little son as well." Reuben rubbed the back of his neck trying to regain his composure.

"Overcome by shock, I stumbled toward the exit. The doctor tried his best to get me to wait and call someone to come get me, but I just pushed him aside. When I reached the front steps of the hospital, I stood there in a torrential rain, screamin' into the dark, stormy night. I remember yellin' at God, demandin' to know why He would let the sweetest, most gentle woman I'd ever known die. Then I screamed at Him for taking my innocent little son." Reuben's face grew pale, and he lowered his head into his hands.

Paralyzed with emotion, Claire bit her lower lip trying not to burst out crying. Her own memories rose up like a tidal wave rushing over her, bringing with it the salty taste of countless shed tears since the night she lost Randall. But she still had her son. She hadn't been left totally alone like Reuben. As hard as things had been, her heart swelled with thankfulness that she hadn't lost her son as well.

Reuben's pain and look of exhaustion broke Claire's heart, and she tried to convince him to stop.

"Claire, sweet lady, I need to do this. For me but also for you. I've come to realize that at some point we need to verbalize our pain, our anger, and our confusion over the loss of those we love. When we do that, and if we're willing to allow God to be part of it, that's when I believe we can begin to experience healing." Reuben eased himself back into his chair.

"The pain will always be with us, Claire, but I can tell you that if we allow Him to, God will ease the fierceness of it. He becomes the healer of our heart. And I've also learned that as time passes, He can use that pain and loss to help others who've suffered in similar ways. I'll leave it up to you. Do you want me to keep going?"

Claire's mouth had gone dry. She nodded for him to continue. She ached to know how he had walked through all that sorrow and become the person she knew today.

"At some point I collapsed onto the steps, drenched from the rain, but not havin' the will to get up," Reuben said, his voice just above a whisper. "Sometime later I vaguely sensed the rain had stopped momentarily, and the doctor was standin' behind me asking me to come back inside. He went on to say he had called George, and he was on his way to get me. I remember snarlin' at the doctor that I didn't want his help, and I didn't want to see George. I just wanted to be alone. Alone like I would be from then on and like I had been my entire life. Then I yelled at him to get away from me." Reuben's hands shook and he rubbed them together trying to get control.

"I'm sorry, Claire," he said, choking out the words. "Even after all these years, I remember it as though it were today." The look on his face was the picture of a shattered heart.

"Oh Reuben, I'm so sorry. So very sorry. I know exactly how you feel. I just thought your life had not seen any pain," she murmured. "You have such a peace about you."

Would she ever come to a place of peace in her life? She wasn't sure. This man, her dear friend, had been through so much. The loss of both parents and then to lose the love of his life and his son. How had he become the man he was now?

"Reuben, this is so painful for you. Please, don't feel you have to go on."

"I want to finish the story, Claire. It's never easy, but I want you to hear it. Are you okay with that?" She nodded for him to continue.

In a low voice, Reuben said, "I felt the doctor pat my shoulder, then heard the splashin' of his footsteps as he left me. I had not moved from the rain soaked steps. I was hunched over my knees, my shoes were filled with water, and my clothes were saturated. Memories of the war overwhelmed me. I had tried so hard to erase those scenes, but in the darkness of that moment, they were back . . . hauntin' me more than ever before.

"When Lois became a part of my life, her love and gentle ways had helped the memories of Nam fade somewhat. But when I lost her and our baby, it was like the most vicious storm I could imagine, all those gory images hittin' me head on. Images of mothers clutchin' their children. All dead. All lyin' in the mud. Always the mud. It never seemed to go away."

Claire gasped at the horror of what was still haunting her friend. She too had thoughts of images that haunted her. Images of the car hitting Randall and dragging his broken body down the highway. She clasped her hand over her mouth to keep from crying out. She had not seen it first-hand like Reuben had, but it was just as real to her.

"I can still hear my scream piercin' that dark rainy night, 'No! Not my wife! Not my child!' And the only answer was the thunder as it echoed back at me.

"Then more questions assaulted me, and I couldn't hold in my anger at God. I shook my fist in the air yellin' at Him. 'Haven't I seen enough death for a lifetime? Didn't I do enough to try and help others? Why, God? Why would You do this to me? To my family?' I started hurling questions at God. 'Is it because I've never paid much attention to You? Do You hate me that much? Why don't You just take me too? That's fine with me since I have nothing to live for now.' I was boiling mad by then. That's when I slammed my fist on the concrete step. I didn't know until later I had broken it."

Recognizing the emotional strain on her dear friend, Claire again tried to convince him to stop.

Determined to continue, he went on. "I don't know how long I was out there on those steps until George came and helped me up. I do remember that the lightning lit up the darkness and thunder cracked above me. The rain had started again. Then I felt George's strong arms help me stand as he said, 'C'mon, buddy, let's get out of this stuff. We got enough of it in Nam, didn't we?'

"I vaguely remember him taking me to the emergency room to get my hand treated. On leavin' the hospital, he tried to get me to go home with him or to let him stay with me, but I just wanted to be alone. George got me in my house, then he hugged me good-bye. I dropped onto the sofa, weariness and sorrow overwhelmin' me. Sadly, I didn't consider that George had to be grievin' too. He had lost his youngest sister.

"Just before I fell asleep, I realized for the first time how much my hand hurt. But even in my groggy state of mind I knew it would eventually heal. My heart though, seared as it was with the pain of loss, I feared would never heal.

"Memories of Vietnam again filled my mind. Scenes I had tried time and again to erase came out of hiding. The same shroud of darkness that held them wrapped itself around me in a new agony.

"It's hard to say this but there comes a time in war where you train yourself to tuck your emotions in a safe place where one day you'll be able to feel again. In the heat of battle, there is no time to reflect or to grieve. Mortar rounds are dropping everywhere. Friends, buddies being blown to pieces. No time to comfort them or even be there for their last breath. Only the thought of survival.

"Just like those times in battle, I wasn't able to be there with the love of my life or my newborn son. I hadn't been there to comfort her or our little boy. In Vietnam I always had the gut feeling I would make it. I would survive. At the moment I lost my wife and child, I had no such thoughts. My heart had died that night. I couldn't imagine life without Lois or the son I would never get to know. Once again, I was alone, and this time I was more alone than I had ever been in the past.

"In the two years after I'd lost Lois and little David, I pretty much had given up on life. I lived alone in a shack in the woods. I only did enough odd jobs to support myself. Most of the time I just fished, hunted, and tinkered with odds and ends of small machinery. It was an okay kind of life for me durin' those days.

"Then George put me in touch with Henry Bedwell. He needed some work done around his place, and George had told him I could fix or build anything. I had no idea what was ahead of me the first day I went to work for Henry."

Claire saw the familiar sparkle return to Reuben's eyes and she sat up straighter in her chair in anticipation. She felt like a child again in this very house listening to her grandfather's stories. "So who was Henry Bedwell, Reuben?"

Reuben stroked his beard and his brilliant blue eyes glistened. "Well now, Henry Bedwell was a man who had lost his wife and little girl in a house fire and didn't care whether he lived or died. World War II had just begun, so he joined the army. While fighting in France, Henry was seriously wounded from an enemy artillery explosion. His platoon commander, also wounded, carried him on his back through a hailstorm of ongoing shrapnel to reach the medics. Sadly, Henry's wounds required amputation of both his legs. Lyin' in his army hospital bed, he cried out to God to help him. His prayer was answered when one of his young army doctors began visitin' Henry after finishing his rounds. He not only helped Henry's wounds to heal but also helped his heart find healin' in the days ahead.

"That young doctor started sharin' with Henry how much Jesus loved him and that in God's scheme of things, there is a perfect purpose for all He allows.

"As Henry and I got to know each other, he shared more of his story with me. He told me that no matter how tired that doctor was after a long, gruelin' day, he would come by to check on him. He'd read something from the Bible to Henry then pray for him to experience God's great love, peace, and comfort even in his difficult circumstances."

Spellbound by Henry's story, Claire twirled a lock of her hair the way she had done as a child listening to Potch. "Then what happened, Reuben?"

"When he recovered enough to leave the hospital, they sent him to a tiny village in England. Lord and Lady Crenshaw had opened their manor to recoverin' soldiers, both English and American. That's where he began the long process of learnin' how to care for himself.

"Watching Henry make the best of his life taught me some valuable lessons. We developed a strong and binding friendship.

Watchin' him live life to the fullest," Reuben said, choking back tears, "had a profound effect on me."

He grew quiet for a moment and stared into the fire. Claire stayed still, not wanting to break the moment.

"Are you ready for the conclusion to that part of my life?" Reuben said with a smile.

Claire nodded her answer.

"Henry became a mentor to me. I hung on every word he said. But I saw someone most people would pity living a contented, peaceful life—from a wheelchair. It changed me. The walls I'd build around me were beginning to crumble, and the anger and bitterness began to melt.

"Then late one afternoon I listened as this man shared that God loved me so much He allowed His own Son to die for me so I could have a brand new life. Desperately needin' such a life, I knelt before this legless man and poured out my heart to God askin' Him to let Jesus come into my life and love me like He loved Henry.

"At that moment, Claire, I became a new person. Light filled my eyes, hope filled my heart, and I saw life as I had never known it could be. I was so overcome by God's love for me, I just started tryin' to love the people around me just like Henry had done for me.

"Before old Henry went to meet his Savior, he whispered to me, 'God means your life to count for something, son. Give to others what you were given yourself, and your legacy will be eternal."

Reuben put another log on the fire, stoking it as he said, "Remember you asked me if I thought a dog would be good for Mason? Let me tell you why I feel it could help him. After accepting Jesus as my Savior, my life began to turn around, and I began to once again find joy and contentment—but I was still lonely. Then this dog found his way into my life. For some reason he had chosen me and kept appearin' at odd times.

"One day when I was cuttin' wood, I spied him out of the corner of my eye. It was blisterin' cold, and I'd been at it for a couple of hours. That dog stayed right there on that cold ground the whole time.

"I decided to take a break and warm up. I went to my truck,

climbed in, and turned on the heat. I got my thermos and poured myself a cup of coffee. Well, that dog sauntered over and sat on that cold ground staring straight at me. It was downright spooky the way he looked at me. Like he wanted to say, 'Hey, I'm here for you.' Sounds crazy, huh? So I opened the door, and he hopped right up— spillin' coffee all over both of us.

"Today people say they get a rescue dog. I'm here to tell you, it's the dogs that rescue us more than the other way around. I named him Scamp. I'm convinced God sent him to me. And you know what? Before I knew it, I had a family, and that family just keeps growing. It's made up of every age, race, and creed. I am a man blessed beyond anything I could have imagined. That's my story. And now it's gettin' late, sweet lady, and we're both tired."

Reuben insisted on helping Claire do the dishes before leaving. Their conversation turned to lighter topics, but Claire knew the memory of this evening would be one she would always cherish.

~ 46 ~

STARING OUT HIS OFFICE WINDOW, SETH found himself massaging his temples, his longtime stress reliever.

Hadn't he made peace with himself about his time in Mason Falls? The time since Thanksgiving at Claire's had flown by. He enjoyed spending occasional time with her and Mason, often in the warm company of Helen and Mac or Reuben. His time with Reuben was so important to him. Yet with all this, another phone call from Chad Peters had unsettled him again. It also awakened the longing for Kansas City that he tried to hide from those around him. What was his true reason for wanting to be there? Rain drops plopped against the window like a minor chord across his heart.

He thought about the positive things he'd learned here from Dr. Mac, especially about interacting with patients. Couldn't he demonstrate Dr. Mac's art of medicine in the science of medicine arena?

He had to admit that during his clinic rotation time at the Hawthorn Clinic, he'd found it rather cold emotionally. Everyone did their job well, but he'd never sensed the warmth and unhurried time that was given to patients here. In Dr. Mac's practice, Seth noticed the efforts made to make patients comfortable and feel more at ease. Of course, to be honest with himself, he'd never given this part of medicine much thought when he'd done the rotation with the younger Dr. Hawthorn. He'd been so excited to get that opportunity, he'd probably overlooked any deficiencies. Now he could honestly see the incredible impact "hands on" medicine played in the doctor-patient relationship. The simple pat on an arm or shoulder or taking a few extra minutes just to listen could actually help the healing process.

And under Reuben's encouraging instruction, Seth had started reading the Gospel of John in the Bible. The words were like food to his hungry soul. He pictured the man Jesus walking through the countryside kicking at the rocks along the roads, talking and laughing with His companions, sweat drenching His clothing and dust blowing through His hair. He would have been a rugged man with calloused hands like Reuben's from working as a carpenter. But there was something else about Him. This man, the son of God, walked the earth He had formed, experiencing life with those He had created. Jesus had looked straight into the hearts of those around Him and knew their specific needs.

Seth let his mind wander back to those long ago days. What would it have been like to gaze into the eyes of the One who knew you better than you knew yourself? But wasn't that what had happened to him? Seth still couldn't explain it, but he'd never been as sure of anything in his life as the fact that he had met Jesus and become a changed man.

The weight of anger, confusion, and heartache he'd carried for so long had been lifted from him. He knew there would always be scars from those years, but he was free. A whole new life stretched out before him. When Reuben told Seth that the book of Luke was written by a physician, he couldn't wait to discover what a man of science had to say about Jesus. What he'd read struck him to his core.

Jesus loved people. It didn't matter if they were rich or poor, powerful or slaves. If they needed His healing touch and reached out to Him, He reached out in compassion to meet their needs. A picture formed in Seth's mind of what he'd been reading in the Bible about Jesus healing people and caring for their needs. What hit him right between the eyes as a physician himself was the account in Luke of Jesus reaching out to touch a man with leprosy. Seth had never seen anyone with leprosy, but he'd seen plenty of pictures in his medical books. It was a terrible disease, disfiguring a person to such a degree they might become unrecognizable.

Jesus could have just spoken to the man but He showed His compassion by reaching out to touch him. Seth wondered what the man's skin felt like—rough and leathery or slick and smooth? Was there a foul stench due to decay? Would he, a doctor, choose to touch or embrace a person with this disease the way Jesus did?

The whole concept of Jesus's healings was transforming Seth as a physician. Regret for all the times he'd left a patient without offering words of encouragement or comfort weighed on his heart. He had been more of a robot than a healer. He knew if he did go back to Kansas City, he had more to offer patients than simply a diagnosis. He could offer them what Reuben was always talking about. Reuben said to give them heaven! Let the love of Jesus flow through him. That's the light that shines.

Jesus didn't set up practice with some high scale group of healers or in a beautiful building. He just walked along the same dusty roads the average person walked. Questions kept swimming around in Seth's mind. Did he belong in Kansas City or did he belong in Mason Falls? Was it his pride that demanded a position in the well-respected clinic? Did he think he was too good a doctor to practice in this small town?

When the time came to make a decision, he hoped God would make the answer clear to him.

~ 47 ~

WINTER IN THE OZARKS STIRRED CLAIRE's joyful anticipation of Christmas. Snow wasn't typical this time of year but with all her heart, Claire wished this year would be different. She wanted her son, who had never seen snow, to feel the wonder of the soft flakes on his face as he experienced it on their first Christmas in their new home.

Claire found herself checking her watch again. Robyn was driving in from the airport during this busy holiday travel time. Claire wanted to pick her up, but as usual, Robyn reported she was quite able to drive herself. Claire didn't doubt that, but the drive back together would have been a great time to catch up for the two of them. She was glad they would have a little time to spend together this afternoon since Mason was at Helen's making Christmas cookies.

Another glance at her watch reminded her Robyn would arrive soon. She looked around her wonderful old house and sensed the precious moments it had collected and saved. The Christmas tree looked beautiful, gifts were wrapped, and much of the food preparation was complete. She was excited about tomorrow night, Christmas Eve, when they all would go to the barn for a surprise. Reuben had built a fire pit, and Claire had filled some of her grandmother's jelly jars with sand, adding a small candle to each one. Tomorrow night she would light them to line the path to the barn.

"Thank you, Potch and Honey, for not only this house but for all the memories. Tears filled her eyes at the thought of her grandparents standing here with her. They would be so thrilled to see their home filled with the people who would be celebrating this Christmas together.

Wiping her tears, she made herself return to her to-do list. She was finishing the last item on her list when she heard a car in the driveway. She rushed outside to welcome her friend. Engulfed in welcoming hugs, they both cried, then laughed. They were together again!

Claire helped Robyn carry her luggage into the house. Robyn stood silent for several minutes then squealed with joy. "Girlfriend, you definitely have the touch! It's all so beautiful."

Robyn insisted on a walk-through to see all the decorations. Then she and Claire headed toward the kitchen to make tea. Being together again brought back memories of so many times they had shared just like this one. They settled in at the kitchen table, contentedly picking up old conversations and adding new ones.

Tea and conversation time was interrupted by the doorbell and Mason rushing in loaded with cardboard boxes sure to be filled with wonderful goodies and Helen following right behind him. After placing the boxes carefully on the table, Mason made a beeline to Robyn. He came close to knocking her down in his enthusiasm, but she grabbed him up swinging him around until they both had to sit down. Claire and Helen smiled at their enthusiastic greeting. Hugs were given all around before Helen said her goodbyes, assuring them she and Mac would see them all tomorrow.

~ ~ ~

Christmas Eve day arrived with clouds that hinted of snow. After breakfast Mason pulled a chair up to the large window in the living room and stared at the sky. His mind was in his own world hoping for the flakes to come. The day was busy with preparations but also filled with joy and anticipation. Everyone was given a task to help move things forward. Seth called to see what he could do to help. Claire said, "Get Mason out of the house for a while. We need to get the 'surprise' ready."

"I'm on the way, fair lady. Have no fear."

Claire couldn't help but laugh. "Get yourself over here immediately, Mister." It seemed only seconds before the doorbell rang.

Mason yelled, "Hey, Mom, Dr. Seth is here!"

Leading Mason out of the house, Seth said, "Don't worry, I've got this."

With perfect timing, the air filled with snowflakes to the delight of all. Robyn was almost as entranced as Mason with the beauty of the falling snow. Claire demonstrated the fine art of catching snowflakes with your tongue. Even Seth joined in. As the snow continued to fall, dusting the ground, Seth challenged Mason to follow his snowprint trail to the meadow. With the challenge accepted, man and boy headed out for their adventure.

Claire and Robyn both breathed a sigh of relief and began getting things ready for the evening. Mac and Helen were on their way to bring something special to Claire. When they arrived, Claire and Robyn went out to meet them, eager to find out what they were bringing. The "something" was quite large, covered with a tarp, and took up most of the back of Mac's jeep. With all hands helping, they carried it to the barn.

When Mac brushed off the snow and removed the tarp, Claire gasped. Overwhelmed, she gazed at a beautiful wooden creche. She hadn't thought of it in years, but then memories of helping Potch and Honey set it up on Christmas Eve flooded her. It wasn't until she was grown that she had been told that Potch had made each piece. And now Mac was telling her that Potch had entrusted the creche to him and Helen with the hope that one day it would go to Claire.

Tears flowed all around as Robyn, Mac, and Helen watched Claire cradle each well-oiled piece. Mac walked over, put his arms around her, and said, "Your granddaddy would be so thrilled to have you accept this gift. He put his heart and soul into every inch of this work of art."

Claire waved Helen over and wrapped her arms around them both, her emotions overwhelming her. When she finally was able to speak, she held their hands and said, "Thank you both. I am overwhelmed with joy and appreciation for the two of you doing this for me. You are my family!"

Herself choking back tears, Helen said, "This is a special way to celebrate this very special evening. Claire, I truly believe your Potch and Honey are rejoicing in Heaven at this very moment."

~ ~ ~

Later that evening after a fine meal together, everyone bundled up and walked the lighted path to the barn. Mason could barely contain his excitement as he looked in wonder at the luminaries lighting the way and the dancing flames in the fire pit in front of the barn doors. The fire wasn't as large as the bonfire from the scrap wood in the fall that had excited Mason, but it was much better for roasting marshmallows. Reuben had slipped way and gotten the fire started while everyone was getting into coats, hats, scarves, and gloves. Claire, Robyn, and Helen had cookies and thermoses of hot cocoa and coffee already laid out. Mason dragged Seth directly to the S'mores makings.

After enjoying their feast around the fire, they moved into the barn to sit on hay bales Reuben had arranged at Claire's direction. The fire danced and give light and a little warmth. Mac read the Christmas story in the second chapter of Luke from Potch's worn and well-read Bible. When he finished, Mason told everyone that this was just like the night baby Jesus was born. Reuben brought out his guitar, and Helen in her beautiful soprano voice led them in singing *Silent Night* and flowing into other favorite carols. Bringing the night of song to a close, Mason led Mac, Reuben, and Seth in a rousing rendition of *Rudolph the Red Nosed Reindeer*. As they took their combined bow, Mason proudly exclaimed, "We guys sure sing great! "

Once their friends had left and both Robyn and Mason were tucked in their respective beds, Claire's mind replayed the special moments of the day before she drifted off. Moments that would be long remembered with the added blessing that there were still many more times to come to add to her library of "cherished memories" in their new home.

~ 48 ~

AT THE END OF A BUSY day at the clinic, everyone had gone home except Seth. Sitting at his desk, he reached into the middle drawer and pulled out a small black Moleskin notebook. A deep sigh escaped him as he opened the volume. Flipping through the pages, he found the entry for his Kansas City-Mason Falls pro and con list.

The list had grown since receiving the most recent call from Chad at the Hawthorn clinic. It now filled several pages. He had divided it into separate entries, one for Kansas City and one for Mason Falls.

He glanced down the list for Kansas City. Under pro he had written: *nice restaurants, Nelson Atkins Art Museum, and Loose Park.* He'd run many a mile in all kinds of weather in that park. An entry for Westport stirred memories of an occasional night out, the perfect hangout place for the under forty age group. Season tickets for the Kansas City Royals and Chiefs had a star beside it. This would be his gift to himself. It was something he had dreamed of on those long nights covering the ER or making rounds when he fought exhaustion, trying to stay alert.

Most of the entries related to medicine. Taking call every fifth weekend had two stars beside it. He found himself at times trying to imagine having that much time off. And if he did, what would he do with it?

He scanned through several notes related to interactions with colleagues. Seth had no regrets of going into family practice. But being around different specialists stoked a fire in him, making him want to grow and be the best he could be.

Turning to the con list, the jolt of what he saw stunned him. Using his finger to move down the list, Seth read one name after

338

another of the people he had come to care about. At the top of the list he had written "Leaving."

Swiveling his chair, he gazed at the maple tree outside his office window. The brilliance of spring green was accentuated by the dark brown, almost black of the trunk. Its beauty touched a place deep inside him. He didn't understand why but it made him more reflective.

Seth turned the pages in the Moleskin until he came to the entries for Mason Falls. Once again he began to scan what he had written under "pro." The first thing was that there didn't seem to be any strangers in this town. The second thing he had written was that when he walked into a store everyone called him by name or they called him Doc. In parentheses, he had noted that in KC, he was just another customer. Next, he had written that his patients were also becoming friends. His eyes fell on a list of special relationships that had developed: Reuben, Claire, Mason, Mac and Helen.

Several notes reminded him of areas of change in his perspective of small town medical care. Some were related to his misconceptions. He had thought there wouldn't be enough challenging and varied medical conditions in a small town to keep his passion alive. He'd pictured monotonous days seeing cases of sore throats, runny noses, and the occasional case of poison ivy. But this proved to be just the opposite in cases he was seeing.

In one surprising comment he had written that the need to treat conditions such as cancer as opposed to just diagnosing the disease and then referring the patient to an oncologist had both challenged and honed his medical skills. He had also noted that his increased diagnostic abilities boosted his confidence about the quality of care he could give his patients. As Seth reflected on this, he realized that more than anything, he had learned how important it was to dig deeper in establishing doctor-patient rapport.

Seth laid the book down and got up to stretch. He felt hungry, so he walked to the break room. The deserted halls and empty rooms felt a little strange after the activities and sounds of the day. He grabbed a drink from the fridge, the can cold in his hand. He popped the tab, took a long swallow, and peered in to see what might be left to snack on. Finding leftover cheese dip, Seth put some in a bowl, set it in the microwave, and punched in thirty seconds on the timer. Scrounging through the cabinets, he discovered an almost empty Fritos bag then went to retrieve the dip. His growling stomach complained of neglect just as he put everything on the small Formica-top table. He had often wondered just how many years that table had been there. He made a mental note to ask Sodie Tucker, the unofficial clinic historian.

The taste of warm cheese and the crunch of the chips helped ease his hunger, but it also became clear he needed more. A giant burger at The Singing Dog Café would be just the ticket. Seth gulped down the rest of his drink and cleaned up his mess.

When he returned to his office to turn off the light, Seth noticed the little Moleskin journal, still open. He picked it up, stuffed it in his shirt pocket, and walked to the back door.

The Singing Dog Café's unspoken welcome to all who ventured through the door was, 'Beware, frantic premises, enter at your own risk!' Seth opened the door preparing himself for the first blast of noise.

Nothing. No one. In place of the usual deafening roar, quiet filled the place. Seth peered around the room but saw no one. Just as he turned to leave, he heard a voice from the kitchen area.

"Hey, Doc. Don't leave. We're open, believe it or not." Hap Carter, the owner, came around the corner, still in his apron. Hap reached out to shake hands with Seth.

"You're surprised," he said, "aren't you, Doc? Once in a great while we'll have a night like this. Had three couples earlier, and they reacted just like you. Kind of nice though, isn't it?" Hap grinned at Seth. "Go ahead and sit down. You want the usual to drink?" Seth nodded. "Take a look at the menu, I'll be right back."

True to his word, Hap returned with Seth's usual sweet tea. It had become almost an addiction with him.

"You order whatever you want. Just because it's slow doesn't mean we weren't ready for a bigger crowd."

"I already know, Hap. I want your giant burger and fries. I'm starved tonight. It's been a long day."

"You got it, Doc. You sit there and unwind, and I'll make one for you that you won't forget!"

Seth couldn't believe the peacefulness in the place. He bowed his head and thanked God for the quiet, the food, and for Hap. He remembered his little notebook and retrieved it from his pocket.

Finding the place where he'd left off, he read the next entry. *More responsible for things I would've referred to a specialist in the city.* What was it Mac had said about that? Something like in Kansas City or any large town with lots of specialists, he would only be a gatekeeper. Seth thought about this. He set fractured bones rather than send the patient to an orthopedist miles away. He treated skin lesions without the need to send the patient to a dermatologist. He enjoyed the opportunities to help his patients this way.

Another entry made Seth chuckle. He'd written, *I even like making house calls. Never would have thought that could happen.*

Approaching footsteps made Seth look up to see Hap coming his way. The smell of grilled onions reached him before the beaming proprietor of the café did. Hap set the enormous plate of food down in front of him.

"You just take your time and enjoy your food, Doc. This burger is my secret concoction, and I only serve it when the mood hits me." The man turned to leave, whistling a tune Seth didn't recognize.

Once Seth had eaten the burger down to just a bite or two left, he glanced again at his Moleskin. He flipped the pages to the con list for Mason Falls.

The list consisted of four entries for medicine. The first was his continued frustration with Mac not wanting to start electronic medical records until the laws demanded it. Second was the lack of a full-fledged lab. Then there was the call schedule. None of the other residents he knew did every other night and every other weekend. But then no one else was in a town the size of Mason Falls. This led to his last entry, the lack of any specialists or a hospital which meant sending patients to Granville when hospitalization was necessary and that meant a twenty minute drive each way to make rounds when he was taking call.

Seth took one more bite of his burger and looked around the

empty room. A strange sensation rippled through him like a shock wave. The differences between his two lists revealed something he hadn't seen before. The things pulling him to Kansas City were more self-centered. What drew him to Mason Falls focused on others. The dilemma boiled down to a fact he couldn't ignore. His heart resided in Mason Falls with the people he cared for. If he was honest with himself, he knew now it was his pride that drew him to Kansas City. Still holding what remained of his burger, Seth's appetite vanished. Sitting in the quiet café, he had never been so alone as at that moment. Bowing his head, he whispered a prayer. *"Father, You've told me in the Bible to trust You with all my heart and not to rely on my own understanding. And that when I do, You'll guide me and put me on the right path. I really need Your guidance right now. Please show me where You want me to be."*

～ 49 ～

THE SPRING DAYS WERE BEAUTIFUL, BUT Claire found herself still struggling despite her resolve to move life forward in a positive direction for herself and for Mason. She thought about the many happy moments in their lives, but still Claire felt an emptiness in her heart and a reluctance to step outside her own small world. This was not what she wanted Mason to see. She decided she and Mason needed some time with the McQuarrys and quickly punched in Helen's number.

"Oh Claire, it's good to hear your voice! This is crazy. I've had you on my mind for the last several days. I kept thinking, Helen, you need to call Claire and see how she and that precious boy are doing." Then she cried out, "Oh my goodness, can you give me a sec to turn the burner down? I have a pot of soup getting ready to boil over."

Claire went out on the back porch and curled up in her favorite wicker chair.

"Sorry about that. I got there just in time. It would've been a big mess! Say, why don't you and our boy come for dinner. I made enough for an army."

Claire didn't hesitate, "That would be wonderful, Helen. To be honest, I was thinking Mason and I needed a little time with you and Mac."

"Well, that sounds perfect, young lady. You and Mason come for dinner."

They set the time for dinner at six since it was Saturday and not a school night for Mason. After ending the call with Helen, Claire realized the tension in her shoulders had eased and her spirit felt lifted. Walking back into the house another realization popped into her thoughts. She had this same sensation every time she interacted with either Helen or Reuben. *Funny,* she thought, *I wonder why?*

After Claire told Mason they were having dinner with the McQuarrys, the next few hours were peppered with one question, "Mom, is it time yet?"

When they pulled into the McQuarry driveway, Mac greeted them clad in a pair of jeans, a checkered shirt, and his broad brimmed Tilly hat. That hat signaled gardening or fishing. He held a hoe in one hand, so probably gardening.

Claire gave Mac a big hug before going to help Helen in the kitchen. The aroma of homemade bread filled the room. She also smelled something sweet, probably Helen's apple crisp. It was one of Mason's favorites. Helen asked Claire to help her set the table on the screened porch since the evening was pleasantly warm. A few minutes later they were seated at the table, and Mason surprised them by asking if he could say the blessing.

"Let's all hold hands," he said with an air of authority. *"Dear God, thanks so much for this food. But most of all thank You for my mom and for Dr. Mac and Mrs. Mac. Especially for Mrs. Mac making this yummy dinner for us. In Jesus's name, amen!"*

Claire watched her son. He was growing up so fast. And he seemed so comfortable here with the McQuarrys. He never asked to pray at home, but now that she thought about it, he did always hesitate and lower his head for a moment before he would start eating. In that moment she realized that her son wanted to pray but wasn't sure if his mother would approve. *How had she not thought of that before?*

After dessert, Mac turned to Mason and said, "What about us two men get a little more gardening done while the ladies do their thing." Grinning from ear to ear, an excited young boy let out a big "you bet"! Claire and Helen looked at one another before both saying, "But it's getting dark!"

"Ladies, a lot of work can be done in a little time with good help like Mason," Mac said as he and Mason headed out to the garden.

"Goodness that boy is growing up so fast," Helen said, shaking her head as she headed to the sink. The two of them worked non-stop getting the kitchen in order, then poured themselves another glass of iced tea and went to sit on the porch.

Helen sat in her special chair, and Claire took the porch swing. She loved the creaking sound, and the gentle swaying always seemed to bring her peace. Just what she needed.

Helen gave Claire's knee a pat and said, "I have a feeling there is something you'd like to talk about. Would it by chance be about our young doctor?"

Startled by her friend's astute insight, Claire couldn't find words to respond. She simply sat there pushing the swing back and forth with one foot, wishing the guys would come from the garden and she wouldn't have to answer.

"I've wondered for some time when you and I might have this conversation."

Claire released a deep sigh and said, "I think he cares for me more than just as a friend, and I don't know what to do about it."

"And what do you want from me, dear?"

Claire stopped the swing. Helen moved to sit beside her. Placing an arm around Claire's shoulders, Helen held Claire while the tears flowed.

"Thank you for mothering me, Helen. You've helped fill one of the empty places in my heart. Honey was always that person for me before she died. I haven't had anyone since then until now. You've become even more special to me, and special to Mason, since we've moved here. Thank you."

Helen drew Claire into a hug and said, "I'm thankful I can be here for you, dear girl. Mac and I have loved you since the first day your daddy brought you to see us when you were just a little girl. I'm always here for you."

"I know you are and thank you for that. I confess I have been thinking you might be able to give me some advice regarding Seth. I know you care a lot for him too. But today I was just feeling the need for your good company! Stretch my world a little bit, you know. Thank you so much for inviting us to dinner. This evening has been just what Mason and I both needed.

~ 50 ~

THE STACK OF CHARTS PILED UP on his desk challenged Seth's patience. Why did Angus McQuarry have to be so stubborn about not going to electronic medical records until he faced the deadline? Meanwhile, Seth faced this mountain of paper charts that seemed to take forever to work through. Of course, Mac would say, "Shoot, son, they're not that bad. I can get through mine in half the time you do."

Seth's reply remained the same. "That may be true for you, Mac. That's how you've always done it. But for me, it's just plain torture."

Seth was still stewing over this ongoing dilemma when his phone rang. "Dr. Bradley here."

"Bradley, this is Marvin Hawthorn in Kansas City. Do you have a few minutes?"

Seth nearly knocked the pile of charts over as he said, "Dr. Hawthorn, certainly, sir. How are you?"

"Fine, fine, but I have limited time, so let's get down to business. I want to talk to you about the possibility of you coming to Kansas City after your commitment is complete. Are you interested?"

Seth sat at his desk, momentarily shell shocked. "Sir, ah, yes sir, I am very interested."

"Fine, I want to ask you some questions. My son said he remembered you from your interview with us but also from your rotation with him. I will say that he was very impressed."

"Thank you, sir. It means a lot to me to hear that. I thoroughly enjoyed my time with him."

"Yes, yes, glad to hear that. Now, let's get to the point of this call. I have three questions I want to ask you. First, what are you wanting in your practice?"

Seth ran his hand through his hair trying to collect his thoughts. "I would have to say what I want most is a place where I can put my training to the best use and to grow as a physician." Seth swallowed and tried to keep from tapping his foot, his nerves on edge.

"Um, . . . okay, second question. What are your goals?"

Seth rubbed the back of his neck trying to pull together an answer. "My first and foremost goal would be giving my patients the very best care I can. Because of that goal and my love of learning not just from textbooks but from others, I would count it advantageous to gain from the experience of other physicians in the clinic. Something I'm learning from Dr. Angus McQuarry, the man I work for here, is the importance of what he calls the art of medicine. In all honesty, I initially thought it was just an old fashioned idea. But I have to say it's capturing more and more of my thoughts on patient care."

"Very interesting, Bradley. I like your willingness to consider concepts out of your comfort zone. Final question, what is it that tugs at your heart in life and in medicine. In other words, what is your passion?"

Seth felt the trickle of perspiration down his forehead and wiped it from above his eye. His thoughts seemed to hang in limbo for a very long time, but he prayed it was more like seconds.

"Dr. Hawthorn, for so long now it's simply been to complete my training, get established, and practice medicine. I hadn't considered it from that point forward. But that's an insightful question to pursue if you will allow me."

"I like an honest answer. Just don't come back and try to snow me. Deal? Tell you what, I'll call you in, oh let's say about three months. Think you can find your passion between now and then?"

"Yes sir, find my passion. To be honest I'm really glad you asked that question. It's about time I knew."

Both men laughed and said their good-byes.

The conversation stirred up emotions Seth had been fighting hard to ignore.

~ 51 ~

Mabel's coffee shop bustled with the early morning crowd. This particular day though had a different dynamic from the normal clientele. The construction workers, farmers, and older men who usually started their day at Mabel's had been overrun with young moms and their little ones. Their lively chatter, the cries of numerous babies, and the shrieks from toddlers unleashed a force that had the roughest of men silently staring in disbelief at the bedlam.

Having dropped Mason at a friend's house to play, Claire had claimed a table for two in the corner at the back. Karen Simpson should appear any moment.

Mabel's typical bad mood escalated from all the noise and chaos.

She heard the woman lash out at a burly man wearing a Mason County Road Department tee shirt who simply asked about his order. "I'll get to you when I'm good and ready," she snapped. A few minutes later she watched in disbelief as another hulk of a man cringed under Mabel's angry glare because he'd asked for a refill on his coffee. "Can't you people wait your dang turn?" The coffee shop turned deathly quiet.

Long after her time with Karen, Claire couldn't get Mabel off her mind. Returning home, she made the beds, started a load of wash, and continued analyzing the owner of the coffee shop. She attacked the kitchen sink with a vengeance as she puzzled over why Mabel couldn't see she was hurting herself as well as everyone around her. Had she suffered some major blow that had caused her to be so angry? Mabel's words were biting and sarcastic. She'd become hardened toward everyone and everything around her.

An image of the woman flashed in Claire's mind, and she

crumpled to the floor. "Am I becoming like that?" she cried out. "Why am I afraid to give life and love a second chance?"

She sat there on the floor for a long time. How long she didn't know. Taking hold of a kitchen chair she pulled herself into a standing position.

"I am not going to become another Mabel Porter!" she shouted into the empty house. Grabbing her keys she headed to the door. She knew exactly where she was going. She needed help.

~ ~ ~

Claire stood at the front door and rang the doorbell. When no one answered, she turned to leave. She felt the weight of her emotions dragging her down the front porch steps when she heard Helen call out to her.

"Claire, wait. Don't go." The older woman stepped quickly toward her and the two embraced with an affectionate hug.

"I happened to look out the window," Helen said, trying to catch her breath, "and saw you leaving." Her eyes were fixed on her young friend.

"Claire, you're pale as a ghost! What's wrong, sweetheart? Come on, let's go inside and talk." Helen settled Claire into a comfortable chair before moving into the kitchen to put water in the tea kettle.

Hearing the uncontrollable sobs coming from the living room, she turned the burner to low and rushed to check on the young woman who was like a granddaughter to her.

Helen perched herself on the arm of Claire's chair and stroked her hair.

"There, there, sweetheart, let it all out, whatever is bothering you," she whispered. "You just take all the time you need." Holding Claire's cold hands, she caressed them sharing the warmth of her own.

As her sobs began to lessen, Claire's eyes turned to her friend. "I'm so sorry I lost it like that."

"Don't you worry about that or about me. We're like family, aren't we?" she said, patting Claire's hand. "I'll go make us some of your peppermint tea, then we'll talk."

Helen returned with the tea and set one of the cups on the

small side table next to Claire's chair then sat down on the sofa across from her. Neither spoke for several minutes letting a comfortable silence surround them.

"I went to Mabel's this morning to meet Karen Simpson. I got there early and found a table. The place was a zoo, more so than usual because of all of the young moms with their small children. Anyway, as I sat there waiting for Karen, I watched Mabel. She was on a rampage. I've never seen her like that." Claire's voice faltered and her face scrunched into a frown as she hesitated.

"Helen, I saw myself in Mabel if I don't change. Something hard must have caused her to become the way she is now. I don't want that to be me," Claire cried out in despair.

"Come here, sweetheart, and sit by me," Helen said, patting the space on the sofa beside her.

Like an obedient child Claire made her way to the sofa and curled up next to her friend. Helen put her arm around the trembling young woman holding her close. "Sweet girl, we won't let you become like that," she murmured. "I know just who you need right now."

Claire shifted her body so she could see Helen.

"Did you say 'who I need right now'? I don't understand."

"Claire, it's time you meet the only person who can ever love you unconditionally, the only one who can meet all your needs. He alone can take your hurt, your loss, and fill your life with true joy. His name is Jesus and He loves you, Claire Westfield, so much that He was willing to die for you."

Claire stared across the room trying to get her thoughts together. She didn't want to offend this precious lady, but she wasn't sure she was ready for the Jesus talk either. She loved Helen, and she'd been such an important part of her life. She guessed it wouldn't hurt to hear her out.

"Sweetheart, you've been running away from God for a long time. Your grandmother believed it started when your mother sent you off to boarding school that first time," Helen said, patting Claire's knee.

"We both noticed a change in you when you came here that Christmas. It was like you'd built a wall to protect yourself from getting too close to anyone." A faraway look came over Helen's face as though she'd been transported back to that exact moment.

"That's when Ruby, or Honey, as you called her, and I started praying in earnest for you." Tears filled Helen's eyes, and she paused to wipe them away. "After that it seemed each time you came for a visit, we sensed that wall had gotten higher and stronger. You seemed more open after a few days here, and we still had some wonderful times together. Didn't we?" Claire nodded, a look of sadness covering her face.

"You've had a lot of painful losses in your young life, but you are not like Mabel Porter." Helen's face turned a rosy pink. "And I'm here to tell you there's no way I'm going to stand by and see you become like her! That would be just too sad."

Claire had never seen such feistiness in Helen McQuarry. It took everything she had to control the laughter building up inside her.

"I'm telling you there are too many years of prayer invested in you to let you keep running away from the only answer to becoming who you were created to be." Helen sat quietly for a moment.

"No matter how many times you run away from God, He will always run after you. He longs to bring you back so you can have a relationship with Him. That's why He let His own son die for you. Think about how you would feel if Mason got lost. You wouldn't just sit and wait, would you? No, you would be determined to go after him. Why? Because of your love for your child."

Helen took a long breath. "Well, that's just how God feels about you." Claire sat very still, a look of exhaustion in her eyes and her posture.

"Claire, sweetheart, all you have to do is accept God's love for you, confess that you've left Him out of your life, and He will help you release the pain of Randall's death and the lack of your mother's involvement in your life."

"I don't know how to do that, Helen. And I don't know if I want to do it." Claire sighed and covered her face with her hands trying to process what her friend was saying.

"It's not rocket science, Claire. He made it very simple.

Remember how you used to climb up in your daddy's lap and tell him about your day or whisper a secret in his ear? That's all you have to do. God is your heavenly father and He loves to hold His children and hear them tell Him they need Him."

Claire didn't want to hurt her friend, but she needed to get away. She couldn't make a decision like this right now. She needed time to think, alone.

"Thank you, Helen, for being there for me. I . . . need some time to think. To be by myself. I hope you understand. I love you, but I need to go." She leaned over and gave Helen a kiss on the cheek.

As she left, she heard her friend shout, "Run after her, Jesus! Don't let her get away!"

Turning to her natural instinct in dealing with frustration, Claire drove home, changed into her running clothes, and headed out for a run. Trying to get Helen's words out of her mind, she ran faster. But the words kept hammering at her. "You've been running away from God for a long time." Claire increased her pace. "You built a wall around yourself." The words pounded in her head matching her steps. "The wall got higher and stronger."

Having pushed herself to the limit, she slowed to a walk. Her body was exhausted, her mind was fleeing from the truth, but her heart had to confess that Helen was right. She'd been running away emotionally her entire life. She had to admit that her physical running masked the emotions she was trying to run away from.

Walking back to the house rather than running gave her time to sort through the last couple of hours. What was it that Helen had said as Claire left? She stopped walking, trying to remember her friend's exact words. Something about Jesus coming after her? She thought she could almost hear Helen's usually soft voice shout out the words, "Run after her, Jesus. Don't let her get away." Claire couldn't help but laugh. It was so out of character for Helen, the picture of Southern gentility.

"So, Jesus," Claire said aloud, "were You running after me like my sweet friend asked You to?"

When she reached the house, she went around to the back porch, stepped inside to get a glass of water, and returned to sit on the porch swing. She sat for a long time thinking back on conversations she'd had with Potch and Honey as a child and even into her teen years. Claire knew they had a strong faith in God. And as best she understood, they lived it out. God was a very real part of their lives. So why had she run away from their God? Was it because of her mother? Had she blamed God for the lack of love she'd received from her?

She pondered the thought, wondering if maybe that was part of it. And then her dad died. Had she blamed God for that? She knew she'd blamed God for Randall's death. But it wasn't God who killed Randall. It was that drunk driver. She thought about Mason and how he talked easily about Jesus being his best friend.

Claire's thoughts went back to the time Reuben had shared his story with her. He had so many reasons he could've used to stay angry, but instead he accepted God's love for him. With all his losses, Reuben was a man filled with love for his Creator, and he radiated joy and peace.

Claire walked to the pasture fence and leaned her arms on the top rail. She watched the cows grazing. Several bluebirds flew by and a red-headed woodpecker was hard at work on a tree limb. Its pecking was the only sound.

She thought of the changes she'd seen in Seth's life. He was a new person. It was like he had a light shining through him. She still found herself amazed at the man he was becoming.

These people she cared for were so different from each other, but the one common denominator was their faith. Had she been so blind she couldn't see that it was God who had filled up all the hurt places in their lives. Even her own little boy had seen the light in them and reached out to its warmth. The light had to be about Jesus.

Helen's words to her earlier flooded Claire's mind. "Jesus is the only one who can replace all your hurt and loss and fill your life with true joy."

Claire continued to pace back and forth along the fence row. She saw darkening clouds beginning to fill the sky. It made her think of the scene that morning at the coffee shop, but instead of seeing Mabel's face as she was lashing out at those around her, the face she saw was her own.

"God, are You trying to tell me something about myself?" Her voice broke the silence. *"I'm so sorry for all the times I've blamed You for everything that's happened to me. I'm sorry for being so angry at You. Forgive me, God. I need You to show me how to live again. Jesus, I want You to be in my life. I can't go on the way I am now. Help me know You the way my son and my friends do. And thank You for loving me so much You were willing to give Your own life for me."*

Kneeling there in the grass, Claire poured out all the pain of the past and the uncertainty of the future. She forgave her mother for the wasted years and lack of relationship. And she forgave the man who had killed her husband, her son's father. A sense of warmth she couldn't explain rushed over her like a loving embrace, and she began to cry.

She knew she'd carry some scars from these wounds. But she remembered Reuben telling her that scars are the badges of healing and to wear them as proof of having lived through the pain. She kneeled there in the quiet, feeling each beat of her heart.

Claire walked back to the porch swing, sat down, and dialed Helen's number. While waiting for her friend to answer, she looked up to see the dark clouds had vanished and a brilliant blue sky was all around her. Her face glowed with anticipation. When she heard the familiar voice, she smiled and said, "I went on a long run after leaving you, Helen. Guess who ran after me?"

～ 52 ～

CLAIRE WAS STILL COMING TO TERMS with her new relationship with God. She felt like she was taking baby steps, but she was taking steps to let His light into her life. For some reason, she had not yet talked to Seth about what had happened to her. They saw each other occasionally and had dinner together at Mac and Helen's, so she wasn't sure why she had been silent about her new-found faith. She stood in front of the washing machine with an armload of wet linens thinking about this. She realized she had not talked to Reuben about it either. It still felt tender and new to her.

Her thoughts were pulled from her contemplation when the noise from her son's room grew louder by the minute. She dropped the linens in the dryer, set the dryer timer, and headed upstairs, taking two steps at a time. Claire threw open the door to Mason's room. "What in the world are you doing, young man? I want an answer right now. Why were you yelling? And why are you throwing stuff all over the place?"

Her son scowled at her, arms crossed against his chest. Claire couldn't remember him ever looking so angry.

"Have you counted to ten, Mom?" he snarled. "You always say you do that so you won't yell at me. I don't think you did it today."

"Don't you get sassy with me, Mason. Go sit on your bed and tell me what's going on. Now!"

Mason plopped onto his bed, his body shaking with anger. "I was yelling 'cause I was really mad at you. I want you to like Dr. Seth the way he likes you. And I can tell he likes you a lot. And I still think he looks at you the way Daddy always did."

"Mason, I . . ."

"No, Mom, don't say that's not true 'cause it is true. Why can't you be happy again?" He stood and took a tentative step toward her then reached out and put his hand in hers.

"Mom, I'll always miss Daddy, but I think he'd like Dr. Seth. And I know Daddy would want you to be happy and to have someone be with you since he can't be here."

Claire felt paralyzed, overwhelmed with the insight of her young son. She struggled to find the right words and the courage to even speak.

"Sweetheart, it's just not that easy. It's a grown-up thing," she said. "And you're not old enough to understand." She moved toward her son to hug him, but he turned away, going instead to his pup tent, the place he always said made him feel safe. As he lowered the flap of the tent, he whispered, "I didn't want to be mean to you, but you don't understand the hurting in my heart."

Choking back her tears, Claire made her way to her own room and flung herself across the bed, smothering her cries in her pillow.

Dusk had cast its shadow through the windows when Claire awoke. Rubbing her eyes, groggy from sleep, she went into mother mode. Where was her son? How had she let herself fall asleep? Was he okay? When she gently pushed his bedroom door open, a sigh of relief escaped her. He too had given way to emotional exhaustion. A soft snore ushered from the tent.

"*Oh, God, what am I going to do?*" she whispered. "*I need help. Would You show me what to do?*" As she stepped back into the hall, she realized she'd truly opened her heart and turned to God for help.

～ 53 ～

HAULING THEIR GEAR FROM SETH'S CAR to the creek proved to be an adventure in itself on this beautiful summer day. Mason talked nonstop while either dragging his fishing rod, poking Seth in the back with it, or using it to swat flies.

"Mason," Seth said, adjusting the backpack, "You have to pay attention to your rod, buddy. You're going to break the thing if you keep treating it like a stick."

Mason ducked his head.

"Hey now, you're not in trouble. You just need to pay attention. Okay?" Seth flipped the boy's ball cap backwards and patted the top of his head. "Let's go get those fish and show them whose boss."

"I'm sorry, Dr. Seth. I'll be more careful."

"Thanks, buddy. You're a great kid! Did you know that?"

Looking at the boy's bright eyes and wide grin, minus another tooth, Seth's mind raced with thoughts he'd never considered. Maybe he did have it in him to be a dad someday. And could it possibly include this impish fishing partner?

Seth told Mason to pick out where he thought the fish would be waiting for them as they moved along the creek bank. Mason took his role seriously, choosing one place after another but changing his mind.

"This is it, Dr. Seth! I just know it's the best place we've seen. Can I bait the hooks? Please, please! Dr. Mac taught me how, and he says I'm really good with worms!"

Seth tried not to laugh but lost the battle. "Sure thing, ol' buddy. You go right ahead. Just be careful of the hooks. I'm not much of a worm man myself." Mason's face beamed his gratitude as he dug his fingers into the coffee can filled with dirt and worms.

"Dr. Mac calls me his worm man. So now I can be your worm man too."

Dumping the backpack on a fallen tree, Seth started getting their rods ready. When he looked up, he found himself staring straight at a large worm Mason was dangling in front of his face.

"We ought to catch a really, really big fish with this one, huh, Dr. Seth?"

"Whoa there, big guy, not quite so close. But yeah, I think that one will work real well."

Standing on the creek bank a few feet from Mason, Seth couldn't help but smile. It was a rare moment seeing this little guy so quiet and focused. Seth had overheard Mac ask around the office for the names of some babysitters for the boy. Mac and Helen wanted to take Claire out to lunch. Before he realized what he was doing, Seth had volunteered.

He'd never done anything one-on-one with a child. Moments before hitting the panic button, he decided to get some ideas from Mac and jumped on the suggestion of fishing. He'd hoped it would keep Mason occupied. It had been the perfect choice. When he'd asked Mason to go fishing with him, Mason had hopped up and down squealing with delight. He'd run circles around Seth shouting, "Do you really mean it, Dr. Seth? Just you and me? Really?"

"Sure, I mean it. Just the two of us." A warm glow had spread over Seth when he saw how something so simple as fishing could bring so much joy.

After helping his pint-sized partner cast several times with no fish biting, he could see the disappointment in the boy's eyes. "Let's walk down the bank to that big rock and try there for a while." After two casts with no luck, Seth was afraid the little guy was going to break into tears as he cast the third time. But no sooner had the line hit the water than a good-sized smallmouth bass grabbed Mason's worm and gave him a fight for all he was worth.

Seth watched Mason reel in the fish. "Easy does it, Mason, just keep going at it nice and slow." Seth kneeled close to the water, net ready. "You're almost there, buddy, just a few more feet, then ease that monster onto the bank if I don't get him in this net." He had never seen such a serious look on Mason's face. When the fish was within arm's length, Seth reached out and let the fish plop into the net.

Seth swept Mason into his arms juggling the fish and the fishing rod. The boy's whoop pierced the silence as he slapped Seth a high-five. Mason's grin said it all as Seth took a couple of quick photos with his phone. The boy's exuberance captivated him. He decided to send the photos to Claire's phone.

"I am proud to be your fishing buddy, young Mr. Westfield. This sure is a fine fish but don't you think we should let him go? Who knows, we might even catch him again."

"You bet!" Mason shouted. After releasing the fish back into the water, Seth stuck out his hand to Mason. The boy beamed as they shook hands.

The earlier question came back to Seth again as he watched the little guy. Could he be a father, a dad, to this child? He was about Mason's age when his grandfather died, leaving just him and Gran, and, of course, he never knew his father.

"I'm starvin'," Mason shouted. "Can we have those snacks Mom sent with us?"

"Sounds like a great idea to me! Fishing sure makes men hungry. And besides we need to celebrate!" Seth chuckled at the sight of his charge puffing out his chest and standing a little taller when being referred to as a man.

Claire had insisted on putting together a backpack filled with all kinds of snacks. When he and Mason looked into the bag, they both broke out laughing. "Your mom sure doesn't want us to go hungry, does she?" Seth pitched Mason an apple with a look that dared him to finish first.

In record time, Mason had eaten the apple down to the core and jerked the bag into his lap, digging through it like a squirrel after nuts.

"You better save some for me, dude, or you're going to start getting your own line out of the trees." Seth reached over and grabbed the bag with one strong pull. Did he just call the boy dude? He couldn't remember ever using that word before. This must be what happens when you become totally relaxed, which was exactly how he felt.

Cramming an Oreo in his mouth, Mason walked to the creek and practiced skipping rocks across the water. Seth sat on the ground leaning against a tree and stretched out his legs in front of him. It would be nice to take advantage of a few moment's break. But as he sat watching Mason, the scene made his heart ache for the child. The boy's dad should be the one here with him today, not some family acquaintance. Seth stood and walked toward Mason and placed a hand on his shoulder.

"You're getting really good at that."

"Yeah, I know. Do you like my mom?"

Startled by the question, Seth tried to clear his throat. "I do. I like her very much." Seth felt a small, wet hand close around his own. The two stood in silence for some time. Then Mason began to cry.

"She used to smile . . . all the time." He sniffled, and wiped his hand across his nose. "And she, she, laughed a lot too."

"How about we go sit down for a while, okay?" He put an arm around Mason's shoulder and felt him slump against his side. Seth wanted to find the right words. "It's hard to see her when she gets sad, isn't it?" He reached out and patted Mason's arm, then pulled him into a hug.

"You see, I kind of understand how you feel because I never knew my dad. Never even saw him. And the same was true with my mother."

Mason's eyes widened as he stared at his friend. He scooted closer and whispered. "I'm really sorry, Dr. Seth." He hung his head and said, "It's just . . . I don't like Mom . . . being this way." Mason jumped up and ran toward the creek. Picking up a handful of rocks, he started hurling them, one after another into the water, each splash like the echo of his anger.

"I want my daddy to come back!" he shouted. "And I want my mommy to be happy like she used to be!"

Seth held his arms out. "Come here, buddy." The impact of the child flinging himself into Seth's arms almost knocked the breath out of him. He kneeled in front of Mason and said, "I'm kind of new to this, but let's pray for your mom."

Mason nodded and said, "That would be good, Dr. Seth." Seth put words to the feelings in his heart. *"Jesus, Mason and I would like to ask You to help his mom be happy again. Help her let You take her sadness away so she and Mason can find joy in their life here. Amen."*

"Thanks, Dr. Seth, that makes me feel better. When we still lived in our other house before we moved here, I'd go in my daddy's closet when Mommy was asleep on the couch. I liked going in there so I could smell my daddy again. He smelled like shaving stuff when he went to work and like coffee when he came home from work. He loved to drink coffee.

"I didn't know about praying back then. I'd put one of his sweaters on me, and it felt like having my daddy's arms around me. But what I liked best was holding his stessascope. I could remember listening to his heart with it."

Mason sighed and said, "Can we always be fishing buddies, Dr. Seth?"

"I sure hope so, Mason, I sure hope so."

～ 54 ～

RAINY DAYS WERE A GOLD MINE for Mabel Porter. Claire breathed a sigh of relief as she spotted the last empty booth in the coffee shop. Her friend Karen Simpson should be here any moment. Stepping up her pace, she moved across the busy room. She reached the open booth at the same time as did a rough looking man well over six feet tall. As she started to back away, the man removed his camouflage ball cap and motioned her to take the booth.

"Thank you so much," she said.

"No problem, ma'am. You have a good day."

Claire still found herself surprised by the generosity and manners of so many of the people she met in Mason Falls. They had become living examples for her about not judging others by the way they looked or what they did for a living.

Reuben was the first to come to mind. His weather-beaten skin, neck-length silver hair, and workman's rough hands couldn't begin to describe the inner man she had come to love. And Karen's husband, Hank, had an MBA from Wharton's School of Business. Who would have guessed that about the owner of a small town hardware store?

"Hey there." Karen's almost childlike voice broke through Claire's musing. Karen slipped into the booth. Wiping at her rain soaked jacket, she said, "Quite a downpour out there, huh?"

"It sure is," Claire laughed. "I thought we might see Noah's Ark float by."

A new waitress approached them with glasses of water and asked for their order. Claire and Karen gave each other a relieved look that Mabel must be busy in the kitchen. While waiting for their coffee and food, they caught up on kids, Claire's latest projects at her house, and Karen's volunteer work at the local homeless shelter.

When the new girl returned with their coffee and blueberry muffins, Claire noticed the girl's hands shaking. Claire asked, "Are you okay?" Glancing at the name tag, she said, "Jodi, is something wrong?" Claire feared the girl would break into tears.

"I . . . I'm sorry. I just can't seem to do anything right. Miss Mabel yells at me every time I see her. I'm not sure I can stay at this job, but I've got to work. I've got a baby. I've just got to keep a job."

Claire squeezed the young woman's hand. "Jodi, that's just Mabel. You know she's like that with everyone, even customers. Try not to take it personally and just do your job." Claire smiled at her as she caught sight of the formidable owner heading their way. While Mabel slapped down plates of food at the next table, Claire winked at Karen signaling she had a plan. Karen's face turned pale.

"Jodi, you've done an excellent job of serving us. Hasn't she, Karen?"

Karen's face froze, but after a nod from Claire, she replied. "Yes, she's done a very nice job."

Jodi's reddened face and a trickle of tears were thanks enough.

Teaming up in defense of Jodi seemed to take the relationship with Karen to a new level. Claire saw it in her eyes and the way her shoulders relaxed. They had discovered a deeper foundation for their friendship.

After paying their bills, they stood outside the coffee shop, thankful the rain had moved on. Karen said, "Do you think we could do this more often, maybe even once a week?"

Claire's mind raced through the countless scenarios of her relationship with Robyn. For Karen, Claire was becoming her Robyn in their growing friendship. Claire replied, "That's a wonderful idea, Karen! With Mason back in school—second grade already—I've certainly got the time. And we do make a good team, don't we? Who knows, maybe we can keep helping Jodi and even win Mabel over."

Karen's face flushed with relief. "Thank you. I need someone to encourage me to step out of my comfort zone. I'm too much of an introvert."

Claire pulled her into a big hug. "Not anymore, girlfriend. You spoke out for Jodi in front of Mabel Porter. That's what I call gutsy! Same time, same place next week?" They hugged again, smiling as they went their separate ways.

~ ~ ~

Unlike the week before when she and Karen met, Claire awoke to a clear and beautiful morning that held the crispness of fall. Throwing on her robe she bounced down the stairs to turn the Keurig on and heat the oven for the cinnamon rolls. Helen had come for a visit yesterday and loaded them down with some of her yummy treats. She placed the rolls on a cookie sheet while the oven was pre-heating then ran back up the stairs to wake up her son.

Sitting on the bed beside him, she slowly rubbed his back and whispered, "Good morning, Tiger. Time to get up. It's a school day, and the sun is finally shining." Mason groaned and turned to face the wall.

"I have a special breakfast for you. I'm getting ready to put some of Mrs. Mac's cinnamon rolls in the oven." Before she could sit up, Mason jumped out of bed. "Really, Mom, you're not just trying to get me up?"

"Really, Tiger. By the time you shower, the house should be filled with the smell of cinnamon." Walking back down to the kitchen, she thought about asking Helen for a freezer full of rolls. They worked like a dream on a sleepyhead like Mason. And the funny thing is that Helen would take her up on the request. She loved Mason like a grandson.

Looking forward to the morning ahead, she slid the rolls into the oven and set the timer. She brewed herself a cup of coffee, stirred in a little hazelnut creamer, and sat down at the table. The warm scent of cinnamon and yeast tickled her nose. Where was her boy? She wanted one of those rolls as much as he did.

Mason tromped down the stairs, each step growing louder than the last. Claire still didn't understand the nuances of boys and their love of noise and roughhousing with each other. Growing up in a girls' school, she wasn't exposed to the behavior of young boys. She had come to realize that these things seemed to be inherent to most boys, not just Mason. Raising an eyebrow at the sight of her son standing in the doorway, she knew his teacher was in for quite a day.

His choice of clothes reflected the mischievous grin filling his face. The neon green tee shirt yelled, "Here I am, ready for anything." His baggy, bright red knee-length shorts were beyond reason as a match with the shirt. He would be a handful today. Maybe she should jot a note to Miss Kendall to be on her guard. Mason had topped off his creative look by choosing his black Nikes with yellow stripes. Claire shook her head and handed him a plate with two rolls. Her son had no taste in fashion, but he glowed, in more ways than one, in anticipation of the day ahead.

"So, Tiger, anything special happening at school today?" Claire winced again at his brightness.

"Not really. But J.J. and me and some other guys are gonna play soccer at recess. I'm so glad Dr. Seth coached our team again this summer. Mom, why don't we see Dr. Seth much anymore? Are you mad at each other?"

"No, sweetheart, we aren't mad at each other. It's hard to explain friendships with grown-ups sometimes, Mason."

Mason stared at Claire as he ate his second cinnamon roll. "Well, it seems to me you guys were really starting to like each other."

Claire stood and gathered their plates. Moving to the sink, she began scrubbing them. "Mason, it's almost time for you to leave. Let's talk about this later. Run and get your backpack so I can put your lunch in it."

The walk to the school bus had been somber in comparison to her son's attire and initial attitude that morning. She felt a bit of guilt about the conversation concerning Seth. Maybe she needed to reconsider her uneasiness about their relationship. She pondered the change in Seth. He definitely was more outgoing and relaxed, happier.

The McQuarrys had invited the three of them to dinner not long ago. Sitting around the table afterwards, drinking coffee and eating Helen's famous devil's food cake with her snow peak frosting, Claire had enjoyed the time with Seth. He could be quite funny when he let himself. There was a sparkle in his eyes as he kept them laughing with some of his stories from his residency program. Looking down at her watch, she gasped at the time. She ran back to the house, took a quick shower, blew her hair dry, and put on the minimum makeup. It was coffee day at Mabel's with Karen.

~ ~ ~

Claire arrived before Karen and looked for a table or booth. Sure enough, a booth emptied just as she walked in. Jodi was clearing the dishes and wiping down the table. She smiled when she saw Claire and motioned her over to the booth.

"How are things going?" Claire whispered.

"Not great, but I'm doing better, I guess. I made it through the week. That's progress. Thanks again for what you and your friend did. It helped." Jodi glanced around to make sure there was no sign of Mabel.

"We meant what we said, Jodi. You did a great job." Claire patted her arm. "Karen should be here any minute, but you can go ahead and bring me coffee." Jodi grinned, picked up the tray of dirty dishes and headed to the kitchen.

Karen walked over to the booth at the same time Jodi returned with Claire's coffee. "Would you like coffee too?" Jodi asked.

"I not only would like it, I really, really need it!" All three laughed.

The kitchen door flew open and Mabel moved in the room like a tank ready to destroy anything in her path. She was dragging a shaggy, black and white dog with sorrowful eyes behind her.

"Anyone here own this dog?" Mabel shouted, her hands on her hips. No reply. Rough, hardworking men cowered much like the dog when she scowled at them. "This mutt's been hangin' around for a week. If nobody knows who he belongs to or claims him, I'm callin' the Sheriff."

Claire watched the poor dog begin to tremble and cower at the woman's feet. Before she realized what she was doing, she stood up, marched over to Mabel and snatched the rope from her. "I'll take the dog." Her own forcefulness shocked her. "Even a throw-away dog deserves a chance." Claire turned, dog in tow, and walked back to Karen. "Let's go. Would you get the check today please? I've got to get out of here before I say something I'll regret."

Karen grabbed their purses and went to the register to pay. Applause and whistles broke out around the room as Claire lead the shivering dog out the door.

The two women stood outside the coffee shop. Neither spoke. When the dog whimpered and nudged her leg, Claire stared at him, or her. She wasn't sure which. When the dog kept whimpering, she reached down to pet its head. The fur was matted and dirty. She sighed and wondered what in the world she'd been thinking.

"Karen, would you go with me to the hardware store to see if Reuben is around? I'd like to get his take on this poor creature." Her friend nodded, and they walked the short distance to her husband's business.

When they arrived, Karen suggested they go to the back door. They would know immediately if Reuben was there. They smiled at the sight of the old green truck. Karen unlocked the door to the building and said, "Wait in the office, and I'll go out front and get Reuben and Hank." Moments later all three walked into the office. The look of surprise on the men's faces made Claire and Karen laugh.

"What in the world have you two been up to?" Hank asked with a startled look.

Reuben chuckled, "My, my, you ladies are turning this poor town upside down of late. You know word's all over town about how you put Mabel in her place last week. I can't wait to hear about this episode. So, who do we have here?" he asked, bending down on one knee and slowly extending his hand, palm up, to the shaking dog.

"All we know," Claire said softly, "is that no one in the coffee shop recognized him, and he's been hanging around the back of Mabel's for about a week. Probably trying to find food is my guess."

Reuben moved his hand a little closer. The dog trembled but didn't move. "That's a good boy, fella. I'm not going to hurt you." After a moment or two went by, Reuben laid his open hand under the dog's chin and began scratching. Moving his hand slowly, he stroked the dog's shoulder then sat on the floor and scooted back a foot or so. He sat there speaking in a low voice. A few minutes went by and Reuben continued to speak to the dog in hushed tones. Not wanting to break the moment, the others stood and watched. When the dog leaned forward to lick Reuben's hand, Claire gave Reuben a big smile. Hank took Karen's hand when he saw her eyes shiny with tears.

"This poor thing has known love at some point in his life," Reuben said, continuing to stroke the matted fur. "What are you planning to do with him, Claire?"

"I honestly don't know. I just couldn't see him taken off by the Sheriff and maybe taken to the pound. It was something in his eyes, like he was pleading for help. It really got to me." Claire felt Karen's arm around her shoulders.

Reuben eased himself into a standing position. The dog looked up and gave a slight wag of his tail. Reuben reached down and scratched him behind one ear. The tail wagged again with more vigor. Four sets of eyes smiled at each other. The women hugged. The men slapped each other's shoulder.

"Do you want my idea about the next move?" Reuben asked.

"Of course, that's why I brought him here." At the sound of her voice, the dog took a step toward her, sat, and seemed to search her face for the answer. "What's he doing?" Claire stood very still.

Reuben's laugh came with such gusto the others couldn't help but join him.

"Well, sweet lady, I think you've got yourself a dog. And I'm pretty darn sure he's going to take to Mason in a heartbeat." Rubbing a finger under one eye, he studied the dog still sitting at Claire's feet.

"Here's what I would suggest. Let me take him by Doc Kennedy's. He's been in practice forever. Really knows his stuff. If anyone can size up this fella, he can. We'll leave him overnight to give Doc some time with him. Kinda put him through the tests as to disposition and whatever else he needs to check. Then if he feels confident he'd make you and the boy a good dog, you can have him give this guy his shots and a much needed bath and a haircut."

Reuben bent down and patted the dog's back. It nuzzled Reuben's hand but didn't move from Claire. "We need to change those plans a bit. I think you're goin' to need to come with me. Doesn't look like he has any plans of leavin' without you." Laughter filled the room once more, and Claire bent to give the dog a pat but got her hand licked instead.

After thanking Hank and Karen and promising to let Karen know whatever happened next, she took the grungy rope and led her companion to Reuben's truck. Reuben opened the door for Claire, and the dog immediately leaped into the front seat, taking a place between the two of them.

~ ~ ~

The next morning Claire could think of nothing but the dog. Had he passed Dr. Kennedy's tests? Would she even know what to do with a dog? Would it like Mason as much as it seemed to like her? What in the world was she thinking?

After walking Mason to the school bus, she retrieved her phone from her jacket pocket and dialed Reuben while she was walking. She let it ring several times but there was no answer. Her forehead furrowed, and she stuffed her hands back in her pockets. The chill in the air warned fall was nearing its end.

She threw her jacket in a chair near the front door and took off her boots. It was crazy for her to feel this way. She'd rarely been around dogs or any animals for that matter, except when visiting Potch and Honey. No sooner had she sat down in Potch's chair than Reuben called.

"Hi, Reuben. What's the verdict?" She twirled a piece of her hair nervously.

"Well, looks like if you want her, she's yours!" Reuben said with a chuckle.

"I do, I can't believe I'm saying this but I really do want . . . did you say her?"

"It's a female all right. Guess we all assumed male and none of us thought to check. And to relieve any fears, yes, she's been spayed.

"Claire, I can't count the wonderful stories I've heard from people about their rescue dogs, and you've heard my story. Doc Kennedy and I both feel she would be a good companion for Mason. And personally, I think for you too. Do you want to pick her up here or have me bring her to you? Doc also made out a list of what you'll need. You can pick everything up at Farmer's Supply."

Claire decided it made more sense for her to get the food, crate, and other items on Doc Kennedy's list and then let Reuben bring the dog out. The lengthy list brought back memories of the day she found out she was pregnant. She'd rushed from the doctor's office and shopped most of the afternoon. Before clicking off her phone, she made Reuben promise he would be at her house when Mason got home. "I want you to be a part of this momentous occasion," she declared. Reuben thanked her and said he wouldn't want to miss it.

~ ~ ~

Claire had never been in the Farmer's Supply. She could've driven to Walmart in Granville, but she was running short on time. If she didn't find all she needed here, she and Mason would go to Granville after dinner. The smells that greeted her when she walked in the store were like none she'd ever experienced. She gazed around the large space feeling completely out of her comfort zone.

"May I help you, ma'am?"

She turned toward the voice and looked straight at the guy with the camouflage ball cap who'd given her the booth at Mabel's. His eyes said he recognized her too.

"Well, hello again," she smiled.

He gave her a shy smile before asking, "Can I help you, ma'am?"

"I sure hope so. I'm out of my territory, but I was hoping to find some items I need. Remember the dog I stormed off with from Mabel's? Well, I'm keeping her. I've never owned a dog, so I'm here with a list from Doc Kennedy for supplies."

The man grinned at her and said, "Right this way, ma'am, We've got pretty much anything you could need." He allowed her to go before him and motioned to a section on their right with a large sign that read Dog Supplies. The man grabbed a flatbed cart parked nearby and said, "Tell me what's on your list, and we'll have you fixed up in no time."

Claire asked him his name.

"Um, it's Trevor, ma'am, Trevor Jenkins." He tipped his hat as he spoke.

"Hi, Trevor. Nice to officially meet you. I'm Claire Westfield." She stuck out her hand. Trevor seemed unsure whether he should take it. When he did, he mumbled, "I know, ma'am, everyone knows who you are." That brought a little blush to Claire's cheeks.

Trevor proved to be exactly the right person to help her. When it came to choosing a dog crate, it helped that he'd already seen her new dog and could suggest the proper size. What had seemed a huge undertaking when she had entered the building proved to be an educational and enlightening experience.

When everything was checked off her list, Trevor loaded what she decided to call her doggie layette into the car. She wanted to get the car into the garage before Mason got home so he wouldn't see all this stuff before he met his new friend.

~ ~ ~

Claire saw the school bus edging closer to their stop. She was excited and nervous. Claire had some reservations because she knew nothing about caring for animals, but this still felt like the right decision. The bright yellow bus pulled up and the red arm with STOP popped out of the driver's side of the vehicle to warn any traffic. Noisy chatter greeted her when the bus door opened. She could hear several children call out "Bye, Mason." It warmed her heart that he was making friends.

Her boy jumped off the last step and waved as the bus pulled away. "Hi, Mom." He gave her a quick hug just in case any of his peers on the bus were looking out the rear window. She accepted it but felt a twinge of sadness.

They talked nonstop on the walk home. Mason barely took a breath as he told her about their soccer game at school and how he'd scored a couple of goals.

As they reached the house, they heard the rumble of a truck coming up behind them. Mason turned to see who it was. "Hey, Mom, it's Mr. Reuben!" His face beamed as he waved his arms in greeting. The truck chugged to a stop, and Reuben stepped out.

Mason ran and jumped into Reuben's outstretched arms. "I sure have missed you, Mr. Reuben," he said with a huge smile.

"Well, little buddy, that goes both ways. I've sure missed you too." Reuben gave Claire a nod to alert her he had the dog. He put a friendly hand on Mason's head and said, "Your mom has something for you. She asked me to bring it by."

Mason turned toward his mother with a questioning look.

Claire took Mason's hand and led him to the truck. Reuben motioned her toward the passenger side. "I have someone I want you to meet, sweetheart." She opened the door. Curled up on the floor lay a dog she barely recognized. She gasped in surprise. Could this be the same animal she'd rescued from Mabel? Reuben smiled and nodded to her.

Mason just stood there, mouth open, looking from one adult to the other. "She's all yours, sweetheart. All you have to do is come up with a name and love her."

"Mom, do you really mean I can keep her?"

"Yes, that's exactly what I mean."

"Well, young man," Reuben said, "I think it's time to get this girl out of the truck and give you two a chance to get to know each other. He gently lifted the dog out and set her on the ground. She was wearing a new collar and leash. Handing the leash to Mason, he said, "Mason Westfield meet your dog. She's a mighty fine girl and needs you to take care of her. Do you think you're able to do that?"

Nodding his head several times, Mason said, "Oh, yes sir, I sure am. I can't believe it. I never thought in my whole life I'd have my very own dog. Thank you, Mr. Reuben."

"Whoa there! This fine girl is here because your momma is quite a lady. She rescued this dog from being sent to the pound. In my book that makes her a hero. So, you thank your momma, not me."

"Thank you, Mom, thank you so much. I just can't believe I have my very own dog."

The two hugged for a moment until they felt the dog wedge herself between them and paw at their legs. Kneeling down together, they shared the wet kisses of the newest member of their family.

"Can I take the leash off of her so we can run around?"

Claire looked to Reuben for an answer. "I think she'd like that, Mason," he said. "Just stay close by. Okay?"

"I will!"

Claire and Reuben laughed as boy and dog played. Reuben put an arm around her shoulder and said, "Way to go, Mom. You hit a home run. I think they're going to be a good fit. And she cleaned up really nice, didn't she?"

"I think she's beautiful. She doesn't even resemble the dog I dragged out of Mabel's. Did Doc Kennedy say how old she might be or what breed?"

"Well, he's pretty certain she's around two. As to breed, she's part Border Collie for sure. That's a real plus. Those dogs are bred to protect and herd." Reuben flashed her a grin. "She'll take good care of that rambunctious boy of yours."

"Hey, Mom," Mason shouted. "I decided what I'm gonna name her!" Boy and dog dashed across the yard then tumbled onto the ground in front of them.

"Mom, you've always told me names are special and important. I want her to have a really special name. I got to thinking that if we hadn't moved here from San Francisco, we never would've found each other, so I'm gonna name her Cisco!"

"That's the perfect name for her, Mason, and so creative. I'm impressed." She pulled him into a hug. Cisco maneuvered her way in between them once again, ready to thank them with more wet kisses.

Reuben grinned at the scene before him. Cisco barked and ran circles around Mason and Claire, her tail waving like a flag.

After unloading all the stuff from the car, the guys started putting the crate together in the mud room. Claire had insisted Reuben stay for dinner. Scrounging through the fridge she decided to heat up her special spaghetti sauce. While Reuben helped her son learn the responsibilities of caring for his new friend, she started boiling water for the pasta and tearing lettuce for a salad. She discovered a package of rolls in the freezer and stuck them in the oven, then set the table. The water wouldn't be ready for a few minutes, so she went to see how things were going with Cisco.

When Claire got to the mud room door, Mason looked up and grinned. "We got the crate together, Mom. And I think she likes it. Especially that soft bed part that you got her." Kneeling down beside her son, she tousled his hair, which was in much need of a haircut again. Cisco moved next to her, laying her head on Claire's leg as though she was trying to thank her. Claire ran her hand over the dog's now silky fur. "That's a good girl, Cisco. No one's going to be mean to you anymore. You're home now." A deep contented sound accompanied another lick of Claire's hand.

Reuben and Mason started getting her food and water set out. Her tail swished back and forth across Mason's legs as she lapped up the water. Reuben instructed him on how much food to give her and wrote it down for him while he fed his dog. As Claire turned back to the kitchen, she heard the older man giving directions on how to put Cisco's rabies tag and ID tag on the bright red collar she was wearing. Claire smiled as she dropped the pasta in the boiling water.

∾ 55 ∾

EVERY TIME SETH THOUGHT OF CLAIRE his heart skipped a beat. Standing in the cool water of the creek quieted his spirit. He threw his line as Mac had taught him and gracefully reeled it in. His mind centered on the woman who filled more and more of his thoughts. She had moved into a part of his life he had kept locked up for almost a decade. And now, he had no idea how to respond to her being there.

Life as he had known it had broken into pieces like a jigsaw puzzle. He had no clue where to start to put the puzzle back together. But the fact that he didn't want to return to the puzzle of his old life struck him to his core.

He thought back to when Claire and Mason had gone to San Francisco. He had worked with a vengeance to fill his free time. Going fishing with Mac helped, but it didn't fill the void and, of course, he had worked hard helping Reuben finish the physical renovations at Claire's house. He had also planted some boxwood shrubs, helped Reuben with odd jobs, and learned a new skill in refinishing the hardwood floors. The changes Claire had made in the old house since then, along with Reuben's expert craftsmanship, were stunning.

He laughed out loud recalling his soccer coaching adventures with Mason, J.J., and the other kids the past two summers.

His mind went back to the conversation he and Reuben had sitting on Claire's front porch while they were taking a break on one of their work days. Reuben picked up on Seth's pensive mood.

"What's eating at the young doctor today?" the older man had asked. "Something heavy seems to be weighing on your mind."

Before Seth could stop himself, he had spilled his deepest

thoughts about Claire to the man beside him. Something about Reuben Walker made people do that. Seth saw it happen a lot. It didn't matter if the person was a prominent part of the community or someone living in Swamp Town, they couldn't help but open their lives to him. People instinctively trusted Reuben. Seth knew that from his own encounters with the man. When a person looked into Reuben's eyes, they saw compassion and unconditional love.

Seth had rubbed his sweaty hands together waiting for his friend to respond. Their conversation came back to him clearly.

"Have you heard the account of how God created everything, including man and woman, Seth?"

"Yeah, I kind of heard it piecemeal over the years, but I have never read it in the Bible." Seth remembered squirming under his friend's penetrating gaze.

'Well, the main thing to know is that God made a man and a woman to complete each other emotionally and physically, but most of all, they need to be one spiritually. If you truly care for Claire, the most important thing you can do right now is pray for her and for yourself."

Seth had stared at his friend in confusion. "Pray for Claire," he said in a raspy voice. "Reuben, I'm still learning to pray at all."

Seth laughed out loud thinking back on that day.

Reuben had reached over and given Seth a friendly slap to his knee. "Shoot, son, praying isn't so hard. It's just talking to your new best friend! Even a small child can pray. And in God's eyes right now, spiritually, you're like a small child."

Seth had paced along the wide planks of the porch. "Man, this makes it sound really serious. I just thought maybe I'd ask her out on an actual date, but praying ... well, I don't know."

"Seth, the second most important decision you will make in your life is choosing a wife. You've already made the most important decision of accepting God's gift of his unconditional love through Jesus.

"You see, God pursues a relationship with us to reveal to us our deepest needs and His ability to meet those needs. What I'm trying to get you to see is this. If you're having strong feelings for Claire, you need to include God in the equation," Reuben had said.

"Son, don't you think askin' God to give wisdom to both of you would help build a better framework for a relationship to grow?"

Seth smiled, thinking of the many changes in his life over such a short time. He had learned to fish, opened himself to Jesus, and coached five and six year olds in soccer. All things he could never imagine himself doing. Now if he could just figure out his relationship with Claire. He stood knee deep in the creek now and noticed the silence of the world around him. He could honestly say for the first time in his life he knew what it meant to be at peace. As a gentle breeze touched his face, he whispered a prayer for Claire that God would touch her life and give her the same peace he had found.

～ 56 ～

THE STAFF AT THE CLINIC EXPECTED a usual day to unfold when they came to work that morning. Things were settling down after all the excitement of the Thanksgiving and Christmas holidays and the new year was starting out well except Mac seemed to be in a mood sometimes. The schedule looked to be light to normal. The atmosphere in the small kitchen as they drank their coffee or tea was more like a family gathering than a workplace. Sodie Tucker kept them in stitches over the latest antics of her two mischievous cats. Mac added his hearty laugh to the general laughter that filled the small room before one by one each person left to begin the new day.

Seth scanned his list of appointments and whispered a prayer for the day. "*Help me be sensitive to each person and their specific needs, Jesus.*"

Willie Tuckett was first on the list of patients in for a check-up. "Tell you what, Willie," Seth said, "how about me stopping by your place after work. That way I can check out your oxygen set-up and make sure everything is working properly during this cold weather."

"You'uns would do that for me, come to my house?"

"Sure, I will. We're almost neighbors, aren't we?" Seth patted the old man's shoulder and helped him off the exam table. "I'm glad to see you are doing better now that you quit smoking. I'm real proud of you, Willie."

~ ~ ~

Among the many visits that morning of colds, a sprained ankle, hypertension, and the usual follow-up visits on chronic illnesses, he also diagnosed another Brown Recluse spider bite he estimated to be two days old. Although he'd never seen one during his residency, Mac had brought him in on a case when Seth had first arrived. He'd wanted Seth to get a clear picture and understanding of what the small but vicious creature was capable of doing. Seth now knew Mac's warning that the spiders were quite common in this area to be true, even this late in the season, in indoor spaces. But he'd also come to realize he was getting quite good at not only recognizing the bite but treating it.

The highlight of the morning though was the checkup for Jasper and Opal Mae's baby, Justine, named after Seth's nurse. She was healthy, happy, and alert to everything around her. Seth and Nurse Justine took turns holding her. He blew up a pink balloon and tied the string around her chubby wrist. Baby Justine squealed with delight as the balloon danced around her.

When Seth walked them out of the exam room, he noticed Mac coming down the hall. His pace was slow, almost lethargic. Seth hoped he hadn't taken on too much today. When the older man came close enough, Seth stepped forward and said, "Mac, are you doing okay? I can see some of your folks if you need me to."

Mac's gruff reply made it clear Seth had stepped over the line. But he'd keep an eye on his boss and, if need be, call Helen, the only person who could deal with the man's stubbornness.

By noon the men had each seen fifteen patients. Seth made his second mistake of the day by asking Mac if maybe he should take the afternoon off and reschedule or let Seth fill in for him.

Thunder roared from the mouth of Angus McQuarry as he informed his protégé that he could still out work him. "I'll see you promptly at two o'clock!" The door slammed behind him, leaving both nurses and Nell staring at Seth.

Kay Harper, Mac's nurse, whispered, "What in the world has gotten into him today?"

Seth shook his head and walked out the back door and got in his car. He needed to clear his head and try to understand what might have set off his mentor. Lunch at the Singing Dog Café ought to help.

~ ~ ~

True to his word, Dr. Mac arrived at the clinic promptly at two o'clock and shed his coat without a word. The staff gave him plenty of space and made no mention of that morning's episode between the two doctors.

It was midafternoon, and Seth had just walked out of exam room two to record his examination of Athlene Henry when he heard a loud thud. Turning to see what had happened, he saw Mac lying on the floor.

Shoving his recorder in his pocket as he ran toward his friend, he shouted for Kay.

"Get the crash cart, stat." Kay whirled around, ran into a room and seconds later was on her knees placing a cuff around Mac's arm.

"Blood pressure is 80 over 60, Doctor."

"Justine, get some pillows and get his feet up."

Seth, kneeling by his friend, began a rapid assessment to make sure he was breathing. He listened to his heart and lungs, then felt for a pulse in his neck and noted it was slow, around 30.

He and Kay exchanged a concerned look.

"Justine, call 911, now!"

Seth continued his exam. Besides the very low heart rate, Mac was cool and sweaty. He remained conscious with no slurring of speech. There had been no signs of localized weakness on either side, so the possibility of a stroke could be eliminated. Mac had no complaints of chest pain to suggest a heart attack.

While waiting on the ambulance, Seth ordered Justine to apply the AED so they could get an EKG reading. It showed Mac to be in complete heart block.

"Blood pressure's now 100 over 70, heart rate up to 45, pulse ox is 92%, and his finger-stick blood sugar is 124," Kay reported.

"Justine, call the ambulance and confirm they have an external pacemaker on board just in case we need it."

The scream of the ambulance siren pierced the air around them. In moments, three men rushed through the clinic back door.

While they checked Mac's vitals again, Seth briefed them on his assessment.

"Dr. McQuarry's skin color has improved, and he's started asking what happened," Seth told the paramedics. "There's also been no sign of pain. He probably doesn't need the external pacemaker at this point as long as his BP stays satisfactory."

The paramedics placed Mac on the stretcher and began rolling him toward the clinic entrance.

Helen, followed by Sodie who had run to get her, burst through the door. Her face pale and eyes wide, she rushed to her husband's side. Seth turned to her and pulled her into a hug. "We're on top of this, Helen. I'm riding with him in the ambulance. Kay and Justine, will one of you bring her in your car?" Seth gave Helen another hug and followed the stretcher outside. As he passed Nell at the door, he said, "Reschedule patients, Nell. I'll get back with you after I know more."

Justine put her arm around Helen as they watched the ambulance tear out of the parking lot, lights flashing and siren blaring. "Come on, Mrs. Mac, let's get you to the hospital. He's in good hands." Kay followed them to Justine's car and got in the back seat.

As Justine was helping her get in the car, Helen cried out to Nell who was still standing in the doorway, "Please call Claire. Tell her what's happened and see if she can meet me there."

"I'm going to make the call right now, Mrs. Mac," Nell said, her voice trembling.

~ ~ ~

Helen sat between Justine and Kay in the waiting area at Granville General Hospital. Justine had asked a nurse for a warm blanket to put around her charge. The older woman was shaking from fear and the frigid room temperature.

Within half an hour of their arrival, Claire came race-walking down the hall to get to her friend. When she bent to hug her, Helen began to cry.

"I can't be strong any longer," she said, her words coming out in spurts.

Justine moved to another chair to allow Claire to sit by Helen. Claire stroked Helen's shoulder.

"I – I – can't – lose – him, Claire."

"Helen, he's being well cared for. You know Seth will do everything he can for Mac," she kissed her friend's cheek and wrapped an arm around her shoulder.

"What did you do with our boy, Claire?" Helen's voice was still shaky but a small amount of light came to her eyes when she mentioned Mason.

"I took him to J.J.'s." Reassured, Helen rested her head on Claire's shoulder.

~ ~ ~

After what seemed like hours, Seth walked toward the four women. His face unreadable.

Helen stood and he took her in his arms, holding her for a long moment. "Rough day, huh?" he said in a gentle voice. She nodded.

"Well, here's what we found," he said, helping her sit down. He pulled a nearby chair in front of her and took her hands in his as he began to explain.

"First of all, I want you to know Mac is stable. We confirmed that he is in complete heart block and in view of his history of tick bites, we suspect the etiology is Lyme disease, which can cause a heart block. While winter cases of Lyme are not common, they do happen. We have drawn blood tests for Lyme disease and have started him on antibiotics while awaiting the results that should give us an answer."

Seth gave her hands a gentle squeeze, waiting a moment before going on. "If it is Lyme, that diagnosis would also account for all the aches and pains he told us he's been having of late. I called in Dr. Phillip Redman, a cardiologist, who examined Mac and took him to the cath lab where he installed a temporary pacemaker. He will be scheduled later for a permanent one if necessary. Dr. Redman and I also will consult with an infectious disease specialist if the blood test does not point to Lyme disease."

Seth stroked Helen's hands, giving her a moment to take it all in.

"Helen, do you have any questions right now?"

She shook her head no, a dazed look in her eyes. "My brain isn't working real well right now," she said.

"I know it's hard to keep up with all this at one time. I'll plan to be with you as much as possible. And, Helen, just as soon as we can, we'll get you back to see him."

Helen smiled at the news and patted his hand. "Thank you so much, Seth. I know Mac has probably never told you this, but maybe you need to know how much he thinks of you." Her voice cracked with emotion. "You've become the son we never had, dear boy."

When she began to cry, releasing all the fears and anxiety, Seth pushed the chair back, knelt in front of her and wrapped his arms around her trembling body.

"Helen, you know I haven't had much experience when it comes to praying, but may I say one for Mac and for you?"

When she nodded for him to go on, Seth took her hands in his once again. "*God, I want to bring Dr. Mac and Helen before You. You already know what's going on, but we just want to ask You to take special care of Dr. Mac right now. And please give Helen the comfort and peace that only comes from You at times like this.*"

Seth hesitated, then said, "*And, God, help me and the other physicians have Your discernment as we care for Mac. Thank You, Jesus.*"

Seth left to go check on Mac and to find out if Helen could see him. Kay and Justine were encouraged by Helen to go on home to their waiting families. Claire promised to call them when they got the results and asked one of them to be sure and call Nell. She planned to call Reuben as soon as Helen could spend some time with her husband.

~ ~ ~

Even from a distance the two women could see the smile on Seth's face as he motioned for them to come to him. Claire helped Helen up, letting the blanket fall to the chair. The three met halfway, and Seth and Claire walked on either side of their friend, anxious to see her reunited with her husband. Claire reached behind Helen and gave Seth's arm a squeeze. The look in her eyes said "I'm proud of you."

~ 57 ~

"You sure are gloomy this afternoon," Claire said, "What's the matter with my Tiger this fine spring day? Hard day at school?" Claire tried to touch her son's shoulder but he squirmed out of her reach.

"I don't want to talk about it. You don't care anyway," came Mason's sulky reply.

"Just one minute, young man. You will not speak to me in that tone of voice," Claire shot back before she could control herself. Her son's escalating outbursts were wreaking havoc on her other emotions. She couldn't decide if this was another phase in a little boy's journey on the rocky road to manhood or just plain insolence. Whatever it was, she'd about had enough.

Throwing his backpack on the floor, Mason glared at her and ran to his room and slammed the door.

Claire was momentarily stunned at his outburst. She ran up the stairs and as soon as she opened his door, Mason flung himself into her arms. Claire caressed her son's silky hair then bent to kiss the top of his head.

"I'm sorry, Mom. I was really mad about something that happened at school."

"Do you want to tell me what made you feel that way?" Claire pulled back enough to look in his eyes.

"At recess a bunch of the guys were talking about a camping trip they were going on with their dads. They said they didn't invite me 'cause I don't have a dad."

"I'm so sorry, Mason. I know that hurt. They don't understand how that makes you feel."

Mason pulled back from Claire. There was grief in his eyes,

but determination on his face. "Mom," he said, "I want to ask Dr. Seth to go on that camping trip with me. It wouldn't be the same as having my own dad, but I really like Dr. Seth. I want to go on that trip, Mom, so please say yes."

Claire nodded just as a shaft of light filtered through the window and lit up her son's upturned face.

"Can I go call him?"

"Not right now, Mason, Dr. Seth is still at work."

Mason tugged at her hand. "I think we should call the office and ask Miss Nell to give him a note inviting him to dinner. Please, Mom."

"Oh, okay." She'd lost the battle but maybe it was a necessary loss.

Mason ran down the stairs two at a time. By the time she walked through the door, she heard her son talking to someone on the phone. Turning at the sound of her entrance, he smiled and said, "Here's my mom, Miss Nell. Thank you for doing this for me." A huge grin spread across his face as he held out the phone to Claire.

"Hi, Nell, yes, I'm fine. How about you? So, what did my guy ask you to do?" Claire looked at Mason as she listened to Nell. "Okay, just shorten all that to an invitation to come to dinner here tonight."

After thanking Nell, she turned to her son. "I shortened your very long and detailed message, my little man. Now, if we're having a guest for dinner, I think we better get cleaned up. While I get a quick shower, I want you to go and get your backpack where you left it and then play with Cisco. I'll call you when it's your turn."

~ ~ ~

The shower was just what she needed to quiet her spirit. All the drama with Mason was enough for one day, but now she had to find her way through the layers of emotions Seth Bradley brought into her world. She let the hot water cascade over her, feeling the tension in her shoulders begin to ease. Why couldn't she relax and give the man a chance? It had been more than three years since her husband had died.

The bond Seth and Mason had formed touched her deeply because it was genuine. A year or so after Randall's death, there had been a couple of men who had tried to get to her through her son, and it repulsed her. She could see now that she had locked her heart and hidden the key, maybe even from herself. Could she find that key and perhaps open the door again? She wasn't sure. But one thing she knew for certain—Seth was not trying to get to her through her son.

Claire was in the kitchen scrounging around for something to make for dinner without having to go to the store when her phone rang. "Hello," she said, glancing at the caller name. "Seth, guess you got our message."

"I did. Must say I was taken by surprise. Does this mean we can be friends again?"

"Seth, we haven't stopped being friends. I just . . . oh, I don't know, have been confused. It's all me, and I do want to apologize. But I need to be honest too. Tonight is about Mason wanting to ask you to do something for him." Claire ran her hand through her hair trying to get her nerves under control.

"Claire, don't you know I'd do anything in my power for Mason. You don't have to invite me to dinner, just ask me."

Claire sat down on the kitchen floor and pulled her legs together, Indian style. It took everything in her to keep from crying. "Thank you, Seth. That means so much to me," she said, clearing her throat. "I still want you to come for dinner. And if it's okay, I'll let Mason ask you what he's wanting you to do. Will six thirty work for you?"

~ ~ ~

When she heard Cisco bark and Mason shriek, she looked at the clock. Two hours had somehow come and gone. She hadn't gotten around to putting on makeup after her shower. At least she had on clean jeans and a decent shirt. Dinner would be lasagna, salad, and yeast rolls. She ran to her bedroom and found her lipstick, just a little color she told herself.

Taking a deep breath, she marched toward the front door. She hadn't seen Seth in close to a month but there was no reason to tremble like a school girl going on her first date. She stepped onto the front porch and her heart jumped. Mason and Seth were throwing a Frisbee back and forth to each other while Cisco ran from one to the other hoping one of them would not make the catch. At that moment, Mason overreached and missed it. Cisco dashed in and an instant later had her prize. The guys pleaded with her to bring it back, but each time they got close, she dashed out of their way, thoroughly enjoying her victory.

Seth waved when he caught sight of Claire sitting on the top step of the porch. She smiled and waved back. He really was so good with Mason. And she had to admit she'd missed him being around.

Mason hopped on Seth's back for his famous piggyback ride. Both of them were red faced from running but the glow in their eyes said far more. They loved being together.

"Ms. Westfield, I've brought your boy home," Seth said, with an exaggerated bow, causing Mason to tumble onto the ground right in front of his mother. They all laughed as Cisco joined in the fun, barking and running circles around the guys.

While Seth and her son washed up, Claire took the lasagna out of the oven and checked the rolls. Memories poured into her mind of all the times she'd done this in the past while Randall and Mason were the ones washing up. But she resisted the thoughts, shoving them into a special corner of her heart. Randall was gone. But Seth was here. Shock rippled through her veins when she realized how comfortably Seth occupied the empty spaces in their lives.

Dinner preparations fell into an easy flow. While Claire placed lasagna on each of the plates, Mason fed Cisco then had her lie down on her bed. Seth volunteered to fill the water glasses while Claire dished up the salad and put the rolls in a basket. The normalcy of the moment touched Claire. She was thankful that conversation was never difficult with Mason around.

At dinner he kept them laughing with tall stories of his escapades at school. About halfway through dinner, his eyes flitted to Claire with an obvious question.

"Seth, I think Mason has a question he wants to ask you," she said, winking at her son.

"Oh, he does, does he?" Seth grinned. "Well, let's have it, my man."

The importance of his request was clear on Mason's face. "Dr. Seth, I know you're a really busy man, but would you take me on a camping trip with some of the guys and their dads?" Fear of the two letter word answer etched the boy's face.

"When is this camping trip, buddy?"

Mason told him the date. Seth pulled out his phone and checked his calendar, a serious look on his face.

"Well," he said in a deep voice, "it looks like I'm . . . free! I would consider it a great honor to go on that trip with a very good friend." Mason propelled himself into Seth's arms followed by a high five.

Claire mouthed a quick thank you when Seth turned to smile at her. His eyes told her all she needed to know.

∼ 58 ∼

Seth stood at his office door going over a chart when he felt his phone vibrate. The name Dr. Marvin Hawthorn blazed across the screen. Seth went to his desk and answered his phone.

"Dr. Hawthorn, what a pleasant surprise. How are you, sir?"

"Quite well, thank you," the man said in a brusk voice. "I was going through some notes on my calendar and had one to call you and see if you're still interested in pursuing a possible position with our clinic. So where are you at this point, young man?"

Seth's pulse seemed to jump through his skin, but he pulled himself together knowing Hawthorn's no nonsense reputation.

"I am still interested, sir. And I appreciate you keeping me in mind."

"By my calculations you're coming up on the time when you need to start making some decisions about your future plans. Is that correct?"

Trying to juggle the shock of this call and the truth of the man's comments, Seth's brain struggled in connecting with his tongue. Could it actually be that his commitment in Mason Falls was that close to being finished? Where had the time gone? And why hadn't he realized it was this close to decision time?

"Dr. Bradley, are you there?"

"Yes, forgive me. To be honest it shocked me to realize how quickly my time here has gone by."

"Hmm," the older man muttered, "that can be good and bad. Good for you and possibly bad for me, if that means you've found your niche where you are." After a long pause Hawthorn said, "Well, are you interested in coming up here in the next two to three weeks for a visit?"

"Yes sir, I'm very interested." Somehow Seth didn't feel as excited as he tried to sound. What was wrong with him? Wasn't this what he'd dreamed of and worked for all these years? He should be pumping his fist in the air and shouting to the world, "Yes! I'm almost there." He'd get excited when it sank in, wouldn't he?

After agreeing to check his schedule and contact Hawthorn's office manager to make arrangements for the visit, Seth sat at his desk trying to take in what all this meant.

He sighed. Mac was back at the clinic after a few weeks recovery time from his Lyme's disease, but he wasn't feeling well today and had taken the day off. Seth was still a little worried about him. He sighed again. His goal was within reach, if he wanted it. But right now, he had a patient waiting for him in exam room three.

~ ~ ~

Mr. Tony Wilcox sat on the exam table like a cold marble statue, arms crossed against his chest, a scowl on his face.

"Good morning, Mr. Wilcox. I took a look at your chart, and it tells me you're having some stomach issues. How about describing what's going on for me?"

The man's face turned dark red. "I didn't come in here to pay you to ask me what's wrong. Ain't that supposed to be your job, mister high and mighty doctor? I don't care much for your type. Thinkin' you're so much smarter than the rest of us. You tell me what's wrong."

Seth moved to the lone chair in the room and sat down, hoping it might help the man feel less threatened. He waited a few moments before speaking.

"Mr. Wilcox, I assure you I don't think of myself as high and mighty or smarter than anyone else. I had to work very long, hard hours to become a doctor. And the reason I did was because I wanted to help people who are ill and hurting. Do you think we might start over?

"Hi, Tony, I'm Seth. How about you and me talking about how you're feeling and what's hurting your stomach?"

Seth crossed his leg and ran one hand along the arm of the chair. "What kind of work do you do, Tony?"

Tony glared at his shoes but mumbled, "I work for the town street department."

"Really! Man, I want to tell you what a great job you guys are doing out on 5th Street. I drove over that way to see my friend Possum Guthrie the other day and was really impressed with the street work being done."

Tony glanced over at Seth. "You're friends with old Possum?"

"Sure am. He's one of my best friends. We like to go fishing together and just kinda hang out. I admire Possum. He's got a heart of gold."

Seth noticed Tony swallow hard while staring at his boots. "Well, maybe if you're friends with old Possum I got you wrong. I don't come to see no Doc unless I really need to. Makes me real nervous."

His exam of Tony Wilcox proved to be a fairly benign diagnosis of reflux. By the time he scrawled out a prescription and handed it to Tony, people would have thought them to be longtime friends.

Seth had learned what a few kind words and a relaxed attitude could do to settle a patient's fears and establish a relationship. In this case, it helped set a good tone for a long and grueling day. Mac wasn't feeling well and had taken the day off, so Seth was covering for both of them. Familiar memories of covering the ER at Saint Luke's followed him throughout the day.

What few moments he had between patients found him reflecting on Dr. Hawthorn's call. He promised himself a long run after work to sort through the questions and emotions rumbling around in his head and especially in his heart.

～ 59 ～

ANGUS McQUARRY HAD BEEN A BEAR since returning from being "under the weather" as he referred to his bout with Lyme disease. He still did not have his full strength back after several months, and he would not admit it. Seth had postponed his trip to Kansas City until summer rolled around. He wanted to make sure Mac was up to seeing patients on the Thursday and Friday while he was gone. His plan was to stay through the weekend and catch up with a couple of residency buddies if all went well with Mac. Now the time was here, and he found himself cruising the winding back roads of the Ozarks, heading to the interstate highway.

The four and a half hour trip would be a breeze even in Old Red. He felt like he was gliding across the miles. He had to admit he was nervous about this visit. He wasn't sure how he would react to being back in the city or in the plush clinic of Hawthorn and Hawthorn. A part of him could hardly wait to get there. But he was also concerned about Mac and several of his patients.

Mac was worrying him. He just wasn't his usual self. Maybe it was just that he didn't feel well but he'd been really irritable with everyone in the clinic. What got under Seth's skin the most was the older man questioning everything Seth did, checking in on him like a first year resident. This trip was coming at the perfect time. He needed a break from Angus McQuarry and small town life.

He hadn't told Claire what he was doing. Not that he owed it to her. They weren't actually dating, but they had been spending a fair amount of time together since the camping trip with Mason, which turned out to be a lot of fun. Was it better for them if they didn't know what he was doing? Probably, he told himself. It was a tricky dilemma. One he wasn't sure he had handled correctly. He didn't even know if he'd be offered a position, he reasoned, so why put them on edge about something that may not happen.

"All righty," he said aloud, "you need to relax, enjoy the scenery, and take a break from all the chaos of the last few months." He rolled down his window allowing the early morning air to rustle his hair and calm his spirit. He soon found himself reliving his favorite daydream. He was driving a restored Austin-Healy sports car. The top was down, the wind smacked him in the face, and he loved the feel of it. He promised himself someday he would be driving that dream car.

~ ~ ~

Eleanor Allen, Dr. Hawthorn's office manager, had made reservations for him at the Sheraton Hotel on the Plaza. As a struggling resident, this well-known area in Kansas City seemed a faraway dream. He had gone there only a few times with some of the other guys at the hospital who wanted to get coffee or occasionally a beer.

He smiled as he remembered saving money to treat himself on his birthday or Christmas to an incredible steak dinner at the Plaza III Steakhouse. His salivary glands began to work overtime just thinking about it. His favorite place for seafood was Bristol Seafood & Steak. Chad Peters had told him the restaurant had moved out to 119th and Nall. If he had any free time that would be on his list of things to do. Last but by no means least was Loose Park. He'd thrown his running shoes and shorts in for some early morning runs. He knew every inch of that trail. Running there had been his stress reliever. No matter how early he had to get up or how late he might have to go, the Loose Park trail was like a trusted friend during his residency days. Usually he was exhausted or frazzled when he got there, but the trail never let him down.

Seth glanced at his watch as he approached Grandview just on the outskirts of Kansas City. Three hours and forty-five minutes. He'd made great time. Watching for the 435 loop he merged into the left lane of traffic. Adrenaline rushed through him. Maybe this was what people who have families experience when returning home for a visit.

Seth checked in at the Sheraton and went to his room to

freshen up. When he opened the door, he found that the clinic had reserved a beautifully decorated suite for him. He closed the door and let out a whistle. He'd never set foot in a place like this. The décor made him grin with satisfaction. He put his hanging bag in the closet and took in every detail of the room. He walked over to the windows to see the incredible view of the famous Country Club Plaza.

"So this is how the well-to-do folks live," he muttered. Falling back on the king size bed, he realized how easy it would be to get used to this lifestyle. After a quick shower, Seth slipped into a pair of neat khaki slacks, white shirt, his favorite navy and red striped tie and a navy blazer. He wasn't taking any chances on the dress code. This struck a good middle, not under dressed but not too formal. He remembered Gran telling him as a young teen that dressing properly for a meeting showed respect for the person who was interviewing you.

"You taught me well, Gran," he said with a smile. "Thanks for taking a thrown away baby boy and molding him into a man. I owe you so much and miss you every day." Seth rubbed a hand across his eyes and stepped into the hall. What would the next two days bring?

The air was warm and humid as he walked from the parking garage to the main entrance of the Hawthorn Clinic. He wiped the perspiration that trickled down one cheek. Better make the men's room his first stop, he told himself. With the humidity, he needed a splash of cold water to regain a fresh look before meeting with Dr. Hawthorn.

Seth checked in with the receptionist and was given the go ahead to take the elevator up to the second floor where Marvin Hawthorn and his son Corbin's offices and exam rooms were located. The next two floors up housed the associate offices of numerous physicians.

Seth punched the Level 2 button in the elevator and straightened his tie. Just as he finished checking his newly shined shoes, the elevator stopped and the second floor light lit up. As he stepped out of the elevator, he uttered a quiet prayer. "*Lord, I'm going to trust You to show me what I need to know during this time in the clinic and with the Hawthorns.*"

Eleanor Allen was the first person to greet him as he opened the door to Marvin Hawthorn's outer office.

"Dr. Bradley, so nice to see you again." She stood and walked around her desk to welcome him with a warm handshake. "Dr. Hawthorn is with a patient but shouldn't be much longer. May I get you a drink while you wait?"

Seth declined the offer and chose a *Newsweek* magazine to read instead. Eleanor asked a few questions about how his time in Mason Falls was going then excused herself to get back to her work. Seth found it impossible to focus on the magazine. His thoughts bounced back and forth between what this day might bring and how things were going in the clinic back home.

Startled by the realization of that last thought, he stood and walked across the room to stare out the large windows spanning an entire wall. A city sprawled before him, tempting everything in him to claim it as his own.

He heard a door open and turned to see the distinguished Dr. Marvin Hawthorn walking toward him. After a few moments of small talk, the older man suggested they move to his office.

Seth breathed another quick prayer to calm his nervousness.

Dr. Hawthorn was cordial but lived up to his reputation of getting to the point quickly. He began with numerous questions related to what experience Seth had gained during his time with Dr. McQuarry.

There was a brief reprieve for Seth when the man stood and walked to the windows. He stared over the city before him just as Seth had done earlier.

Marvin Hawthorn said, "Dr. Bradley, you have passed a very deliberate and extremely difficult barrage of questions that I ask every man and woman I consider for a position here. And I must say you have done so with flying colors."

For the first time since the questions began, Seth could take a complete breath. "Thank you, sir, that means a lot." In the quietness now filling his heart, he thanked the one he knew to be responsible.

Hawthorn walked back to his desk and sat down. "Now, that's the good news, but the hard part comes next. I want you to know something at the outset of my next question. I believe I may have mentioned it to you on the phone. Over the years, I have developed a quite keen perception for knowing when someone is trying to, shall we say, put something over on me. So are you ready to answer another question?"

His heart pounding Seth said, "Yes sir, I am."

"Well then, Dr. Seth Bradley, tell me two things, what is it that tugs at your heart in life and in medicine?"

Seth hadn't felt this nervous since he assisted in his first surgery. A vivid memory of willing himself not to faint was just how he felt right now.

He sat up straighter in his chair, then said, "Sir, I never knew my parents. I was raised by my grandmother who died of cancer when I was nineteen. My answer to what tugs at my heart in life would have to be finding a place where I can belong and someday to have a family of my own."

He hesitated as he gathered his thoughts. "I'm not sure I could have given you an answer to what tugs at my heart in medicine if you'd asked me that before I went to Mason Falls. But the answer is quite clear to me now.

"Sir, I went to Mason Falls an angry young man. My disappointment in not being able to be considered for a position with your clinic ate at me. I'd made a commitment to pay back my rural practice loan by going to a small town for three years. That was the right thing for me to do, and I was going to do it even though I didn't want to. But what I've learned since being there, I wouldn't trade for anything."

Seth leaned forward, willing this highly regarded man before him to hear the words of his heart. *Give me wisdom, Lord*, he prayed in silence.

"Dr. Hawthorn, what tugs at my heart in medicine is the honor and privilege my patients give me when they put their trust in me. That has given me a sense of joy and fulfillment I never expected."

Seth sat back in the chair.

Marvin Hawthorn said nothing but stood and walked back to the long bank of windows. He once again gazed at the prestigious buildings before him. When he returned to his desk, he stood at the corner and looked at Seth for a long moment. "Dr. Bradley, thank you for coming. I appreciate your candor." He reached out to shake hands. "I've made arrangements for you to meet with my son Corbin, then he and a couple of others will take you to lunch."

Seth nodded. "Thank you, sir. I appreciate your time." He turned to go, feeling like a total failure. Just as he reached the door, he heard Marvin Hawthorn call his name.

"Seth . . . I heard your heart."

~ 60 ~

THE SOOTHING VOICE OF NELL MEYERS helped ease Claire's nerves. "Nell, this is Claire Westfield. Any chance I can get Mason in to see Seth or Mac? He's having a hard time with some kind of rash. I've done everything I can think to do but no change. I'm probably hitting the panic button, but I don't know what else I can do for him."

Nell's hesitation was so out of the ordinary that Claire asked, "Is something wrong at the clinic, Nell?"

"Umm, not really," she said. "It's just with Dr. Bradley in Kansas City, Dr. Mac is swamped. But let me see what I can work out. I know Dr. Mac will want to see Mason. I just need to see the best place to plug him in."

Claire's heart skipped a beat at the mention of Kansas City. She recovered quickly and said, "Nell, I could take Mason to the ER in Granville if it would help."

"No," came the firm reply. "Just give me another second. Okay, how about right at closing time? Be here a few minutes before five. And you still may have to wait a bit. I sure wish Dr. Bradley was here."

Claire had the same thought herself.

When Claire and Mason showed up right before five, the clinic still had two patients in the waiting room. She wondered how many might still be in exam rooms. Mason curled up next to her on what looked like an old church pew, an obvious sign her little guy didn't feel good. Stroking his hair, she wrestled with the question that continued to gnaw at her. Why hadn't Seth told her about Kansas City?

She scolded herself for thinking he owed her an explanation, but the truth hurt. He hadn't given up on his desire to go to Kansas City once he completed his commitment here. Looking down at her son and knowing how much he cared for Seth brought her to the verge of tears. Would he now have to lose another person who'd become an important part of his young life?

She checked her watch. Five-thirty. The other two patients had been called back some time ago. She hoped Kay would come get them soon.

Several minutes later, Kay opened the door and motioned them back.

"Well, this fella isn't his spunky self, is he?" Kay said, nudging the boy up on the scale. "Let's see how much you've grown, Mason, so you can tell Dr. Mac. As she adjusted the machine for height and weight, Mason seemed lost in some other place. A blank stare clouded his usually bright, mischievous eyes.

Mac ambled down the hall as Mason stepped off the scale. Claire noticed how weary he looked. She knew he hadn't been feeling well, but it had been a couple of weeks since she'd seen him. Disappointment and a touch of anger grabbed hold of her. Why would Seth go on a trip when Mac obviously wasn't feeling well? Maybe Seth wasn't the man she thought he was.

Mac gave a weak grin as he tousled Mason's hair. "Hi there, partner. Looks like you and I are both not feeling too great. Let's go check you out, okay? Mason slipped a hand into Mac's as the two of them went to a room. Claire followed, taking a mental snap shot of the tall man and small boy.

Mac picked up Mason and set him on the exam table, but Claire noticed the effort it took.

"So, my favorite fishing buddy is having some problems. We can't have that, now can we? Mac rubbed his stethoscope on his lab coat warming it up before asking the child to lift his shirt.

"I'm just going to take a listen to what's going on inside of you, partner. Breathe in real deep for me. Good job, Mason. You're a very good patient."

Mac continued his exam, checking ears, eyes, and throat. "Claire, when did you notice the red bumps on his waist and arms and legs?" He took a sucker from a glass jar next to the sink and handed it to Mason. "This always helps make things a little better!"

"I think it started a couple of days ago, but it's gotten worse, and he scratches almost constantly. I know this may sound crazy, Mac, but I was afraid it might be measles even though he's had his immunizations. I tried everything I could think of, but he seems to be getting worse."

"It's okay, Mom, it's a case of chiggers. We see them every year. Chiggers are tiny red mites that get under the skin and itch like the dickens. The timing is right because it usually takes twenty-four to forty-eight hours to manifest."

Mac turned to the boy on the exam table and said, "You haven't by any chance been picking blackberries have you, Mason?"

Mason's eyes widened and a spark of life glowed in them. "How did you know, Dr. Mac? I've been findin' bunches of those things along our road. They sure do taste good."

Mac patted him on the shoulder, "I agree with that, old buddy, but from now on your mom needs to spray you real good with insect repellant before you go berry picking."

Turning to Claire, he said, "I want to give him a good once over while you're here and check for ticks. Those are another issue this time of year. I'll have Kay come in and you can wait in my office. Then I'll meet you in there."

~ ~ ~

When Mac entered his office, he gave her a thumbs up.

"No ticks. That's good news. We sure don't want him to get Lyme disease or Rocky Mountain Spotted Fever. A couple of things we need to talk about so you can be up to speed on this type of thing.

"First, it's very important to keep him from scratching the chigger bites. And let me tell you that's not easy." Mac gave a little chuckle. "Those little critters can drive you crazy. If he keeps scratching, he's likely to get impetigo, so keep his fingernails trimmed. You might want to give him Benadryl, especially before bed. That will make him drowsy and help him sleep. And last of all, I'll write you a prescription for a steroid cream for the bites. Use this twice a day. And make sure both of you use insect repellant when you go outside. Keep me posted and call if he doesn't start showing some improvement." Mac stood and walked around the desk. Giving Claire a hug, he said, "He's going to be fine. It's part of life around here. And, Claire, be sure you check for ticks at bath time. That's very important."

Claire returned the hug and said, "Angus McQuarry, you take care of yourself too. You look very tired."

"I plan on doing just that as soon as Seth gets back," Mac said, giving her a tired grin.

~ 61 ~

SETH HAD MUCH TO THINK ABOUT on the trip back to Mason Falls. One moment his thoughts were filled with the pampering and flattery he'd received and the next he was missing the small town he'd come to care about. Marvin Hawthorn's son Corbin had taken Seth to his favorite restaurants, The Plaza III Steakhouse and Bristol Seafood, and Friday night the other senior partner, Dr. Henry Ridgeway, had invited him to his private box to watch a Royals game. All three men had given Seth the impression the position was his if he wanted it. Their words were encouraging, and Seth had felt comfortable with each of them. With the clinic's reputation as one of the top in the nation as well as the city, Seth could hardly get his mind around the idea that they had a genuine interest in him.

The wind from his open windows whipped his hair and stung his eyes. His thoughts were like a boomerang zooming in one direction only to return to him with a jolt. Some struck him hard. Could he take an offer if given one? What about Mason Falls and the people depending on him? What about Mac and Reuben? And most of all what about Claire and Mason?

As he entered the Ozark mountain range, he began watching for one of the many lookout points where he could pull over. Several miles later he spotted one and eased Old Red off the road. He got out of the car and stood gazing at the view. A large red-tailed hawk flew by in front of him, its piercing cry the only sound he heard. Seth watched in awe as the bird soared around him making wide circles in the sky. He wondered if it was searching for its mate. But what struck him most was the ease and grace the bird displayed. It knew what it was created to do and where it belonged.

He turned to go but looked back over his shoulder one last

time. In a final swoop, the hawk seemed to head straight for him at an incredible speed. It came so close Seth raised his hands, fearing it might attack him. As he peered through his fingers, he saw the hawk hover in midair and look at him. A moment later its wings lifted it once more into a wind current, and it was gone.

Seth lowered his hands and leaned against the rock retaining wall. He strained to see the hawk again, but the moment was over.

He slid into his car and started the engine. What had just happened? It was the strangest thing he'd ever experienced. As Seth pulled back out on the road, he voiced his question. *"Lord, were You trying to tell me something in what just took place?"*

In the quietness of the moment, he was struck by a thought. God's creature, a red-tailed hawk, seemed to be demonstrating the need to be at peace where the Creator had placed him. Seth's hands clutched the steering wheel, and he willed himself to breathe.

Each mile took him further from Kansas City and all the experiences and emotions that had captured him through the weekend. His time with his fellow residents, Chad Peters and Mark Riley, had been like igniting a match that glowed brighter with every scenario they used to convince him this was where he belonged. Seth pulled over to get gas and something to drink at an old combination gas station and mom and pop café. He stretched his legs while Old Red guzzled the gas.

He noticed a picnic table off to the side under a large shade tree. He moved his car out of the way and walked over to the table with his Coke and Snickers. He sat on the table, resting his feet on the bench beneath it. He couldn't help but compare the bustling pace of the city life he'd just experienced to the slow, easygoing pace he was returning to. Munching on his Snickers, he wondered what Claire and Mason had done these few days. And was Mac feeling any better? He was concerned for the man he'd come to admire. Something wasn't right, but Mac wouldn't confide in him. After licking the last bit of chocolate from the candy wrapper, Seth hopped off the table and tossed the wrapper in the trash can.

~ ~ ~

By the time Seth reached the outskirts of Mason Falls, his head felt like it had been a punching bag for his emotions.

～ 62 ～

GUILT WORRIED HIM. SINCE HIS RETURN from Kansas City, he couldn't get rid of the unshakable need to apologize to Claire. He had rationalized not telling her he was going for fear that it would only cause her needless worry, especially since he didn't know if he would be offered a position. But was that really why he didn't tell her?

He and Claire cared for each other. He was sure of that. They hadn't come to grips with how serious a relationship they had, but he felt convinced it was more than casual. He made up his mind that tonight after work he would man up and go see her. He needed to apologize for not telling her about his trip. Their friendship was far more important than his pride. A thought struck him that made him smile. There would be a stop he would make before going out to her place.

That afternoon Seth found himself day dreaming between patients. He rehearsed over and over in his mind what he'd say when Claire opened the door. The schedule dragged on for what seemed like forever, and Seth found himself checking his watch repeatedly.

When the last patient left and the last chart had been dictated, he rushed out the back door. He drove to the stop he intended to make and was in and out in a matter of minutes. "Now," he mumbled, "comes the humbling part."

～ ～ ～

No sooner had Seth stepped out of the car than Mason and Cisco came charging down the front steps.

"Hi ya, Dr. Seth!" Boy and dog ran circles around him, laughing each time he reached out pretending to try and catch one of them.

Then he saw Claire appear on the porch. She looked like a

school girl in shorts and a tee shirt with her hair in a ponytail. He smiled as he walked up to the porch.

"Well, this is a surprise," she said.

Seth heard the cool tone in her words.

"Yeah, I guess it is. I need to talk to you if you have a moment."

"Hey, Dr. Seth, what's that flower for?"

"It was a surprise for your mom, buddy."

Mason said, "Uh oh. Does that mean you love my mom, Dr. Seth? When my daddy brought Mom flowers he always said, 'Love you, Babe.'" He stared back and forth between his mom and Seth waiting for an answer.

"Hey, buddy, how about you and Cisco go play and give your mom and me a few minutes, okay."

A look of understanding flashed across the boy's face, and he and his dog ran toward the barn.

A slow smile spread across Claire's face. "Sorry. Out of the mouths of babes, you know. They haven't developed any filters yet."

"It's okay," he said, handing her a single dark red rose tied with a turquoise ribbon, her favorite color.

"I came to apologize. And I want to ask your forgiveness."

A confused look spread across Claire's face.

"For not telling you I was making a trip to Kansas City to meet with a clinic. I felt terrible about it the entire weekend. Will you forgive me, Claire?" His eyes never strayed from hers, trying to read her thoughts. "I should have had the courtesy to let you know and I'm sorry."

"You don't owe me any explanation, Seth, but it was very thoughtful of you to come by and apologize." She ducked her head then said, "The rose is lovely, and I forgive you."

Seth let out a sigh of relief and smiled at her. "Thank you, that means a lot. Well, guess I'll head home."

He had almost gotten to his car when he heard her call his name. When he turned to look back, she was moving toward him.

"I have a confession to make too." Her green eyes stared straight into his. "I was really angry at you when I found out you were gone. Most of all because you left when Mac was not doing very well."

"I can understand how that looked. I had put off the trip a while to make sure he was feeling better, and he assured me he felt fine. He insisted I go." Seth hesitated, "In retrospect, you're probably right. I should've stayed here," he said, his thoughts pulling him in two directions.

"Claire, there's a fine line for a man between doing what he knows he should do and what he shouldn't do. And it boils down to the male ego, I guess. We don't like to admit our weakness. When Mac insisted he felt up to seeing patients those two days I would be out of the clinic, I accepted his decision."

Claire reached out and laid a hand on his arm. "Guess it's my turn to apologize and ask forgiveness. I'm sorry for not trusting you. Forgive me?"

Without thinking, Seth drew her into his arms, holding her close. It felt wonderful holding her. She didn't pull away. Taking her face in his hands, he bent down and kissed her. She leaned her head against his chest, and the world around them seemed to him to glow.

When she pulled back, he wanted to draw her close again, but instead he gently caressed her cheek then brought her hand to his lips with a gentle kiss.

Looking up at him, she touched his lips and said, "I better go check on Mason. Seth, I . . . don't know what to say."

"You don't need to say anything. Let's give ourselves time to think this through." The look of relief in her eyes told him he had done the right thing.

~ 63 ~

CLAIRE THOUGHT SHE HEARD HER PHONE ring, but she was in the middle of giving Cisco a bath while Mason was at school, so she didn't check it. She'd found the old wash tub her grandparents had used for their dogs. Childhood memories flooded her mind. Dog washing day, as Honey called it, had been one of Claire's favorite experiences. Honey would tell her to get her swimsuit on and together they would tackle the job. Their dogs, Cider, a large German Shepherd, and Molly, a Border Collie, loved their baths.

Claire's job was to hook up the water hose and fill the tub. Once Honey coerced one of the dogs into the tub with a piece of cheese, Claire was to spray the dog while Honey rubbed some shampoo in its fur. But being sprayed was the dogs' least favorite part of the process. By the time both Cider and Molly's cleanliness met Honey's approval, both Honey and Claire were as wet as the dogs.

She smiled at the memories. Spending summers with Potch and Honey had meant everything to Claire. Her mother would've been repulsed by the whole scene, and if she had been there, she wouldn't have allowed Claire to be a part of it. It was a sad thought. Claire willed herself to push it from her mind.

Once Cisco was dried off, Claire put her in the house. She didn't want to go through another episode like the one after Cisco's first bath when Claire had found her rolling in a pile of cow manure. Although soaked to the skin, she retrieved her phone and saw that the call had been from Robyn. She dialed the number and went to sit on the porch swing where the nice breeze would dry her off.

"Hey there, girlfriend, what were you doing? I let this thing ring for what seemed like forever." Robyn said in a carefree tone. "I've been missing you and my Tiger something awful."

Claire couldn't help but laugh. "Hi yourself. You wouldn't believe me if I told you."

"Try me," came the quick reply.

"Remember when we were kids and I'd come back to school and tell you all the stuff I did here with my grandparents? Well, I've been reliving one of those times today."

Claire grinned as she went on. "I was giving Mason's dog, Cisco, a bath in that same old wash tub I used to tell you about. And right now I'm sitting on the porch swing, and I'm soaking wet! What are you doing, my big city attorney friend?"

It felt good to be laughing again with her best friend in the world as though they were still those silly school friends so many years ago. Robyn seemed relaxed and unhurried, Claire noticed, totally out of character for her Type A friend.

After several minutes of conversation, Robyn said, "Are you up for some company? I'm in need of a break and some time with my two favorite people."

"Oh, Robyn, that would be wonderful! We've both missed you so much. When do you want to come?"

"I have a case that should be completed soon. Don't say anything to Mason yet, but I should be able to give you a definite time frame by the end of this week."

Claire filled her friend in on the latest ups and downs with Mason. They laughed at the boy's antics and grieved together over the rough places.

"Well, I better get back to it. But before I go, what's the latest on that gorgeous young doctor?"

Claire knew her friend well enough to know exactly the look on her face as she asked her question. Her dark eyes would zero in on Claire like a torpedo and there would be a funny smirk across her face.

"Things are fine now, but he had been in my doghouse. I didn't tell you because I really needed to sort things out first," she answered.

"Spill it 'cause there is no way we're closing this conversation with that statement. My client can wait a few more minutes. Give it up, girlfriend."

Claire hesitated, wondering what she was ready to share. She walked down the steps and started around the yard enjoying the bit of cool under the large shade trees planted so long ago by her twice great grandparents. What a gift they had left her.

"Robyn, I was angry that he went to Kansas City a few weeks ago and didn't bother to tell me. Then I felt guilty for being upset at him. I mean it's not like we're officially dating. We kind of have a relationship, but it's more friendship than anything else."

Claire was surprised that her very outspoken friend said nothing. It wasn't like her at all. She was always ready to take on the world as just another case. Why wasn't she reacting?

"Hey, you're the one who asked about him. Why aren't you saying anything?"

After a long pause Robyn asked, "If he's only a friend should he be expected to check in with you about what he does? I know that sounds harsh, but, Claire, it seems like you need to make some decisions about this guy."

"You're right, as usual. I guess what set me off was the reason he went. I had to take Mason to the clinic, and the receptionist told me Seth was in Kansas City. Then Dr. Mac said a clinic up there is interested in him. That's where he's always planned to go when he's finished here."

Tears slipped down her cheeks and she wiped them away with her hand. Silence from Robyn was rare, but at this moment Claire was thankful for it.

"Robyn, I'm afraid to let myself fall in love again. Seth's a good man, and he cares for Mason. My son hangs on every word he speaks." She walked over to the wooden fence separating the back yard from the pasture on the other side and leaned against it.

"Do you feel guilty about moving ahead with life because Randall can't?" Robyn's voice was soft and gentle. "It's okay for you to start a new life, Claire. Randall would want you to find someone, not only for you but to give Mason a father."

"I believe that, and we are getting settled here, making a home and a life. If Seth is going to eventually move to Kansas City, where does that leave us? I want to stay here and to raise my son in this type of environment. I just don't have any answers right now."

"I understand, sweet friend. It'll all work out, Claire. You just have to hold on to that."

～ 64 ～

CLAIRE LOVED MORNINGS LIKE THIS WITH a slight chill in the air but not too cold to work in her flower beds. She zipped up her jacket, pulled on her gloves, and headed for the shed. Cherished memories of working alongside her grandparents on her visits here again played across her mind like a favorite old movie. She had helped build the cozy little structure and she'd always thought it looked like a giant doll house.

Potch and Honey were meticulous in everything they did. She smiled as she remembered Honey's favorite saying, "A place for everything and everything in its place." The door creaked as she opened it just as it had when she was a girl. She could oil the hinges, but it just wouldn't be the same. She loved that sound, but for the first time, she wondered why her grandparents had never oiled it. Now that she thought about it that was totally out of character for them. Had they liked the sound too, or had they left it because they knew she liked it?

A rich earthy smell from bags of mulch and potting soil always greeted her when she opened the door, and she inhaled it with pleasure. The thought of preparing the garden for fall filled her with joy and anticipation. She cleaned out summer beds, trimmed the fall asters and camellias, and prepared the beds for mulch. Just when she was ready for a break, her phone started ringing. A quick glance told her it was Mason's school.

"This is Claire Westfield," she said. After listening for a few moments, she said, "Yes, of course, I'll come in. Thank you." She slumped to the ground, pulled her knees up to her chest, and dropped her head to rest on them. "Oh, Mason baby, what is going on with you?"

Returning to the shed, she hung up her gardening spade, laid her gloves on the work table, and set the bag of mulch under a row of shelves. All she knew was that Miss Kendall wanted to see her over the children's lunch break. And it was important. The churning in her stomach increased with every scenario that went through her mind.

By the time Claire cleaned up and tried to look presentable, her nerves were shot. The least the woman could have done was say exactly what the problem was. She would make that point to Miss Kendall. It couldn't be worse than not knowing and going through the myriad of options out there for little boys. Or could it?

Claire pulled into the parking lot of the school still fuming. When she got out of the car, the urge to kick the door closed almost won out, but she didn't know who might see her outburst, so she shut it with great force instead. She decided she'd take out her frustrations on the vehicle at home. In her remote location, she could slam, kick, or pound the thing and no one would know she'd thrown an adult temper tantrum. Claire struggled to get her emotions under control. One minute she wanted to scream and the next she wanted to cry. And then her mind prowled through all the possibilities . . . again.

Miss Kendall had asked her to come to the counselor's office. It would be a place they could have privacy. That comment alone had driven Claire's stress level up several notches. She checked in at the principal's office and was told she could go straight to the counselor's office.

She knocked on the door marked Counselor and waited. Moments later a frazzled looking Miss Kendall approached and opened the door.

"Thank you so much for coming, Mrs. Westfield. I hated to have to call you, but this latest incidence is concerning. Mason got into a pretty bad fight. He literally erupted and punched another boy at recess."

Claire had never seen the woman look so shaken. At that moment all she wanted to do was grab her son and run back to her other life, the life before all this. Instead she heard her shaky voice ask for details.

"Neither boy will say what started it. That's why I called you. I thought maybe together we could get Mason to explain what sent him over the edge."

It took everything Claire had to keep from asking the teacher if she had called the other boy's parents.

"So, you're saying Mason is the one in trouble but you don't even know whether the other boy provoked him?"

Miss Kendall's face turned a deep pink, and she kept rubbing her hands. "I guess you could look at it that way. But your son is the one who gave the other boy a bloody nose. And I did try to reach that child's parents, but there was no answer. Mrs. Westfield, I want to get to the bottom of this for both boys. I just thought you could get Mason to tell us what happened."

Claire could see the torment in the woman's eyes. She didn't seem angry, just weary and frustrated. "I'll do my best."

Miss Kendal dialed a number and said, "Roberta, this is Mary Kendall. Would you please send Mason Westfield to the Counselor's office? And have Sherman Hopkins wait with you in the school office." She hung up the phone and let out a deep sigh.

Neither woman spoke while they waited on one little boy to make his appearance.

When they heard a slight knock on the door, Claire caught her breath, willing herself to keep her composure. The horrified look on her son's face when the teacher opened the door would stay with Claire a long time.

Miss Kendal immediately took control and asked Mason to sit in a monstrous leather chair in one corner of the room.

Claire felt tears sting her eyes as she watched her son almost swallowed up by its size. He gave Claire a dazed look before staring at his feet dangling over its edge.

The teacher said nothing for what seemed a very long time to Claire, and she was certain seemed even longer to her son. When his teacher spoke again her voice was soft, but her words were measured and held authority.

"Mason, I asked your mother to come in so the three of us could talk about what happened at recess. That was a pretty bad fight, wasn't it?" Mason only nodded, continuing to stare at his feet.

"We need you to tell us why you punched Sherman. Did he do something to you or say something that hurt you or made you mad?" Mary Kendall looked at Claire, her eyes telling her it was her turn."

Claire went to kneel beside her child. "Sweetheart, your teacher and I just want to know why you got so angry. You've never done anything like this before. There has to be a reason. Please tell us what happened."

"Are you mad at me, Mommy?" Mason asked.

Claire's words caught in her throat. She shook her head no and wrapped her arms around the small boy in the large chair.

"I just want to understand what happened, sweetheart. You've never hit anyone before. Please tell me why it happened."

Mason looked at his mother then his teacher. "Sherman kept making fun of me saying my daddy didn't like me or my mom so he left us. And he got the other kids to say the same stuff. When I told him my daddy died, he just laughed and said it was 'cause he didn't want to be around me and my mom—that's why he died. So, I told him to take it back, but he wouldn't. Then I punched him until he finally said, 'Okay, I take it back.'"

Mary Kendall's eyes narrowed as she looked at Claire. "Thank you, Mason. Why don't you go back to the office and wait for us there?"

Mason took a tentative step toward the door then turned and threw himself into his mother's arms. Holding him close she felt his small body shake as the tears began to flow.

"I'm sorry I got so mad at him, Mommy. And I know I shouldn't have hit him, but I'm not goin' to let anybody talk about my daddy like that."

When he pulled back and looked at her, Claire saw determination in his eyes. "Mason, I appreciate you standing up for your daddy, but you need to find other ways to deal with people who say hurtful things. We'll talk about that at home."

"Miss Kendall, Mason and I will abide by whatever discipline you and the school feel is appropriate. I am going to assume that Sherman Hopkins will also be disciplined for the hateful remarks he made. I will wait to hear back from you."

When Claire turned to leave, Mason flung his arms around her begging to go with her. "That's up to your teacher, Mason. And you owe her and Sherman an apology."

Mason's face went pale. "I'll apologize to Miss Kendall, but I'm not goin' to say I'm sorry to Sherman. At least . . . not yet. He was really mean to me, Mom."

The two women looked at each other hoping the other had a solution. Miss Kendall stood up and moved toward Mason, who began to back away. "Mason, you will stay in school today, as will Sherman. Until we decide on what your discipline is to be, the two of you will move your desks up front next to mine. For anything that we do requiring a partner, the two of you will be partners until the end of the grading period. Maybe that is one way you can learn to get along and hopefully learn to respect each other.

"Thank you for coming in, Mrs. Westfield. We will all get through this and hopefully become better people because of it."

Claire nodded and hugged her son. These were the times she desperately wanted a man in her life and the first person she thought of was Seth. Could she be bold enough to call him and ask his opinion?

Sitting in her car she went back over the last thirty minutes piece by piece. Then it hit her. Today was Thursday, Seth's afternoon off. She got out her phone and tapped his number.

Seth's phone when straight to voice mail. Icy fingers of loneliness wrapped around her the way they had when the reality of Randall's death hit her. She put the key in the ignition and just as she started the car, her phone rang. One large tear ran down her cheek when Seth's name appeared on the caller ID.

"Seth, are you free? I need to talk to you please."

"Claire, what in the world's wrong?" His voice was filled with concern. "I'll come to you. Where are you?"

"I'm at the school but getting ready to leave. Can we meet at the city park? It's about Mason. I need your advice."

When Claire pulled into a parking place at the park, she saw Seth sitting at one of the picnic tables. There was no one else there, which was unusual. She opened the car door. Seth saw her and started walking toward her. When he reached her, without realizing what she was doing, she collapsed into his outstretched arms and began to weep. The strength of his arms around her eased the shaking and slowed the pounding in her heart.

"Claire, my sweet friend," he whispered in her ear, "I'm always here for you."

The kindness in his voice, the scent of his aftershave, and the warmth of his body stirred emotions she thought were gone forever. She had forgotten the magnetism of a man's embrace. Longing filled her for the first time since her husband's death.

Seth took her hand and led her to the table where he'd been sitting. "Thought you might need a cup of hot tea to settle your nerves," he said with a small smile. He handed her a Styrofoam cup.

Claire nodded gratefully. As she swallowed the hot liquid, she saw the compassion in his warm brown eyes. Her heart felt safe with this man. He was a true friend. And at that moment, she once again could imagine him becoming more than just a friend.

~ 65 ~

Sleep wouldn't come no matter how many times she punched her pillow, switched sides, or adjusted the sheets and blanket. She crawled out of bed and gave the alarm clock a quick glance . . . eleven-thirty.

Grabbing her robe, Claire went downstairs and padded toward her grandfather's chair. When she was lonely, frustrated, or hurting, she'd always found a measure of comfort there. Potch had soothed her hurts, calmed her fears, and spoken words of comfort when her little girl world seemed to be falling apart. Tonight confusion kept her from sleep. The emotions she'd experienced sitting with Seth at the park rattled her.

She'd been touched by his willingness to sit and listen. He didn't try to rush her or make light of her feelings. His tenderness and concern for her and for Mason soothed her in ways she'd never experienced, even from Potch or Randall. Randall had been a wonderful husband, but the sting of knowing she'd never been the main focus of his life still hurt her.

Today with Seth she knew without a doubt she was his only priority for that moment. And she didn't know what to do with the feelings that welled up inside her. She'd give almost anything to be sitting here with Potch. She could hear his deep, slow drawl. Could he answer all her questions now like he did when she was a child? No, today's questions were not those of a little girl. These were questions of a woman trying to understand her heart.

Claire tiptoed out the back door. Standing there in the night air with millions of stars blinking back at her, she felt very small and vulnerable. Is God really up there like Helen, Reuben, and now Seth believe? Of course, they believe God's also living inside them

418

too. It seemed like a strange concept to her. If there is a God why would He want to live in us? Why would He want to live in me? Can't He see what a mess my life is right now? Who would want that? I do believe that Jesus ran after me when Helen called out to Him. But what have I done with that realization?

Claire sighed and turned to go back in the house. Just before she opened the door, she turned and looked once more at the beauty of the night.

"*I know You're there, God, but to be honest I don't know how to deal with You. I'm willing to trust You.*" Claire laughed. "*And just so You know, I still feel strange talking to You like this.*"

The house welcomed her with a feeling of peace. She moved quietly up the stairs trying not to wake her sleeping son.

~ 66 ~

SATURDAY MORNING PROVED TO BE A perfect late fall day for a picnic. Claire hadn't told Mason what they were doing just in case Seth had to take call for Mac, who was still feeling the effects of his bout with Lyme disease. When her phone rang, she held her breath.

"Looks like a great day for a picnic!" Seth said. "We're good to go."

"Yay! Mason's going to be so excited. Thanks, Seth. Your idea may be just what he needs."

"I'll pick you up around eleven. Be sure and bring bug spray," he said, his words cheerful and carefree even about the potential of insects.

"Okay, see you then." Claire felt herself getting caught up in his enthusiasm. "Hope I can keep the secret until you get here." They were both laughing as they hung up. Maybe they needed this picnic as much as Mason did.

While her son watched cartoons, she packed everything that didn't need to be put in the ice chest in her picnic basket. She managed to get it to the front porch without Mason seeing her. For once she didn't mind him being glued to the TV screen.

At ten-thirty Claire brought clothes down and insisted her son get dressed. His eyes never once moved from his show, but he changed from his pj's into jeans and a tee shirt. One more obstacle she could check off her list.

At the sound of the doorbell, Mason yelled, "I'll get it, Mom!" When he opened the door, he let out a happy shout. "Hey, Mom, it's Dr. Seth! Whatcha doing here, Coach?" Mason said, his face lighting up with a huge smile.

"Oh, nothing much. Just thought maybe you and your mom

420

would go on a picnic with me. But if you aren't interested, I can always go sit by myself in my little green house," Seth teased with a forlorn look.

"No! Don't do that. Me and Mom will go with you. And," he asked in a pleading voice, "can Cisco come too?"

"Hmm, let me think about that." Seth scrunched his face into a serious scowl. "I think I can fit the four of us into Old Red. Yes, she can go." He picked Mason up, throwing him over his shoulder, and grabbed the picnic basket.

On hearing the commotion, Claire came to the door in time to see her son squirming and laughing as Seth hauled him to his car. She couldn't help but smile.

"Hey, Coach," Mason said, fastening his seat belt. "Are we going to the falls? That's where everybody goes for a picnic."

Seth said, "You're right, buddy, but we aren't going there this time. I checked out a really neat spot Reuben told me about. That way it'll be just you, your mom, and me. Oh yeah, and you too, Cisco." At that the dog hung over the seat and gave Seth a wet lick up the side of his face.

"Ugh, thanks a lot, girl!" Seth said, wiping the slobber from his cheek. "I like you too!" Cisco wagged her tail with enthusiasm. "Let's get this show on the road before I get anymore slobbery kisses from Cisco!"

"I know what we should do," Mason said. "We do this in music class. So, Mom you start singin' that song *She'll Be Comin' Round the Mountain* first then I start singin' it, and then Coach comes in. So we're all singin' at different times. It's crazy but fun. Okay?"

Seth rolled his eyes and Claire scrunched her lips and raised her eyebrows. Then they both laughed. Claire surprised herself by starting with the first round and the guys followed at the appointed times. Her old inhibition about singing in front of people seemed to be gone.

Claire's emotions soared as they sang together. The joy in this shabby little car outweighed anything they'd ever experienced in her beautiful BMW. Singing at the top of her lungs, she soaked in the beauty of fall all around them. The color was so beautiful. If only she could find and hold on to the same in her soul. A new life was why she had come here. She and Mason had made progress toward the new life, but they weren't there yet. After all wasn't the reason they were on this outing an attempt to help her little boy deal with the pain of his loss and the torment of thoughtless children?

She glanced at Seth. Even when she'd held him at arm's length for weeks and even months at a time, he'd remained a true friend. He was a much warmer person than when they first met. Now his eyes seemed to shine with some kind of intangible light that permeated his spirit. She wanted to spend time alone with him and ply him with questions. It was like a battle because just as she would start to bring up his changes, something in her shut down, making her retreat. She'd never been afraid to approach something she didn't understand before. Why now? It puzzled her.

"Hey, Mom, why'd you stop singing? You messed us up."

"Oh, sorry, had something on my mind." Claire kept her gaze straight ahead but noticed Seth's sideways glances.

A few minutes later Seth turned the car down a narrow tree-lined path and pulled into an area wide enough to park and to turn around when they were ready to leave.

"Well, here we are! Reuben's secret fishing hole, which is also a great place to picnic," he said. "There's a large outcropping of rocks down by the creek just made for picnics."

Seth hopped out of the car and ran to the other side to open the door for Claire. "My grandmother taught me to be a gentleman, Mason. Opening a door for a lady is a really good thing for us guys to do. Will you remember to do that for your mom?"

"Uh, I guess so. Dr. Mac told me the same thing but do I just do it for Mom or do I have to do it for girls too?" Mason's contorted expression told the two adults it would be a while before he was ready to go that far.

"For now," Seth said with a chuckle, "just focus on your mom. Okay?"

"And Mrs. Mac too." Mason's face lit up at his own idea.

"You're going to be a good man one day, Mason Westfield." Seth put out his fist and his young friend completed the punch.

The guys began throwing sticks for Cisco, whose energy never seemed to run low. When asked if they could throw the sticks in the water for the dog to retrieve, Claire hesitated, but Seth assured her that Cisco would be dry by the time they left. If need be, he had some old towels in the trunk they could use to dry her.

Mason let out a whoop and threw the stick. Cisco barked as she jumped in the water then proudly brought the stick and dropped it at Mason's feet as a thank you.

Seth sat down beside Claire on the blanket she'd spread out, and they laughed at the antics of the boy and his dog. "It's the perfect spot for today, Seth," she said as she watched her son. "Thank you for everything." She felt the warm, gentle touch of his hand as it covered hers, and she didn't move her hand away.

When they had talked at the park, they'd decided to not be in any hurry for Seth to speak to Mason about what happened at school. Both were convinced the day needed to be low key. Seth would let the conversation happen at the right time.

"Claire, I want you to know I take your request seriously," he said in a soft voice, "and I'm honored not only that you asked me but that you put that much trust in me. It's very humbling.

"I'm assuming you know how much I care for Mason," he said. He looked at her and added, "and for you."

Claire thought her heart might stop beating. It wasn't a proclamation of love by any means, but it felt closer than she would've imagined. What should she do with it? Was she ready to move forward in this relationship?

Seth seemed to sense her confusion and slowly removed his hand. "I'm saying the two of you are important to me. I also want to be up front with you about something." He hesitated for a moment, rubbing his hands down the legs of his jeans.

"I'm still really new at all this, but from the minute you asked me, I started asking God to prepare Mason for our conversation and me as well. From what I've been learning, God's the perfect father who knows everything about us and loves us unconditionally. I just thought it couldn't hurt to include Him in this. The bottom line is that little guy's well-being. Don't you think?"

His comments did surprise her. She'd never really heard people she socialized with talk about God. But the pleading look in his eyes won her over and she nodded. Vague memories of her grandparents talking to her about God flitted through her thoughts. They'd never been pushy about what they believed, but she'd always known how important God was in their lives. Seth must be feeling the same way. She could accept that.

The warmth of the sun caressed her face and the giggles from her son rolling on the ground with his dog opened her heart to her friend's request. "Seth, just don't start preaching to him. Okay?"

Seth startled her by bursting into laughter. "No problem there, Momma," he said, after catching his breath. "I don't know enough to preach, believe me. I guess I just wanted you to know I wasn't coming into this on my own. I wanted someone much wiser than I am to give me the right words. Does that sound okay with you?"

"Yes, that sounds fine," she whispered.

Claire gave Seth the task of helping Mason clean up while she got lunch ready. She'd handed him a new container of Handi Wipes and pointed to her son and the dog. Boy and dog had become magnets for dirt after getting wet and rolling around in the grass.

With Cisco on her leash fastened to a nearby tree branch, the three of them sat on the blanket ready to dive into the food Claire had packed. Out of the corner of her eye, she noticed Seth bow his head for a moment before grabbing a plate and Mason did the same.

"This looks wonderful, Claire. You do good picnics! Invite me anytime, okay?" They all laughed, and Cisco joined in with several barks. To the dog's delight, Mason tossed her a doggie biscuit.

"Hey, guys," Mason shouted, sitting cross-legged on the blanket, "this is just like us being a family!"

Seth choked on his mouthful of sandwich and gave Claire an embarrassed grin.

"This pimento cheese is fantastic," he blurted out. "I'm not usually a fan but this is great."

"It's my grandmother's recipe. She was quite a cook," Claire said as she tried to regain her own composure. "She'd be so happy that you like it."

Seth winked at her letting her know he understood what had just happened.

She was glad when the guys went back to eating. She enjoyed watching the two of them inhale the food. In a bitter sweet moment, she thought of similar times when she'd watched Randall and Mason do the same thing. And it still made all the work worth the effort.

The day proved to be all fall should be. Just the right amount of sunshine and an unhurried pace. Claire busied herself putting the remaining food back in the ice chest. The guys were getting the fishing rods ready to do some serious "catching" Mason had informed her.

She declined their invitation to join them, opting for a possible nap instead. Whether she could fall asleep while wondering if this would be when Seth would talk to her son was another question. But she had been convinced they needed time alone.

Lying on her back with her jacket rolled up for a pillow, Claire's thoughts turned to the trust factor she'd developed for Seth. By allowing him to step into a larger role in her son's life, she'd opened a door she had thought would be closed for years to come. One minute it felt strange and she questioned every aspect of their relationship, especially when she wasn't with Seth, and the next minute it seemed so comfortable. She did find herself thinking of him more and more often.

Numerous times of late she'd considered calling Robyn for some female insight, but her fingers froze when she went to tap her number. She knew without hesitation what her friend would say. "That a girl, Claire! Step out there and take a chance!"

They were so different. Robyn needed a man in her life, but she wouldn't commit to just one. She hopped from one to the other to the point even Claire had trouble keeping up with the name of Mr. Most Recent, as she called them. She yawned, giving way to the sun's embrace.

~ 67 ~

SETH AND MASON STOOD AT THE creek bank with hopes as high as the sun above them that today would be their lucky day. Seth had learned well under Mac and Reuben's tutoring. And for the first time, he could see for himself why Reuben considered this the perfect fishing hole.

Mason stood near enough they could still carry on a conversation, but there was enough space between them not to get their lines tangled up. Seth's focus on fishing, however, was distracted by his need to come up with a good way to bring up the school issue. He'd wrestled with it a good part of the night before and came to the conclusion there wasn't an easy way to approach the subject. Lost in his own thoughts, he jumped when a voice beside him asked, "Can I tell you somethin', Coach?"

The boy's eyes that had been so full of excitement only minutes before were now filled with tears. Seth kneeled in the dirt and opened his arms. Mason began to cry and threw himself at Seth, wrapping his arms around his friend's neck.

"I've been really bad, Coach," he said between tears. "I got into a fight with a kid named Sherman at school. I punched him and gave him a bloody nose. And there's other stuff too." The boy's tears were soaking Seth's shirt. He forced himself to wait until the sobbing faded before speaking. He sat in the dirt, holding a boy who reminded him of himself at that age. A boy always having to defend himself for why he didn't have his dad around.

"Sorry, Coach." Mason ran a hand across his face but didn't look at Seth. His cheeks were pink with embarrassment as he made an awkward attempt to stand.

Seth said, "Let's go sit on that old tree trunk and talk."

426

Seth pulled two cans of ginger ale out of a small ice chest and handed one to Mason. "I think I know you well enough, buddy, that you didn't just go up and punch this kid. So spill the details. What'd he do that set you off?" Seth took a long swig of the cold drink and waited.

Mason popped open his can and seemed to be waiting for his answer to rise out with the bubbles. After staring at the ground and kicking the rocks around him, he said, "Sherman was makin' fun of me 'cause I don't have a dad. He told the other kids it was 'cause my dad didn't like me or my mom. And even when I told him my daddy died, he still said it was 'cause he didn't want to be with us." Mason bent down, grabbed a good size rock, and threw it hard into the water causing the soda he was still holding to splash on his shirt.

"Was this the first time Sherman said this to you?"

"No, he does it all the time. It's not always about my daddy. He says a lot of mean things to me and then gets the other kids to do the same thing." Mason's face turned pale, and he threw his can of ginger ale down and smashed it with his foot.

"Hey, buddy, look at me, okay. Have you told all this to your mom?"

For a long moment the boy sat motionless. "No," he said.

"Is there a reason why you haven't told her what was going on at school?"

"I didn't wanna make her feel bad. I was tryin' to take care of it by myself," he said, ducking his head. "Guess I didn't do a very good job."

"I'd like to tell you a story, buddy, of another boy about your age who went through some of the same things. This guy lived with his grandparents and could never even remember meeting his mom and dad. You see, one day when he was a little baby his mom showed up at her parent's house with him. His mom stayed there for a few days, then without saying anything, just went away. She hadn't even given her baby a name. Can you guess who that baby was?" Seth asked, his voice a little above a whisper.

Mason's eyes grew wide as he stared at the man before him. "Was it you, Dr. Seth? Were you that baby?"

Seth reached out and ran his hand along the boy's shoulder then nodded. "Yes, I was that baby boy who grew up never knowing his parents. The hardest thing though was neither of them caring enough to give me a name.

"Mason, you had a dad who loved you so much. And he never would've chosen to leave you. And your mom loves you with all her heart.

"I know exactly what you're dealing with, buddy. Kids can be mean. Sometimes they don't realize how much their words are hurting someone. Kids were always asking me why I lived with my grandparents." He stood and motioned for Mason to follow him. They walked closer to the creek, and Seth picked up a handful of pebbles. He hurled one pebble after another across the water. "Were you afraid to talk to your mom about Sherman and the other kids making fun of you?" he asked, glancing at the boy from the corner of his eye.

Mason nodded his head then bent down and scooped up his own hand full of pebbles.

"Do you and your mom ever just talk about your favorite memories of your dad?" Seth asked.

"Not very often," Mason said, gazing across the creek. "It makes her sad, and I don't want to upset her. I tried to talk to her about Daddy the night before I punched Sherman, but she got that sad look on her face, so I went up to my room and went to bed."

"I understand, Mason. Hey, buddy, you stay right here where I can see you," Seth said, patting the top of Mason's head, "while I go tell your mom we're going to fish a little longer."

Claire was probably anxious to know how things were going. He found her asleep on the blanket where they'd eaten lunch. He didn't want to wake her and turned to leave when he heard a groggy, "How'd it go?"

"I didn't mean to wake you," he said, sitting down next to her. "We've had a good talk. I learned some things that might help. Do you think we could talk later tonight after he goes to bed?"

He reached out and took her hand when he saw the fear in her eyes. "It's okay, nothing earth shaking but it does answer some questions. You and I need to talk." She nodded but clung to his hand. "Claire, I'm here for you both. I'll help in any way I can. Trust me?" Her eyes told him she would.

"We're going to fish a little longer. Want to come watch? Or we might even let you try to catch one," he said in a playful tone. He stood, giving her his hand to help her up. She stumbled as she tried to stand and fell against him. He drew her close and held her for a moment, wanting to hold her like this forever. He was certain he saw a hint of longing in her eyes. Then she pulled back and started toward the creek.

~ ~ ~

Seth declined the offer of dinner when he took Claire and Mason home. Everything in him wanted to say yes, but his gut told him he and Claire needed some space. He'd meet her later to fill her in on his conversation with Mason.

When he got back to his house, he scanned the frig for something he could whip up with little effort but nothing enticed him. He opened the freezer door, took out a frozen supreme pizza, and turned the oven to 400 degrees.

While the oven heated, he went to take quick shower. He smelled of fish and sweat. He wasn't typically one for singing in the shower. He surprised himself by belting out his favorite country song. When he ran out of words for the song, his thoughts turned to the afternoon with Mason. He felt pretty good about their conversation, as good as he could he guessed, since he had no fatherly experience.

~ ~ ~

By nine o'clock he began to wonder if Claire had changed her mind about calling. He paced from one room to another. When his phone did ring, he pounced on it, chiding himself for acting like a lovesick teenager.

He grabbed his windbreaker and keys and headed to his car. Claire had apologized for calling so late. She wanted to make sure her son was sound asleep. She suggested they could sit out on the porch to give them an extra measure of privacy in case Mason woke up.

Seth pulled into the parking area and breathed a sigh of relief when he remembered Mason's bedroom was on the back side of the house. He'd been afraid his car lights might wake the boy. Claire met him on the porch with two mugs of coffee.

"Thanks for coming," she said in a low voice. "You've really gone over and above with this, Seth. I want you to know how much it means to me."

They sat in two rockers her grandfather had made. Countless stars dotted the night sky, and only the soulful lament of two doves broke the stillness around them.

"Claire," Seth said, "like I mentioned earlier, my time with Mason didn't uncover any earth shattering revelations. From what he told me though, there seem to be two consistent concerns he has, and they are both for you. First and foremost, he carries a very real concern for you and your well-being. He senses that talking about things related to Randall or the times you had as a family makes you sad, so he turns his thoughts inward."

Seth saw the pain his words had given her. He took her hand and said, "Your little guy has a heart as big as that moon shining down on us right now. He adores you and even as a child wants to protect you over his own needs. Claire, he's been holding in his need to talk to you about his daddy because he knows it's hard on you. He said he'd tried to talk to you about a special memory of Randall, but you looked sad. So, he kept it inside, and I'm pretty sure holding all that in is what is causing him to lash out verbally—and physically like when the kid at school teased him."

Her hand began to quiver, and she pulled it away. "Please believe me when I tell you as a physician this isn't unusual. Mason is not blaming you or angry with you."

Even in the half-light filtering through the living room window, he could see that she was shaking. He got up and wrapped his jacket around her then bent to cup her face in his hands. "Claire, in his little boy heart and mind, he's trying to take Randall's place. He wants to protect you. He's trying to be your champion," Seth leaned down and kissed the top of her head. "One day he will be an incredible husband."

He leaned back against the cold wall of the house giving Claire a little space. She needed time to absorb his comments. In his heart, he cried out to God *Please don't let her think she's a failure as a mother.*

He didn't know how long they stayed there, neither of them saying anything, before Claire stood and turned to him. "Thank you, Seth. I appreciate all you've done. It means a lot. I guess I just need some time to process all this."

"Claire, may I say one thing before I leave?" She nodded. "You are a wonderful mother who cares deeply for her son." He reached out and stroked her hair, the silky feel of it slipping through his fingers. "Please believe that." She looked at him, then went inside.

He replayed the conversation over and over as he drove back to his house. One minute he knew it was right to have been honest with Claire. Then almost immediately he wondered if he had said more than she needed to know.

~ 68 ~

THE TWO LIFELONG FRIENDS SAT AT the kitchen table sharing stories with Mason of their years at the boarding school. Mason's eyes widened as he watched the two women's laughter bring them to tears. Robyn's unexpected visit reminded Claire of the joy of receiving a beautifully wrapped gift. Even Claire's move more than halfway across country didn't diminish the connection they'd built over the years.

Robyn's visit was passing quickly. They made the most of last Saturday when they had taken Mason to Granville to see the latest kid's movie. The three ventured out for walks with Cisco tagging along, usually down to the creek, in the afternoons when Mason got home from school. Neither one of them could believe he was in the third grade. This Friday was a perfect day for an afternoon walk.

"I love watching that boy with his dog," Robyn said, in a dreamy tone. "It's like watching a real life version of Tom Sawyer or Huckleberry Finn."

"Watch how many times I can make this rock skip," Mason shouted. "Dr. Seth and Dr.Mac say I'm getting close to being a champion rock skipper."

Both women burst into applause, yelling, "Bravo! Bravo!" Mason's face glowed with pride. Cisco barked her approval, jumping on him so hard it knocked both of them into the water.

The women went to lend a hand but found themselves soaked instead by Cisco's vigorous shaking.

"Well, that made a mess, y'all" Mason said, the picture of a pint size philosopher.

"Oh, no!" Robyn cried out, placing a hand on her forehead like she might faint. "I've lost my best guy to the hillbilly culture! When did you start saying y'all?"

Mason gave her a questioning look. "I don't know, Aunt Robbie. It's just how we talk here. Can I still be your best guy even if I say it?"

Seeing the boy's concerned look, Robyn threw her arms around him. "Mason Westfield, I lost my heart to you the day you were born. Y'all will always be my best guy," she said, tickling him.

~ ~ ~

Claire heard Mason shriek,

"Mom! I need you!"

Claire ran from her bedroom, taking the stairs two at a time. She nearly slipped before her foot touched the bottom step. "What's wrong, Mason? Are you hurt?"

"Nothin's wrong, Mom. I just need to ask you somethin'. Why's your face so red? You look kinda scared," he said with a quizzical look.

"Mason Westfield, don't you ever shriek at me again unless it's for a real emergency. Do you understand? You scared me half to death." Claire lowered herself to sit on the bottom step and catch her breath. "I think you owe me an apology." Her heart pounding, she drew in several breaths while cradling her head in her hands.

"I just wanted to ask if Aunt Robbie could borrow your jeans again. Sorry I scared you. She wants just me and her to spend this morning together. She said you can go do somethin' by yourself. I guess for big people that must be fun."

"That's fine," she stammered. "I'll take the jeans to her. Go play in your room until Robyn's ready."

Mason ran up the stairs and slammed the door. "What is it with the door slamming?" Claire muttered as she returned to her bedroom. Another issue she'd have to address, but she didn't feel up to it right now.

With jeans and the same tennis shoes she had loaned Robyn before in her hand, she knocked on the door of Robyn's room.

"Come on in, whoever you are," came the sassy reply.

"Hey, here are the jeans and shoes you requested." Claire sat on the end of the unmade bed.

"I didn't ask for those. I never want to see them again, remember?" Robyn continued brushing her hair but turned to look at Claire. "Girl, what's wrong with you?"

Claire stared out the window, a look of defeat settling across her face. "I don't know, Robyn. Sometimes I get so frustrated. I feel like a failure as a mom. Did you hear Mason shrieking at me then slamming his door when I sent him to his room?"

"Yeah, I did, but my word, that doesn't mean you're a failure. Look at me. Sometimes I lose cases. Does it sting? You better believe it. But that comes with the job—win some, lose some. Same is going to be true with you.

"And Mason plays a part in all this too, you know. He's just a kid. Kids blow up when they don't get their way or get out of line."

Robyn went to sit beside Claire on the bed. "Remember when we were in boarding school and some teacher or our housemother would get onto us? Remember our screaming spot?"

Claire looked at her friend and nodded. How could she not remember? Those days were forever etched in her memory.

"We'd go out there in the woods and scream at the top of our lungs." Robyn grinned, her dark eyes shining with mischief. "Why? Just to get rid of our childish frustrations. We knew better than to let Old Barlow hear us!"

Claire couldn't help but giggle at the picture of the two of them. Why they had never been found out had always amazed them. But maybe Old Barlow had known all along.

"I think you just gave me an idea. What if I give Mason my permission to go out to the barn to let out his frustrations?"

"Bingo! Sounds like a perfect fit for that boy of yours! Okay, since we've got that settled, why is it I'm supposed to put on those awful things again?"

"The young man now in his room informed me the two of you are spending this morning together, and you would need them. And that I'm going to do something by myself."

"Well, he sure is getting ahead of himself, isn't he? I did tell him I'd ask if I could have some one-on-one time with him. But I don't have a clue why he wants me to climb back into those jeans.

Those plans are new to me. You okay with them?"

"Oh, sure." Claire stood to leave. "Right now I think it's just what we all need. See you downstairs."

While Robyn finished dressing, Claire knocked on her son's door. "Mason, meet me in the kitchen while Aunt Robbie gets dressed. We need to talk."

Standing at the large kitchen window waiting for her son, she watched two squirrels playing on the porch railing. It dawned on her it was their version of give and take. One would snatch an acorn from the floor and scurry up the railing. It would then either let go of the acorn or the second little critter would take it from the first. They continued the back and forth game for several minutes until one grabbed the prize and ran up the tree. She decided to take a lesson from the furry little creatures on her porch.

"Sweetheart, let's go out to the barn. There's something I want us to talk about while you wait on Aunt Robbie."

~ ~ ~

Mason reached almost above his head to unlatch the large, battered barn door. "What're we doing in here?" he said, his face a mix between frown and curiosity.

Claire motioned him toward the stack of hay bales. The alfalfa hay, with its pungent yet slightly tangy smell, filled the barn. She could picture Potch, even after all these years, standing right here declaring his pride in raising the best hay in the county. When Pete Tompkins asked her to lease the land for some of his cattle and permission to cut the hay and buy it, she agreed immediately. It accomplished several things for Claire and helped Pete out as well.

The main thing she liked was the place would continue to be kept up in honor of her grandparents' great love for the land and the heritage they cherished. Pete was a kind and honest man she could trust. It would help him keep his cattle well fed and give her a little extra money to put away in a college fund for Mason. Her son's excitement alone made it the right decision. He loved sitting on the rock wall just watching the cattle graze. When Pete had told Mason that in the spring there would be little calves romping around the pasture, her son's excitement confirmed her decision.

Pete had also asked if he could rent space in the barn to store the hay. When he told Mason it would make for great hay forts and tunnels, there was no way Claire could say no. Her child's eyes had glowed with anticipation.

"I wanted to talk to you about something, sweetie," she said, watching him chew on a piece of hay like he'd seen Pete do.

"You and I have been having some . . . let's say, cranky times lately. Do you agree?" Mason dropped his head and nodded.

"Well, I have an idea. When you get to feeling that way and, say, want to slam the door to your room or just get rid of those cranky feelings because you're upset, how about coming out here to do it?"

Claire picked a piece of hay out of the bale she was sitting on and ran it under her nose, sniffing the rich scent. Then she popped it in her mouth sucking on it like a straw. Out of the corner of her eye she saw her son's expression turn to one of amazement as he watched her.

"Aunt Robbie reminded me that when we were in boarding school, we had a place where we could just go and yell or stomp our feet and get rid of all our mixed up feelings. So how about this barn being your own place to get the crankiness out? How does that sound to you?"

Staring in disbelief, his gray-green eyes questioned if this was real. Climbing to the top of several bales he let out a shriek that shattered Claire's nerves. Clasping her hands over her ears, she endured his test.

"That's a great idea, Mom. So, this is like my own special place?"

Claire nodded. "But there are a couple of rules," she said, watching his eyes narrow. "First, you have to ask my permission to go to the barn and second, you have to tell me your reason. Understood?"

Hoping down from the bales, he ran to throw his arms around her neck.

"Gosh, I have my very own barn! This is too cool. Thanks, Mom. Sometimes us guys need a place like this."

There it was again. Her little guy sounding more and more like a big guy. She was determined to embrace every moment of their time together—even the tough ones.

When Claire left the house, she had no idea what she would do or where she would go.

A new project was what she needed, but what would it be? She decided to go check out the town library. It was a lovely little native stone building that had been here as long as she could remember. Maybe she could find something to read to stimulate her creative juices.

~ ~ ~

"So, Tiger, what're we going to do with our time?" Robyn asked, once again in a pair of Claire's jeans. She poked him in the ribs, then tried to lay a big kiss on him.

"Aw, Aunt Robbie, I'm gettin' too big for that!" Mason said, squirming out of her hold.

"Never, ever, Tiger. But let's get us a plan for the morning. We're to meet your mom at noon at Mabel's for lunch."

"I know, let's go to my barn! My mom gave it to me this mornin' for my own special place. We can build a hay fort with a tunnel to get to it. That'll be so fun, won't it?'

Robyn tried to conceal her lack of zeal for dragging hay bales around, but she had told him to choose what he wanted to do. After what seemed like hours to Robyn, they had finished not only the fort but the tunnel. Standing there admiring their efforts, she had to admit it looked really good. She tried to convince him to go to the house for something to drink, but to no avail.

"Okay, so I'll go get us some lemonade and bring it out here. Does that work for you?"

His grin said it all, and she turned to go.

"Thanks, Aunt Robbie! I'll think of you every time I'm out here. This is so fun."

"You're welcome, Tiger. And you know what? I had fun making it with you. Bet you never thought you'd see me crawling around in a bunch of smelly hay, did you? I'll be right back with the lemonade."

Mason crawled back through the tunnel and into the fort. He liked how he felt safe inside it. He wished Billy could be here. They could play cowboys or maybe pirates, but he was too far away, so he'd ask J.J. to come over and play. He'd probably like it too.

"Hey, anyone here? I left this really good fort and tunnel builder in here. I wonder where he could have gone?"

Robyn walked around kicking at loose hay on the floor.

"Hmm, I know this is where I left him. I sure thought he wanted this delicious lemonade. Guess I'll just have to drink it all myself."

"Boo! I'm still here. Can you see me?" Mason giggled.

"I give up, where are you?"

"Right here!" Mason popped his head out of the top of the fort.

"Well, come on out, boy, this here lemonade is gonna get warm." She plunked herself down on a hay bale. "What'd you think of my Southern drawl?" Robyn chuckled, "I've been practicing just for you."

"You sounded funny, Aunt Robbie! Come in the fort. We can have our drinks in here."

Leaning over the open top of the fort, she handed him the two plastic glasses. Robyn heard him laughing as she wiggled her way through the tunnel.

"Here I am!" She brushed stray pieces of hay out of her hair and blew one off her upper lip.

"This smells good. Thanks, Aunt Robbie."

"Better than this old hay?" she asked, her eyes crinkling as she smiled.

"Hmm, I'm not sure. I really like the hay smell." He handed her one of the glasses.

"Mason Westfield, I do believe you have the makings of a very good politician."

The two of them sat on the hay covered floor and looked around at the end results of their hard work. It made the lemonade taste even better.

"You know you're the only person in the world that could get me to do this, don't you?" Robyn said, patting his leg.

An impish grin lit up his face. "Um huh." He studied her for a moment obviously weighing his thoughts. He said, "Aunt Robbie, do you think Dr. Seth likes my mom?"

Robyn, who had just taken a drink, nearly sputtered it all over herself. Trying to regain control, she put on her best analyzing attorney look.

"My goodness, that's a very interesting question, I must say." Deciding to toss it back in his court she said, "What do you think?"

Mason dug his feet back and forth in the hay. "I'm pretty sure he does. I watch the way he looks at her. One time I told Mom that he looked at her the way Daddy used to. She said that wasn't true, but I think it is." His questioning eyes grew wide waiting for her answer.

"Mason, sweetheart, that's a hard question for me since I haven't seen them together that much. I do agree that Dr. Seth seems to like your mom, but I'm not sure I can give you an answer whether it's the same way your daddy looked at her."

The boy stared into his now empty glass for a long moment. When he looked up, his eyes spoke from his heart. He wanted there to be a relationship between the two.

Robyn scooted over to sit beside him. Putting her arm around him she pulled him close. "You really like Dr. Seth, don't you?"

"I do like him a lot, Aunt Robbie. And I really want Mom to like him too."

As his tears began to fall, Robyn rubbed his back to help soothe his pain. There were no easy answers for times like this. No need to try and come up with them. Right now, a small boy hurt for his loss and for all that might have been. He also longed for what might be in the future.

She felt almost as certain as the child that Seth Bradley was smitten with Claire. But she didn't want to get Mason's hopes up to only have them dashed if things didn't work out. Time would tell.

"I'm glad Mom let me have this barn," he said, breaking into her thoughts. "She said it's for when I get cranky or mad. I guess I get that way kinda a lot. Sometimes I just feel mad about everything." He turned to look at her. "Is that cause my daddy died?"

Robyn bit her lower lip. This was getting to be a pretty heavy conversation. "Tiger, those are things you really need to talk to your mom about. You need to tell her when you feel those things. If anyone would understand, it's your mom because she lost your daddy too. But since you asked me, I would say yes. When you lose someone you love so much, it hurts for a long time. And sometimes because you're hurting inside, you may act mad on the outside."

"I have an idea!" He stood up and raised his arms above his head. "Stand up, Aunt Robbie. Now raise your arms." In his deepest voice he proclaimed, "This hay fort is goin' to be where nothin' bad can happen and where nobody can get taken away!"

Mason dropped his arms and gave Robyn a fierce hug. "That means we built a place that makes you happy when you're sad or when you're mad. Thanks for helpin' me, Aunt Robbie. I sure wish you could live here with us. And since you have to leave soon, we need to do one more thing."

"And just what would that be, kind sir?"

"I'll show you!" Mason ran up to a pile of loose hay, grabbed an arm load and threw it all over Robyn. "Hay fight!" he yelled and ran for another arm load.

"Oh, now you've done it, you rascal. Prepare for war!"

The hay fight finale stretched her tolerance level. But determined to make it a memorable time for him, she gave it her all.

Chasing around the barn throwing hay at each other was one thing, but jumping into a large pile of the stuff did her in. It was the point of no return.

"Oh my goodness. I just noticed the time. As much as I hate to break up this party, we need to get cleaned up and go meet your mom for lunch."

Mason kicked at the loose hay, muttering under his breath, "Just when we were having fun."

"I thought we'd been having fun all morning, mister. Let's have a good attitude, okay?" He grumbled something under his breath but moved toward the ladder.

"Thanks for sharing your barn with me," she said, bending down to kiss his cheek. "Come here." Opening her arms to him, she was engulfed by his embrace. "I love you, Tiger."

"Love you most." Mason shot back with a smile.

Robyn sent Mason for a much needed but unwanted shower

after their time in the barn. She couldn't wait for her shower to get rid of the smell and itchy feeling from all that hay.

~ ~ ~

Claire arrived at Mabel's first. It wasn't too full for a Saturday. She found a booth where she could see Mason and Robyn when they came in. A new girl waited on her, and she ordered iced tea. The lunch crowd began filling up the place, surprising her at how busy it was. She nodded at a few people she had met but realized how isolated she'd been since moving to Mason Falls. Her life had revolved around her son, finishing the house, and a couple of friends. And of course, the McQuarrys and Reuben. And Seth. The thought struck her that the people in the café probably thought of her as a snobby, big city girl who couldn't be bothered to get to know small town people. Claire felt her face flush. Even though she had made friends with Karen, Hank's wife, and Cindi, J.J.'s mom, she had been so focused on her own issues, she had inadvertently built a wall between herself and the people she had chosen to live among. The sound of her son's voice startled her as she was stewing over her inappropriate behavior.

"Hi ya, Mom. Wow, you won't believe what we did! Aunt Robbie is so cool."

Words tumbled out of Mason's mouth almost faster than she could catch them. "Slow down, Tiger," she laughed. "I can't keep up with you." The two slipped into the booth, Mason sliding in next to Claire. "So bottom line, you had a good time, right?"

Staring at his mother with a shocked look he said, "No way!" Claire's expression showed surprise. "We had an awesome time! Didn't we?" He and Robyn slapped each other a high-five.

"That we did. One that I can say with total truthfulness I will never forget!" Robyn gave Claire a look that said they would talk later.

Before conversation could continue, Mabel Porter appeared out of nowhere. "What'd y'all want to eat?"

"We really haven't had a chance to look at the menu," Claire said. "If we could have a few more minutes that would be great."

"I'll be back in five minutes. Be ready. I'm too busy for ya'll to be sittin' here lollygagging. Understand?" All three grabbed a menu and ducked their heads.

"I can't read all this yet," Mason whispered, "but I sure don't wanna get in trouble with her. Quick, Mom, does she have a grilled cheese sandwich?"

"Is she for real?" Robyn leaned toward Claire, "How does she keep people coming with that kind of attitude?"

"People around here just know that's the way she is, I guess. She's something else for sure. Oops, here she comes." Claire ordered the grilled cheese for Mason with chocolate milk and BLT's for her and Robyn, plus coffee for Robyn.

As Mabel turned to leave, she glared at Claire and snapped, "Where's that whippersnapper of a doctor you're seeing?" When Claire choked on her iced tea and started coughing, Mabel stormed toward the kitchen.

"That woman is one piece of work!" Robyn said, loud enough that those at nearby tables stared at her.

The rest of their lunch was uneventful. Both women breathed a sigh of relief as they walked out into the sunshine.

~ 69 ~

AFTER TUCKING MASON IN BED THAT evening, Claire and Robyn made tea, collected a couple of cozy afghans to ward off the fall air, and went to sit on the back porch. Claire had recently hired Reuben to screen it in for her to keep the pesky mosquitos out. It had been a good decision, and tonight proved it.

Robyn brought her closest friend up to date on her most interesting news at work, including the likelihood of her being offered a position as a partner.

"And remember the guy I told you about?" Robyn said with a sly smile.

"Um, which one among the many was that?" Claire teased.

"Okay, I know it's hard to keep up with me, girl, but I have mentioned him more than any of the others. It's Lenard, but he goes by Len."

Claire nodded, "I remember you saying something about him."

"Well, we're spending more and more time together. Nothing really serious going on but he's . . . special. He's fun to be with. We laugh a lot. But there's more to him than the guys I usually go out with. He's thoughtful and kind. And he treats me with such respect and gentleness. I don't think I've ever known anyone like him."

"Wow!" Claire said. "I never imagined hearing you say anything like that about a guy. Do you consider yourselves dating or just friends?"

Robyn thought for a long moment. "I think I'd have to say dating. We see each other every chance we get." Her usual business manner faded, and her honey-brown skin glowed from the touch of moonlight.

Both sat in the quiet. Night sounds Claire had come to love

engulfed them. The sound of an owl in the large Red Oak tree, the soft mooing of her neighbor's cattle in the pasture, and the eerie howl of a distant coyote.

"Claire," Robyn said, her voice just above a whisper, "I answered your questions about Len. Tell me where you and Seth are in your relationship."

She knew the question would arise at some point in her friend's visit and realized it would not be an easy one to answer.

"We've become good friends."

Robyn said, "Go on."

Claire laughed, remembering all the secrets Robyn had pulled from her over the years.

"Guess I might as well give in. You always get the information from me anyway." She pushed the porch swing with her foot, the creaking sound comforting as usual.

"I've come to appreciate what a good man he is in so many ways. He was raised by his grandmother; his mother abandoned him when he was a baby and he never knew anything about his father." Claire found the words hard to say without tears forming in her eyes.

"I've seen him make some significant changes in the way he sees this place. At first, he had a dislike for everything about small town life. But now he seems to see the good things. People have come to love him as a person and trust him as their doctor. I hope he realizes that.

"Regarding the two of us, it's still a big question. I'd say we've moved forward but how far I'm not sure. He and Mason adore each other, there's no question about that."

"Girlfriend! Get to the good stuff. Are you dating? Has he kissed you? Do you want things to move forward?" Robyn's exuberance threw Claire into a fit of laughter.

"What?"

Her friend's look reminded Claire of their days as silly, lovesick teenagers.

"Okay! Yes, he kissed me only days before you got here. I wouldn't say we're officially dating, but we see each other quite a bit between Mason wanting him to come over and the McQuarrys inviting the three of us to their house.

"I'm not sure what to make of his new found faith in God, but I have to admit he's been a different person. Finding God really does seem to have made him so much happier and peaceful."

Claire's jaw clenched. Why could Robyn still pull things out of her she would never tell anyone else? Her friend had certainly chosen the right profession. Another reminder of why people feared her in the court room.

"Claire, that sounds like good things."

Thoughts tumbled around in Claire's mind as she processed her friend's comment.

"I do agree. What I've seen happen in Seth and watching Helen and Reuben has affected my thinking."

Claire stood and looked into the cloudy night sky. Only an occasional star could be seen, and the moon was only a sliver. "I've never really felt the need for God in the past, Robyn. And to be honest, I'm still angry at Him for letting Randall die. But something keeps drawing me to Honey's old Bible."

Robyn curled her legs under her in the chair and with her typical attorney gaze, her eyes zeroed in on every motion.

"It talks a lot about God's love for us, Robyn, even in difficult times. I guess I can see why people would be drawn to that kind of love. I believe I even had a little experience of my own after talking to Helen one day."

Claire stared again at the night sky, recalling her experience. She wondered if the Creator, a perfect being, really could love her, an imperfect being for sure, unconditionally.

"Girlfriend, this is getting way too serious and deep for me. Either we change the subject, or we go to bed."

"You're right," Claire laughed. "Your turn to guide the conversation."

"Great. Because I want to be brought up to date on this business of him thinking about moving to Kansas City. We haven't talked about that yet."

Claire filled her friend in on what details she knew. They

discussed what it would look like if he took the offer. Robyn, not one to ease into questions she deemed important, bluntly asked her if she would stay in Mason Falls minus Seth Bradley.

Robyn had no sooner gotten the words out of her mouth than Claire sat up, an anxious look on her face. "Did you hear that?" She stood and moved toward the door. "I'll be right back. I'm going to go check on Mason."

When she returned, the anxious look had disappeared from her face. "Guess I overreacted. I didn't want Mason to hear our conversation. He would be crushed if he thought Seth was leaving. He was sound asleep, thank goodness."

Upstairs the sobs of one small boy were heard only by his faithful companion who sought to dry his tears by licking his face.

~ 70 ~

THE DAY CAME TO AN END, and Seth needed a long run to work out his frustrations. Just as he picked up his gym bag to go change into his running clothes, his phone rang. His first reaction was to ignore it, then he recognized the area code for Kansas City. "This is Seth Bradley," he said.

"Dr. Bradley, Marvin Hawthorn. Glad I caught you. I'm on my way out of town for a few days and wanted to touch base with you before I leave. Do you have a few minutes?"

"Yes sir, of course." Seth dropped the gym bag in a chair and went back to sit at his desk. This could be the defining moment in his life, his career. Keep breathing, he told himself.

"Bradley, I've put off this call because I sense we have a dilemma. I'll just get to the point. Corbin, Henry, and I are all in agreement on extending you an offer to join our clinic." The man gave Seth a moment to let the offer sink in.

Seth wasn't sure he could breathe. It seemed all the years of preparation were fighting to control his thoughts. He felt overwhelmed, exhilarated, and numb all at the same time.

"Sir," he said, willing himself to regain his composure, "that is . . . such an honor."

"You're an impressive young man, Dr. Bradley. But now I need to tell you my concern. Seth, the last words I said to you were, 'I heard your heart.' Do you remember that?"

"Yes sir, I do," he replied, feeling a knot in the pit of his stomach.

The older man hesitated then said, "The offer is there for you, but here's what I want you to do. I want you to take the next month and do some serious thinking about the right answer. This is too important for a hasty decision. My concern for you, Seth," Marvin

Hawthorn paused, seeming to weigh his next words, "is that your heart has found a home in Mason Falls. As an outsider that's what came across loud and clear to me." He went on to say, "What I believe neither of us wants is to discover several months or even a year or so later, that a wrong decision was made. If you come, I want it to be the right fit for both of us."

Seth felt the escalation of his heart rate and took a deep breath, trying to calm himself.

"Thank you, sir, for the call and the offer. I will do as you have asked."

"One last thing," Hawthorn said. "Are you a praying man, Seth?"

Seth swallowed hard. "Yes sir, I am."

"Then I suggest you do so over the next month. And Seth, I will join you."

～ 71 ～

CLAIRE AND ROBYN, DISTRACTED BY PREPARATIONS for dinner that night, hadn't noticed how listless Mason had been most of the day. He and Cisco watched cartoons until Claire told him to turn the TV off. Grumbling to himself, Mason stomped upstairs and pulled out a large box of Legos.

Cisco curled up beside him as he built space ships.

Mason's favorite people were all coming for dinner, but he couldn't get excited. All he could think about was what he'd overheard his mother say the night before to Aunt Robbie. Dr. Seth might be moving away. In his little boy mind, he'd decided it was all his mother's fault.

"I hate you, Mommy," he said under his breath. "If you'd be in love and marry him, he would stay here with us. But you're making him go away, and now I'll never have another daddy."

Midafternoon Mason stomped back downstairs and told Claire he and Cisco were going to the barn. Both women, still in the middle of preparations for the evening meal, nodded while continuing what they were doing.

The barn was warm and stuffy. Mason soon tired of chasing his dog around the bales of hay. "Let's go for a walk, girl." The dog's tail began to wag, and she ran to the barn door and waited until her master caught up.

"Let's go chase some squirrels, or maybe we'll find a rabbit." Mason patted her head, and they ran toward the pasture. Cisco loved the pasture and the cows. The Border Collie part of her couldn't help but herd the animals into a group. Mason laughed, watching her hunker low to the ground and sneak up on the cows, then move them to exactly where she wanted them. She would turn and wait for his whistle, the signal to release them. After several times, they both grew bored with the cows, and Mason headed toward the creek. He knew he shouldn't go there alone. Still angry with his mother, he decided he'd go anyway.

Before long Cisco spotted a large rabbit and set out after it.

"Go get it, girl," Mason yelled, chasing his dog.

The rabbit escaped, and Cisco returned to her master with a defeated look in her eyes.

"It's okay, Cisco. You gave that ol' rabbit a good chase." The two stretched out in the warm grass and moments later both had drifted into sleep.

~ ~ ~

Claire was on the verge of panic when her guests began to arrive. She couldn't find her son. She'd checked the barn and his room. She and Robyn had shouted for him until they were both hoarse, but no response.

When she told her friends her concern, they gathered in the living room to come up with a plan. Helen said they needed to pray before they did anything. Claire wasn't sure if it would help, but right now she was desperate.

Helen and Reuben asked God to give them wisdom in where to look for Mason.

"We need to split up and cover the most likely places first, then meet back here," Reuben said, taking control. Mac and Helen, y'all stay here in case he comes back while we're gone.

"Claire, you and Robyn check out the creek with Seth. I'll break out a little further since I know the property better than you do."

"Reuben," Claire said, her voice trembling, "take my cell phone since you don't have one. That way we can stay in touch."

"I don't know how to use one of those things," Reuben answered.

Seth took Claire's phone and handed it to Reuben and said, "I'll give you a crash course in technology."

Helen wrapped her arms around Claire and whispered, "I'll be praying for you and for our boy. Don't give in to fear, Claire." Helen held her close, stroking her hair. "One of your grandmother's favorite verses was in the book of Psalms. It says, 'When I am afraid, I will trust in God.' Trust God, dear Claire, trust."

~ ~ ~

Storm clouds had formed on the horizon as the half light of the evening crept across the sky. The four checked in by phone and decided to return to the house. Claire could barely put one foot in front of the other, and Seth put an arm around her to steady her. Robyn reached out and took her hand.

They all gathered in the living room and found places to sit. Seth said, "I think it's time to call the police, Claire. We need to form a search party before it gets any later."

Sitting on the sofa between Helen and Robyn, Claire nodded. Her face was pale, and her body couldn't stop shaking. Mac took the afghan from her grandfather's chair and draped it around her. He kissed the top of her head and patted her shoulder.

Seth dialed 911 and explained their need for a search party. "They will issue the call immediately, Claire. The sheriff's leaving now. They'll also call in the search and rescue dogs."

Helen went to the kitchen to make Claire some tea to try and warm her up. She put on a pot of coffee for what looked to be a long night, and she prayed, "*Oh, God, protect this precious child. Keep him in Your loving care. Help us be strong for Claire and use us to bring her Your comfort.*"

She took a tray of coffee and tea to the others just as the sheriff arrived. Claire was still shaking so hard she couldn't speak, so Robyn gave the sheriff a time frame of their afternoon.

"Ms. Westfield, we're going to do everything in our power to find your boy. We've sent out an alert and in the next few minutes there should be a large group of people arriving to start the search. The sheriff put his hand on her shoulder and said, "The more people involved, the greater chance we have of finding your son.

"We'll be bringing dogs and that helps a lot. We're going to need a piece of your child's clothing or maybe something he sleeps with, say, a teddy bear."

Claire asked Robyn to go upstairs and get Mason's much loved bear, Po. "I'm certain he has his dog, Cisco, with him."

"That's a good thing, Ms. Westfield. Dogs have a keen sense of hearing, so let's hope when his dog hears our calls, he'll return the call, so to speak."

The noise of approaching cars made Claire jump. In a matter of minutes, the yard was filled with volunteers.

Seth moved toward Claire and kneeled in front of her. Taking her hand in his, he warmed it with his own, stroking it gently. His heart ached for her. He felt torn. Should he stay with her or go with the others to search? He longed to stay and comfort her, but something in him demanded he go. He asked himself what a father would do in this situation. Then he knew without a doubt. He would go and search for his boy.

"Claire," he said, his voice tender, "I want to stay here with you, but I need to go help find him." He kissed her forehead then stood to join the others.

"Wait!" She stood on shaky legs and walked toward him. "I'm not sitting here while everyone else goes to look for my child. I'm going too and that's all there is to it."

She went over to Helen, leaned down and said, "Pray, Helen. Pray for Mason."

~ ~ ~

Slipping on a windbreaker, she let her thoughts acknowledge that Seth cared deeply for her and for her son. The decision he'd made to go help find her child showed her beyond a doubt he had a father's heart. And that was the greatest gift he could have given her.

"There's no way I'm staying here if you're going," Robyn called out, and ran after her friend, jerking a jacket off the coat rack.

Claire, Seth, and Robyn moved toward the large crowd of people who stood listening to the sheriff's instructions.

"We're going to cover as much territory as possible tonight. To do that we'll form a kind of grid. For those of you who have done this before, try and hook up with someone who's new to this." The sheriff stopped for a moment when the search and rescue van with the dogs arrived.

"Okay, we're ready, so listen up! Once we are all on the other side of that fence," he pointed to the pasture beyond it. "You will form a straight line across the field. Each person will extend their arms out to their sides and toward the person on your right and on your left." He hesitated a moment while the handlers tried to quiet the dogs.

"That will give you an idea of what will be your territory. That way we can spread across the field and pick up on any possible clues. Does everyone have a flashlight? If not raise your hand and my deputy will give you one." A few hands shot up.

"One last thing. Reuben Walker and Ms. Westfield, the mother of Mason, the boy we're looking for, are forming a separate group. Reuben's very familiar with this property, and he will be taking his group to some areas he's concerned about. I need maybe fifteen of you to go with him. Reuben, would you lead us in prayer for Mason and for all these kind folks who are wanting to help this little guy get back to his momma?" One by one men removed their hats and bowed their heads.

"*Father, we come to You right now asking that You go before us in this search for Mason. You know exactly where he is, and we ask You to keep him safe until we can bring him back to his mother. Thank You for each one of these people who have answered the call to help us find Mason. Keep them safe tonight. Thank You, Father, for Your constant love.*" In unison the group said a loud amen.

Claire's body shook as many of the people came by to give her an encouraging word before disappearing into the night. A strong arm wrapped around her shoulder and the voice whispered, "It's time to go find your boy." Seth took her hand and turned on his flashlight.

Their group followed the sheriff's instructions, spreading out in a line looking for any clues that Mason had come this way.

~ ~ ~

Memories of her grandfather's warnings to her growing up plagued her thoughts. Places he'd strictly forbidden her to go or explore because of how dangerous they could be. She was thankful Reuben knew this land as well as Potch had known it.

~ ~ ~

Mason curled up closer to Cisco, her thick fur warming him from the cool night air. She licked his face, and he wondered if she was trying to tell him it would be okay. "It was that darn rabbit that made us get lost, huh, Cisco. Let's don't ever chase rabbits again. I don't like being out here at night." He cuddled up closer to his dog and buried his face in her fur, releasing the tears he'd tried so hard to keep from coming. "Do you think someone will find us, girl?" he whimpered. "I'm scared, and I want Mommy. I'm really tired, girl. You stand guard, okay? I'm goin' to take a little nap." Mason yawned and laid his head against his dog.

~ ~ ~

"I've been all over this land for years," Reuben told Seth. "We need to think like a scared little boy getting caught in the dark and not knowing what to do or where to go. There are two places he might have gotten to. We'll try the closest one." Reuben held his hand up for the team to stop and explained his plan.

"The two areas we're going to are not easy. You need to keep your flashlights in a position where you can see where your next step will be but also be able to have a broader vision of where we are. It's rough terrain with a fair amount of brush, rocks, and low hanging tree limbs."

Seth felt uneasy and totally out of his comfort zone. He was born a city boy and this went way beyond anything he'd ever done. But he was determined to help find Mason and put him in his mother's arms where he belonged. He said a prayer and continued in the direction Reuben had pointed out to them.

He couldn't believe how dark it was out in the middle of nowhere. There were a few stars out now, and at least it wasn't raining. He was thankful for that.

Glancing at the time on his phone he couldn't believe they'd been out here searching for close to two hours. Shining his flashlight to either side he saw the bluffs Reuben had told him about.

"Stop," Reuben shouted, "Okay, once again let's call Mason's name in unison." After numerous calls there still was no response.

"We'll take a quick break. Drink water and eat something. I'm going to do a little scouting up next to the bluffs."

Without hesitation Seth said, "I'm going with you."

Claire and Robyn huddled together. Robyn put an arm around

her friend trying to keep her from shivering but nothing seemed to help. The only thing that could help her was finding her son.

~ ~ ~

When Reuben and Seth returned, they were alone.

Trudging through the next area made the one they'd just come from seemed like nothing. The brush was thick and prickly, tearing at their clothes and scratching at their hands and faces. Claire wanted to scream, but she knew staying at the house would've been far worse. At least she was doing something to bring her little man home.

"Oh, Tiger, where are you?" From a place deep in her soul, words came tumbling out of her mouth in a quiet plea. "*God, I said once that I would trust You. I know I have not really done that, but I'm at a place where I must. Please help us find my little boy. I can't go on if I lose him too.*" Her legs ached and felt too heavy to take another step. She rubbed her neck, tense and knotted from all her stress. "*I know I've ignored You and was so angry at You for a long time because of Randall's death. But I have nowhere else to go. All I can say is please, God, keep my little boy safe and let us find him.*"

Reuben called for another short break. Their team was exhausted but not one person had complained. Claire and Robyn found a large rock to sit on and made room for Seth to sit down when he came to check on Claire. A few moments later, he began massaging her shoulders. There seemed to be no need for words between them.

When Reuben told the team it was time to start up again, he gathered them into a circle with Claire next to him. "I know you're discouraged, Claire, and I think I can speak for each of us. We are too. But we are not giving up. Are we?" He looked around the circle at eighteen weary faces. Every one of them shook their heads. They were in for the duration.

"This will be the most difficult part of our trip. Be careful of the terrain. There are lots of loose rocks and fallen tree limbs, so watch your step." Taking off his cap, he bowed his head. Everyone followed his example once again.

"*We're physically and emotionally tired, Jesus. Our hearts are heavy for Claire and for little Mason. But You said, 'Bring the little children to me.' So right now, we're going to trust that You are caring for Mason while we do our part to find him. Guide us to where he is. Thank You."*

Over the next hour they helped each other climb over boulders and fallen trees. They called out for Mason until their throats were dry and raw.

Out of nowhere Seth heard the howl of what he guessed was a coyote. But what was that other sound? Could it have been crying? There it was again!

Seth started running in the direction of the sound. "Mason!" he yelled. Nothing. "Mason, it's me, Seth!"

Then he heard a dog barking for all it was worth. "That a girl, Cisco, keep it up!" he shouted. "I'm coming, Mason. Hold on, buddy."

The cries got louder, closer. "I want my mommy! I want Dr. Seth!"

"We're coming, Mason. We're coming."

A quivering voice in the darkness said, "Dr. Seth? Is that really you?"

"You better believe it," Seth called out just before he was almost knocked down by one small boy and one good-sized dog. Claire ran to them and dropped to the ground, opening her arms to her son. Robyn was right behind her.

Mason threw himself into his mother's outstretched arms. "Oh, Mommy, I was so scared. I'm sorry. I didn't mean to get lost. We were chasing a rabbit." Robyn wrapped her arms around both of them. "I'm so glad to see you and Aunt Robbie and Dr. Seth."

When Claire let her son come up for air from holding him like she'd never let him go, he said, "Who are all those people? Why are they crying? Look there's Mr. Reuben! Why is everyone here, Mom?"

"We'll tell you all about it tomorrow, sweetheart."

Reuben led the group back toward the house. One of the volunteers notified the sheriff that Mason had been found and was safe. Mason clung to Claire with one hand and Seth with the other, looking over his shoulder to make sure Aunt Robbie was behind him. When his legs finally gave out, Seth picked him up and carried him.

"Dr. Seth, don't go to that city place. Please stay here with me and Mommy."

Seth glanced at Claire not knowing what to say. "We'll talk about that another time, buddy."

Moments later Seth looked down at Mason, now sound asleep, as a sliver of moonlight crossed the boy's face.

He turned and smiled at Claire. She reached out and grasped his hand in hers.

~ 72 ~

"I DON'T WANT YOU TO LEAVE, Aunt Robbie!" Mason wailed. "Can't you move here," he pleaded, "and be with us?"

Robyn sat down on the sofa, pulling the boy onto her lap. His arms reached around her neck holding on to her in a desperate embrace.

"Tiger, you know I can't do that. I wish I could but San Francisco is where I belong." His small body shook with each new sob, and she drew him close. She stroked his silky hair in an effort to calm him. When the sobs began to melt away, she kissed the top of his head.

"Tiger, I'm going to make you a promise." Mason looked up and stared into her eyes. "I'm going to work out a plan with your mom and my people at work where I can come see you more often. It's called making a schedule. That way we don't have to be separated for so long," she said with a hug. "You and your mom are all the family I have, and I miss you so much." She planted a kiss on his cheek and noticed the twinkle in his eyes had returned.

Claire knew how much Mason wanted to go with them to the airport, but Robyn had asked if they could have some time alone. The McQuarrys had invited the three of them plus Reuben and Seth over for dinner the night before. Seth had overheard their conversation and volunteered to take Mason for the day. Still feeling overprotective of her son since he had gotten lost, she'd hesitated to leave him, but Seth assured her he would take good care of him. And her mother's heart knew it would make Robyn's leaving a lot easier on her son, so she agreed.

~ ~ ~

Robyn's rental car had been dropped off the day before at the company's agency in Granville, and her suitcases were loaded in the trunk of Claire's car. Once in the car, Robyn, with her typical cut-to-the-chase personality, wasted no time getting to the reason she wanted them alone.

"We have an hour and a half before we get to the airport, and I have some things I want to say."

Claire tried to hold back her laughter, but it spilled out anyway. She'd seen this look before. It was what she called Robyn's bad momma attorney look. Her friend's dark eyes seemed to drill through the other person's most hidden thoughts.

"Okay, get it out. But I think I already know where you're headed. It's about Seth, isn't it?"

"How'd you know?"

"You're not the only one who has keen insight, girlfriend!" She laughed. "Go ahead and get it out before you pop."

"Touché!" she said. "This week's been eye opening for me when it comes to you. You're building yourself a family here." Robyn's mood turned pensive, and she gazed out the window.

When she looked back at Claire a slight twinge of sadness covered her face.

"I have to admit I feel jealous. The McQuarrys are wonderful, and they fill your parent-grandparent need so well. Then there's Reuben. He's like a wise and caring uncle," she said, staring out the window again. "I want you to know how happy I am for you and Mason. I wasn't sure this move would be the best thing for either of you, but I'm admitting I was wrong."

Claire reached over and squeezed her friend's hand. "Thank you, Robyn. That means so much to me."

"I'm glad, but that's not all I want to say. This is where it might seem like I'm meddling, so let me finish before you reply. Watching Seth during all the trauma of Mason getting lost made quite an impression on me. He's a very good man, Claire," she said. "I saw a kind and gentle man who cares a great deal for both of you. And when he kneeled in front of you and promised to find Mason, well, I almost lost it."

Claire steered the car onto the shoulder of the road and

reached out to hug her dearest friend. There had been many times in their lives when the only person either of them could turn to was the other.

Robyn said, "Don't take Seth Bradley for granted, Claire. A man like him doesn't come along very often. He adores you. It's written all over his face. And the way he relates to your son makes it clear he loves that boy of yours."

They rode in comfortable silence for several miles, their life-time friendship giving them permission for solitary moments.

As they approached the airport, Robyn put a hand on Claire's arm and said, "I have something I'd like to mention."

When Claire nodded, she went on, "We've always been more than best friends. Our bond is stronger than most sisters." They both smiled knowing it was true. "So, because of that I want to be up front with you. It's time for you to release the past and open the door to your future and to Mason's."

~ ~ ~

Driving back home, Claire realized Robyn was right. It was time for her to open the door to her future. She was no longer a wide-eyed college girl dazzled by the handsome medical student. She had tasted the sweetness of life but also its sorrow. Maybe the question she needed to answer was did she have the cour-age to open her heart to love again and to once more enjoy that sweetness?

On the outskirts of town, Claire pulled into an empty parking lot to call Seth and let him know she was back. When he answered, she heard laughter in his voice and in the background making it dif-ficult to understand him.

"Hold on," he said, "I'll move to another area. Sorry about that. We're out at Reuben's. Are you back in town?"

"I'm in the parking lot of Sander's grocery store. Sounds like you all are having fun."

"You've got that right. We've had a blast. We're finishing a little project. Why don't you meet us out here?"

Claire drove down the long, narrow road to Reuben's with her window rolled down, enjoying the brisk air and appreciating her warm sweater. Everything was peaceful and quiet. She loved these moments. They were so different from what Robyn would be returning to.

When she got out of her car at Reuben's, she heard voices and laughter in the barn. Claire found Reuben, Seth, and Mason working at a large work bench reserved for Reuben's carpentry work. "Hi there," she called out. Three sets of eyes looked at her from happy faces.

Mason darted to his mother's outstretched arms, planting an excited kiss on her cheek. "Come see what I made!" He beamed as he dragged her to the table.

The two men had the same goofy smiles on their faces as her son. It must have been very much a guys' day.

"Ta da!" Mason said, glowing with pride as he pointed to a funny looking little wooden house. "It's a blue bird house, and I made it all by myself! What do you think, Mom?"

"I think it's the best bird house I've ever seen."

"Us guys had an awesome day! I wanted to go with you, Mom, but I'm sure glad I stayed here with Dr. Seth and Mister Reuben." His grin confirmed his words.

Reuben insisted they all stay for dinner and promised to grill the best steaks in the county. He also sent the three of them off for a walk down to the creek on his place. "It might even challenge Mason Creek for beauty," he said with a grin.

Mason ran ahead lost in his little boy world. After picking up a long thin branch, he seemed to have entered his own pirate adventure, swishing the branch back and forth like a sword.

As a touch of wind swirled her hair, Claire seemed to be in a daydream herself. When she reached out to brush her hair from her face, she felt the touch of Seth's hand brushing it back for her. She looked at him and something hard inside her began to melt. When he lifted her chin and kissed her gently, an overwhelming sense of longing filled her.

"Claire Westfield, I think I'm falling in love with you," he whispered.

Before she could get her mind around those words, her son's

excited shouts broke the spell as he ran toward them. Seth caressed her cheek before heading toward Mason. "What's up, buddy?" he called out.

"You gotta come quick and see what I found!" Mason yelled and turned to head back to the creek.

Seth ran down the path behind the boy and Claire followed. When she reached them, both were kneeling by the creek, their heads touching while they grabbed at something in the water.

"What is it, Mason? Is something wrong?"

Two smiling faces looked up at her. "I found a zillion crawdads," her son said, "and they're huge!"

"That's a pretty exciting discovery, Mason!"

Seth grinned at her. "This is big stuff, Momma!" He winked at her and went back to helping her boy catch crawdads. Holding them carefully so not to get pinched, each bragged about who had caught the biggest before releasing them into the water.

Claire pulled out her phone and took a video of the guys intent on their task. When Seth turned and looked at her with a silly, boyish grin, a sudden rush of joy enveloped her.

~ ~ ~

Reuben proved himself to be quite a good cook, and his steaks matched his bragging rights. After helping with the dishes, they said their goodbyes, and Seth insisted on following Claire to her house. Mason's day caught up with him by the time she reached the main highway. Claire looked in the rear view mirror at her boy, a slight smile stretched across his sleeping face.

Seth carried the sleeping child up to his room, and Claire slipped off Mason's clothes, leaving him in his tee shirt and boxers. She pulled the sheet over him, then leaned down and kissed his cheek. "Sleep well, Tiger."

She met Seth downstairs. It was one of those perfect nights in the Ozarks. The night sky dotted with stars, a full moon, and the sounds of nature all around them. They sat side by side quietly in the porch swing.

Seth broke the silence. "Claire, I'd like to tell you something if that's all right." She twisted her body to see him better and noticed a nervous look in his dark eyes. "I meant what I said earlier today. Your friendship means so much to me. I've never said this to anyone else, but I can't hold it inside any longer. My feelings for you go beyond being friends. I am falling in love with you."

In the moonlight Claire could see the depth of emotion in his eyes. She took his hand and held it, enjoying its warmth, and the warmth she felt in her heart.

"Seth, I don't know what to say. I also care for you as a friend." She saw a pained look cross his face, and she reached out to touch it. "I . . . think I have feelings for you too."

Releasing his hand, she stood and moved to the railing and stared into the night sky. "One of the things I'm struggling with is your plan to leave Mason Falls. I'm just getting settled here and to be honest, I don't see myself moving. I love this place, and I want to watch my son grow up here."

Seth stood and moved close to her. "I understand that I do have a major decision to make about my future. I guess I'd like to know if there's a chance that our relationship could go to the next step before I make the decision."

Claire saw the longing in his eyes. That same longing was tugging at her heart.

When he drew her to him, she wrapped her arms around him and closed her eyes.

"Will you give us a chance?" he whispered.

She stepped back and locking her eyes to his, she said, "I want to, Seth, but it's not just about us. There's a little boy to consider. I don't want him to get his hopes up for something that might not happen."

"I know, Claire, and I understand. We both have a lot to sort through."

She stood on tiptoe to give him a gentle kiss.

~ 73 ~

THE DAY SEEMED TO DRAG BY and she checked her watch one more time. Blowing a wisp of hair out of her eyes, she brushed the remaining hay from her jeans and sweater. She loved to surprise her son and today was one of those times.

Fall in the Ozarks could be a glorious season. And this year's long fall had been magnificent. The mountains seemed to shout, "Look at us! We're putting on a show of color you won't soon forget!" The day was chilly, but the barn, well insulated with all the bales of hay Pete Tompkins had stashed in it, had a toasty warm feeling. She could hardly wait to share the afternoon with her child. Everything was ready, so she decided to start the walk up the road to meet him. He thought he was now too big for his mom to come to the bus stop, but she wasn't ready to give up those special moments just yet.

The bus had come a little earlier than usual, and Mason was already walking down the road, kicking at the gravel with the toe of his shoe. Even from a distance Claire sensed moodiness in him. Something must have gone wrong at school. If so, she was glad she'd prepared something special for him.

He kept his head down, staring at the road, not noticing her approach.

When she called out to him, his solemn look startled her. She wanted to run to him and pull him into her arms the way she had when he was little. But her little boy was disappearing before her eyes each day. He was growing taller and more subdued in his behavior.

Tucking her hands in her jacket pockets, she walked alongside him. "How was your day, sweetheart?"

He looked at her then turned his eyes back to the gravel on the road. "So, so. Nothing special," he said, stone-faced.

She decided not to push, hoping her surprise would help him open up.

When they reached the house, he headed toward the front door.

"Wait up, Tiger. I need you to come into the barn for a minute."

Mason scowled. "I'm getting too big for you to call me that anymore, Mom."

"Tell you what, I'll work on not calling you that in front of other people, but as the person who gave birth to you, I reserve the right to call you Tiger any time I choose. Now, we are going into the barn, so wipe that scowl off your face."

She turned and marched toward the barn, wondering if it would even be worth all her effort.

Opening the barn door, she sucked in the pungent smell of the hay again, enjoying the way it tickled her nose. She looked over her shoulder to see Mason's expression and knew her effort had been worth it.

"Wow! Mom, this is so cool." His eyes lit up and his grin spread all over his face.

She'd spent most of the morning cleaning out one of the stalls and moving new bales of hay into it to use as a table, complete with a red bandana style tablecloth. There were two old wooden benches, one on either side, for them to sit on.

She had put a small wooden table in one corner, and she'd brought an extension cord to plug in a coffee pot filled with apple cider. Next to it were two mugs, a small tray with two caramel apples, and a plate of oatmeal cookies.

"Thanks, Mom," he said, but a pained look crept over his face. "I . . . don't think I deserve this," he said, turning a piece of hay over and over with his fingers.

"I don't understand. Why wouldn't you deserve it?"

Mason raised his eyes to look into hers. "I got in trouble at school. A guy was calling me names. I tried not to pay any attention, but I did push him down when he wouldn't stop. A teacher saw it and told the principal it wasn't really my fault. I still had to apologize and ask the guy to forgive me. And that's not the only reason I don't deserve all this," he said, looking down at his feet. "You know when I got lost and scared you so bad? Well, I need to ask you to forgive me for something I said. I'd kind of forgotten about it until I had to ask that kid to forgive me.

Claire stared at him with a confused look.

"The night before I got lost, I was really mad at you. I had come back downstairs, and I heard you and Aunt Robbie talking about Dr. Seth maybe moving away. I got mad and blamed you. I thought if you'd fall in love with him, then he wouldn't leave." Mason hung his head.

"The next day when I was playing in my room, I was thinking about Dr. Seth maybe moving, and I said I hated you and it would be all your fault if he left. But Mommy, I didn't mean to run away or get lost, I promise. It really was chasing the rabbit like I said. And I didn't really mean what I said. I'm so sorry." Big tears began to slide down his cheeks.

Claire stood and motioned for her son to follow her. She led him to a pile of loose hay and pulled him down next to her.

"And that's been bothering you," she said, searching his face, "all this time?" He nodded his head but wouldn't look at her.

Drawing him into her arms, she stroked his hair. "Sweetheart, I forgive you. And I do understand that what you heard was hard for you. I know how much you care for Dr. Seth. But, sweetheart, please try to trust me when things come up that you don't understand. And don't be afraid to tell me you overheard something and ask me what it means. Okay?" Holding him close, she kissed the top of his head.

"Will you forgive me, Mom, for saying I hate you?"

"Of course! You're still my Tiger!" She jumped up pulling him up with her. "Now, I don't know about you, but I'm ready to take on one of those caramel apples."

~ ~ ~

Later that night, after getting her son tucked into bed, Claire made a cup of hot chocolate and took it out to the porch. The chill of the night stung her face, and she wrapped the blanket she'd brought tighter around her. Stars shimmered against the dark sky like they were dancing around the moon. These were the moments she treasured. This was when she could be real with herself.

There was a difference now though. She wasn't totally alone, although it would look that way to others. Now the One who knew her better than she knew herself was Jesus, and He was right here with her sharing this night. She loved the closeness she felt with Him. So much had changed for her since the night Mason was lost. Now she felt the freedom she had to pour out her heart and know that He cared, that He knew the answers to her questions before she ever asked them. And she had so many questions right now. Her son had shared his heart and his hurt with her in the barn that afternoon. Sitting alone in the darkness she wondered if she could do the same with the One who had changed her life forever. Peace flooded her heart, and she knew He would show her what to do.

~ 74 ~

SETH SAT AT HIS DESK, EXHAUSTED. Not only had the day been packed with semi-emergencies, but he was on call. That meant heading to Granville General Hospital at least twenty minutes away.

He guessed he'd do a drive-thru dinner on the way. It was either now or after he finished rounds, which tonight might turn into three hours. What he really wanted was a large steak, medium rare, with a baked potato and a salad. Maybe he'd do one on the grill tomorrow night if it wasn't too cold, and his mouth watered at the thought.

He knew he wasn't just physically exhausted because of how hectic the day had been. What had taken place over the noon break had added a new dimension to an already perplexing dilemma. Midmorning Nell Meyers caught him right before he went to do a skin biopsy in the procedure room. She'd gotten a call from Helen that she and Mac wanted Seth to come over for lunch. They had something to talk to him about. Thinking it had to do with Mac's recovery, he made the short walk to their house as soon as the last patient for morning appointments left the building.

Seth sat down to lunch at Helen and Mac's, ready to hear why they had wanted to see him, but Helen wanted them to enjoy lunch before they got down to shop talk.

After finishing the last bite of Helen's famous apple crisp, Mac got down to business.

"Helen and I have, after many long hours of conversation," Mac winked at his wife, "come to a mutual decision. Seth, we both agree that you've become like a son to us. You've also proved yourself to be a fine physician as I've watched you mature in your practice of medicine. Most of all, I've seen you grow to care for and even come to love many of your patients. That was a major concern I had for you when you first came to Mason Falls."

"Thank you, Mac, I appreciate that. Looking back, I was pretty full of myself," Seth said with a chuckle. "You've taught me so much about caring for our patients in ways that don't come from a textbook."

"Well, that's enough of patting each other on the back," came Mac's gruff reply. "Helen and I have something we want to ask you to think about. Dealing with my Lyme disease and its aftereffects has made us talk about where we are at this stage of our lives." Mac turned to look at his wife and patted her hand. "We've determined that it's time for me to slow down."

Picking up Helen's hand, he kissed it before turning back to Seth. "This precious lady has put up with a lot over the years I've been in practice. In all that time, we've had far too few opportunities to get away and focus on each other.

"So all that to say we want to offer my practice to you. I would still like to come in two or three mornings a week, at least in the beginning. Whatever would work best with you would be fine. But I want to be flexible enough to take more extended time off to travel or just do things with Helen."

The outright shock of Mac's words turned Seth's world upside down.

"I don't know what to say, Mac. To be honest I thought you'd work till you dropped."

Mac laughed and said, "Well, young man, I almost did! But I've been given a second chance, and I plan to take it!"

Helen's face lit up as she stood and wrapped her arms around the man she'd loved most of her life.

"So, here's the plan we came up with." Mac leaned forward, his look all business. "First, there will be no buy-in fee. I'm counting the time you've been working for me as that part paid in full."

Seth stared at his boss wide-eyed.

"Over the next three years," Mac continued, "you can rent the building with the payments going toward the purchase price, should you choose to buy it."

Mac and Helen held hands and their eyes twinkled as they watched the look of unbelief cover Seth's face.

"I . . . don't know what to say," he stammered.

"We don't want you to say anything right now," Helen said. "Just give it some thought and ask God to give you wisdom in making the right decision."

Seth bowed his head trying to keep back the tears. "This is such a generous offer," he said his voice shaking. "I'm overwhelmed."

He stood and walked around the table to shake Mac's hand, but Helen got to him first. "We love you, Seth Bradley," she said, pulling him into a hug.

Mac grasped his hand and held it, "We know this doesn't fit your original plans, and we both want you to know we understand if you choose not to accept it." In an unusual sign of affection, Mac put his hand on Seth's shoulder and squeezed it.

～ 75 ～

REUBEN'S CALL THE NIGHT BEFORE OPENED a door Seth knew he needed to walk through. Helping his friend out on the project he'd mentioned would also give Seth the opportunity to talk about his own dilemma. He was facing one of the biggest decisions of his life, and his friend's practical wisdom was an asset he valued.

Pulling on an old pair of jeans, his favorite work shirt, a warm jacket, and his new work boots, Seth headed to the kitchen. He filled the Keurig with fresh water and put two slices of bread in the oven to make some toast, stuck three slices of bacon in the microwave, and cracked a couple of eggs to scramble.

Cooking hadn't been something he enjoyed doing until recently. But he'd learned to appreciate the creative aspect of putting a meal together and the tantalizing aromas awakened a whole new world to him. After downing his scrambled eggs, toast, and bacon, he ran hot water in the sink and added some dish soap. He chuckled aloud at his favorite part of cooking for himself. He still found it hard to believe how much he enjoyed washing dishes. The house hadn't come with a dishwasher, so he had to wash them by hand. It had taken him a while to recognize that the simplicity of the task was what relaxed him, and he had a finished product when the work was done.

Grabbing his Royal's cap, he headed out to Old Red. The smell of smoke lingered in the crisp air. Someone nearby had been burning wood. He inhaled the pungent smell as he got in the car. He and Reuben had agreed to meet at the clinic.

When Reuben called and asked if he'd help him, Seth considered it an honor that his friend trusted him and his newly learned skills enough to be part of the project. A couple from Granville had commissioned Reuben to build an elaborate hutch that would become home for a very old and exquisite set of china. They'd placed a special order for Desert Ironwood from Arizona and had it shipped to their home. Reuben's description of its contrasting colors and marbled or burl figuring stirred Seth's curiosity. Watching his friend take a piece of wood and fashion it into something of beauty had opened another new world to him. He'd learned so much from the man. But more than anything, he'd gained a new perspective on life. And the insight of someone older and wiser than himself was what he needed right now.

Driving to Granville was the perfect solution for both of them. He could get his friend's advice on the way over and back, and it wouldn't interrupt their work when they got to Reuben's place.

~ ~ ~

As the truck bounced along the winding country road, Seth updated Reuben on the offers from the Hawthorn clinic and from Mac. Staring out the window at the passing landscape, he winced at the knot in his gut. He'd been on a road similar to this one when he came to Mason Falls. And with each new mile, he remembered feeling like he was leaving his hopes and dreams behind him.

Thinking back on it, he couldn't believe the time had gone so quickly. And now the question was, if he left this town he'd come to love, would he be turning his back on a new set of hopes and dreams?

Reuben shoved his hat to the back of his head and rubbed a hand across his brow.

"You know, Seth, I once read a quote that said, 'Choices are the hinges of destiny.'" Glancing over at Seth he went on, "I wish I knew who said that. Now as I see it, the hinges are what connect the present to the future. Have you considered that Mason Falls is the hinge to your future?"

They sat in silence, both weighing the significance of the question. "It seems to me," Reuben said, his weathered face breaking into a half smile, "you have a mighty fine opportunity for a good future right here. Main thing is, have you asked God where He wants to use you?"

Seth stared out the window before answering. "I've kind of asked Him to help me know what to do."

Reuben turned and gave him a look. "Seth, you either give it to Him or you go your own way. Seems to me this is a mighty important decision to be takin' on all by yourself."

Ducking his head like a chastened school boy, he knew his friend was right. He'd been trying to make a life-changing decision based on his own emotions that seemed to change from one day to the next.

"You're the only one who can make this choice, son," Reuben said. "Think about it this way. The light shines best in the darkness, doesn't it?" Seth nodded in agreement. "Well, right now your confusion is your darkness. I'd say the most important thing you can do is not to get ahead of the light. And since you became a man of faith, that light needs to be Jesus. He's the light that shines inside us. He's the one who shows us the right path to take."

Seth knew his friend's words were true. He'd been wandering around in his dark, secluded closet of confusion, afraid to open the door and let life and love surprise him. Reuben was right. He was a new man, not the one who came here with his plan carved in stone.

Staring at the walls of jagged limestone bluffs as they drove along the narrow road, a thought struck him. Stone was a hard taskmaster. It didn't change easily and any changes had to be hammered and chiseled away. His heart had been like this wall of stone when he came to Mason Falls. He'd shut people out of his life for so many years, he hadn't known how to respond until Reuben, the McQuarrys, Claire, Mason, and even his patients had each chiseled their way into his life.

With every bump in the road, he pictured the impact a person, or the town itself, had made on him. When he came to Mason Falls, he'd craved what a large, well-known clinic in an incredible city could offer him. Was he willing to exchange that prestige and all his old dreams for what he'd found in one small town nestled in the Ozark Mountains?

The few red and yellow leaves left on the trees glistened with dew in the early morning light. A sense of awe flooded his soul.

Had God just confirmed to him the beauty and wonder of the life he could have here? He knew then, without any doubt, that the relationships he'd made here far outweighed anything he would gain in Kansas City.

Seth glanced over at Reuben who was humming some tune Seth had never heard. "Reuben, I think Jesus just turned on the light." The heavy weight he'd been carrying around for months evaporated in one simple moment of truth. Mason Falls was where he belonged.

It was so clear to him now. The answer to every reason he'd gone into medicine could be found right here. He wanted to make a significant difference in the life and care of his patients.

But as the truck continued to rumble down the road, Seth's heart began to beat faster. Caring for his patients was only part of what drew him to stay.

Kansas City offered an incredible career opportunity, but it couldn't match the woman and boy who had captured his heart. Reuben glanced over at Seth. "Are you going to keep it to yourself or let me in on what's making you grin like a sixteen year old on his first date?"

"I've made my decision, Reuben. I'm taking Mac's offer and staying right here."

Grabbing his friend's hat, he stuck it on his own head and said, "I think it's about time I get me one of these things." He clapped Reuben on the shoulder. "This is where I belong."

"Well, that was a snap decision. Don't you think you should take more time?"

"I think I've known what I need—and want—to do for quite a while. Pride has had its hook in me for a very long time, Reuben. I'm ashamed of how self-centered I've been all these years. And I'm thankful God's given me a wakeup call to a whole new way of life."

When he looked over at his friend, he saw tears in his eyes.

～ 76 ～

Seth awakened with one thing on his mind, the picnic for Claire. He'd been making plans for a couple of weeks, even research-ing recipes online. He had called Claire and asked if she'd like to go out for a nice dinner. But he didn't tell her where. Helen had agreed to keep Mason, and Reuben had said he would help with some of the last minute details.

Now the day was here and Seth's excitement had him jump-ing out of bed instead of sleeping in. The first item on his agenda was to meet with Hap and Madge Carter at The Singing Dog Café. He felt confident they'd been able to get all the ingredients for the recipes he'd chosen since they hadn't called to tell him oth-erwise. But it wouldn't hurt to go by. The restaurant wasn't open this early but he knew Hap and Madge got there by five thirty every morning.

As he climbed in Old Red, he said a silent prayer that the weather would hold until this night was over.

The town square was completely deserted when he arrived. He knocked several times before he saw Hap emerge from The Singing Dog kitchen.

"Well, well, you're up bright and early, Doc. I figured you'd try and sleep in on a Saturday. Come on in and have a cup of coffee with me, and I'll give you a run down. I think you're going to be pleased.

"The Mrs. and I made those recipes for ourselves the other night, and they're real tasty." Hap grinned. "Have to tell you we were a little uneasy about it when we started. Never heard of a lot of those things, but it came together real good."

Seth breathed a sigh of relief. "Hap, thanks so much for all

475

you're doing. It really does mean a lot to me. And thanks for the coffee. It's great as always."

"Why don't you come to the back door this evening when you pick up the food? That way you won't get caught by someone wanting to get some free advice or just one of those folks who'll talk your ears off."

Seth grinned, "That's probably wise advice, Hap. I'll do that. Thanks. See you at four thirty."

~ ~ ~

Reuben helped Seth set up the picnic site. Seth had split a good size supply of wood for the make shift fire pit and had the blisters to prove it. Reuben promised to finish the final details by five o'clock. Seth would pick up the food at the same time, then drive over to get Claire.

"Looks like this will be a very romantic moment. Women love surprises. You've done well, my boy. You've loosened up since your early days in Mason Falls. It's noticeable."

Seth reached over and gave his friend a playful punch on the arm. "People thought I was a little stiff, huh?"

"Well, I guess you could say that." Reuben's face broke into a smile. "But I can tell you that no one thinks that anymore. You've made some big changes, Seth. And people think highly of you as a doctor and as a man."

With their tasks finished, Seth helped his friend carry tools and supplies back to his truck and then decided to go for a quick run to make the time pass a little faster.

~ ~ ~

The run had been a good idea. He felt relaxed and ready for the evening. He took a long, hot shower then put on gray slacks and a navy blue sweater over a white shirt. He grabbed his coat and headed out the door.

Seth knocked on the back door of The Singing Dog Café at exactly four thirty. Hap had the food ready in a special insulated chest. Seth paid him and thanked him for all the effort he'd put into doing a special order.

The drive to Claire's gave him time to think back on their

friendship and some of the memories they'd made together. A smile crept across his face, and he decided that could be a good focus for their dinner conversation.

When Claire opened the door the sight of her melted all his anxious thoughts. "You look beautiful," he said. Then he noticed she had on high heels. "Uh, Claire, you might want to get a pair of low heeled shoes to take with us and a warm coat. I thought we'd go for a little walk before dinner."

"That sounds great! I'll be right back."

Seth couldn't help but laugh out loud.

"What are you laughing about, mister?" she shouted from her room.

"Just you," he said. "Just you."

When she came back down stairs, he pulled her into a hug.

"What?"

"I'll tell you later. Let's get going."

When they arrived at the parking area for the Falls, Claire said, "Now I see why I needed flat shoes."

Seth went to the trunk and pulled out the chest full of food and a blanket. "I thought we'd have a picnic!" His dark eyes held a flicker of mystery as his lips curved into a wide smile.

"Well, aren't you the sneaky one! You also arranged for Helen and Mac to invite Mason over too, didn't you?"

Seth nodded and motioned for them to start walking. He handed the blanket to her. "This is heavy!" he joked with a little shake of the food chest. Truthfully, the blisters on his hands stung something awful, but he smiled at the beautiful woman beside him. She was worth every effort he'd made to pull this evening together.

When they reached their favorite spot near the Falls, Claire gasped. A fire was going in the fire pit and near it was a small table for two draped with a white table cloth and two chairs with white chair covers and warm burgundy lap blankets draped over the back. A vase with a single red rose stood near a candle waiting to be lit.

Reuben had made everything ready.

"It's so amazing, Seth. I've never seen anything so beautiful or special." She moved toward him and slipped into the warmth of his embrace.

"Look, Seth," she said, a touch of awe in her voice, "Another one of God's masterpieces." They pulled back from each other to watch the explosion of color starting to fill the sky.

Turning them from the glorious expanse, he took her face in his hands giving her a gentle kiss before ushering her to the table.

He pulled out a chair for her and lit the candle while she admired the softness and warmth of the lap blanket.

When Seth opened the chest, Claire said, "Don't tell me you did the cooking too."

"I wish. But I didn't want to take any chances. My culinary skills are a long way from perfection." Placing a tray on the table with a flourish, Seth said, "For our appetizer we have Black Olive Tapenade with Figs and Mint."

Claire raised her eyebrows and grinned. "Are you serious?"

"I am. And here's what will really be hard to believe. I had Hap and Madge Carter cater everything. Of course, I haven't tasted it yet." They both broke into laughter.

Sampling bagel chips loaded with the tapenade, they concluded the Carters might need to expand into catering.

"How did you come up with the recipe?" She toasted him with another bagel chip spread with the mixture.

"I went to Google. Where else? I scrolled through things until I found something interesting that sounded like what you might eat in San Francisco."

Claire covered his hand with hers. "That was so thoughtful. Thank you."

"Are you ready to try the main course?" he asked. "For the main course, my lady, we have the most wonderful crab cakes you will ever taste. And to go with them we have selected quinoa salad with snap peas."

Claire's eyes danced with delight. "Oh my goodness, I can't wait. Seth, this is really too much!"

Seth turned their conversation to the memories they'd made together. How stiff and business like she thought he was when they first met. Then all the good times and meals they had shared with the McQuarrys and often Reuben. How he couldn't have made it through that first soccer practice without her. The picnic when he had talked to Mason about him getting into the fight. The Thanksgiving and Christmas celebration gatherings at her home. The day Mason got lost and the emotions connected to that scary time.

Seth poured her a cup of her peppermint tea from the carefully packed thermos and brought out the famous Madge Carter pralines for dessert. They moved to a log by the fire, sharing laughter and tears. They talked of their sorrows, their pain, and their losses. And they looked back on more happy moments they'd shared.

Seth got another log for the fire and brought the blanket to wrap around Claire's shoulders. When he put an arm around her and drew her close, she nestled next to him. He knew it was where she belonged.

"Seth, I have something I want to tell you," she turned her face to look into his eyes. "I want to thank you for being such a large part of my asking Jesus into my life. You and Helen helped me see I could never get over the past on my own."

She smiled up at him and caressed his cheek with her hand. "I'm ready to move forward in my life."

"I'm so happy for you, Claire. I know from experience how different life can be once that choice is made."

Seth stoked the fire one more time. He pulled her close and turned her face to him. "I love you, Claire, with all my heart. I don't want to live my life apart from you and Mason."

In words just above a whisper, he heard her say, "I love you too, Seth, more than I ever imagined possible."

As tears began to trickle down her face, he held her close, kissing each one. When the tears subsided, he moved out of their embrace and dropped to his knee in front of her. He drew a box out of his jacket pocket and took her left hand in his.

"Claire, I came to Mason Falls a broken man," he said, struggling to keep his composure. "I'd let the pain and loneliness of the past years make me focus on myself more than on others.

I thought I deserved more than what this small town had to offer. But what I've discovered is that I don't feel worthy of all this town has given me."

He drew her hand to his lips and kissed it. "But most of all, I never imagined that it would be in this small town that I would find the woman I want to spend the rest of my life with. Claire, I love you with all that I am. I would consider it the greatest honor of my life if you and Mason would share your lives with me."

Opening the box, he said, "This ring is my most cherished possession. It's my grandmother's wedding ring and it would make her very pleased to know that I have found the woman I want to wear it. Will you marry me, Claire?"

With a joy that had taken her breath away, Claire threw her arms around him. "Yes, Seth, oh yes!" She felt her heart beat faster as she listened to the words she would cherish forever. "Claire Westfield, I will love you and your incredible son all the days of my life."

~ ~ ~

The night air was cool, the fire had burned down to embers, and the large moon seemed to watch over the man and woman who, with a kiss, had sealed their love beneath its glow.

Seth's arms wrapped around her, they stood watching the last of the embers burn down, not wanting the moment to come to an end.

"I want to tell you something," Claire said as she turned to look into his eyes. "I've made a decision. Whatever you decide to do about staying here or taking the offer in Kansas City, I'll support you." She stood on tiptoe to kiss him.

He searched her face looking for the slightest hesitation in her eyes. He saw none.

"Let's get you to the car, then we can talk."

She stared at him trying to understand his lack of response to what she'd told him. "But what about the table and everything?" she said.

"Shh, I'll come back later. Right now, I want to get you in the car before you get too cold! You're shivering."

The warmth felt good when Seth started the car. Old Red might be old but its heater worked great. He took her hands in his, rubbing them to restore more warmth. Worry lines creased his brow. "I'm sorry it got so cold. I guess the doctor side of me kind of took over. I don't want you to think that what you said didn't touch me. It did more than you could imagine because I know how much you love Mason Falls. Thank you for what you said. I could tell it came from your heart." He squeezed her hand. "And I know it was a huge decision, which makes me cherish it even more."

Reaching over, he put his arm around her and pulled her close. "I have something to tell you as well. I made my own decision a few days ago. I called Dr. Hawthorn and told him I would respectfully have to decline his offer. I also told him I had found the place where I belong."

Claire laid her head against his chest and cried. When she looked up, she held his gaze. "You're certain about this? It's what you want to do?" He nodded, his eyes confirming it was true.

"The interesting thing is Dr. Hawthorn told me he knew what my answer would be. At the end of my previous phone call with him, he asked me if I was a praying man. When I said yes, he suggested we both pray that God would give us a clear answer. And now we know He did."

Lifting her hands to his lips, Seth said, "I wouldn't change life here with you and Mason for all the elite clinics in the country. "Now let's talk about how we tell everyone," he grinned. "We're getting married! That's big news!"

Driving back into town they decided to tell Mason, then let him share the news with the others. When they got to the McQuarry's, Seth parked out front while Claire called Robyn and asked her friend to call her back in forty-five minutes. Seth called Reuben to see if he could meet them at the McQuarry's at the same time.

Claire and Seth told Mason, Helen, and Mac about the surprise picnic, minus the details of the proposal. They asked Mason if he'd like to go get a hot fudge sundae before coming back to say goodnight to Mac and Helen before heading home. Mac raised his eyebrow and Helen cocked her head. Claire said, "We'll be back in half an hour."

Mason was full of stories of what he'd done with Dr. Mac and Mrs. Mac. He and Mrs. Mac had made gingerbread. Dr. Mac was teaching him how to tie flies for fishing. They were also teaching him to play dominoes.

Claire and Seth gave each other a relieved look when they went to Braum's and saw they were the only customers. They got their sundaes and found a booth as far to the back as they could get. When Mason was almost finished with his, Claire said they wanted to talk to him about something. He looked up with fudge and whipped cream on the tip of his nose and both sides of his face. Mason looked from one to the other. "Am I in trouble?" he said, a concerned look crossing his face.

Seth and Claire had decided she would be the one to share the news. "No, sweetie. You're not in trouble. Dr. Seth and I have news we are so excited to tell you. You are the first to know. Seth has asked me to marry him!"

The joy and excitement on Mason's face would be indelibly printed in her mind for the rest of her life. Mason jumped to his feet, ice cream forgotten. Yelps of "All right!" destroyed the quiet of the place. Pumping his arm, he shouted "Yes" over and over. Employees stared in their direction. Seth mouthed, "Sorry."

Mason threw his arms around them both. "It's really, really true? Dr. Seth is going to be my dad?"

They were all laughing and crying at the same time. Seth scooped him up in his arms. "I would count it the highest honor of my life, buddy. Well, except for your mom saying yes she'll marry me."

Driving back to the McQuarrys, they explained their plan to Mason. They would keep the secret until Mr. Reuben arrived and Aunt Robbie called before telling anyone. "Do you think you can keep the secret until then?" Claire asked, reaching over the seat to take his hand.

When he nodded, Seth slapped him a backwards high five. "Then how about you being the one to tell everyone when it's time?"

Claire thought her son was going to cry. But he sucked in his breath, and her little man as she called him, grew a few inches in his journey to manhood.

On the drive back to the McQuarrys, Mason grew quiet. "Dr. Seth, when do I get to call you dad?"

Seth cleared his throat and with a glance at Claire said, "Well, how about after the wedding ceremony?"

"That's not going to be a long time from now is it?"

"Not if I have any say in things, buddy! I'd do it tomorrow if it was up to me." Seth's laughter broke the tension in the car. "But you see, Mason, us guys need to keep in mind that things like weddings are very important to women. And they should be to us as well. A wedding's the way two people start a brand new life together. Now our wedding is going to be even more important because there are three of us getting ready to start a new family."

"I like that!" Mason ducked his head and whispered, "I've wanted us to be a family for a long, long time."

~ ~ ~

When they drove up to the McQuarry's, they breathed a sigh of relief to see Reuben was already there. In a few minutes Robyn would be calling. Seth said, "Okay, buddy, now wait for your mom's signal, the wink, then it's all up to you."

"Gotch ya. I've been workin' on not smiling too much when we go inside."

Claire and Seth laughed, and said in unison, "Us too."

The three of them had only been inside a few minutes when Claire's cell phone rang. "Hey, Robyn, thanks for calling back. Yes, everything's fine. Mason just has something he wants to tell you, the McQuarrys, and Reuben. I'll put him on. She put the phone on speaker and with a wink handed it to her son.

"Hey, Aunt Robbie. Yeah, I'm doing good. I have something special I want to tell all of y'all." His eyes lit up and he grinned at the people in the room.

"My mom and Dr. Seth are getting married!" Robyn's squeals of delight came through the phone as though she were right there with them.

Mason handed the phone back to his mom while he got high fives from Reuben and Mac, and hugs and kisses more times than usual from Helen.

"Girlfriend, that's wonderful! I'm so happy for all three of you. I can't wait to hear all about the details so you call me later, okay? Right now, you need to celebrate!"

"Before you hang up, Robyn, will you be my maid of honor again?"

"You better believe it! No way I'm missing out on being part of this wedding. I love you, sweet friend, and I'm absolutely thrilled for all of you. Call me later, okay?"

Over the next hour they celebrated with hugs and laughter. Helen volunteered their home for the wedding or reception if they wanted it after Claire and Seth said they wanted a small, intimate ceremony with close friends and a few of Seth's patients.

As everyone was getting ready to leave, they took a moment to bow their heads for Reuben to offer a prayer.

"Father, we come to You with full and happy hearts at the news of this wedding. What a joy to see what You have accomplished in each of their lives. We thank You for Your goodness, and ask Your blessing on Seth, Claire, and Mason. May this bond of love establish them as a family for now and forever."

⌒ 77 ⌒

ON THE DRIVE BACK TO CLAIRE'S, Seth looked over his shoulder at the sleeping boy in the back seat. His heart warmed at the thought of not only marrying the incredible woman beside him but of having this boy as his son.

When they arrived at the house, he carried the still sleeping Mason upstairs. Claire brushed by him to get the bed turned back. "Want me to go put some coffee on while you get him in his pj's?" he said, lowering the boy onto the bed.

Claire whispered, "I think I'll just get his jeans off and let him sleep like this. And coffee sounds great."

As Seth headed toward the door, Claire called out in a hushed tone, "And maybe on this special night start a fire in the living room fireplace? Please!"

He walked back to her, kissed her, and murmured, "Sounds wonderful."

The smells of coffee and burning wood greeted her as she left her son's room. Memories of the evening still held her mind captive. Her heart was full of love for the man waiting for her downstairs. It had been a magical evening.

She curled up next to Seth on the sofa. The light from the fire created a warm glow around them and the quiet surrounded them like a cocoon. Seth took her hand in his while they sipped their coffee and talked about plans for the wedding.

"What would you think about having the wedding here at Thanksgiving? There's such a history of lifetime love in this home. Wouldn't it be special to begin a marriage and a family right here?"

Seth looked at the flecks of gold in her green eyes caught by the firelight. "I'd say that kind of heritage makes this the perfect place for our wedding!"

He cradled her face in his hands and kissed her until they broke into laughter.

"I was beginning to think I'd have to resuscitate both of us!" Seth said.

After catching their breath, he said, "Oh, I wanted to let you know I got a few minutes with Reuben before we left and asked if he would be my best man. It really touched him."

They talked of the people in their lives and the impact each one had made on them.

"Seth, would you be okay with taking Helen up on having the reception at their house? She's been such a help to me, letting us stay with them when we got here, and all the times they've kept Mason for me. I think it would mean a lot to her."

"She'd enjoy all that, wouldn't she?" He grinned. "I can see her now, pulling out all the stops and probably drawing Mac into it by giving him a long honey do list."

They giggled at the thought of Angus McQuarry wearing an apron and dutifully working through all of Helen's detailed requests. The happy hours evaporated before them until they both began to yawn. Seth looked at his watch. It was time to call it a night.

~ ~ ~

Claire knew sleep wouldn't come yet. She padded down the stairs to watch the fire burn down and to call Robyn. She knew she'd regret staying up so late tomorrow morning, but tonight was too full of joy and anticipation to try and sleep.

So much had happened during the time they'd been here. She thought of Seth's words to her earlier that evening. "I was a broken man when I came here." They had so much in common when it came to brokenness.

She walked to the fireplace and poked at the logs with the stoker. What was it Reuben had said to her about God working in our lives even when we're unaware of Him? As the fire began to crackle again, she remembered his words. "God works in unique ways to bring us to Himself. And sometimes He takes us out of our comfort zone to do it."

Returning to the sofa, she curled up where she and Seth had been and inhaled the faint scent of his aftershave. They had so much to be thankful for. Now she needed to call Robyn to let her know she and Seth were planning to have the wedding over the Thanksgiving weekend.

When she'd called Robyn back, her friend was giddy with excitement. She'd also promised to clear her schedule to allow extra time so she could stay with Mason while Claire and Seth went on their honeymoon. Claire was hesitant about her taking off so much time but gave in when Robyn insisted. Mason would be thrilled, but they decided to keep that a secret.

When sunlight burst through the living room windows, she found herself still curled up on the sofa where she'd fallen asleep under her grandmother's afghan. The house was quiet, and she was filled with happiness. Today was going to be a coffee day. She'd need something stronger than tea. It had been a long night, but oh what a special one.

Before the coffee had finished brewing, she heard her son clomping down the stairs. She laughed when he strode into the kitchen in his tee shirt and boxers, his hair going several directions.

"Mom," he said, his voice groggy, "did I dream it or are you and Dr. Seth getting married?"

Taking him by the hands she danced him around the kitchen. "We're getting married, silly. It wasn't a dream. It's very real." She kissed the top of his head and said, "I'm whipped. Seth and I stayed up late making plans, and then I called Robyn. Let's shower and get dressed and go to Mabel's for breakfast."

"Yay, I'm starving. I'll go shower while you drink your coffee."

The sound of stairs creaking told her Mason was running up them, probably two at a time. Sitting at the kitchen table she wondered how it would feel to have that much energy again.

~ ~ ~

Mabel's was filled with people as usual. Claire and Mason found a two person table in the corner. She hoped the noise wouldn't be as loud there.

As they waited for a server, Claire noticed Mabel and Jodi, the young woman Claire had befriended, were the only ones waiting tables. She could hear impatient customers saying things.

"Sweetheart, you wait right here. I'll be back." Claire walked to the kitchen door, pushed it open, and stepped into Mabel's territory. When she reappeared, she was wearing an apron with Mabel's Café printed on the front. She had an order pad in her hand, and she started at the table closest to her.

"How may I help you all? We're a little short-staffed today, but we'll get you your order as quickly as we can."

People all across the room stared as Claire, business-like but very cordial, began taking orders and handing them through the kitchen window to the cook, filling waters, and clearing tables.

Out of the corner of her eye, she saw the shocked look on Mabel's face and caught the wink Jodi gave her. When all the customers had their orders taken, Claire went to sit down with her son. As soon as she sat, folks began to applaud and smile at her. Mason's face glowed with pride as he too clapped to honor his mother. Claire's face turned a bright red as she nodded her thanks.

As customers finished their meal and went to pay their bill, they stopped to tell Claire thank you and what a kind thing she'd done.

When she and Mason had finished their breakfast and walked over to the cash register, Claire wasn't sure what kind of response or more likely, reaction, to expect from Mabel.

In her typical gruff voice Mabel said, "No charge today."

Claire thanked her and turned to go.

"Why'd you do that?" Mabel said.

"Well, you were short of help and had more than two people could take care of. That's all." Claire smiled and turned to leave.

"Miss Mabel, my mom and Dr. Seth just got engaged to be married. Why don't you come to the wedding? We'll send you an invitation. Oh, the pancakes were the best ever." His grin lit up his face, and he took his mother's hand, leading her to the door.

If there was one person Claire would not have invited to her wedding, it would be Mabel Porter. Now she had to figure out how to talk to her son without hurting his feelings.

"Sweetheart, what made you ask Miss Mabel to come to our wedding?"

Mason stopped and his eyes narrowed as he searched his mother's face. "Do you not want her to come to the wedding?"

Claire gazed into her son's probing eyes as she searched for the right words.

"Mom, I thought it would be nice to invite her. She doesn't seem to have much to be happy about and weddings make people happy, don't they?"

Mason's childish reasoning stung Claire's heart. Her son was now teaching her. Somewhere in her grandmother's Bible she'd read about a child leading an adult. Her son had just done that.

"You're right, sweetheart. I'm very proud of you for wanting to help Miss Mabel. How about you addressing the invitation envelope when the time comes?"

The bear hug she received made the idea of Mabel Porter at her wedding worth it.

~ ~ ~

Time seemed to pass both fast and slow. Her calendar became filled with things that needed to be done. She started keeping additional to do lists on note cards she could tuck in her purse or pockets. Helen had been thrilled at the idea of having the reception at their home, just as Claire and Seth had expected. Each day was filled with an air of joyous activity.

Invitations were sent to Jasper and Opal Mae Hobbs, Possum Gutherie and Willie Tuckett along with their wives, Fred Lawson, Hank and Karen Simpson, the Harrisons including J.J., the entire clinic staff, and of course, Mabel Porter, for a total of twenty-five guests.

The guest list was miniscule in comparison to the one Claire had put together when she and Randall had married. But it felt more like family than trying to cover all the bases from a society stand point. The list made her smile, and her heart fluttered with a fresh sense of what community had come to mean to her.

~ ~ ~

Claire awakened with an unsettled sense of dread. Today was

to be a busy day of last minute details. They were three days away from the wedding. Robyn was flying in today and had insisted as usual on renting a car. Claire tried to shake the dark cloud hanging over her with a long hot shower. No change. She told herself it was just wedding jitters, although she thought at her age and a second marriage that sounded silly.

The house was immaculate and Mason had been so thoughtful about keeping his stuff picked up. Most of what she needed to do were small things, but they took time. She breathed a simple prayer asking God to quiet her heart and fill it instead with His peace.

Her phone rang just as she finished a late breakfast. "Hi, Helen. What's up?" When she heard Helen's words her face went pale, and she had to sit down to steady herself. "Yes, I'll come right over."

Grabbing her car keys, she called for Mason to come down and go with her to Helen's. She went into the garage and shouted "Why now?" Her hand shook as she tried to put the key into the ignition. Waves of emotion flooded over her, and she felt she was drowning. "God, why now? I can't do this!"

She sat motionless for several minutes trying to get enough control that she could drive to Helen's. Mason ran into the garage, opened the door, and plopped in the back seat. At least he was in a good mood.

~ ~ ~

Mason ran to the backyard where Mac was raking leaves. Helen stood at the front door, waiting for her. Claire fell into her friend's arms and cried. Helen drew her into the house and held her until the tears turned to sobs then took her by the hand and led her to the kitchen booth. She put a china cup with hot tea in front of her and motioned for her to sit down.

Claire thought she must've been sitting there for hours before she could finally get words to come out of her mouth.

"When did she get here?" She felt hollow inside, except for the anger that made her stomach churn.

"She said she got here late last night. She's staying at a hotel in Granville." Helen's eyes brimmed with sympathy. "Sweetheart, I know this is such a shock. Whatever you want me to do to help, I will." She reached over to stroke Claire's shaking hands.

"She couldn't have known about the wedding. Why is she here?"

"No, of course she didn't know you were getting married. She just said she'd been thinking of you and didn't know where you were, so she came to see me to find out how to reach you. I've told your mother nothing at this point, Claire."

The two sat in silence. Claire's thoughts hidden under a shroud of painful memories known only to herself.

"Helen, what am I going to do?"

Helen moved to sit next to her on the other side of the booth. Putting an arm around her young friend she held her, letting Claire's heart release pain from so many years of neglect.

"I don't know if I even want to see her again. She's my physical mother, but I don't know her." Claire put her head in her hands. "And she certainly doesn't know me. It's been years since I've heard anything from her. And what about Mason?" she cried out, her words catching in her throat. "He has no memories of his own grandmother! Do I throw that at him right now when all our lives are getting ready to change? I really thought I'd let all these feelings go, but here they are again."

Helen waited patiently allowing Claire to vent her anger and hurt.

"Sweetheart, it's your decision to make, and I would encourage you to do two things. First of all, ask God to speak to your heart. Forgiveness can only come as we allow Him to work in us, and the second thing is to talk with Seth. You're getting ready to marry him, and he needs to walk through this with you. This is a time when you need his wisdom and perspective as your soon-to-be husband." Helen placed a hand on Claire's shoulder gently stroking it. "A marriage is meant to be two people coming together as one in making decisions. Lean on him, Claire. Trust him to help you and to support you."

After taking Claire's hand and praying for her, Helen said, "Now what can I do today to help you get the house ready?" Helen gave her a hug.

The drive back to her place gave Claire the time and solitude she needed to process her conversation with Helen. Little by little she felt some of the shock, anger, and pain diminish.

The decision to let Mac take Mason out to do some errands helped to relieve some of her stress. She needed time to think how to tell him about the grandmother he'd never known.

When she drove up to the house, she felt a peace come over her. Sitting there in the car she thought of her son and his comment about why he'd asked Mabel to the wedding. Her mother had everything the world could give her, but Claire had a feeling her mother was much like Mabel in that neither had much to be truly happy about.

She would talk to Seth and get his thoughts on what she should do. But it just might be that her son had shown her the way.

～ Epilogue ～

Their honeymoon in Montreal was quickly coming to an end. It had been like a wonderful dream but very soon she'd have to open her eyes to reality. Sitting at the small table at what had become their favorite little coffee shop, Claire stared out the window at the historic Hotel Le St-James where they were staying. It towered over the nearby businesses.

"Hey there, beautiful lady," Seth said, "you seem very far away. And as newlyweds, I'm supposed to be the focus of your attention."

Her cheeks flushed as she smiled at him. "I'm so sorry, sweetheart, I hadn't meant to let my thoughts wander like that. You are my main focus. I just drifted for a moment."

"So, are you going to tell me where those thoughts have taken you?"

Her eyes brightened and she said, "Just reminising about a lot of things. Like you remembering that random conversation we had months ago when I told you I'd always wanted to visit Montreal. You scored a lot of points with this choice for our honeymoon!"

Leaning across the table she kissed him, still in a joyous daze to think they were husband and wife.

"I have to admit," he said with a mischievous grin, "I was pretty proud of myself. And what else has been going through that mind of yours?"

Claire laughed and gave him an affectionate pat on his arm. "I thought of how Reuben looked like a proud father standing there as your best man."

"Well, that's what he's become for me, my best friend and my spiritual father."

"Isn't it amazing how God's put all these special people in our lives? Mac and Helen were so happy for us," Claire said. "He's used each of them to help fill the void and the losses in our past. He's given us people to love who love us back!"

Seth moved his chair closer to hers and put an arm around her. "It is amazing, Mrs. Bradley," he whispered, "and so are you. And He's been there in ways we didn't even know we needed Him." Claire nodded.

A dreamy look crossed her face. "Were you as pleased with the way the wedding turned out as I was? It was so simple, but I loved it."

"If you say so. All I could see was you and how beautiful you were."

"You're turning into a real flirt, Seth Bradley."

"Yeah, and I hope to spend the rest of my life flirting with you."

She smiled and tucked a strand of hair behind one ear.

"And remember how proud Mason felt when he walked me down the aisle?" She reached out to take her new husband's hand.

"And when the pastor pronounced us husband and wife and Mason rushed over to us and yelled, 'Hey, everyone, Dr. Seth's my new dad!'"

Seth said, "And when he took a piece of cake for himself and for Mabel and sat down and ate it with her, I was so proud of him.

"It was a big day for our little guy. Not only did he get a dad but he met his grandmother for the first time. I meant to tell you more about our meeting and his reaction to my mother, but then a honeymoon kind of filled my every thought," she said with a happy laugh. "The timing of my mother's arrival was so shocking to me. I really wasn't sure I could face her. I felt so much anger and hurt that I thought I had put behind me. Helen praying for me helped, and remembering Mason's sweet reason for inviting Mabel to our wedding flooded my mind.

"Talking to you about your experience with your mother helped me come to better terms with my situation. You said if we are to turn over hard things to God, this certainly needed to be turned over. You were right. It was time for me to truly let all those negative emotions go.

"You know I met Mother at the hotel where she was staying.

There was not a lot to say. I told her Mason and I were living in Potch and Honey's house and that Helen was bringing Mason to meet with us after he got out of school. When I told her I was getting married, she really didn't say anything except she hoped I would be happy.

"Helen arrived with Mason and left us to be together. The night before I had explained to Mason that he was going to meet his grandmother after school the next day. He was very subdued when Helen walked him over to us and greeted my mother. He shook hands with her and was very polite. He answered the few questions she asked him about school. Then she said it was nice to see us and that she was leaving in the morning for a trip to Paris. She patted Mason on the head and kissed my cheek.

"My little boy's growing up and becoming quite astute when it comes to relationships. He seems to have taken the meeting in stride."

Claire stirred a little more cream into her coffee and broke off a bite of her croissant.

"Mason did tell me he was glad he'd met his grandmother," she said, her face clouding with sadness. "He even gave her a bit of a hug. I thought that was a big step for a child who'd never even seen her before."

Just then a young couple, staring into each other's eyes, bumped against their table. Coffee splashed across the table, and Claire and Seth jumped to escape it. Their cups crashed onto the floor in a hundred pieces.

Their waitress rushed to help them. "*Escuses-moi, Madame, Monsieur, je suis tellement desolee.* I mean, I am so sorry this has happened to you!"

They assured the waitress no harm was done, and she efficiently cleaned the table and returned with two fresh cups of coffee for them. Seth asked Claire to finish the account of Mason and his grandmother.

"There's not much more to tell except that later he confided to me that she might be his grandmother, but he'd adopted Mac and Helen as his real grandparents." She smiled and said, "That's when he wanted to know if it was okay with me for him to ask them if he could start calling them by the names he'd chosen for them."

"So what did you say?"

"That it was fine with me. My mother has made her own life. I'm at a place I can release her to be who she is. She'll never be a steady part of our lives, but Mac and Helen will be."

Claire noticed a couple with ice skates slung over their shoulders walking past the café window, probably on their way to the nearby ice rink. Was it only yesterday she and Seth had been there for their "last dance on the ice," as Seth had called it. A vivid picture came to mind of the golden evening light that cast its glow across the buildings and the ice, announcing the coming of dusk. She thought too of the warmth of her hands in those of her husband's as he'd drawn her close and whispered, "I'll never forget this moment, Claire Bradley." Tiny twinkle lights flickered in the trees that surrounded the rink as they swayed to the rhythm of the music, lost in the magic of their own private world. She would cherish this memory the rest of her life.

"Hello, calling Claire. Have you left again?"

She laughed. "This time I was reliving our last dance on the ice. Sorry. Where were we?"

"About releasing your mom, and Mac and Helen being a steady part of our lives. Then you drifted away. Did Mason tell you what happened with Mac and Helen?"

"He did. He was so excited that they said yes and liked his names for them. Mac is G-Mac and Helen is My-G. The G of course is for grandpa and grandma."

"I bet that made their day," he said. "Mason's quite a guy, Claire. I'm so honored to be a part of his life forever."

She covered his hand with hers then turned and watched people passing by the coffee shop. Their body language spoke volumes. Most were in a hurry to get somewhere. Maybe it was home or to get some shopping done or to catch the next cab or bus. They were cold from the wind and a light snow that sprinkled their coats and jackets. Others, like the couple who bumped into their table, had eyes and attention only for one another. Everyone had their own story.

When she turned back to look into her new husband's eyes, a sense of warmth filled her heart. She was no longer alone. She, Seth, and Mason were beginning a story of their own.

About the Author

ANNE ARKINS IS THE MOTHER OF four grown children, grandmother to twelve, and great-grandmother to one. While following her passion as a homemaker, she has found time to be a mentor to younger women, Bible study teacher in her church, a published songwriter, Family Life marriage conference speaker along with her husband, Jim, and  the co-author with Gary Harrell of the best-selling book, *While They Were Sleeping*, a guide for praying 12 character traits in children.

She and Jim, a retired family physician, live in Northwest Arkansas.

(c) 2021 Matthew Arkins

Made in the USA
Las Vegas, NV
11 August 2021